Also by Vaddey Ratner

In the Shadow of the Banyan

MUSIC
of the
GHOSTS

Vaddey Ratner

TOUCHSTONE
New York   London   Toronto   Sydney   New Delhi

T

Touchstone
An Imprint of Simon & Schuster, Inc.
1230 Avenue of the Americas
New York, NY 10020

First Touchstone hardcover edition April 2017

TOUCHSTONE and colophon are registered trademarks of Simon & Schuster, Inc.

For information about special discounts for bulk purchases, please contact Simon & Schuster Special Sales at 1-866-506-1949 or business@simonandschuster.com.

The Simon & Schuster Speakers Bureau can bring authors to your live event. For more information or to book an event, contact the Simon & Schuster Speakers Bureau at 1-866-248-3049 or visit our website at www.simonspeakers.com.

Interior design by Jill Putorti

Manufactured in the United States of America

10 9 8 7 6 5 4 3 2 1

Library of Congress Cataloging-in-Publication Data

Names: Ratner, Vaddey, author.
Title: Music of the ghosts / Vaddey Ratner.
Description: First Touchstone hardcover edition. | New York, NY : Touchstone, 2017.
Identifiers: LCCN 2016026793 (print) | LCCN 2016033313 (ebook) | ISBN 9781476795782 (hardcover : acid-free paper) | ISBN 9781476795799 (softcover : acid-free paper) | ISBN 9781476795805 (eBook)|
Subjects: LCSH: Cambodia—History—20th century—Fiction. | Refugees—Cambodia—Fiction. | GSAFD: Autobiographical fiction.
Classification: LCC PS3618.A876 M87 2017 (print) | LCC PS3618.A876 (ebook) | DDC 813/.6--dc23.
LC record available at https://lccn.loc.gov/2016026793.

ISBN 978-1-4767-9578-2
ISBN 978-1-4767-9580-5 (ebook)

To the lives, and the beauty, that inspired these pages

Prelude

Suteera wakes amidst the high grass to a tremor several meters away. She is confused for the first few seconds, thinking it music, the quiver of a plucked string. One of those ancient-looking instruments her father used to play for her when she was very little, a lullaby to help her sleep. She's forgotten its name. She's forgotten many things—the taste of real food, her father's voice, who she was before her mother and brother died, before hunger and fear.

The tremor continues. She stills herself to listen. It seems to be coming from the next field, but she can't see past the rise of dirt in front of her. She shouldn't be scared, she tells herself. Her aunt is sleeping beside her on the hard earth, cushioned by a layer of patted-down grass, and all around, dispersed among stalks and blades, the other members of their group are lost in dreams. It is twilight, the sky a muted gold. Soon, when it's completely dark, they will wake and continue their headlong flight out of Cambodia toward the border with Thailand. But despite the distance they've covered, Suteera can't shake the feeling of being pursued. Haunted.

It wasn't long ago that Khmer Rouge soldiers, retreating from a battle lost to the invading Vietnamese troops, had forced their entire village into the jungle. Halfway through the journey, her grandparents, lacking the strength to go on, urged Suteera and their youngest daughter, Amara, to continue without them. Her aunt promised to return as soon as they found help, though they all knew this wasn't possible, could never be. Days or maybe weeks later, they emerged from the dense jungle and found themselves in the middle of rice fields spiked with the dry cut stalks of crops long harvested. The sun was setting fast, a big shimmering globe straddling the horizon, tinting the sky and earth with its fiery hue. It must have just rained—an out-of-season shower, Suteera thought—because in the far distance there appeared the faint arc of a rainbow. Suteera weaved her steps around the bodies of a family, their possessions scattered haphazardly, among which was a ripped pillow overflowing with gold and precious jewels. The soldiers said they could take what they wanted. But the villagers shook their heads and scurried past the corpses.

Frightened, Suteera grabbed the arm of a young soldier walking beside her. He let her cling to him and murmured that she should stick close to the bodies, step over them if she could, because this was the safest path. These people were shot, he told her, pointing out how the bodies were completely intact, no limbs blown off, each one whole. He whistled a lullaby to soothe her—or maybe to keep himself calm—and softened his footsteps. They'd decided to cut across the rice fields instead of taking the wide, open road some distance away, because roads like those were more likely to be planted with mines and explosives. Suteera looked over her shoulder and saw Amara furtively bending down to pick up something. *Don't*, she wanted to tell her aunt. *Don't steal from the dead.* But too late. A flash of gold necklace dangled from Amara's clenched fist as she quickly slipped it into her shirt pocket. Suteera faced front again, holding tighter to the soldier's hand, eyes on the distant rainbow. They crossed one field into the next, following the trail of more bodies, more families, more gold. Suddenly they heard faint music in the woods ahead. Some kind of string instrument. A lute perhaps, said someone, one of the older gentlemen who still remembered such sounds. There must've been a hut nearby, a farmer and his family, tenders of these fields. Everyone was certain of it. Those in front quickened their steps. Then, without warning, the fields lifted in explosion. Earth and flesh shattered. Blood sprayed the dried yellow stalks.

Now there's only Suteera, and her young aunt, and the few who were far enough away when the mines exploded. The rest were killed. Who, or what, had made that sound? Was it a person, some kind of forest spirit, the rustle of bamboo leaves, the vibration of cicadas? Their joint hallucination? They'll never know.

Suteera listens again for the sound that woke her. Maybe she's imagined it. Another hallucination, she thinks. Beside her, Amara curls in the grass, her breathing calmed by sleep. Like this, with her eyes closed and her face in repose, Amara looks like a child herself, not someone left with the responsibility of caring for another. As far as they know, they are the only ones in the family to have survived. They have no idea what happened to her father, if he lived or died. He'd disappeared long ago, the first to vanish. Suteera knows she and Amara are lucky to have each other. Most of the others in the group are alone, their loved ones murdered or lost to hunger, disease. Maybe this is why they've all decided to take their chances crossing the border. There's nothing, no one, to tie them to their homeland. There is no more home, only this land of open graves.

Her aunt takes a deep breath, turns the other way, continues sleeping, one arm swung over their scant belongings as if to guard against field rats that might try to invade the rice pot with the gold necklace inside. When Amara dropped the necklace into the pot while the rice was bubbling away, she explained that this would keep it safe from bandits and border guards. The thieves would never think to look inside a lump of rice no bigger than Suteera's bony fist. Her aunt had been careful to make the lump look natural, eating around it, spooning it out in a seemingly abandoned way, leaving uneven edges. The necklace would keep them alive, she told Suteera. They could trade it for food and shelter once across the border. *The ghosts won't leave us alone*, Suteera thought. *They'll follow us wherever we go.*

The tremor resumes, more like scraping now—like the rasp of metal against rock, nothing at all like music. She hears whistling and knows right away it's the young soldier. Comrade Chea, she used to call him. Now it's just Chea. He's the only one of the band of Khmer Rouge to survive, while his leaders, those who had gone ahead, died in the blasts. He'd been relegated to the back to guard over the slow movers like

Suteera and her aunt. He was the youngest of the seven and seemed the least like a soldier, might even have been a new recruit, plucked from the fields a few months before when fighting started with the Vietnamese. She gets up and walks toward him through the tall grass.

Chea stops whistling when he sees her. She squats down, chin on her knees, watching him sharpen his knife against a rock half buried in the earth. When the mines exploded, he'd picked her up as if she were a toddler and run for cover behind the trunk of a palm they'd passed, her aunt and the others scrambling to follow, keeping to the course they'd already trod. Then, when all was silent again, the earth resettled, and the dead stayed dead, Chea tossed aside his gun. It was useless, he said, depleted of ammunition since their last battle with the Vietnamese. He'd had enough of this, he went on, without passion or emphasis, in the same tone he'd used when guiding Suteera's steps among the bodies. He'd yet to kill another human being outside the battlefield, but he'd seen enough of death. He wanted no more of this place. Chea knew the way to Thailand. Before the war, he'd traversed the jungle many times, guiding young water buffaloes and ponies to the border to trade. It was the most he'd said. He started walking, retracing his steps out of the rice fields and back to the narrow dirt path where they'd started. He waited. Who wanted to come? They all did. Who else could they have followed? The dead stay dead. Days ago he was their captor and now he is their protector and guide, his knife the only weapon against possible bandits, wild animals, imagined sounds.

"I thought I heard music," Suteera tells him.

They have formed a kind of bond. He looks to be about her aunt's age—no, several years younger, maybe only seventeen or eighteen, and Suteera is thirteen, if what people are saying is true: that it's 1979, and they've endured this hell for four years. She's certain a lifetime has passed. But it hardly matters how old she is or how old she was before all this, before she lived alongside corpses, borrowing from their expired breath, stealing from them to feed herself. She knows she may not live tomorrow.

"Out here," Chea says, his voice gentle, as if not to frighten her, "there's only music of the ghosts."

First Movement

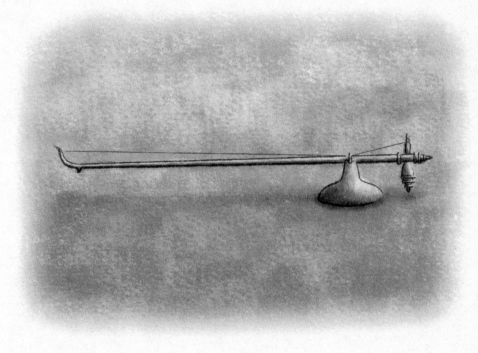

First Movement

He feels his way in the confined space of the wooden cottage, hands groping in the dark, searching among the shadows through the blurred vision of his one good eye for the *sadiev*. The lute has called out to him in his dream, plucking its way persistently into his consciousness, until he's awake, aware of its presence beside him. His fingers find the instrument. It lies aslant on the bamboo bed, deeply reposed in its dreamlessness. His fingers inadvertently brush against the single copper string, coaxing a soft *ktock*, similar to the click of a baby's tongue. The Old Musician is almost blind, his left eye damaged long ago by a bludgeon and his right by age. He relies much on his senses to see, and now he sees her, feels her presence, not as a ghostly apparition overwhelming the tiny space of his cottage, nor as a thought occupying his mind, but as a longing on the verge of utterance, incarnation. He feels her move toward him. She who will inherit the *sadiev*, this ancient instrument used to invoke the spirits of the dead, as if in that solitary note, he has called her to him.

He lifts the lute to his chest, rousing it from its muted sleep, holding it as he often held his small daughter a lifetime ago, her heart against his heart, her tiny head resting on his shoulder. Of all that he's tried to forget, he allows himself, without reservation, without guilt, the reprieve of this one memory. The curve of her neck against his, paired in the concave and convex of tenderness, as if they were two organs of a single anatomy.

Why are you so soft? he'd ask, and always she'd exclaim, *Because I have spinning moonlets!* He'd laugh then at the sagacity with which she articulated her illogic, as if it were some scientific truth or ancient wisdom whose profound meaning eluded him. Later, at an age when she could've explained the mystery of her pronouncement, he reminded her of those words, but she'd forgotten she'd even uttered them. *Oh, Papa, I'm not a baby anymore*. She spoke with a maturity that pierced him to the core. She might as well have said, *Oh, Papa, I don't need you anymore*. Her eyes, he remembers, took on the detachment of one who'd learned to live with her abandonment, and he grieved her lost innocence, yearned for his baby girl, for the complete trust with which she'd once regarded him.

Something fluid and irrepressible rushes from deep within him and pools behind his eyes. He tries pushing it back. He can't allow himself the consolation of such emotion. Sorrow is the entitlement of the inculpable. He has no claim on it, no right to grief. After all, what has he lost? Nothing. Nothing he wasn't willing to give up then. Still, he can't help but feel it, whatever it may be, sorrow or repentance. It flows out of him, like the season's accumulated rain, meandering through the gorges and gullies of his disfigured face, cutting deeper into the geography of his guilt.

He runs his fingertips along the thin ridge, where the lesion has long healed. The scar, a shade lighter than the rest of his brown skin, extends crosswise from the bridge of his nose to his lower left cheek, giving the impression of two conjoined countenances, the left half dominated by his cataract eye, the right by smaller grooves and slash marks.

If his daughter saw him now, would she compare the jaggedness of his face to the surface of the moon? How would she describe the crudeness of his appearance? Would she see poetry in it? Find some consolably mysterious expression for its irreparable ruin? He never did make the connection between the softness of her skin and her imaginary moonlets. Now he is left to guess she probably associated the distant velvety appearance of the full moon with the caress of sleep, the lure of dreams that causes one's body to relax and soften. But even this is too rational a deduction, for he cannot trust his memories of the full moon to make such a leap. The last moon he saw clearly was more than two decades ago, the evening Sokhon died in Slak Daek, one among many of Pol Pot's secret security prisons across the country, each known only by their coded euphemism as *sala*. School. That evening, at Sala Slak Daek, the moon was bathed not in gentle porous light but in the glaring hue of Sokhon's blood. Blood that now tinges his one-eyed vision and sometimes alters the tone and texture of his memories, the truth.

He closes both eyes, for the effort of keeping them open has begun to strain the muscles and nerves of the right one, as if the left eye, unaware of its uselessness, its compromised existence, continues to strive as the right eye does. Sometimes he thinks this is the sum of his predicament: he is dead but his body has yet to be aware of his death.

He reaches into the pocket of his cotton tunic hanging on a bamboo peg above his pillow and withdraws a cone-shaped plectrum made to put over the fingertip. In the old days, this would be crafted from bronze or, if one was a wealthy enough musician, from silver or gold. But this plectrum is fashioned out of a recycled bullet casing. *Art from war*, said Narunn, the man who gave it to him, a doctor who treats the poor and sometimes victims of violence and torture; who, upon examining his eyes, informed him that the cataract covering his left pupil was caused by untreated "hyphema." An English word, the Old Musician noted. A medical term. A vision clouded by spilled blood. Or as the young doctor explained, *Hemorrhaging in the front of your eye, between the cornea and the iris. Caused by blunt trauma. I believe yours happened at a time when there was no means of treatment.* The doctor did not inquire what might've been the source of the trauma, as if the lesions and scars on the Old Musician intimated the blunt force of ideology, that politics is not mere rhetoric in this place of wars and revolutions and violent coups but a bludgeon with which to forge one's destiny.

Indeed the doctor was kind enough not to interrogate. Instead he revealed to the Old Musician that the brass plectrum was made by a young woman who'd lost half her face in an acid attack, who worked to reconstruct her life, if not her visage, by learning to make jewelry in a rehabilitation program for the maimed and the handicapped. *Hope is a kind of jewel, don't you think?* his young friend pondered aloud. *At once metal-hard and malleable . . .*

Certainly it is the only recyclable currency, the Old Musician thinks, in a country where chaos can suddenly descend and everything, including human life, loses all value.

He places the plectrum over the tip of the ring finger of his right hand, the brass heavy and cool against his nailless skin. It refuses to grow back, the nail of this one finger, the lunula destroyed, a moon permanently obliterated by one smash of his interrogator's pistol. The other fingernails are thick and deformed, some filling only half of the nail beds. He's often surprised that he can still feel with these digits, as if the injuries they sustained decades ago heighten their wariness of contact, sabotage.

He tilts the *sadiev* so that it lies diagonally across his torso, the open side of the cut-gourd sound box now covering the area of his chest where his heartbeats are most pronounced, its domed chamber capturing his every tremor and stirring.

Ksae diev, some call it. He dislikes it, the harshness of the *ks* against his throat, as if the solidity of the first consonant pressed against the evanescence of the second inevitably leads to a betrayal of sound. He much prefers *sadiev*, the syllables melting into each other so that it's barely a whisper, delicate and fleeting, much like the echo it produces.

Eyes still closed, he takes a deep breath as he would before every performance, diving past the noise in his head, the surging memories, his plagued conscience, until he reaches only silence. Then tenderly, with the ring finger of his right hand, the brass plectrum securely in place, he begins to pluck the lower part of the string, while higher up the fingers of his left weave an intricate dance. He plays the song he wrote for his daughter, upon her entry into his world, into his solitary existence as a musician. *I thought I was alone. I walked the universe, looking for another . . .* He remembers the day he brought her home from the hospital, her breath so tenuous still that he wanted to buttress it with notes and words. *I came upon a reflection . . . and saw you standing at the fringes of my dream.*

He adjusts the *sadiev* slightly on his chest. He often dreams of her. Not his daughter. But the little girl to whom this lute rightly belongs. Except she's no longer a little girl, the three-year-old he once met . . . He wonders about the person she's become, the woman she's grown into. He dares not confuse one with the other, the young daughter he lost long ago and the woman he now waits to meet. They're not the same person, he reminds himself. They are not. *And you, you are not him.* Can never be him. The father she lost.

Sometimes, though, his memory rebels. It contrives a game, tricking him into believing that the past can be altered, that he can make up for the missing years, give her back what he stole from her. He can amend— atone. But for what exactly? A betrayal of oneself, one's conscience? Was that what he'd hoped when he decided to write to her? To seek forgiveness for his crimes? Or was it simply, as he said, that he wished to return the musical instruments her father had left for her?

He thinks again of the letter, not what it said, but what it was on the verge of saying, what it almost revealed. *I knew your father. ~~He and I were~~* . . . His failing eyesight had required him to enlist the help of the young doctor to write those words. He told Dr. Narunn to cross out the incomplete sentence. When he'd finished dictating the rest of the letter, the doctor wanted to copy it onto fresh, clean paper, without the crossed-out words. The Old Musician would not allow it. He'd send it as it was, with the mistake, as if he wanted her to see the duplicity of his mind, the treachery of his thoughts. *~~He and I were~~* . . . What they were—men, animals, two sides of a single reality—was destroyed with one deliberate stroke, the laceration made by a moving blade.

He glides the fingers of his left hand closer to the gourd sound box, producing a periodic overtone, like an echo or a ripple in the pond. *I thought I was alone. I walked the universe, looking for your footsteps. I heard my heart echo . . . and felt you knocking on the edge of my dream.*

The quality of each note—its resonance and tone—varies as he slides the half-cut gourd across his chest. He plucks faster and harder, reaching a crescendo. Then, in three distinct notes, he concludes the song.

Teera studies the clouds caressing the wing of the plane. They seem to be in no hurry, gliding at an imperceptible speed, melting into one another like fragments of a childhood memory. *We're going so fast it seems we're sitting still*, her aunt Amara said on their plane ride together as refugees journeying to America. Teera didn't understand it then—the idea that speed could be stillness. She thinks now that what her aunt probably meant by "stillness" is suspension of the senses: you're thrust forward at such incredible speed you're left paralyzed, unable to feel, to absorb all that's happening around you.

It's been more than half an hour since the plane took off from Kuala Lumpur, leaving the colorful landscape of duty-free shops for the blankness of transboundary skies. They've reached cruising altitude, the captain announces. Teera feels herself hurtling. Toward what, she doesn't know. The future and the past lie in borderless proximity.

She turns her face from the window and, closing her eyes, leans back in her seat. Pressing the oversize shoulder bag against her abdomen, she tries to draw from it some sense of anchor, even as she's fully aware that its contents are the very reason for this headlong flight. Her mind leaps through the events of the past months—her aunt's death, the Buddhist cremation ceremony in the depths of Minnesota winter, the unexpected letter from the strange old musician, quitting her job as a grant writer at a community arts center, and now this trip halfway across the world. A year ago Teera couldn't have imagined a life without Amara or this journey she's taking alone to a land they'd risked everything to escape.

Srok Khmer. That's how Cambodians refer to the country in their own language. Never Cambodia, for Cambodia is synonymous with war and revolution and genocide. But Srok Khmer is a place that exists in the geography of the heart, in the longing for what is lost. For Teera, it is no bigger than her childhood home, and the more time passes the smaller still it becomes, like a star whose light diminishes with increasing distance. The rest—the destruction, the killing, and all that was lost—she does not, *will* not, associate with her small private Cambodia. That was Pol Pot's Democratic Kampuchea. Her country disappeared with her family.

A woman's voice over the intercom announces that breakfast will now be served. A flurry of activities ensues as passengers let down the tray tables in front of them in anticipation of the meal.

She's gathered from the snippets of conversations around her that for many overseas Cambodians this is a pilgrimage they take every year they can since the UN-sponsored election a decade ago in 1993. Amidst flight attendants serving food and refreshment, the Cambodian-Americans freely exchange information about their lives. They seem obsessively curious to know what part of America others are from, as if the name of a city or town would pinpoint the exact cause of their isolation.

They reminisce about the old days—the years before the war, before "ar-Pot," always the pejorative prefix denoting their contempt for Pol Pot, which, to all of them, to every Cambodian, including Teera herself, is more than the man or the monster but has become the epithet of an era. *Where were you during ar-Pot?*

In her most pessimistic moments, Teera feels this is the triumph of evil—the name that lives on alongside those of heroes and saints, written in history books, casually pronounced on the lips of adults and children alike, gaining magnitude and permanency in our collective awareness, even as our sensibility becomes immune to all the name subsumes.

"I was in Battambang," says a man across the aisle to his newfound traveling companion. "Awful, awful place. Many deaths there. How about you?"

Teera knows they won't venture beyond the names of provinces, the scant remembrances and quick summaries of their family's ordeals. The horrors they experienced might be expressed only in the one question that runs common in all the conversations she's hazarded upon: *Do you still have family back there?* Often a head shake will say it all. But Teera knows these same people, like the Cambodians in Minnesota, will have ready answers if asked by outsiders. *Many times we almost died. But luckily we survived the killing fields.*

Stock phrases, picked up from television and newspaper, recycled words, compressed and distilled of all ambiguities, leaving no doubt as to who was innocent and who was guilty. *We are Khmers, but these Khmer Rouge, who knows what they were! Real Cambodians would never have killed other Cambodians!*

As for Terra, she keeps quiet and saves her thoughts for paper and pen, her private journey with words, the music of her distilled emotion pulsing through her. She hears it now in the beating of her heart, the rhythm of her own breath.

He puts down the *sadiev*, his gesture tentative, as if lulling a child back to sleep. Behind him in the upper corner of his bamboo bed, among bundles of clothes, crouch the lute's companions, the *sralai*, a kind of oboe, and the *sampho*, a small barrel drum. Made during the revolutionary years, these instruments are younger and newer than the *sadiev*. He feels profound tenderness toward all three, for even in their inanimate silence they appear sentient, conscious of his existence, his history and transgression, yet forgiving, always answering his invocation, offering him the music he seeks for his own healing. For nearly two and a half decades they've been his traveling companions, his only family. Now, he senses, they must part company, he toward his long-overdue demise and they toward love's reclamation.

It's been more than six weeks since he wrote to her about these instruments, and in these shadowy hours, he senses he is about to meet her, and in her face he will recognize the reflection of a dead man.

He hears the first soft chime of the meditation bell at the temple. He takes a deep breath, freeing his mind momentarily of the noise of his thoughts. Even if it brings him only fleeting peace, the act of inhaling and exhaling makes him aware that perhaps his body, like the bell itself, is just another instrument, hollow and mute on its own, yet capable of producing a whole range of tones and pitches when struck. That the clatter and buzz of his mind are not permanent, as he sometimes believes, but self-induced vibrations, transient and hallucinatory.

Ours is a false existence, the monks will soon intone, a variation of the same Buddhist chant they recite day and night. *Suffering and despair are nothing more than illusions. Let go of desires and attachments, and inner peace shall be attained . . .*

He'd like to take comfort in these words, except that by the same logic, peace, or whatever consolation he allows himself, is also an illusion. He can't deny the miseries around him. The limbless men begging at the entrance of every market, their legs or arms blown to pieces by explosives buried in a road or rice field. The ragged old widows wandering the city streets, their minds deranged because they've lost entire families, might've witnessed the executions of their children. The orphans roaming the landfills, scavenging through the refuse for food, for any scraps that will numb their hunger or hide their bone nakedness. They are real, these peripheral, splintered lives, their struggles far from the false manifestations of his tormented conscience. Meditation only makes him see them all the more clearly. The only illusion would be if he allowed himself to believe he'd played no part in the present misery.

What's incredible, preposterous, is the fortuity of his situation. How is it that he's come to be given refuge at a temple, a place whose belief and way of life he once shunned, whose inhabitants the soldiers of his espoused revolution disrobed and annihilated?

If karma is as he understands—the certainty that he'll pay for his crimes—then a temple is the last place he'd expect to be offered a home. How then has he arrived where he is, given sanctuary by men whose brethren his soldiers murdered? What wrinkles or variances in the laws of karma have delivered him to this enclave of mercy, when his actions should've warranted him a punished existence?

At the fall of the regime in the early days of 1979, upon his release from Slak Daek, he headed for the jungle—to nurse his injuries, to hide his shame. For some months he existed in complete isolation, until he could bear it no longer. If he must live out the remains of his days, then he would do so in the company of humans, not the ghosts that had followed him there, the mutilated faces and mangled screams of those slaughtered in Slak Daek. So he emerged from the forests and returned to the world of the living, what was left of it. He went to a village where he knew no one, where no one would recognize him behind the scars of his shattered self. There he built a quiet life, and for many years earned his keep through music, playing the instruments, mostly at funerals and spirit-invoking ceremonies. It was during one such occasion—the funeral of a village chief—that, in a newspaper used to wrap his payment of fried fish and rice, he came upon an article describing the calls to establish a tribunal to try those responsible for the "crimes committed during the Khmer Rouge regime."

Khmer Rouge—he tested the words on his tongue, seeing himself as others would see him if they knew his past. He searched the oil and spice stains saturating the newspaper, turning the once solid-black letters diaphanous, but he did not find his name.

How was he to consider himself? he wondered, letting the flies feast on the rice and fish fallen to the ground. A victim or a perpetrator? He'd believed in the cause he was fighting for, and then, without warning, was shoved into that hellhole for a crime against the Organization, a crime he wasn't aware of but was made to confess again and again. He was a traitor, his torturers had wanted him to admit, a viper slithering and scheming in that insidious *ksae kbot*, that endless "string of betrayals" to which his name was bound along with hundreds—*thousands*—of others. *You can corroborate*, the interrogator would inform him coolly. *Or you can lie there on the tile floor, chew your own tail, like the snake that you are, until there's nothing left, except your head—and the traitorous thoughts you hide there!* A padded club would land on his temple, his head clanging and buzzing, blood flowing out of his ears, pushing against his eyes. *So what will it be? Live or die?* Over and over he'd chosen survival, some part of him foolishly believing his life was still worth something, that he still *had* a life.

Now, years later confronted with his own culpability, he realized all that had remained then was his conscience, the only possible source of truth worthy of his sacrifice. But he'd betrayed that too.

He wiped away the grease and food bits from the newspaper, folded it neatly, and slipped it into his pocket. It was clear what he had to do.

He left his quiet village and came to Phnom Penh. If there was to be a tribunal, he was prepared to turn himself in, be among the first to come forward and face the condemnation of his people and the world, not because he wished to set a moral example for others, but because he believed the initial wrath would be unsparing, merciless. They would be seen for what they were—monsters. They would be convicted of genocide, crimes against humanity, and thrown in jail to rot and die.

Here he caught himself. *Jail?* After what he had endured in Slak Daek, jail would be a farce, a travesty not only of justice but of punishment itself. What inhumanity could he be made to suffer that he hadn't already endured in those macabre cells? He had only to think of it to recall each pain in its intensity and realness, as if somewhere in his skin, amidst the complex, regenerative structures of his cells, hid the contour of his torturer's sadistic malice, twitching and thrashing like a whip, inflicting new lesions upon the old.

Imprisonment, lifetime or otherwise, would be all too light a sentence compared to what he had already known in Slak Daek, too small a reprisal for the magnitude of his crimes. What about death then? What was left of his despicable life that could recompense for the lives he'd taken and the countless more he must've unwittingly harmed or destroyed? Death would be an even easier escape.

Besides, the very fact he'd lived through Slak Daek meant death had rejected him. It had spat him out, as if it found no niche or nook in its vast storehouse of offenders for one as vile as he, as if death only obliged with its punctuality those who understood the value of life.

If there was to be any justice, he was convinced he would have to mete out his own punishment. *Just as well,* he thought. Since that initial appeal he'd read in the newspaper, there was still no tribunal. In the meantime, one by one, Pol Pot and some of those most responsible had died. Others, like himself, were quickly growing old, and before long would be too feeble to stand trial. When it became obvious the tribunal would not happen for many more years, there was only one place for him to go.

Finally he faced it, sitting one morning on a street corner outside the wall of Wat Nagara, a temple on the edge of the Mekong. It was at this temple that Sokhon had immersed himself in meditation, the life of a young novice. It had once been his beloved childhood home. A group of novice monks, returning from their alms walk at dawn, encountered the Old Musician playing the *sadiev* and, out of pity for a disfigured, homeless elder, offered him food from their alms. That evening, having sought the permission of the abbot, the same group of novices invited him to spend the night on the temple grounds, away from the stench and filth and danger of the streets. They offered him the wooden cottage belonging to the temple sweeper who had recently passed. *Stay as long as you like*, the abbot told him. *We could use a musician.* So he stayed, fed and clothed by a daily tenet of generosity, protected by a shared belief that a temple is where one quietly seeks ablution and forgiveness, where peace of mind may be found through silent reflection. *Who among us, dear old man, has not been touched by tragedy?* the abbot asked, sensing the weight of his affliction. *Who among us does not bear the burden of survival?* The other monks echoed, *Whatever your transgression, you've paid for it with your injuries.*

If they knew his past, they would see that his injuries—his partial blindness and physical disfigurement—convey not just transgression but a bodily dossier of unconfessed crimes. *It's time you merit a better karma.* They encouraged him to join the sangha, their spiritual community of ritual contemplation. *Let go of the troubles of the world and you'll find the peace you seek.*

He declined. He'd come to the temple not to escape retribution but to put himself at the gates of forgiveness, knowing full well that he could never be forgiven, that he did not deserve the charity and kindness he received, that his only salvation was in the realization of his own worthlessness, his evil and monstrosity. This was to be his deserved punishment—to live the rest of his days in self-condemnation, self-loathing.

Or so he thought.

A young Malaysian flight attendant in a blue flowered batik dress—a *kabeya*, Teera remembers from an article in the in-flight magazine—leans forward, pushing the heavy compact metal cart with her slender frame. She asks the elderly couple sitting next to Teera what they'd like. They don't understand. Teera isn't at all surprised these two old people can't speak English, though she noticed earlier that they carry American passports. Like many elderly Cambodians she's come across, they may have never, aside from this trip, ventured outside their community.

The flight attendant repeats the meal choices, raising her voice slightly as if the old couple were hard of hearing: "Beef fried rice or mushroom omelet?—Asian breakfast or Western," she adds for clarification. Still, they don't understand. Teera tells her, "Fried rice—for both," knowing, without having to confer with the old couple, they'll always prefer rice. It's in their blood. Once they may have even risked their lives to steal a spoonful.

Rice. Mama, rice. Her brother's last words. He was born some months after the Khmer Rouge had taken over. When they left home that April morning in 1975, joining the forced mass exodus out of Phnom Penh, Teera hadn't known her mother was pregnant. *Rin hungry. Tummy hurts.* Hunger was among her baby brother's first words, his first knowledge, and he died as he was just learning to talk. She blinks away the memories.

"And you, ma'am?" the flight attendant asks, her gaze on Teera.

"Coffee, please," she says.

In the first years after their arrival in America, she and Amara did try to put it all behind them. When Amara was asked if the Khmer Rouge regime had been as horrible as portrayed, her answer was always simple. *Yes*. Amara's silence reinforced her own. It built thicker and higher walls, until it seemed the two of them existed in separate cells, prisoners to all they couldn't say.

"What about breakfast?" the flight attendant says.

Teera shakes her head. She wants to explain she's not hungry, but the effort of finding words for her thoughts requires more energy than she can muster. Besides, there are crackers in her bag. She'll nibble on those if needed. She hasn't felt hunger, felt the desire to eat since boarding the flight in Minneapolis more than twenty hours ago. Since Amara's death, really.

"No, just coffee, thanks."

Teera sips the lukewarm diluted liquid, letting the mild bitterness glide down her throat. Next to her, the old woman seems overwhelmed by all the little packages on her tray, unsure what to tackle first. Then, following her husband's lead, she peels the foil cover from the rectangular dish and sniffs the fried rice. The thick smell of reheated grease is overpowering. Again, Teera feels nauseous. She tries holding her breath to block the odor.

The old woman begins to pick out the greasy, stringy beef with her fork and puts it in her husband's dish. Turning to Teera, she says in Khmer, "No teeth left." She smacks her exposed gums together and grins.

In spite of herself, Teera smiles and reluctantly lets down her guard.

"Is this your first time going back, *chao srey*?"

Teera's heart skips a beat. It isn't at all unusual for Cambodians to address one another in familial terms, but she can't remember when she was last called "granddaughter" with such tenderness. An image of the cave where Teera left her grandparents blooms in her mind, its entrance illuminated by the setting sun, giving the impression that it was lit from within. She swallows, wondering as she has countless times over the years how they perished. Who went first—her gentle, diminutive grandmother, or her stoic, once-imposing grandfather? They'd already been starving, their bodies weakened and damaged beyond saving, when she and Amara were forced to abandon them in the cave in order to keep up with the rest of their group as they navigated the jungle. They probably didn't last through the night. They had survived through the regime, through four long, miserable years, only to end up betrayed by life, handed over to death in the middle of nowhere.

Teera takes another sip of the coffee to help ease down the lump in her throat. She gives only a tentative nod to the old woman's inquiry. Already she regrets allowing herself to be seduced by those toothless grins.

"It's our first trip as well," the old woman says. "Now that we're getting on in years we haven't got much time left, as you can see. Soon we'll be too old and sick to travel."

Teera winces, recalling the oncologist's words not long ago. *At this advanced stage, I'm afraid the prognosis is not good.* She remembers him looking from her to Amara as he spoke, unsure who was responsible for whom. When she and her aunt first walked into his office, he'd assumed they were sisters, as Amara's petite frame made her look more like a woman in her late thirties than midforties. *I am truly sorry*, he concluded decisively after what felt like mere seconds. *What could you know!* Teera felt the urge to scream at him, at his useless apologies, the absurdity of it all. For them to have endured indescribable inhumanity only to succumb to something as nameable as pancreatic cancer seemed a mockery of their struggle all these years to rebuild their lives. It was their shared belief that after what they had been through they'd overcome anything, that their survival had purpose and meaning—a *reason*. They were meant to live, damn it, she wanted to tell the smug doctor. Amara was stronger than this. She'd live. Her aunt would fight and live. *You'll see!* Instead, in a tone close to threatening, Teera rasped, *We'll seek a second opinion.* And to Amara, she added shakily, desperately, *A third and fourth, if we need to.* Amara looked at her with pity, as if Teera had been the one with cancer. They left the doctor's office in defeated silence.

Only later, when they were back home, did Amara speak. *If I'd had more time, I might've returned to Cambodia.* Her aunt had chosen her words carefully, speaking in her precise, practiced English. But all Teera could think of was that the verb tense was all wrong. Did Amara not remember anything about the past subjunctive from all those grammar lessons Teera had helped her with? *You're not dead yet*, she wanted to say. *There's still time. You have more time. You do!* Instead, she burst into tears, to which Amara responded, *Oh, Teera, we've been blessed in so many ways. I've had a good life. I got to see you grow up, didn't I? I'll always be grateful for these extra years, for all we've built together here.* Her aunt sounded as if she believed she ought to have died with the others. Teera grew more upset.

In the following days and weeks, Amara, with her characteristic equanimity, proceeded to put her life in order. She resigned from her longtime position as the head of an organization that provided social services to Cambodian immigrants and refugees in Minnesota. She went to a lawyer and made a will to ensure that Teera, her only kin, would receive all her savings and assets, which, including a life insurance policy she'd had the foresight to buy many years earlier, amounted to a small fortune. *Certainly enough to allow you to devote time to your own writing*, she explained matter-of-factly, while Teera listened in stunned dismay. *You must look after yourself, darling. Tend to all that's alive in you, to what's living. And let me tend to the dead.*

Besides the inheritance she'd left for Teera, Amara had bequeathed an amount for the construction of a communal stupa at Wat Nagara, their old family temple. She told Teera she'd already written to the abbot of the temple, expressing her intentions that it serve as a kind of memorial to their family, and to those who had perished during the Khmer Rouge years. Weeks passed, then a month, then two. Amara grew visibly sick, her physical deterioration reducing her to a pale copy of herself. Then one day, sitting Teera down and handing her a small wooden box, Amara said, *If you should ever return to our country, please take a bit of my ashes in this and leave it in the stupa there.* Teera reeled in the midst of her aunt's calm instructions. *But you're still alive!* she wanted to shout, too confused and upset to make sense of her own words, let alone Amara's. *Divide up the ashes?* She felt certain this was sacrilegious—a violation of Buddhist custom and belief, even as she was acutely aware that a divided self was something her aunt had to live with daily since their arrival in America, a reality she struggled to accept as she built her life in a country where she felt she never truly belonged.

If you should ever return . . . Those words angered Teera. They sounded like a betrayal. Why should she? Why would she want to? There would be no one for her to visit or reconnect with. Unless this was Amara's way of saying *she* wanted Teera to return, to take her back and reunite her, if only in spirit, with the rest of the family. Teera couldn't voice her objection. Amara was dying.

Every time she thinks of her inheritance, Teera can't escape the feeling that she's always gotten the better end of life, while her aunt bore the brunt of it, suffered. Died. Is this why she's going back now? To purge her own guilt by fulfilling Amara's unspoken longing for home?

Amara passed at the beginning of the year, three days short of her forty-seventh birthday. Her sudden death sent shock through the Cambodian community, and the tremendous outpouring of grief engendered a kind of collective mourning on a scale befitting a minor celebrity. Teera shouldn't have been surprised. For many years, Amara was a constant fixture in the lives of so many. There was never a birthday, graduation, wedding, or funeral she failed to attend. If invited, which was almost always, she was there to offer her quiet support. Naturally, when news of her death got out, the whole community came to pay respects, gathering at a funeral home in Minneapolis, where the undertaker, familiar with the rites of a Cambodian funeral, arranged a row of chairs for Buddhist monks on the pulpit facing the mourners. They went on to the crematory a few blocks away, where Amara's body was incinerated and the ashes collected in an urn with the efficiency, Teera noted with dismay, of a well-run bakery. The next day they gathered once more at Wat Minnesotaram, the temple in rural Hampton where an evening wake was held. The urn was on display atop a small table beside a photograph of

Amara, accompanied by funerary chants and music meant to ease her aunt's spirit on its journey into the otherworld.

Then, sometime at the end of June, a bit more than half a year after Amara's death, just when Teera felt that everyone had grown accustomed to her aunt's absence and she could begin to mourn privately, a letter arrived from Cambodia. The author of the letter offered his condolences. He had heard of Amara's untimely passing from the abbot of Wat Nagara, the temple where he had sought shelter. To Teera's astonishment, the stranger went on to explain that while he offered his deepest sympathies for her great loss, he was in fact writing in regard to some musical instruments belonging to her father, which he wished to give her. Teera didn't know what to make of it, believing for a moment it might've been an opportunist's vague solicitation for money. She ought to trash it. But something about the letter made her hesitate. Its tone, perhaps. *A tone is the intention of a note*, Amara would say in moments of unbidden remembering, quoting her father, repeating things that had struck her as mysterious or prophetic. The tone of the letter made Teera believe that the stranger's intention was honorable. Sincere.

Three instruments, the letter said, yet it failed to mention what they were. Teera couldn't help but think how ironic it was that, while houses and monuments and entire cities had dissolved and vanished, these instruments, trivial and fragile by comparison, had endured. How had the instruments found their way into this man's care? If indeed they'd once belonged to her father, what would she do with them now? What use could they serve when she could no longer hear her father's music?

She tried repeatedly to put the letter away, stashing it in various drawers, burying it under piles of mail, or filing it randomly in one of the hanging folders at her writing desk so she'd forget its whereabouts, only to retrieve it again and reread the words, its whispers and intimations. *The man knew her father.* They were together, it said, during the final year of the Khmer Rouge regime. Imprisoned, her father had survived almost until the end. *But how? By what means?* Had he made any effort to find them during the prior three years? What was his crime? And, most curiously, why did this man, who claimed to know her father, only now make contact? Who was he? What could he possibly want? Hard as she resisted, Teera couldn't escape the pull of the past.

Truth, she believed, lies in what is said as much as in what isn't, in the same way that a melody not only is a sequence of audible notes but encompasses the spaces and pauses in between. *When listening to music, you must learn to take in even the atmosphere of an echo.*

She wasn't sure whether she'd first recalled these words on her own, or whether, like so much of what she remembered, they'd emerged from Amara's recounting and fused with her own recollections of those early childhood years when she'd follow her father to universities and performance halls to hear him lecture. In any case, these words over time came to invoke for her the cave in which her grandparents had been abandoned to die twenty-four years earlier, in 1979. A cave whose yawning silence must've augmented the sound of their labored breaths, and elongated the pauses in between.

She wondered if the author of the letter would be able to explain what her father might've meant by "atmosphere of an echo." Is it like the inside of a cave, where a person's life is slowly absorbed into the stillness, as a flame is extinguished for lack of oxygen? Or is it like the hollow of a mass grave, where even silence has a tenor, carrying with it the rebuke of the dead, their relentless reproach that the living have yet to honor them with a reply, an answer to why they died, why atrocity such as this was allowed to happen, why it happens still?

Teera finally stowed the stranger's letter in the cedar chest where she kept some of Amara's cherished belongings. Then, taking everyone by surprise, she resigned from her position at the community arts center. It was clear that her friends and colleagues saw the abrupt departure as a kind of denial, her inability to deal with grief or, as some put it, to properly mourn her aunt's death. But Teera knew all too well that grief is an unpredictable, untimely visitor. One can never properly prepare for its arrival. If anything, her sudden resignation kept the door open for grieving so that indeed she might move beyond it.

Now here she is, on a plane, plunging she feels not forward with her life but backward. Once again her mind is overtaken by recollections of another headlong flight—that fraught journey across jungles and battle-fields when, with each dash forward, she would turn to look behind her, gripped by the uncanny feeling that someone or something was pursuing her, calling out her name. She didn't—couldn't—know then that this constant backward glance would come to define her life, her inviolable tie to that land and its ghosts. She will never be free of it. Still, at the time, she tried to outrun it, tried to escape its incessant calling.

Suteera, Suteera . . .

Memories swell, flooding Teera's mind, her vision. She pulls herself up, breaking the surface, breathless with the knowledge of where she's heading and why. Certainly she intends to take Amara's ashes to consecrate the stupa, its construction now completed, as she's learned from the abbot of Wat Nagara, and to reclaim her father's instruments. While she won't admit so aloud, the main reason for her return, and perhaps the only reason, is her father. He is the only one who holds her to the past.

Surely, she'll finally learn from the writer of the letter what happened to him. In the nearly four years of the Khmer Rouge rule, as one death followed another, her father's disappearance never attained that searing ache of a definitive loss. She would search for him everywhere. Even now, decades later, his ghost haunts her most persistently.

She can't help but believe he vanished violently.

He hears her name now in each ring of the meditation bell. The very first time he heard it, the Old Musician thought it a phantom echo, like a soft trill in a musical passage, a familiar reprise of the same few notes in an otherwise erratic melody of his madness.

It was this past May, during Visakha Bochea, a festival celebrating the three most significant events of the Buddha's life—birth, enlightenment, nirvana—when the abbot announced to the whole sangha that a certain Miss Suteera Aung, a Cambodian living in America, had sent a substantial gift for the construction of a large communal stupa on behalf of her aunt.

Suteera Aung. It took the Old Musician a few seconds to recognize it, as the abbot had said the surname second, the form she must have adopted in the United States. *Our benefactor wants the communal stupa to be a place*, the abbot went on, *where those who cannot afford to build a private family stupa can store the remains of loved ones perished during the Pol Pot years. Remains, as described by Miss Suteera Aung, might be the ashes of exhumed skulls and bones, an old photograph, pieces of old clothes, memories of the deceased, our prayers and wishes for them. Anything really . . .*

As the Old Musician listened to the abbot, a wave of calm passed through him. *She's alive.* He was caught between disbelief and the inexplicable sense that he'd known all along. How he could be so sure of such a thing, he can't explain. He only felt he'd been waiting for this moment. What happened next would fall neatly into place, as if the long, twisted course he'd traveled for the past decades suddenly straightened and revealed the only direction left for him to take.

He waited, like a condemned prisoner given time to take stock of his life and ready himself for execution. He wanted to plan it right, to imagine his final moment of reckoning, to anticipate, as he'd often done in Slak Daek, the full extent of agony and pain so that he wouldn't lose the courage to bear it.

After all, he reminded himself, he'd willed this. Days after Visakha Bochea, he went to the abbot and told him the truth, the bits he could bear to tell—that he'd once known Suteera's father, that he'd chosen Wat Nagara knowing that if any family member survived, they would someday come here. In case there was any doubt about his intentions, he made clear he was not seeking to benefit from the connection in any way; he desired neither pity nor recompense of any sort, least of all from the young woman. He repeated that he wished only to return the instruments—the remains of the father she'd lost. Perhaps she would want them kept in the communal stupa once it was built. In any case, they were hers to do with as she saw fit.

The abbot, moved by the story of this broken man who all these years had held on to the only possessions of a dead friend in hopes of returning them to his family, gave him the address in America and said he could write Miss Suteera Aung himself. Then the abbot told him something he hadn't expected to hear: the gift of funds for the construction of the communal stupa came from Miss Suteera's aunt, a longtime patron of the temple until her untimely passing a few months prior, at the beginning of the year. *We knew the aunt was sick*, the abbot said, *but we didn't expect her to go so soon. Her death is a blow to us.* The old monk then added, *It may be that Miss Suteera doesn't want to hear from the ghost of her father at this time. It's hard enough to bury one family member, you see, without exhuming the memory of another. You will understand, of course, if she doesn't wish to reply.*

The Old Musician could only nod. She had not been alone! He did not know if Suteera and her aunt were the only two members of the family to have survived the regime. He assumed this was the case since the abbot mentioned no one else—not her mother, Channara. He dared not ask. His heart quaked at the name alone.

Again, the bell rings, as his recollections swell. It was the end of June when he'd finally decided to write. It is now September, and he has received no word from her. Still, he convinces himself it is only a matter of time before he faces her and confesses, before he looks into her eyes. And only then, only when he sees himself through her, will he know pain worse than any he experienced in Slak Daek. She will be his scourge, her loathing his final and lasting suffering.

The Old Musician turns his face from the dark corners of his cottage toward a patch of gray light filtering through the burlap curtaining his doorway. Even with his eyes closed, he can always feel light, its source and temperament. Its design on his skin, if it intends to soothe or hurt, warm or scorch.

In Slak Daek, blindfolded with a black cloth, he was often taken from his cell in the middle of the night and shoved across the grassless quadrangle to the interrogation room. Though he couldn't see, he would always know the moment he stepped from the natural light of the night cast by the stars or the moon into the fluorescent glare of his torturers' chamber.

The bell issues its final call. The monks have begun their morning chant. In their plaintive incantation on the meaning of existence, the Old Musician hears again and again the allusion to misery and pain. *This cycle to which we are bound . . . spinning in perpetual ignorance and strife . . .* In a little while, alms bowls in hands, they will leave the temple and walk the streets barefoot, pausing in front of a house or shop to receive a family's first proffering of cooked rice and vegetables, food they will bring back to share with him and those who have sought refuge here. *We, who cling and desire . . .* their voices thick, viscous like balm . . . *we, who attach ourselves to this earthly realm, with all its ills and illusions, we cannot escape the wheel of samsara, the ceaseless rotation . . .* Yet, he finds life unbearably kind to him. After all that he destroyed and violated, the sun still rises and offers him its light and colors, the rain still falls and refills his clay cistern, and these monks who intone life to be an inescapable circle of sorrow still see fit to give him food and shelter to ease his suffering. How is it that he, who had such low regard for the sanctity of human life, has lived this long, the charity of old age doled out to him?

He stands up from his bamboo bed and, with one arm stretched out before him, lifts the burlap partition. He steps out into the morning, his eyes open now, and though he can barely make out the rows of monks chanting in the prayer hall, their saffron robes made more brilliant by the sunrise, he knows that their harmonized chanting will give his day solace.

Above him, the wind sweeps through the trees, shaking loose the night's residual rain, and he hears the drops hitting the bamboo trough attached to his cottage in an almost pentatonic succession. Or has she—his daughter, the lute in whose voice she now speaks—called out to him?

What can the author of the letter tell her that he couldn't or wouldn't say from a distance? There has to be more to his shared history with her father than those instruments. He didn't reveal his name, only the curious signature, *Lokta Pleng at Wat Nagara*—"the Old Musician at Nagara Temple"—at the bottom of the page, in a shaky, barely legible scrawl that contrasted with the neat, careful handwriting of the body of the letter, as if he'd grown old and tired in the course of composing it.

"Yes, we're going home," the old couple in the seats next to her echo back and forth, squeezing each other's hand.

Home. They use the word so easily, savoring its single syllable like the taste of palm sugar remembered from long ago.

Amara, in her final days, wasn't so clear about where she wanted to be. *I'd like to reincarnate here*, she'd said in a moment of clarity between the morphine injections given to alleviate her pain. *Here, in Minnesota, where snow covers and erases everything. Where the seasons forgive all our wrongs.* Then later, in another moment, she cried out in anguish, *Take me back, Teera. I want to be with the others. Let me die in Srok Khmer.* This, of course, wasn't possible. A mere three months after she'd been diagnosed with the cancer, Amara took her last breath. There was barely time to find a funeral home, let alone make arrangements to return to their homeland.

At Wat Minnesotaram, where Teera has left the rest of Amara's ashes in an urn, her aunt can slip back and forth between one existence and another. She imagines Amara's ghost sitting in the prayer hall now, calm and collected in death as she'd been in life, neither accepting nor denying her passing but observing with her keen eye the irony of geography—that borrowed landscape of snowy winters and cornfields in which their tropical dream rose from a modest farmhouse into a glittering reality, a sanctuary of gold spires and ornately carved columns, safe from the threats of war and revolution.

Teera leans her head back and closes her eyes. She should've never set foot on the plane. Now there's no changing her mind.

Slak Daek, the Old Musician had written in his letter. How long were he and her father in that chamber of torture together? What were their crimes? What had they done—been accused of? She's read enough to know that out of the thousands of mass grave sites discovered across Cambodia, most were located at or close to the Khmer Rouge security prisons. In Kompong Thom Province alone, which the Old Musician mentioned in his letter as the location of Slak Daek, nearly twenty mass grave sites have been surveyed and are believed to contain the remains of more than 120,000 victims. In Kompong Cham, where Teera and the rest of her family finally ended up after their expulsion from Phnom Penh, sixty-one mass grave sites have been found, with close to 180,000 victims.

In her obsession, her search to understand, Teera will read everything she can get her hands on, the latest findings, and when she comes across a photograph of the remains of the dead, always she wonders if some piece of her family is among the skulls and bones captured in the image. Often she'll gaze at a fractured cranium, look into the hollows of eye sockets, with the unease that it's not the living, the survivors, but the dead who bear witness, their vision unabated, reaching across time, seeing the violence committed, now and again, their warning unheard. Unheeded.

Tightness fills the small space between her brows. Teera pinches her skin to release it. When she opens her eyes again, the low ceiling of the aircraft cabin tilts left and right, and she feels herself whirling in confusion. How much did her father suffer? How did he die? Did they shoot him from behind? Was he allowed to run? Or did they tie his hands and ankles? There were other ways to destroy a person, she remembers. Other methods more effective, more efficient. In his final moments, did her father think of the family? Of her? Or was his killer's face the last he remembered?

She doesn't know why she bothers with such useless queries. They're like holes in a moth-eaten mat, and when she peers into them, they lead only to greater voids.

Teera feels a hand on her arm. She looks up and sees the flight attendant smiling at her. The young woman reminds her to bring her seat to an upright position. The plane has begun its descent into Phnom Penh International Airport. Around her, the Cambodians chatter away in anticipation of the landing. She is suddenly aware that sweat is trickling down the sides of her face. She wipes it away with the base of her palm. She turns toward the window.

A terrain of slender sugar palms and straw huts comes into view, desolate and scarred, the earth a deep saffron color. For some reason, maybe because of the Angkor advertisement she came across earlier, Teera expects to see more green, to be greeted by a lush tropical landscape of coconuts and teaks, emerald rice paddies, lakes and ponds filled with lotus and water lily, rivers embroidered with winged sampans and palm canoes with prows like beaks of birds. Instead, what lies below resembles a battleground, pockmarked by dark-water holes and bomb-crater-like gashes. A fractured geography.

What can it tell her? What lies beneath those patches of gray and brown? What secrets does this wounded earth hold for her that she doesn't already know? Does it conceal in its crevices her father's dying scream, his shattered ideals and dreams, evidence of his alleged crime, the possibility of his redemption, as well as her own?

The plane dips left, dropping in altitude. The city comes into sharper focus. "*That's Phnom Penh?*" someone says, evidently disappointed. "It looks like . . . like nothing."

The city slips in and out of vision in the framed perspective of the small window. It's nothing like what Teera has come to expect of a city. Even from this bird's-eye view, it looks more like a rural town than the capital of a country. Her eyes scan the city's topography, looking for the golden temples and red-tile roofs from the 1960s *National Geographic* features she pored over time and again as a university student, scouring for evidence of her history, the fragments of her home and family. All she discerns now is architectural incongruity, the remnants of prewar edifices patched together with newer, grayer blocks.

The plane tilts right, and Teera catches the glints of a gold-painted rooftop in the distance along a river. Could it be the Royal Palace? And the river—is it the Tonle Sap?

Images of the old Phnom Penh suddenly flood her mind—the layered steeple of the Independence Monument rising out of its circular foundation like the mauve flame of an immense candle; Wat Phnom shimmering in the afternoon sun; the palace grounds dotted with glittering halls and carved pavilions, resembling, she always thought when she was little, a celestial city; the Tonle Sap River brimming with monsoon rains.

The plane swoops down, then touches ground with a light bump. Teera's heart skips a beat. Next to her, the old woman weeps. "We're home," she tells her husband, taking his hand, and he, in return, cups his over hers, fighting back the tears rimming his eyes, his chin trembling.

Teera presses her forehead hard against the window, feeling helpless in the presence of such exposed sentiments. Over the years, she's learned to blanket her feelings in the rhythm of another's language. Even her name has taken on a more pronounceable disguise. Teera instead of Suteera. She's an American. This is no longer her home.

As the plane makes its way smoothly along the runway, her heart lurches, banging against her chest. Again, she clutches her oversize shoulder bag to still herself. Inside are the valuables—her passport, some cash and a couple of credit cards, the small wooden box of Amara's ashes, and the Old Musician's letter.

My dear young lady, I don't know how to properly begin this letter. She's read it so many times she can recall it word for word. *There is so much to say . . .* It isn't a long letter, but the empty spaces between the lines resonate with inexpressible sadness, their parallel sorrows. *I knew your father.* She imagines his pen poised at an angle as he paused in search of the next word, the next sentence, while his mind leapt over countless things he wanted to tell her. ~~He and I were~~ *. . .* The words were crossed out, a single straight line running through them, as if the mistake was immutable, impossible to obliterate or retract by a new beginning. Teera was touched by its honesty, its self-revelation when she first read it. *We were in Kompong Thom together during the last year of Pol Pot's regime, in Sala Slak Daek. A prison. How I survived such a place, I do not know. Why I survived at all is a question that has plagued me until now . . .*

The plane slows, gliding parallel to the terminal building, its reflection undulating in the windowpanes. *Alas, I am an old man, I shall confront death soon enough.*

Teera feels the gears shift and the aircraft coming to a full stop. *I don't know how much time is left, or if it is already too late . . . I have in my possession three musical instruments that once belonged to your father. He would have liked you to have them. He would have liked you to know that some part of him lives, even if only in these instruments.*

In her mind, Teera hears the music of her father's *sadiev*. She doesn't know why, but of all the instruments he played, she remembers the sound of this ancient lute most vividly. Perhaps it's because as a child she grew up listening to her father trying to master it. She remembers a song, not its name but its melody, each note like a drop of predawn rain on bamboo.

She closes her eyes and lets the melody wash over her.

Someone raps on the front of his cottage. The Old Musician opens his eyes. The Venerable Kong Oul stands in the open doorway, a small black umbrella shielding the elder monk from the soft drizzle. "I'm sorry for intruding," the abbot apologizes, his voice unusually deep and authoritative for a man so slight in build.

"I've come to ask for your participation in a ceremony. We have a young couple, the Rattanaks—you know them—whose boy is sick, and they wish to hold a blessing for him."

The Old Musician recalls seeing the couple and their boy some months back. "What's wrong with Makara, Venerable?"

"*Louh pralung*—the parents believe a ghost has lured their son's spirit from his body to a forest, and as such they wish to make an offering of food and music to call the straying spirit back to the body. I'm wondering if you could play your *sadiev*."

"Of course, Venerable."

The abbot furrows his brow. "I've spoken with Dr. Narunn. He said the boy is suffering from drug abuse and recommended he be taken to a proper rehabilitation center, preferably an international one. I've expressed as much to the parents. While they suspect he's indeed using this 'crazy medicine'—as they call it—they believe that the straying of his spirit may be the root of all their son's problems."

Then, brightening, the abbot adds, "We've decided the ceremony should take place ten days from now, which coincides with the boy's birthday. An auspicious day, befitting a ceremony for rebirth, don't you think?"

"Yes, Venerable."

The abbot's eyes stray over to the upper corner of the bamboo bed where the lute leans over the oboe and drum as if whispering in confidence. "You ought to know I wrote to Miss Suteera, informing her that the communal stupa is finished. This was a while ago. I've yet to receive a reply." The abbot hesitates. "It's possible that her spirit has also strayed, journeyed too far to hear your lament. If it's any consolation, my dear old man, I believe these instruments are meant for your keeping. Perhaps their purpose is to aid you in transcending another's suffering."

"You are too kind and wise, Venerable. I rely on your foresight."

The abbot studies him, then, putting out his hand to feel the splattering drops, says, "Ah, if only I had the foresight to know when the rain will clear. I'll let you return to your reverie."

Alone again, the Old Musician tries to picture her in this setting. She whose presence he has sensed these past months, as surely as he felt her father's ghost with him all these years. He straightens and looks around the vast temple grounds, his mind discerning clearly those things his vision can perceive only vaguely from a distance.

The compound is hemmed lengthwise on the east by the Mekong and on the west by a road. A *vihear*, a rectangular prayer hall, rises in the middle of the grounds, wrapped by a spacious white-pillared veranda, with a set of tall double teak doors on each side painted an earthy red and stenciled with gold-enameled lotuses. He was hardly surprised to learn that the whole compound was in ruins when the Venerable Kong Oul found it in the mid-1980s. The Old Musician knew all too well that most of the country's Buddhist temples, along with churches and mosques and other religious edifices, were converted during the regime into warehouses, holding centers, or prisons. He himself had seen to some of these transformations firsthand, turning a blind eye as his young comrades beheaded and toppled statues of the Buddha or used them for target practice. Many times he has wanted to confess to the abbot his role in the regime, but always the Old Musician feels he is pardoned before he opens his mouth.

"I lost every single member of my family," the old monk told him. "I've remained in the sangha, this spiritual fellowship, not so much to worship the gods but to honor the ghosts." When he'd come upon the desecrated temple grounds during a boat ride along the Mekong, what first caught his eye was the remains of a staircase rising from piles of rubble and wooden debris. This partially burnt stairway, ascending to nowhere, moved him profoundly. The abbot set right away on the task of restoring Wat Nagara. "From this, from nothing, where could we go but up? We must rise from the ashes."

Standing where he is, the Old Musician can see past the *vihear*, the cremation pavilion, and the cluster of stupas to the high wall and the two gates that open to the main road. An ancient banyan tree separates the stupas from the clearing where many festivities and celebrations take place. In the dry season the area is bare and brown, but during the rainy season talon grass, known for its tenacious hold on the earth, carpets the slope down to the river, whose sandy shore has all but disappeared, swallowed by the seasonal floods. Presently the concrete stairway, flanked by *naga* balustrades, descends halfway into the water, with the serpents' heads completely submerged, leaving visible only their undulating tails.

Tall, mature frangipanis shade the grounds, some of their branches so bowed as to suggest hammocks, lending to the belief that ghosts and spirits often seek the refuge of these trees for their faintly fragrant blossoms. The Old Musician can't be sure about the ghosts, but he certainly appreciates the trees' ethereal beauty. The flowers fall in a constant stream, enshrouding the stupas and the surrounding pathways. They have a tentative hold on life, these blossoms. For it seems the moment their petals spread open, their beauty in full bloom, they lose their grip on the stems and fall to death. Their descent is made more poignant by a pair of white cotton banners hanging vertically along the front pillars of the cremation pavilion, each bearing in ornate black script a line of funerary *smoat*, poetry sung without music—

As these blossoms wilt away . . .
So my body succumbs to its inevitable end.

That something as beautiful as a flower will also have served its purpose gives him comfort. His time too will surely come.

The Old Musician returns his gaze toward the nearest gate, then the one farther away. Nothing. Not a sound or silhouette. He feels his hope slipping away, its footfalls heavy upon his heart.

There's an interlude, a hiatus of melodic shimmer. He can almost hear it, the sound of sunlight bouncing off the leaves and petals, hitting the soft earth, a medley of notes that recall the rosewood keys of a curved xylophone in a royal court ensemble. He lifts the banana leaves that shelter his supply of firewood and sets them aside. It is a week from Pchum Ben, the festival honoring the dead, and for the past several days, the rains have fallen almost continuously, as if the sky wishes also to remember these otherworldly exiles and itinerants, mourning them with renewed tears, so that between one burst and the next the ground never fully dries but appears steeped in shadows, undefined longings.

Next to the firewood, under a small plastic sheet, nestles an earthen brazier, shaped like a bottle gourd sliced lengthwise and hollowed out, with the bigger basin for the fire, and the smaller, shallower basin for excess cinders and ash. The Old Musician squats down, pulls the partially blackened brazier toward him, and, with a small bundle of twigs held together by dry vines, begins to loosen the moisture-laden ash that has settled like thick batter. If the rain keeps away, the ceremony to call Makara's spirit back to his body will take place today at sunset as scheduled, and by then hopefully the ground will have mostly dried for the procession around the temple.

The Old Musician closes his eyes as he works his twig whisk. Life hums and whirs around him. He's learned to take in his surroundings within the first few moments, as one might learn to discern the form and mood of a song by hearing the first phrase of notes. Considering the blows his head received during those months at Slak Daek, it's a wonder he can still hear. And at the moment he hears everything. Right beside him, an orchestra of insects buzzes in their chamber beneath the firewood. Some forty meters away, the Mekong rushes in full spate. Hidden in the roof of some nearby structure, a gecko rasps, *Tikkaer! Tikkaer!*

A thunderclap rumbles in the north, in the direction of the city. At the far corner of the temple compound the air whistles. A rush of leaves falling from a great height. Something crashes to the ground with a resounding thud, as if following the command of the thunder. A desiccated palm frond, the Old Musician surmises. Not far from him, two adolescent monks on the steps of their *kot*—the wooden cottage on stilts—recite by rote their English lessons, chanting as they would the Buddhist dharma. *My name is Mr. Brown. What is your name? My name is Mr. Smit* . . . In their saffron robes, with their arms and shoulders bare, the interplay of cloth and skin, they remind the Old Musician of a pair of orange-spotted geckos he once glimpsed under the front eave of his cottage. He half expects them to chime, *Tikkaer!* Instead, they reel off back and forth, *How do you do? I'm fine, sankyou.*

Sankyou. He can't help but smile. For most Cambodians, the *th* is difficult to articulate. Likewise, Smit could well be a Khmer name, easily pronounceable, but not Smith. Most people looking at him—an impoverished old musician, disfigured and half-blind—never guess he once spoke this language with great fluency. He wonders whether the saffron-robed Mr. Smith and Mr. Brown will accept his help if offered. Or will they regard him with skepticism, as the young often regard the old? He doesn't blame them, youth with their doubt and distrust. They've inherited a harsh world, and there is much to question. He for one is suspect.

Where do you live? My how is near de market. My how is near de river. House, he wants to correct. *The* market, *the* river.

In Democratic Kampuchea, he forced himself to forget most of the

English he'd learned in his youth. But now, with it used everywhere, he remembers more and more each day, with a speed and ease he didn't think possible. Quite often a word or phrase will skim the surface of his mind, like a stone skipping the stillness of a pond, rippling his memory.

He recalls an English word he learned during his brief sojourn in America in the fall of 1961 when he was a university student. *Heart-strings*. The woman he loved taught it to him. "It could be the perfect English name for the *sadiev*," she said, placing her head on his bare chest as they lay on the narrow bed in his dormitory apartment. "Except the lute has only one string—singular." She was his English tutor, and in class, he had been eager to demonstrate his ability to hear the *s* at the end of a word, which the other Cambodian students in his group found difficult to catch. To him, this barely audible sibilance, more like a sigh than a hiss, denoted not only the plural form but also the plurality of thoughts and ideas, the reverberation of the multitudes. Lying in his arms, she told him what the word meant and how it would be used in a sentence. "*You* are my heartstrings," he said, pulling her even tighter to him, certain of what love meant.

They had met only weeks earlier. At a time when women wore their hair in short, stiff bouffants, she had long, soft curls that had unraveled from a loose knot and spilled down the length of her back as she rushed into the classroom. *A creature born of the wind*, was his first thought. He felt certain if he so much as breathed on those midnight tendrils, she'd upheave and take flight, hair spreading like a cape behind her. She was wildly beautiful.

"In English, it doesn't matter if you're the students and I'm the teacher," she'd said by way of introduction, "it is *you* for everyone. There's no hierarchy, no need to address me as Neak Gru—'Respected Teacher'—or any other such title we Cambodians are so fond of. We're all here to learn, to expand our understanding of ourselves through another language, another rhythm of thought and feeling. Call me Channara!"

More than her beauty, it was her eloquence that had simultaneously stirred and arrested him. Barely eighteen, younger than the group of male students facing her, she possessed a confidence rarely exhibited by a Cambodian woman, let alone one as young as she. On first impression he'd mistaken her self-possession for the arrogance of her social class, but he came to suspect instead that perhaps it was the product of her upbringing abroad.

The daughter of a career diplomat—who served for many years as the most senior advisor at the Cambodian Embassy in Washington, DC—she practically grew up in the United States, speaking English as fluently as she did Khmer and French. That fall, at the start of her freshman year in college, she'd heard that a group of vocational school graduates from Phnom Penh were looking for additional tutoring to help them more quickly master the English language. She brought it to her father's attention and, gaining his permission, volunteered to be their tutor. "A language is more than just a tool of communication," she said to the enthralled group as they advanced in their lessons. "It's a road map to a country's future, encompassing the collective aspiration of its people." She went on to speak of the "language of democracy," explaining the equality of "you" and "I," as if fairness and justice began with the parity of pronouns. It was then that he fell in love with her, this *tevoda* with hair down to the small of her back.

The Old Musician's head suddenly spins at this recollection. He tries to regain his balance, returning his attention to the task at hand, loosening the ash in the brazier. Still his memories come unbidden, rushing headlong, blurring like currents of light. Voices mingle, accelerating, and he finds he can't quite distinguish one from another. Are they real or imagined? Are Mr. Brown and Mr. Smith still reciting their lessons? He hesitates to look, fearing that if he opens his eyes too quickly, the light will assault his vision. Yet, he feels the sensation of his lids fluttering open of their own accord. He forces them closed again. But to his utter confusion, he sees an altered landscape, a dream spreading before him. Rain puddles, each a different shape, glint under the afternoon sun.

A splintered lake? Where is he? What time has he fallen into? Whose consciousness has he invaded?

His temples throb. The soft thuds of quickening footsteps. He recognizes them. He hears her running toward him. "A *tevoda* threw down her mirror, Papa!" his daughter says, ignoring her nanny's repeated calls to return to her room for her afternoon nap. She's inches before him, at once incandescent and corporeal, as if through the trickery of his failing sight, he has transmuted part and parcel of his memory of her into a living whole. "Did you see it, Papa?" It seems they are in the middle of a rainstorm—another bolt of lightning has just cut across the sky. "Oh, the mirror is broken, Papa! Now the *tevoda* is crying." She seems particularly distressed, and he guesses this is why she can't settle down for her nap. He tries to soothe her by explaining electrical discharge in the atmosphere, moisture and condensation, prevailing southwest wind, the habits of monsoons. But this fails to appease her, and, as always, he gives in to her imagination, adopting a playfully exasperated tone, wondering how it is that a *tevoda*—all wise and knowing—can't foresee that a mirror flung from a place as high up as the sky will shatter. His daughter cries, "Oh, Papa, you don't understand! She threw it down so that she could look at it! She wanted to see herself from where we are!"

He is struck by the turn of her mind, her leap and insight, this ability to communicate beyond her tender years, to perceive beyond her small world of nagging nannies and afternoon naps. She stares at him, waiting for his reply, and he wants only to reach out and grasp hold of her, to confirm her realness and solidity. She looks as she always does, sempiternally young, the rain-soaked sunlight limning her white cotton dress. It suddenly hits him that *she* is that *tevoda* they're speaking of, a spirit in the moment of incarnation, staring at the pieces of her shattered mirror, their fragmented world. "Now do you see, Papa?" she pleads, speaking the same exact words she uttered in another life they'd shared together. "Do you see it?"

He nods. *Yes, I see. In blindness, I see . . .*

Heaven, she meant. *Do you see heaven, Papa?*

The Old Musician opens his eyes. She vanishes. Just like that, like a tiny point of light, her presence no bigger than the glint of an arrow piercing his sight. Blinding him all over again. Sorrow blooms inside his chest, tentacular and effulgent, reaching deep into him. The temple grounds return around him, the ashes, the brazier, and he tells himself that she did indeed appear, that some part of her is still here, continues to exist alongside him. He has only to look at these tiny reservoirs, these twinkling liquid mirrors dotting the ground, and he will see her again.

"In blindness," he murmurs aloud, "I see you in your heaven."

Minneapolis, Minnesota. Its foreignness speaks to him of a distance he once traversed. He tries to picture what this place looks like, where it is on the map, how far it might be from Washington, DC. That fall, in 1961, he never had the opportunity to travel and see the rest of America, as he would've liked. The first semester ended with the news of his father's death and his rushed return to Cambodia for the old man's funeral. Once home, he found that his grieving mother had also fallen ill and, despite her insistence that she would be fine on her own, he couldn't leave her. He was her only child, and with his father gone, she had no other immediate family member nearby. So, he made the painful decision to give up his studies in America for the time being. Perhaps he could win another scholarship. It was not impossible. After all, he'd won this one without much knowledge of the English language.

He had been in his fourth year at the School of Arts and Trade, finishing his studies in woodworking—his particular specialty the technique and art of carving traditional Khmer instruments—when he was selected, along with a handful of classmates, for a two-year language immersion course funded by a grant from the United States government. That spring—in '61—he and his classmates enrolled in an intensive English class taught by an Indian teacher from Burma. By the fall, they'd learned enough of the language to feel some confidence when they boarded a Pan Am flight that took them first to Hong Kong, then Honolulu, and finally to the America he'd dreamed of for so long. A land where the endless expressways alone inspired in him inexhaustible optimism and hope.

He couldn't have known then that in a few months' time he would reverse course, speeding along those same expressways back to the airport on a no-return flight to his homeland, to his dismal prospects in a country he'd come to regard after his brush with modernity as a place stuck in time, folded in on itself. He could not permit himself to think of Channara, their severed love, his shattered heart. He could not face her. A good-bye was impossible. As he resigned himself to the task of caring for his mother, he dared not voice his ambition but vowed that one day he would resume his studies in America. It never happened. The country drew him into politics, and politics drew him underground, into the jungle, and war.

Minneapolisminnesota. The Old Musician says the two names as one, letting the syllables roll effortlessly off his tongue, noting the way the letters repeat themselves, like the reflections of a reflection inside a hall of mirrors, as if the place felt a need to confirm its existence through persistent alliteration. If he gets up now and looks into one of the rain puddles, he wonders childishly, will he see this Minneapolisminnesota? Will he see a paradise reflected among the cumuli, and in its pure white serenity will he see her, this Suteera, another *tevoda* reincarnated, grown-up and altogether different from the child she had been, peering down to search for him, for her father?

He places a handful of kindling in the brazier, lights a dried coconut blade, and sticks it into the cluster. Swirls of smoke rise like recalcitrant sprites slow to awaken. A tiny orange-blue flame leaps forth through the dry leaves and branches, a chameleon born of alchemy. The flame grows and multiplies. He adds bigger pieces of wood to the fire and gives it his breath, once and then again. The flames spring higher, the heat reaching his face, reminiscent of the warmth of his daughter's tiny hands cupping his cheeks.

Wake up, Papa, wake up! He recalls those mornings when she would tiptoe into his room and rouse him with a peck on the nose. *Time to practice your music!* When he groaned, she would kiss him all over his face. *You lazy papa!* she'd say, her breath redolent of the sugarcane juice she'd drunk for breakfast. If she kissed him now, he thinks, if she were here as the little girl she was, tenderhearted and joyful, showering him with sweet, scented drops, his scars and injuries would vanish, as the fissures and rifts on a drought-inflicted earth would surely disappear under the monsoon rains. He longs to be whole again.

He gets up and shuffles over to the front of his cottage. He fills his kettle with the rainwater collected in the clay cistern, shuffles back to the brazier, and sets the kettle down over the fire, letting the blackened bottom cover the orange flames like the moon eclipsing the sun.

Will she appear through the far gate? Or the one nearer to him? Sometimes he sees her so clearly his heart stops. *Will she walk? Will she float?* However she arrives, he knows she will appear to him like a vision, her beauty as untamable as her mother's. Even as young as four or five, she'd already become the spitting image of the young Channara, with long, swirling locks tumbling past the small of her back. A little girl, she was more hair than body, more spirit than mass. When she ran she was a blur of moving strands. A current of air. A thought or wish whizzing past. If he's not vigilant—

He gasps, shocked by his own perfidy, the tricks his mind will play with hope and memory.

Suteera, he meant. He is certain of *her* return.

The streets teem with pedestrians, vendors, and vehicles of all sorts. Cars big and small, some with steering wheels on the left, others on the right, pack the narrow lanes littered with detritus. Quite often a vehicle will force its way from the opposite direction, facing the on-coming traffic, with no regard for driving rules and regulations, or even common sense. *Tuk-tuks* sputter next to SUVs emblazoned with giant letters—LEXUS—across the full span of their exteriors, as if making clear their status and origin, should anyone question the satiny frilled synthetic curtains across the tinted windows, and other such oddities, and mistake them for inferior cars. Cyclos, most empty of passengers, roll aimlessly along, a species marching toward its inevitable extinction. Open carriages rigged to motorcycles haul supplies ranging from toilet seats to oversize mattresses to assortments of sharply cut glass and rebar protruding dangerously into the crowds. It's been more than a week— ten days, to be exact—and Teera still can't get used to the contradictions and incongruities, the endless acrobatics.

Mopeds convey cartons of eggs stacked a meter high into the air, plumes of live chickens hanging upside down by their feet, a litter of pigs squirming and squealing in the confines of bamboo netting. Ram-shackle trucks crammed with passengers gurgle next to spotless Land Cruisers carrying foreign aid workers, whose affluent appearances and calm demeanors sharply contrast with the bedraggled populace they've come to help. On sidewalks, shiny glass carts offering noodles and steamed buns vie for space next to crooked wooden shelves hawking

gasoline and antifreeze in reused soda bottles that emit a dirty phos-
phorescent glow. A rainbow of pollutants, poisons, and pickles. You
can't be sure what is what. All seem flammable, a lineup of Molotov
cocktails. Again, Teera is unnerved by how closely it resembles the
mass exodus decades ago when Khmer Rouge soldiers forced everyone
out of their homes toward the countryside, leaving the entire city in
apocalyptic disarray.

Shantytowns fight for their inch of land against sprawling resi-
dential estates and hotel grounds, against sprouting American-style
shopping malls and Chinese-style row houses. Open sewage canals—
clogged with plastic bottles and bags, the blackened water a hothouse
for diseases heaving in the heat and dust—hem the streets boasting
modern clinics and pharmacies. Casinos and nightclubs, thudding with
pop rock and hip-hop music at all hours, cast their neon auras onto
crumbling brick walls of adjacent Buddhist temples. The city evinces a
makeshift existence, a way of life in constant flux, which at any moment
can implode into violence, like the last bloody coup that took place
only six years ago, in 1997, when televised images of gunfire and tanks
and fallen bodies recalled again and again those frightful days of the
Khmer Rouge takeover. Always the potential for another war, another
revolution. Teera fears this every time she emerges from the guarded
enclosure of Hotel Le Royal. Despite the relative calm and stability, she
senses tension everywhere, in the reckoning of these disparate elements
forced into proximity.

"Are you all right?" Mr. Chum asks, glancing at her in the rearview
mirror.

Teera nods. *Chaik knea ros*, the taxi driver said on their first ride together that day from the airport, as if apologizing for the disorder. She
didn't quite grasp it then, but she's beginning to see now that this "getting by together," this attempt at coexistence in the confines of tragedy, is
perhaps a kind of redress, a provisional atonement for the survivors, both
victims and perpetrators, amidst the wreckage and loss.

Eyes back on the road, Mr. Chum maneuvers his *krabey sang*—his "gas-guzzling water buffalo"—around a traffic circle, unperturbed as one motorcycle after another zips past or cuts in front of them. The blue-black 1993 Camry, he proudly told Teera, was "imported" from the United States, from "Cali," parroting the diminutive for California coined by Cambodian-Americans, as if he himself knew that place well. The car had been totaled in a crash and fated for the junkyard but was instead brought here and, like legions of others, refurbished with a second life. There are countless similarly reincarnated blue-black sedans crowding the narrow lanes around them. Their ubiquitous presence reminds Teera, ironically, of the black-clad soldiers who occupied the same streets decades ago as they declared an end to machinery and forced the populace toward a machine-less existence.

Even more ironic, Mr. Chum was one such soldier, an on-the-spot recruit assigned to drive a truck that would relocate city people to the countryside. He had been a commercial driver, forced to take up the revolutionary cause when the Khmer Rouge stopped him in his vehicle loaded with cases of bottled soft drinks. He would either join them, the soldiers informed him, or face being shot for his "capitalist vocation." His work for an import-export company had brought him to Phnom Penh, while his wife and three children remained back in their home province. He joined the Khmer Rouge, believing this would afford him the privilege to reconnect with his family. He never saw his wife and children again. To this day he doesn't know their fates.

When Teera chose him from a crowd of taxi drivers upon her arrival at the Phnom Penh Airport, she knew none of this. While the other drivers jostled one another, fighting to get her attention, Mr. Chum stood off to the side, smiling timidly. She liked him, felt reassured by his serene stillness amidst the noise and movements. What's more, she thought his childlike face—the square jaw and bulbous nose—made him look like an older, darker version of the Chinese film star Jackie Chan, the quintessential good guy. It was only a couple of days after, when he picked her up at the hotel for her first tour of the city, that he proceeded to divulge his history, as if wanting her to know before she decided to further engage his service. She did hesitate for a moment, then remembered she'd once trusted a soldier and he'd saved her life.

Despite his *pravat smoksmanh*—his "complicated background"—Mr. Chum has been nothing but generous and patient, always picking up his cell phone on the first ring when she calls. He's driven her wherever, at the oddest hours, never once questioning her recurring needs to go to the promenade in front of the Royal Palace on a rainy dawn; to the same spot in front of Chaktomuk Theater in the heat of the afternoon, where long ago, she told him, she'd sometimes come for sugarcane juice; or to a ferry crossing to view the confluence of the three rivers.

In less than a week, he's learned to maneuver his vehicle to the unpredictable twists and turns of her memories, the unmapped leaps of her longings. Time and again, they will search for a place she vaguely recalls from childhood, only to discover that it no longer exists, much to his disappointment, as to hers. Presently, they're on their way to visit a temple outside the city, though there are countless others closer in. He does not ask her why, and this is what she appreciates about him most.

At a roundabout, they enter congested traffic. A rail-thin woman taps on their car window, begging for spare change. Mr. Chum rolls down the window and gives her one thousand Cambodian riels, about twenty-five cents, enough for a simple packet of rice and fish. She thanks him, palms together in the traditional *sampeah*. He asks about the small girl strapped to her bosom with a black-and-white checkered *kroma*, the whites of the cotton fabric yellowed with dirt—"Is she your daughter?" No, the woman explains, but she cares for the girl like her own. The parents were close friends, like a sister and brother to her. She hesitates before proceeding, "They've died of AIDS."

Teera, in her oversize sunglasses, sits frozen in place, unable to speak or move a muscle. How should she acknowledge such a revelatory exchange in so transient an encounter? How should she respond in this place where personal tragedy is routine? She shrinks back in her seat, wanting to give the woman the dignity of her confession.

"Hello, madame." The woman mistakes her for a foreigner. Mr. Chum gives a sad chuckle but doesn't explain that Teera is Cambodian.

A way opens up and they move on. Teera is grateful for the escape.

The journey continues. At every pause, they encounter the homeless and the hungry. Sometimes throngs of children in rags press against both sides of their car, bobbing palms joined in *sampeah*, lips moving in continuous plea. If they're too aggressive, Mr. Chum keeps his window up and tries to distract Teera with small talk, often marveling about America—"Everything all shiny and new and gigantic, right? Like the people!"—as if by his mentioning America, Teera would somehow forget she's in Cambodia. At the moment, some children are knocking on her window, appealing to her directly, "Please, madame, little money buy food. Please, madame . . ." They echo one another.

Today more than any other day—perhaps because she's heading out of Phnom Penh for the first time—Teera feels she's on a reverse exodus, journeying not toward a strange, unknown destination but returning to a place where she's become a stranger, where people no longer recognize her as one of their own. They all assume she's a foreigner—Thai, Malaysian, Filipino, some Asian other than Cambodian—and she wishes they could know that she too is *koan Khmer*, a child of this ancient race, that she's come back to a homeland where her home no longer exists, to this land as scarred and ravaged as herself. She wishes they could know that she too went through war and revolution, lost loved ones, survived against incredible odds.

And yet, to put herself next to them, to dig up her past suffering and line it side by side with the hardship they endure daily, their continuing struggle to survive, to think that she and they are the same because they share a history, would be a gross exaggeration of her own plight.

So she stays hidden behind her dark glasses, protected in the borrowed anonymity of being "foreign."

"It's okay," Mr. Chum consoles, as if *she* were the one in need of consolation. "There are too many. You can't help them all."

She nods, pushing back the emotions that compete to find expression on her face. When she can't bear it any longer, she allows herself the solace of knowing that she is among the luckiest—she not only survived, she escaped.

"What are you concocting?"

The Old Musician startles out of his remembrances. He looks up and sees Dr. Narunn standing before him. "I—I was going to have some tea, Venerable." As customary, he addresses the ordained physician by the title used for a monk. He is about to add, *With my evening meal*, but refrains from any mention of food in front of one who adheres to the monastic discipline of no food or drink besides water beyond noon. "I didn't see you coming, Venerable."

"Well, you know, I thought I'd sneak up and steal a cup of whatever you're brewing." Dr. Narunn lowers himself on his haunches, gathering the hems of his saffron robe and tucking them in place. "I'll have a bit of hot water with my condensed milk, please. And a slice of that cake, if you don't mind." He chuckles, his Adam's apple bouncing happily. "I'm parodying myself, of course. The first time I was ordained and had to fast, that was all I could think of—*food*. I imagined what I'd say if people invited me into their kitchens during our alms round! Of course no one did." He lets out a resounding laugh. "I'm not made for this life!"

The Old Musician's mood is instantly cheered by the doctor's presence, the buoyant energy emanating from his friend. There is a nobility to the young man's carriage, an assuredness in each movement. Every year for a month during the rainy season the doctor enters the sangha to meditate and take a respite from the demands of his profession.

"You know," Dr. Narunn says, observing him, "you are constantly squinting now, more than ever before. We really ought to protect what's left of your sight." It was Dr. Narunn whose help the Old Musician had enlisted to write the letter. "Please let me get you a pair of glasses."

"Thank you, Venerable, it is very kind of you." How can he tell the young doctor that his sight cannot be remedied, that his partial blindness is rooted in the betrayal of his mind, not his eyes? "I would feel too disoriented with those modern things on my face." Let others believe he was a stubborn, benighted old peasant, refusing the aid of technology. "Maybe an eye patch to cover the bad eye is better suited for me—more dashing, don't you think?"

"You're right! I don't know why I didn't think of it. It'll certainly strain less if you keep it covered. I'll see what I can find."

"I was only joking, Venerable. You mustn't bother." *The truth is it's best not to be able to see at all. As it is, one already perceives too much suffering . . .*

"Yes, and less easily, but surely one also glimpses the possibilities for change, for transformation."

He's startled by the doctor's response. It happens more and more now that he speaks aloud without realizing it. The line between thought and speech bleeds, and he is back in his cell—*Tell us what you know! Confess! Or else you'll end up like the others!* Blood obscures his vision, seeping down into his skull.

He blinks and sees only Dr. Narunn looking at him intently. He remains silent, terrified of his own mind.

"I've just spoken with the abbot," the young doctor says, changing the subject. "He has some urgent matter to attend to outside the temple. He wants me to take his place and lead the chanting in the evening's ceremony. I understand you are to play your *sadiev*?"

"He's so young, Venerable."

"Pardon me?"

"The boy, I mean."

"I was just as surprised to find out it was our Makara. His parents brought him to my clinic a few weeks ago. He showed all the symptoms of a meth addiction. You'd think he *was* a ghost, not just a person who'd lost his spirit to one."

"He turns twelve today and, I'm told, his parents have chosen his birthday to have this ceremony, to symbolize a rebirth. At this age, Venerable, one hasn't lived long enough to acquire a habit, let alone an addiction."

"Unfortunately, they're younger and younger, the children who've fallen into drugs. One encounters them as young as seven or eight. Meth is a popular drug among the poor youth, like Makara, who turn to it to escape their realities. You can't blame them. Here, in the city especially, they see everything at close range. Fancy houses and fancy cars, flat-screen TVs, digital cameras, computers and laptops, exorbitant wealth in the hands of a few . . ."

The Old Musician is not familiar with some of these. *Flat-screen TVs, digital cameras, laptops.* He repeats the words silently, learning them as he would in his youth any new English words, committing them to memory. They didn't exist a few years ago in Cambodia, and certainly not when he was a young student in America. As for computers, he has seen the one the Venerable Kong Oul has in his study, a small square machine humming and glowing, flipping pictures like some creature of memory sorting through its recollections. He thinks back to the days when monks were barely allowed to own a pair of sandals. How much the world has progressed, despite the failed revolutions. If only he'd had more patience, more faith.

"They're privy to all that excess and glitter," Dr. Narunn continues, his voice becoming taut, "while they themselves have no access to the most basic things. Do you know that the cost of a handgun could buy a family like Makara's enough corrugated tin sheets for a new shelter?" The doctor shakes his head. "Yet, it seems, there are as many handguns as cell phones, because our Excellencies and their children dispense them like playthings to their bodyguards."

It's obvious to the Old Musician why his young friend needs the enclosure of the sangha now and then. To critique the government so openly on the street could get one killed. Assassins could be made on the spot for as little as a few hundred dollars.

"Perhaps you are right," Dr. Narunn concedes, sighing. "There's so much suffering. It's everywhere—inescapable." Despair seems to have supplanted the doctor's earlier hope. "The poor remain poor, trapped in a slum, which is a kind of underworld for the living, if you ask me."

The kettle spews steam from its lid and spout, hissing violently.

"Ah, it's angry at my diatribe!"

They both try to laugh, but disconsolation has joined their company, refusing to leave.

"You should have your tea," Dr. Narunn suggests in a desultory tone. "And also something to eat to sustain your strength through the ceremony—"

The physician stops abruptly, looking up the steps of the prayer hall. "We have a visitor," he says after a moment. "In a white dress and a big floppy sun hat. A foreigner, I think, from the look of her clothing." Whenever they're together the doctor has taken it upon himself to describe those things at a distance. "She's walking up the steps of the *vihear.*"

"Someone we know, Venerable?"

But Dr. Narunn doesn't hear. He stands up, straightens his robe, and, most curiously, checks his appearance, then takes a step forward. "I'll see if she needs any assistance . . ."

Teera dashes up the steps of Hotel Le Royal at a speed that feels to her more like flying, her sandals grazing the red carpet draping the center of the expansive staircase. She keeps her head bowed to avoid eye contact. People come and go, a continuous traffic up and down the stairs. Some greet her as she passes, their familiar tone indicating they recognize her as a fellow guest. From a couple of steps above, the general manager pauses in his chitchat with others to offer—"*Salut! Ça va?*" Teera returns his greeting, using the bit of French she knows, but doesn't slow her steps to allow for conversation. At the top, she turns and gives one last wave to Mr. Chum. She can see he's worried. He doesn't want to leave her like this, but he's forced to move his mud-splotched Camry to make way for a shiny black Mercedes pulling into the arcade of the hotel driveway.

Since fleeing the temple, Teera has encased herself in silence. During the entire drive back to the hotel she shut him out. She hopes he doesn't think her muteness has anything to do with him, that she's dissatisfied with his service or his driving. The past, surely he knows, is tricky terrain, riddled with potholes and pitfalls and unmarked graves. No matter how vigilant you are, you can find yourself in a head-on collision and, amidst the shock and reverberation, catch in the periphery of your vision a phantom of your deepest longing. *In the memory of Music Master . . .*

Teera tilts her woven sun hat forward to hide her face and sails past the doormen dressed in their silk pantaloons and high-collared tunics, each holding a door open for her. They give a slight bow but refrain from saying anything, clearly sensing she's not in the mood to stop and exchange pleasantries.

She panicked. She'd simply panicked. At Wat Nagara, a monk came up behind her on the steps of the prayer hall to greet her, and just as she turned to face him, she caught sight of the stupa, her father's name glittering in gold on its white dome. Teera felt the wind knocked out of her. She couldn't speak. Instead, on impulse, she pretended she was a foreign tourist who didn't know the language and bolted away, leaving the monk completely nonplussed on the steps. Outside she pleaded with Mr. Chum to go, startling him with her emotive outburst, her voice quaking to a breaking point. *Please let's leave—please!*

As they screeched away, the car wheels stirring up water and mud from the puddles left by the recent rains, she glimpsed through the open entrance the whole dedication. *In the memory of Music Master Aung Sokhon and family who lost their lives.* She was utterly unprepared for the devastation, the summary of her loss in that finite phrase. She'd planned this first visit to the temple without letting the abbot or anyone know. She'd even taken care to enter discreetly through one of the smaller side gates, asking Mr. Chum to wait outside by one of the main entrances in front. She wanted to be alone with the ghosts, to seek communion with her loved ones. Instead she came face-to-face with her aloneness, saw it reflected wholly, indelibly, in the engraved invocation.

Teera hurries now through the lobby with its elegant teak furniture and art deco pieces, its gleaming marble floor and high ceiling, a wall boasting two large black-and-white photographs of Jacqueline Kennedy during her historic visit in 1967. When she passes the corner reception bar, Devi, a pretty young waitress she's come to know well, is busy decorating fresh juices with orchids to welcome new arrivals. Teera is tempted to ask for a stiff gin and tonic to loosen the tension in her neck and shoulders. But before Devi looks up, Teera steps into the adjoining veranda, where a couple and their son are enjoying afternoon tea and cake in the air-conditioned coolness. "*Papa, Maman, regardez le lézard!*" the little boy exclaims. Teera has seen them before, a Cambodian-French family, and the way the little boy says "Papa"—round and solid like an embrace—makes her want to weep.

The family smiles at her as she passes, but she's unable to reciprocate, certain that if she lets go of a single muscle, her entire being will unravel.

She pushes open the set of doors and takes the few short steps down to the covered walkway between two swimming pools built to look like a bridge across water. The spacious, blossom-strewn courtyard—bordered by the four colonial-style buildings and shaded under a canopy of giant monkey-pod trees—seems like a world far from the rest of Phnom Penh.

She reaches the rear building and turns right into the warmly lit hallway, the wooden heels of her sandals clicking against the polished black-and-white checkered tiles that remind her of the floor of her childhood home. When she arrives at her room, she fumbles with her key and lock. One of the cleaning girls, noticing her agitation, rushes over and unlocks the door for her. Teera nods her thanks and quickly enters her room. She hangs the "Do Not Disturb" sign outside, closes the door, turns the lock.

Without flicking on the light, she walks into the bathroom, sheds her white cotton dress and sun hat, steps into the claw-foot tub, and, turning the shower knobs, lets the water crash down on her. She weeps, alone and naked in her sorrow.

The monks have emerged from their cramped shelters to take advantage of the lull in the rains, their blurred silhouettes like streaks of turmeric or cinnamon powder scattered across the temple grounds. On a grassy patch between the ceremony hall and the Old Musician's cottage, a group of them engages in a soccer game, robes hitched up to keep the hems from soiling as they roll and kick the worn ball. Nearby another group gathers in a circle with one player in the middle bouncing a shuttlecock on the side of his foot, then projecting it high in the air for another player to receive and continue the choreography.

The Old Musician takes pleasure in the movements and sounds around him. He hears footsteps approaching. Turning, he sees Mr. Brown and Mr. Smith heading for the *vihear*. He angles himself to follow them with his good eye. The two oblates race up the stairway, then emerge at a window at the top of the prayer hall. There they perch side by side, a pair of orange macaws, feet firmly planted on the wooden sills, arms extending straight out on upright knees, their gazes cast toward the river and the geography far beyond.

He wonders whether Mr. Brown and Mr. Smith are contemplating their flights, longing for loftier existence. Both boys are orphans. Mr. Brown's parents died of AIDS, which according to Dr. Narunn has spread with the country's growing sex trade, human trafficking, and drug addiction. Mr. Smith's father, a journalist known for his outspoken criticism of land-grabbing and forced evictions, was shot and killed on a crowded market street by armed men on a motorcycle. A month later,

Mr. Smith's mother suffered the same fate. The two adolescents were recently ordained and will likely remain at the temple until old enough to live on their own.

During the period of Chol Vassa, the "Rain Retreat" from mid-July to the end of October, when the monsoon falls most heavily, Buddhist monks withdraw from the outside world and confine themselves within the temple compound to study and meditate. At this time one also sees the largest number of young men and boys enter the monastery for a temporary ordination that can last as little as three days or as long as three months. The majority of the younger ones are orphans whose parents, like those of Mr. Brown and Mr. Smith, have fallen victim to the myriad diseases of poverty or to the violence of armed politics and personal vendettas. No one will take the children of these victims in, for fear of contagion or retribution. At the temple they find a semblance of family, a roof over their heads, food and nourishment, even if only in the one daily meal. While a few will choose to pursue a serious spiritual path, most stay simply to escape poverty. Nonetheless, the Venerable Kong Oul rarely turns anyone away, believing that education, practical or spiritual, cannot be gained on an empty stomach or while shivering in the rain.

With water from the clay cistern, the Old Musician washes his face, soaks one end of his *kroma* and wipes his arms and torso, splashes his feet and flip-flops clean of dirt, then shuffles back inside to prepare for the ceremony. He finds the white *achar* shirt and the pair of black wraparound pants, the only clothes he owns without patches or stains. Coincidentally, they were a gift from Makara's parents during Krathin, a carnival-like festivity with performances of *chayyam* drums and giant puppets that beckon the entire community and passersby to the temple to make donations. When the Rattanaks handed him the parcel of wrapped clothes, the Old Musician hesitated, reminding them that he isn't a monk. He possesses no spiritual wisdom, nothing he could impart to help ease their difficulties. They told him they expected nothing in return, except his simple wishes—a prayer or two on their behalf to the *tevodas* and deities—that they would always have rice in their pot and a place to sleep, that their son, Makara, would abandon his errant ways and return to school, grow into manhood strong and resourceful.

The Old Musician was moved by their generosity, knowing that the couple has so little to begin with, the wife a vegetable seller and the husband a *motodup* driver who taxis people on his rusted scooter, together earning barely enough to feed themselves and their son. How could they think that one as destitute and vulnerable as he should have the power to alter their circumstances with his wishes? Yet, that they should think so gave him pause. In truth, it prompted in him a small awakening.

He has not turned to religion. Nor has he renewed his belief in camaraderie and brotherhood—the ideology of revolution. Rather the simple gift of clothes, made on the faith that what one gives to another will not be lost, led him to consider that the arbitrariness of birth and circumstance might be altered not through grand schemes of social engineering but through such minute selfless acts, the gestures of empathy we extend to one another in our daily encounters. It's clear to the Old Musician that without the kindness of his fellow human beings he would be left to walk the streets barefoot and naked, abandoned among the city's refuse.

He wishes now for the Rattanaks a fortune as vast as the spirit of munificence they've shown him. He supposes in this way he's learned to pray not as one might to the gods but as one does by simply pausing every now and then to think of others.

He walks to the open doorway and, before lowering the burlap partition to dress in privacy, scans the compound once more. He blinks, again a flash of white appearing before him. If he tells Dr. Narunn about it, he's afraid the young physician will inform him that he's losing sight in the good eye as well, that the white flare he sees with increasing frequency is a kind of phantom cataract before the real condition sets in, before total blindness. No, he must not tell the doctor. He prefers to think it is she who invades his vision, this specter of his sorrow.

He espies her in all he beholds.

The brass knocker echoes in the hallway, followed by a male voice. *Room service!* Teera tightens her bathrobe, gathering the collar for modesty, and opens the door. Samnang, the young man who's brought meals for her before, walks into the room, bearing a tray with a pot of hot water, a caddy of assorted teas, and a steaming bowl of rice porridge, along with a vase of orchid blossoms. Devi trails him as he puts the tray on the coffee table in front of the sofa. The young waitress greets her, palms together in the traditional *sampeah*. "We are all worried, big sister. You didn't look well when you came back from your outing." She steps back so as to be able to face Teera without having to tilt her neck and look up.

At five foot eight, Teera towers over Devi, but she must come off frail or broken in some way to engender the sympathy and protectiveness she's been receiving from the hotel staff.

Devi's eyes flit to the food tray and then back to Teera. "Rice porridge is not very nutritious. It's sick people's food. Are you sick, big sister?" Behind her, Samnang furrows his brow in shared concern.

Teera shakes her head.

"Is there anything else you need?" Devi persists. "Maybe hard-boiled eggs or ground sweet pork to go with it? At least some grilled salted fish?"

"Thank you, but I have everything I need. And really, I'm fine. It was probably just the heat. I'm not used to it yet. The shower was good. I'm feeling much better already."

"You've gone out every day. Maybe you should rest, stay in for a day or two. Just enjoy the hotel—it's beautiful here. Outside there's so much mud and dirt. Srok Khmer is not like America."

Yes, the dirt. As if it were the only thing. Teera signs the bill and hands it back to Samnang. The two bow and leave, and as the heavy wooden door softly closes, she hears rapid whispering back and forth: *If she were plumper, she'd be very beautiful. It's the style over there. What— looking bony and sad? Oh, you boys don't understand trends!—I think big sister's beautiful as she is. I think* you're *beautiful, Devi.* A sudden hush.

Teera imagines Devi blushing. Big sister, they all call her. Even in the States, Cambodians address each other by familial terms. There she thought nothing of it, but here it stabs her every time, this default claim of kinship, this illusion of continuity and wholeness. Maybe Devi knows what she's talking about after all. The dirt here clings to you, crimson and sorrow-tainted, no matter how long you stand under the shower.

Teera walks over to the writing desk near the head of the bed and confronts her reflection in the mirror on the wall. She runs her fingers through her damp hair, regretting all over again that in a moment of rashness, a week or so before making the journey here, she'd taken a pair of scissors and, in the Buddhist act of letting go, chopped off the long strands. It looks better now, thanks to her hairdresser, who, upon seeing her handiwork, lamented, *Oh, your beautiful curls, I just want to faint!* She wonders, though, whether the shoulder-length crop makes her look even thinner, more long-limbed and willowy than she already is. She hasn't been eating or sleeping well for months.

She puffs her cheeks out, imagining a fuller face, a self less spare, less spectral. *Maybe you'd gain some weight with less hair to lug around,* Amara would always tease, hand smoothing Teera's massive waves. *But I can't imagine you looking any other way. You're the spitting image of your mother.* Whenever her aunt said this, Teera felt an echo of another self, as if her body was not hers alone.

She returns to the sofa, drops a bag of Earl Grey into the teapot, and, letting it steep, begins to take slow sips of the rice porridge, her comfort food. When she was a child, starving, even a few spoonfuls of the plain, watery gruel would calm her stomach, lessen the horrible pang. How long ago that was. And yet, no matter how far she has traveled, something as tactile as a knot in her stomach can collapse time and space and plunge her back to the moment when hunger was all she knew.

She pours herself some tea and reaches into her shoulder bag on the floor, pulling out the two books she bought early this morning at the hotel bookshop, the Lonely Planet guide and a collection of essays. Her fingers flip through the guide, stopping at a map of Phnom Penh. She notes that many of the street names are still preceded by the French *rue*, as painted on the road signs. She reads them aloud in succession like the headings of a history lesson that stretches from Cambodia's mythical past to its multifarious present. She locates Duan Penh, where her hotel stands, the avenue named in honor of the legendary widow Lady Penh, whose divine vision supposedly led her to erect a temple on the hill, two blocks east of here, around which grew the eponymous city, Phnom Penh, the "Hill of Lady Penh."

Main roads with names like Confédération de la Russie and Dimitrov jostle those named for royal personae—Sisowath and Norodom and Sihanouk—like revolts against feudalism itself. Phnom Penh is probably the only city in the world where one would find Charles de Gaulle, Josip Broz Tito, Jawaharlal Nehru, Mao Tse-tung, and Abdul Carime all in the same tight geography. This map, she thinks, is a study in the accumulated layers of geopolitics that intertwine here, none completely erasing that which came before.

Teera sets down the guidebook and picks up the volume of essays, letting her index finger trace the letters on the front cover. *Understanding the Cambodian Genocide*. From among the bookshop's offerings, she was attracted by this title, its bold and capitalized confidence, its promise of an explanation. She turns the pages and tentatively begins reading, curling up in the sofa as she did years ago in the armchairs of Cornell's Kroch Library, home to the Asia collections. For hours at a time, she'd pore over old journals and manuscripts from Cambodia, deepening her knowledge of her native tongue, reawakening her childhood love of reading, searching for clues. Despite her aunt's gentle warning, she was drawn to history, captivated by its fluidity and ease with the language of loss. *That was then, this is now*, Amara would remind her. *It's all in the past. We've left that land behind.*

Cambodia. Kampuchea. Srok Khmer. No matter how she says it, Teera knows it will never leave her tongue. It will never leave her, even as she tries to peel it from the memory of her skin. It has stained her. Marked her with the lives lost, those whose faces she's forgotten but whose voices, whose screams and pleas, weave the tenuous boundary between dreams and nightmares. She recalls once again that particular evening, its twilight glow, in which corpses sprawled across rice paddies looked at first glance like families sleeping. Even now, a lifetime later, the dead stalk her, and she, who wishes only for their burial, a restful end to their journey, hears their cries as her own.

She gets up from the sofa and, pulling the double glass doors open, steps onto the balcony. She needs fresh air, the voices and presence of living people. She inhales deeply, her attention immediately drawn to the sounds of paddling and splashing a few yards away in the children's pool. A roly-poly toddler in a sagging two-piece wades sneakily to the far corner of the pool, climbs the edge, tummy pressing against the tiles, leaps to her feet, and bounds off. Water drips from her drenched bikini bottom, leaving a wet trail on the pebbled mosaic floor, like an umbilical cord connecting her to an aqueous origin. A woman, as pale as the toddler is brown, turns from her conversation with a friend and says suddenly, "Luna?" In a split second, she runs after the toddler, whose cherubic form rounds the pillars of the roofed walkway separating the shallow children's pool from the deep pool at the opposite side of the courtyard. "Luna! *Luna*, if you jump again, Mommy's going to—" *Splash!*

Teera goes back inside and shuts the balcony doors, fogging the glass panes with the humidity she's let into the air-conditioned room. She breathes on the glass directly in front of her face, thickening the vapor. Then, with the tip of her forefinger, she draws a straight line, a band of opening, and peers through it, back into the verdant, tangled underbrush of the past.

In his clean new tunic and pants, the Old Musician is transformed from a mendicant to a respectable elder. Such loose-fitting clothes were popular among the leaders of Democratic Kampuchea, except then everything had to be dyed black. Black is simply practical, often worn by peasants when working in the fields. During Democratic Kampuchea, though, black was equated with the peasantry itself, with a way of life that was incorruptible, absolute. Black meant erasure.

The mistake of the party leaders was to believe that people could easily be reeducated, that culture and tradition and history, all thousands of years in the making, could be obliterated in a single angry stroke, like a painter's tableau smeared to suit an abrupt change in perspective. Perhaps it's because these leaders had been so thoroughly transformed by their own reeducation abroad, particularly by Le Cercle Marxiste, in the Paris of the 1950s.

As for himself, besides that brief flirt with America, he had never traveled anywhere else, not to France, where many of the party leaders had studied in their youth; not to Yugoslavia, where Pol Pot had his revolutionary awakening; not even to neighboring Vietnam, where many of his comrades had gone into hiding; none of those countries whose Socialist aspirations he would come to adopt. He was the product of a homegrown education—if there was such a thing, given the deep colonial influence—first learning the basics of reading and writing from the monks at the temple, then continuing primary years and *collège* in public schools based on the French system, which emphasized Western classical studies and often used French as the principal language of instruction.

Perhaps because of this requirement to learn French, the tongue of their former masters, he saw English as a liberating novelty and seized upon the language when it was introduced to him at the School of Arts and Trade. Later, during that last spring at the vocational school before he was to leave for America, when he enrolled in the intensive English class, his Indian teacher from Burma, rumored to be a Communist, spiced up the methodical lessons on syntax and grammar with talk of self-rule, political sovereignty, and equality for all. Concepts inherent not only to Communism, the teacher had rhapsodized, but to democracy as well. Anil Mehta was inspired by events in his homeland, India's progress after independence in establishing a democratic republic.

Looking back on it now, he wonders if his political consciousness first awakened when he was that eager student poring over a copy of *Anglais Vivant d'Angleterre*, as Mr. Mehta, in his philosophical voice, added social and political commentary to sentences from the book, alternating between English and French. Or perhaps it took root much earlier. With music.

The Old Musician pours himself a cup of tea, kept hot in the large thermos that—like the kettle and the other possessions of this cottage—he's inherited from the late temple sweeper. He blows on the steaming liquid, which smells faintly of jasmine, and takes a sip.

Music. Always it followed him, at every stage of his life, nudging its way into all he saw and did, like the unyielding will of the father whom he feared but whose musical genius he could never aspire to, despite the caning to his back.

His father was a man of uncompromising vision. The old man saw music as a kind of sublime blessing, like rain or sunlight, something not to be taken for granted or reserved for the privileged few. While the old man could have made a place for himself among the country's most respected music masters, could have earned enough money to feed the family by playing for the rich and powerful, he would feign chronic rheumatism when invited, claiming he wasn't fit to *entertain*, choosing instead to play for the poor, for whom music was the only antidote to daily struggles. In the beginning, his father would play all kinds of music, from the sacred to the secular. As long as his audience was the needy and the indigent, he'd gladly share his melodies. Then one day, his father stopped playing altogether, except in the capacity of a medium where his *sadiev* became the voice used to communicate with the ghosts and spirits. The old man became impoverished, barely able to feed him and his mother, and he, the ten-year-old son—Tun, as he was called then—had to find his own way in the world.

As an adolescent, he joined an ensemble in which he eventually became known not only for his *sadiev* playing—honed under his father's strict guidance, he must admit—but also for the songs he wrote, the sublime lyrics he sang for the dead in exchange for handouts from the living. If music, as his father believed, is a kind of cure, then destitution, he realized in those dire years when he and his mother existed hand to mouth, was the worst kind of ill. He would use his music to escape it. It was this vow he'd made to himself—not his father's beating—that fueled his discipline, pushing him to excel in his art. Later, even as a respected and sought-after musician, he never forgot his humble beginnings and would align himself with those striving for change, those seeking to make Cambodia a more just and fair society, a modern nation. He joined a political group, attracted to its progressive ideals, and then, when his hometown was bombed by the Americans, became a member of the underground movement, embracing its radical ideology, its anger.

The Old Musician drinks the remains of his tea. A procession of voices floats past his doorway. "Let's go, little one," he murmurs, picking up the lute, waking it from its slumber near the wall. "It's time for the ceremony."

The Rattanaks and their boy, Makara, along with relatives and friends, are gathering in front of the *sala bonh*, the open-air ceremony hall, where the ritual for calling back the spirit will take place. The sun has set, streaking the sky yellow and orange, reminiscent of spirits in flight. Before them, the Mekong darkens, a long, sinuous shroud, boats and sampans swaying on its surface like ornaments tentatively fastened to a tapestry. Suddenly it seems this mighty ancient river, cut deep into the earth centuries ago, could be lifted and shaken loose, smoothed of its wrinkles and creases. At these twilight hours, the world appears insubstantial. Vaporous as a child's etching on a fogged surface, the Old Musician thinks. He remembers. And once again, his daughter's voice comes to him unbidden.

Look what I drew, Papa!—You and me! It was a misty morning, and she nodded at a scene she'd rendered on their car window. *What's this long thing here?* he asked, his mind elsewhere. *A naga serpent?—A caterpillar?* She laughed. *No, you silly old papa. It's a river, with other rivers connecting to it, just like the one in front of us. We're going to travel on it. We're going to go places together.* She must have believed then that she would accompany him on all his journeys. He had been suddenly seized with fear. Would she grow up to love another more than she loved him in that moment? *Here comes our boat!* she exclaimed, adding to the drawing, fingers moving constantly. *With the head of a phoenix! Or should I make it a plane?*

He lifts his hand as if to wipe away the scene. Dr. Narunn appears beside him. "Your path is clear," his young friend assures, obviously mistaking his gesture as an attempt to find his way in the dusk.

He lowers his hand and turns to the ordained doctor. "Who was it, Venerable?"

"I'm sorry?" Dr. Narunn seems perplexed.

"Earlier this afternoon. You said there was a visitor in the prayer hall."

"Oh, yes! No one really. Just as I suspected, a foreigner. Asian, though. Maybe Burmese? Or possibly even Indian—with big, beautiful eyes. In any case, a tourist, who didn't speak a word of Khmer. Didn't speak at all actually!" Dr. Narunn runs a hand over his shorn head, as if suddenly conscious of his exposed scalp. "There she was, doing her own walking meditation, and I came up the steps from behind, a bald man in a dress no less, speaking to her in our peculiar temple dialect—'Would the devotee like to pay homage to Lord Buddha?' Ridiculous, isn't it!" The young doctor laughs, his whole face flushed, obviously embarrassed by the memories of the strange encounter and his even stranger greeting. "I could've sworn she was Khmer, one of us. But she flew off like a creature from another world, her *pralung* fleeing ahead, as the rest of her ran to catch up. I think I scared the living spirit out of our visitor! Wouldn't be surprised if she never set foot at another Khmer temple."

"What does she look like, Venerable?"

"She was very . . ."

"Lovely."

"*Lost*, I was going to say." The doctor narrows his eyes with amused suspicion. "But yes, lovely too. Very much so. Lovely and lost."

With his attuned hearing, the Old Musician recognizes the unmistakable tenor of infatuation in Dr. Narunn's voice, like that of an amorous schoolboy describing a pretty girl he's caught sight of. But, at the moment, he doesn't have the peace of mind to probe further into the doctor's heart, as his own is pounding inside his ears. *She was here.* He's absolutely certain of it now. She stood on this ground. She might even have seen him. *Suteera.* He says her name silently to himself, as if to call her back, then just as suddenly doubts his imagining. Such coincidence borders on madness.

"What did you say?" Dr. Narunn asks.

"Nothing, Venerable." He swallows, sorrow and hope caught in his throat.

The *lok gru achar*—the temple officiant—assigned by the abbot to facilitate the ceremony emerges from the gathered throng and, bowing to Dr. Narunn, says, "Everyone is here, Venerable. We are ready to begin."

The group forms a circle around a banana trunk cut approximately to Makara's height and placed in a clay pot. The tree is wrapped in raw silk and decorated with its own fruits and leaves as well as cubes of sugarcane on bamboo sticks, treats to entice Makara's spirit to return.

Dr. Narunn, as the presiding monk, the main spiritual presence, walks around the effigy and chants the sutra in Pali that commences every act of worship. *Namo tassa bhagavato arahato samma sambuddhassa . . .* An homage to the Buddha. But in his usual style, the young doctor follows it with an interpretation in the vernacular, slightly different from the habitually memorized words—"Let us always honor one who is learned, wise, and compassionate . . ." He sprinkles the ground with lotus-scented water from a bronze bowl to consecrate the area and ward off delinquent sprites that might be gathering to watch, especially ones clever enough to assume the traits of the sick boy and enter his body in order to partake of the food. The Old Musician knows that Dr. Narunn does not subscribe to these superstitions, but as a physician, he is willing to aid in any process of healing, be it conventional or fanciful.

Looking at Makara, the Old Musician wishes he possessed Dr. Narunn's encompassing hopefulness. The teenager resembles a living corpse. Barely able to stand on his own, Makara is propped upright by the elbows, his parents on either side of him. In contrast to his brand-new school uniform of white shirt and black slacks, and recently washed appearance, the twelve-year-old bears all the telltale symptoms, as Dr. Narunn has described, of a meth addict.

In the few short months since the Old Musician last saw him, Makara has suffered great weight loss, rendering him old and skeletal. A few of his front teeth are missing, and those remaining are blackened, decaying against inflamed gums. While it is obvious the Rattanaks have attempted to scrub their son clean for the ceremony, Makara emits not only a nauseating odor from his rotting mouth but the strange musky stench of cat urine from his entire body. What's more, the boy's once youthful face is now ravaged by acne and rashes, some bleeding and infected from what appears to be self-inflicted vicious scratching. Yet, the most shocking change is in the boy's eyes, the way they shift about in apparent paranoia, looking at once vacant and possessed, as if tormented by phantoms only he sees.

If man possessed a monster's soul, this is what it would look like. A

creature peering from within its human frame, terrified by its capacity
to destroy not only others but ultimately itself. Once he too was such
a creature staring at his murky reflection in the pool of his urine after
a prison guard at Slak Daek had beaten him to a pulp. Still, even as he
wished more than anything to die, some mysterious part of him fought
to stand erect, rise to take another blow, another breath. *Why?* He didn't
know. He's not certain if he knows now.

He ponders the ceremony taking place in front him, this tradition
based on the belief that a person's *pralung*—made up of nineteen different traits, each acting like a unique minor spirit on its own, all sharing
a kind of vulnerability—is so fragile that it can be scared into fleeing
at the slightest provocation. If so, then what is the force that stands its
ground and says to death, *Even as I fall, I do not submit to you?* Does it
have a name at all? Perhaps this force, or spirit, draws strength from its
namelessness? He wonders if its invincibility is precisely its unname-
able caprice, its alchemy. That ability, when confronted with the end,
to transform itself into whatever trait a person needs—be it courage,
defiance, or simply stubbornness. *Why won't you die?* another prison
guard, a former soldier of his, once murmured in privacy. *Why are you so
pigheaded?* There was a hint of compassion in the guard's hushed, frus-
trated growl. It was clear the youth believed death was more merciful
than that hellhole. *Why do you still hang on?* Yes, why did he? Why has
he hung on still after all these years?

The Old Musician forces his mind back to Makara. Knowing the
shantytown where the Rattanaks live, he wonders whether the boy
turning to drugs isn't an attempt to hang on to life in some way, just as
he had.

Dr. Narunn climbs the few short steps to the ceremony hall, joined
now by four other younger novices. The monks lower themselves onto
the row of cushions atop the straw mats, with the young doctor taking
the honored middle seat. They each assume a lotus position, facing the
river about ten meters away.

The lute in hand, the Old Musician follows and takes a seat on the straw mat a bit off to one side. A couple of *koan saek*—"parakeets," as they're called, little orphans who mimic a monastic existence by learning to chant and observe basic precepts but who are still too small to be ordained—enter the hall, each carefully balancing a tray with glasses of water for the monks. Kneeling, they put the trays down, bow three times, place a glass in front of each monk, and again bow three times, their heads touching the floor each time. Then, with their backs bent to keep their heads lower than those of the monks, they exit the ceremony hall the same way they came, pausing briefly to offer a glass of water to the Old Musician as well. For a pair of otherwise rambunctious mischiefs, their steps are so perfectly choreographed that they rouse a chuckle from Dr. Narunn, forcing him to break from the solemn demeanor required for the occasion.

The Old Musician draws the brass plectrum from his shirt pocket, slips it around the tip of the ring finger of his right hand, pauses in a moment's concentration, and then plucks the *sadiev*. He lets the copper string vibrate for a second or two before silencing it with the base of his palm. Grasping the cone-shaped knob of the tuning peg, he tightens the string and plucks it again, his head slightly cocked to one side, his torso leaning forward, listening with his entire body. He repeats the steps several times more, tightening and loosening the solitary copper string until it produces the desired pitch, a tone that articulates the essence of the music he has invoked in his head. Tuning, he used to tell his students, is not about fiddling with a cord or peg but searching for the kernel, that core sound around which the rest of the notes and melodies weave themselves.

If he could name that vital force akin to *pralung*—that which had kept him alive all those months in Slak Daek—he would call it music, the incipient resonance from which both the named and nameless emerge.

He lifts the lute, holding it aslant, letting it stretch from his left collarbone to the right side of his abdomen. With the domed sound box over his heart, he begins to coax out a kind of *bampae*—a lullaby—gentle and jaunty, each note mimicking the sound of a child's footfall, a happy skip toward home after a day's careless wandering.

The temple officiant guides Makara and his parents into the ceremony hall. Meanwhile the *mae gru*—a female spiritual medium—leads the relatives and friends in a procession around the hall. Cradling a clay vessel in one arm and waving its lid with the other, the *mae gru* beckons Makara's spirit to enter the vessel, her stylized gestures a kind of dance.

In the countryside, such a procession would weave a path through the forests around the house of the sick person. But here in the city, where life moves at a much faster pace and space is constrained, the group merely circles the ceremony hall thrice.

The *mae gru* snaps the lid over the clay vessel, indicating that she has caught Makara's *pralung*. The Old Musician eases the tempo, weaving a more sedate phrase. Then, with the sound box directly over his heart, he bends the string, plucks, and releases, ending on a ghost note.

March 1974. It's Suteera's eighth birthday, and they're celebrating it with a big party, an unusually huge gathering of family and friends. She doesn't remember it being this grand last year. At some point in the night, her father pulls her aside from the festivities and tells her, in a rather urgent voice, "I'm going off to hide." Suteera laughs, thinking he—her solemn father—is going to take part in the game of hide-and-seek some of the littler children are playing at the moment. But tears flood his eyes and he quickly gathers her into his arms. Then, in a hushed voice, his cheek against hers, lips grazing her hair, he begins to sing, as he would a lullaby when she was smaller to help her sleep, to ease in their separation during the night.

"Your birthday *smoat*," he says when he's finished, releasing her from his warm but shaken grip. It suddenly hits her that this isn't a game, that he is really leaving, and this is his parting gift. She doesn't want it. But how can you return a song that's already been sung, silence a poem already spoken? There's nothing she can do to stop it—to stop herself from turning eight. Suteera wishes there were a clock within reach for her to rewind. But the only ticking she hears is the panic of her own heart. Faster and faster it gallops, as the rest of her stands stock-still. *Wait!* she wants to cry out, but the word lodges in her throat. Choked, she watches her father turn and disappear from sight.

Romvong music rises from the garden overlooking the Mekong, the male singer beckons, and the female vocalist croons her response, the pair weaving their steps and gestures around each other. Grown-ups and

children alike rush to dance. Cheers erupt, and it seems everyone is singing now. The celebration continues late into the night, indifferent to
Suteera's shock and grief, her inarticulate confusion.

The next morning she wakes up thinking it was all a dream. But
when she goes out to look for her father, he's nowhere to be found, his
absence a palpable gloom hanging over their vast estate, silencing the
memories of last night's festivities.

Later in the morning, when it seems the household has resurfaced from
its collective mourning, Suteera hears voices coming from the wooden pavilion by the water. "We remain who we are, Father, at our peril . . ."

"Channara, I didn't give you all that education so that you could run
off to the jungle!"

Her mother and grandfather are in the middle of another tense exchange, while her young aunt Amara listens on silently, forced to stay
put by the two combatants who each want her to take their side. But as
always Amara shows no sign of getting involved, remaining where she is,
if only to bear witness to their words should later one accuse the other of
saying what hasn't been said, as often is the case with Suteera's mother
and grandfather.

Noting Suteera's presence, the formidable patriarch fixes his eyes on
his elder daughter and growls, "I forbid you to follow him. I forbid you,
do you hear?"

Channara retorts, "There are things beyond even your control, Father,
and war is one of them." She sounds as resolved and unafraid in her erect
slenderness as the statesman appears authoritative in his ministerial stance.

Suteera's grandfather issues a warning look. "We'll discuss this later,
like adults, *among* adults." He strides away, brewing with silent fury.

As Suteera approaches the pavilion, Amara gets up to leave, but
Channara gestures for her younger sister to sit back down. "Please," she
pleads, seeming afraid to be alone with her own daughter. "I need you
here . . ." Her words trail.

The three of them remain silent for some time before Channara begins again, turning to young Suteera. "You know, when I came back

from America in 1962, your grandfather had this pavilion built for us, a wedding gift to me and your father." She lets out a tight, bitter laugh. "Perhaps as a reminder that the reason we have a roof over our heads at all is him. He allows it. We're all at the mercy of his generosity, his noblesse oblige. He thinks he's king."

Suteera stares at her mother, not knowing what to say, afraid of sounding stupid or childish. It's tricky to be around her mother when she's in this mood, unpredictable. She can snap at you or shoot a look that can silence you into submission.

Channara glances up at the ornate carving of the mythical Rahu straddling the sun and the moon that lines the edge of the roof. "*Rahu chap chan*," she says, alluding to the ancient tale that inspired the carving. "The sun and moon are destined lovers. Long ago the gods separated them, tore the lovers apart, believing the unification of their opposite qualities would ignite a cosmic war . . ."

It's so like her mother to try to explain everything through stories. She's a writer even when she's not writing. There are of course many legends about the sun and the moon, and Suteera, a child more well read than even most adults around her—the throng of servants working for them—is quite familiar with the tale depicted in the carving, in which the demon Rahu, during the war of the gods, propelled himself between Chandra and Suriya and, when no one was looking, devoured each in turn, causing a total eclipse. But this particular story about the sun and the moon as "destined lovers" torn apart by the gods who feared their union would cause an all-out cosmic war is one Suteera has never heard before. What's more, it doesn't make sense. How could they be *destined* for each other yet easily *torn* apart?

"But once in a long while, their paths will cross . . . and when this happens, Suriya and Chandra will swallow each other, darkening the world with their love."

Suteera suspects this is one of her mother's more ironic interpretations of the ancient tale, published under her pen name, Tun Chan. A male name, Channara explained, so that it's possible for a woman to write and publish. When Suteera's grandfather had agreed to let his elder daughter take up writing, he'd thought nothing would come of it. But to his chagrin, Channara's *reung toan samai*—"modern renderings"—of these complex tales in a series of graphic novels had become especially popular among the illiterate peasants and the urban poor, who, even if they couldn't read and write, could still make sense of the stories through pictures. This was how Suteera herself had learned to read by the age of four, first drawn to the colorful illustrations, and then prompted by curiosity to connect the words to the actions depicted. Her mother says it has been her intention all along to offer some means of education to those with little or no access to schooling, especially women and girls, who, unlike boys, cannot live at the temple and receive instruction from the monks.

"The problem, Suteera," her mother explains, sounding angry, "is when men play at being gods, the consequence is war. You cannot decide another's path without drawing resistance. Sooner or later, there'll be a clash, a collision so dark and huge it'll eclipse any battle we've seen." Her mother pauses, looks at her, and frowns, as if suddenly realizing she's talking to an eight-year-old. "Do you understand what I'm trying to tell you?" She seems annoyed at the whole world, scornful of its ignorance.

Suteera nods, though she's not sure whether what she understands is the same as what her mother intends. A sorcerer of sorts, her mother can weave an entire universe into existence, a world so intriguing you can lose yourself in it for days. But as a child, Suteera still sees her world—the real one she shares with her family—as preferable to any conjured up by words. Suteera understands her mother's story to mean that, even if it seems there's someone or something trying to separate them now, in the end her father will return, they will see him again, and, like the sun and moon, her parents will be reunited.

"Your grandfather may believe himself to be this god-king who decides everyone's fate. But war has come, whether he likes it or not."

Whatever antagonism her mother and grandfather harbor for each other has turned more dangerous in recent months, with Channara abandoning her comic books in favor of writing newspaper articles that criticize the rich and powerful, people like themselves, people Suteera's grandfather knows intimately. The senior statesman sees this as an outright assault against him and has many times ordered his daughter to stop. But Channara keeps at it, arguing that because she's publishing under a fake name—various ones, in fact, for different articles—no one will trace these writings back to her. *You're safe, Father*, she hissed during one of their more seething arguments. *You and your good name*.

"And for all his power and influence, he's no match for it. We'll all be scorched. Few will escape its fire. We have to change, or we'll be torn asunder—"

"What your mother means," interrupts Amara, who hasn't said a word until now, "is that we must look after one another." She glances at Channara disapprovingly, then back at Suteera with a smile. "We must be attentive amidst all the coming and going."

Suteera knows her aunt is attempting to reassure her. Gentle like Suteera's grandmother, Amara is the peacemaker in the family, and in this explosive environment, she strikes Suteera as the bravest. It takes courage to stay composed amidst angry words flying.

"And you," her aunt continues, "mustn't wander off too far by yourself."

At seventeen, her aunt is calmer and wiser than most grown-ups Suteera knows. While Channara is brilliant in many ways, it is Amara who often makes sense when no one else does. Still, Suteera finds it unsettling that neither her mother nor her aunt has spoken yet of her father's absence, that neither seems to be addressing his abrupt departure in the middle of the night. Do they know where he's gone and why? Did the two women plan the big party so that he could take advantage of the commotion to slip away unnoticed? No one sees it necessary to explain what has happened, and Suteera is too afraid to ask. She keeps hoping that she's just imagining things, that in reality her father has gone on a trip to the provinces to talk about music and recruit new talent, and that by nightfall he will return, as he always does.

"I want us to prepare ourselves for it," her mother concludes prophetically.

The spiritual medium leads the group into the ceremony hall and everyone sits down on the straw mats, facing the monks, leaving a respectful aisle in between. Once again the chanting resumes, with Dr. Narunn leading in a baritone, the other monks joining him one by one in succession, their voices merging in layered resonance, like water upon water, a midnight monsoon descending on the Mekong, sonorous and pensive.

Makara appears soothed by the chanting, eyes closed and head lowered, palms together in front of his chest, body twitching every once in a while as if from the residual effect of the drug.

The Old Musician remembers himself during those adolescent years when politics was a kind of intoxicant for a generation heady with the country's newly gained independence. He was only a few years older than Makara is now, but he felt like a man, making his own decisions about the future—where to go to school, what to study, which classmates to fraternize with, which teacher to steer clear of and which to endear himself to. It was 1956, less than three years after Cambodia had won its freedom from France. He was at Chomroeun Vichea, a private school in Phnom Penh, at a time when private schools were a relatively new phenomenon and thus considered inferior to the long-established government public institutions rooted in the French system, where, in order to move up from one level to the next, one must pass the notoriously difficult national examinations. While he had received high marks on all his exams, earning the coveted *diplôme*, he'd nonetheless failed to secure a place in a public *lycée*, as there were a great many more qualified applicants than available seats, often given preferentially to those with wealth and family connections. Having neither money nor family influence, he'd entered Chomroeun Vichea with the help of a friend already at the school. *Prama* . . .

The Old Musician smiles, remembering his friend's pet name. Cambodians are fond of nicknames and diminutives, as if every trait or idiosyncrasy deserves its own appellation, a distinct honor and title. Tun, his own nickname, came from his mother telling him as a young child that he was *tunphlun*—tenderhearted—and thus "tun" was a term of endearment for her son. It seems even back then the students and the teachers all had nicknames, demonstrating, as he would come to realize, a predilection for self-metamorphosis, the ease with which they would later assume one alias after another, to obscure some aspect of their identity as much as to accentuate another.

His friend was part of that growing circle of youth more interested in politics than academic pursuits. The year before, Prama had arrived at the school after he'd failed the state examinations, having abandoned his studies in favor of political meetings. Hearing of Tun's travails, Prama was indignant on his behalf and told him there was still space at Chomroeun Vichea. Prama then convinced his father, a well-to-do silk merchant, to help his friend with the private school fees and tuition. Tun was extremely grateful and felt profoundly beholden to the generous but surly patriarch. Prama's father made clear he expected great things from the studious young lute player, whose talents he'd enjoyed and patronized over the years at various family festivities and religious ceremonies. Tun greatly respected the merchant and feared the debt he would owe this man for the rest of his life. At the same time, he was reassured by the possibility that the patriarch must have truly thought well of him to put forth such investment in his future. A school was only as good as the paths it opened for its students, he reasoned.

Once at Chomroeun Vichea, to his surprise, he quite liked it, was even impressed by it, despite its reputation as a breeding ground for Communists and radicals. While at the time he was not politically active or even inclined, Tun found the atmosphere of open debate dynamic and refreshing, so unlike any school he had known. Soon he came to believe this private institution was indeed striving toward "progressive learning"—as the name Chomroeun Vichea clearly purported—the kind of education that went beyond memorization of standardized knowledge to incorporate a critique of social conditions and spur civic engagement. That particular year, 1956, his friend Prama, using Tun's love of songwriting and Khmer poetry as bait, inveigled him into taking a literature class taught by a relatively new teacher who had quickly gained a reputation for being eloquent, insightful, and inspiring, as well as compassionate and fair in his dealings with students. It soon became clear to Tun that the teacher's reputation was the sole reason Prama had wanted to take the class, given his friend's absolute lack of interest in literature.

During class one morning, Prama, fidgeting with a trickster's restlessness, obviously impatient with the writings of dead Frenchmen, raised his hand to interrupt the teacher's reciting of a prose poem by Rimbaud from the collection titled *Les Illuminations*. "Why is it that we must mimic the tongue that reduced our people to savages?" Prama quipped, as usual teetering between humor and irreverence, pretending he'd completely forgotten this was a course on classic French literature.

Who else were they supposed to read and mimic? Tun wanted to remind his friend. From the seat behind, he snapped Prama's shiny cowlick with a flick of his forefinger, hissing under his breath, "You're going to get yourself *expelled*." But others seemed to concur with Prama. *Yes, why do we seek to master the language of our former masters?*

Instead of slamming the desk or roaring with anger, the more likely response to such insolence, the teacher quietly closed the book he had been reading, looked up slowly, and smiled. He nodded his head a few times, as if to encourage the students to continue their inquiry and critique. The whole class, abandoning Rimbaud's poetic reflection on youth and war, suddenly burst into debate. They pondered the pervasive use of French, particularly in academic and official settings, among the Cambodian intelligentsia in general—even in an avant-garde institution like Chomroeun Vichea—and what that said of the Khmer national identity.

One student asserted that for him it was a matter of pride to speak French, to prove that Cambodians are not the buffoons the colonialists had thought them to be, that the Khmer race, like any human race, was capable of varied linguistic expressions, even the languages of the so-called civilized. No, it was revenge, argued an aspiring writer, a character more irreverent, more dangerously flippant, than his friend Prama. "Because knowing a language well gives you the tools to expose a system of thinking from within!" Then, half jokingly, the would-be novelist explained that while he could never utter expletives in his own "lovely native tongue," he found it was easy to do so in French. Vulgarity, he rationalized, was not part of Cambodians' innate speech, and thus, the only undeniable influence of the French and their erstwhile colonial administration on him and those they subjugated was obscenity, which, in his well-read opinion, was the very essence of colonial practice. "Colonialism, both concept and application, is obscene at best and, ironically, barbaric at worst because it reveals the ignorance of those blind to their own savagery!" The whole class stood up and clapped, rowdy as a crowd watching a street performance.

The teacher said nothing, and it was difficult for the students, even the more astute and perceptive among them, to tell what he thought of their circuitous detour from the subject of French literature. Once the class had settled down again, the instructor, who stood before them with a face as composed and benign as a bodhisattva, returned to Rimbaud's collection and the last lines of "Guerre," the prose poem about the potent dream of war:

Je songe à une Guerre de droit ou de force, de logique bien imprévue.
C'est aussi simple qu'une phrase musicale.

For the first time that morning, Tun felt he understood Rimbaud's poetry, or at least the metaphor. Certainly the allusion to music was something he could grasp. But perhaps what drew him was the way the poem was read, the melody, the tenderness and poignancy, the irony with which the teacher recited the final line.

Teera's father failed to return that night after her birthday, or the next night, or the one after. But true to her words, her mother tried to prepare her for what was to come. Weapons of war, Channara explained when distant howls and roars intermittently broke the almost funereal silence around them. She told Suteera about rockets and bombs and grenades, painting them with her terrible, beautiful words, illustrating them with her graceful hands, her dancelike gestures. Rockets, she said, looked like banana blossoms. They whistled as they flew through the air. Grenades hissed like snakes before exploding. *If one rolls through our gate, you must run from it as fast as you can, Suteera. You must not touch it, go near it, or mistake it for a fruit—a custard apple gone gray.* And bombs? Suteera wanted to know. Bombs were unpredictable, her mother explained. You'd never know when one would drop from the sky, but if it did, you'd feel it—its awful power. Bombs came in all shapes and sizes, gifts from the Americans, who rained them down on towns and villages, killing and injuring hundreds of thousands. *If one lands on our estate, it'd be the end of us.*

In this way the days passed into weeks, the weeks into months, with the screams of war growing louder, at times deafening, until its monstrous presence replaced her father's ghostly absence. *One sees the agony of a people in that woman's face*, her mother wrote in a newspaper about an encounter she'd had with a peasant woman who'd lost half of her face during a rocket attack, and who, with her children, had fled their war-ravaged village to the city, as had the countless refugees living on the streets. *Bullets and rockets rain down on us like a new kind of monsoon.* Her mother's words ricocheted through her grandfather's circles, angering him and others supporting the American intervention.

Only many years later, as an adult, a student of history, did Teera come to understand what her mother had tried to explain about the war—that their small country was caught in the much larger political mayhem of the American conflict in Vietnam, that in 1969 President Nixon authorized a secret bombing campaign on Cambodia in order to destroy Vietnamese Communist forces hiding there, and that by 1973, when Congress finally knew and put a stop to it, the indiscriminate carpet bombing had left hundreds of thousands of Cambodians dead and millions displaced. The United States bombed Indochina with three times the tonnage of bombs used in all of World War II; Cambodia alone was hit with three times more tonnage than Japan.

Knowing this, it's easy for Teera to see now why Cambodians, educated and uneducated alike, were so ready to believe the Khmer Rouge when a mere two years later, on that fateful April morning in 1975, upon seizing the capital, the guerrillas claimed the American warplanes would return to drop more bombs, this time on Phnom Penh itself.

In hindsight, Teera believes that people like her mother and grandfather, those with a deeper understanding of international politics, may have known it was a straight-out lie. Still, even if they'd known, by that time they had no choice but to leave the capital as ordered, joining the entire urban population, now some two million displaced peasants in addition to the seven hundred thousand original city dwellers—a gargantuan mass for so small a city—all forced at gunpoint in the mass evacuation to the countryside.

But for the young Suteera, the chaos began weeks before the Khmer Rouge victory. One night in March, a year after her father had disappeared, just as she grew certain she would never see him again, he suddenly returned, cloaked in the din and chaos of mortar explosions rattling the city. "I've come back to celebrate your birthday," he told her happily, as if he'd only been gone a few days, as if a whole year hadn't passed.

She had the urge to hurt him, to tell him she wasn't a child—*his* child—anymore. She wanted desperately to wound him so he couldn't escape again. But she had the distinct feeling that words, whatever she said, wouldn't make a difference. She couldn't have been more right.

Her father stayed with them for several more days and, on the night of her ninth birthday, vanished again. This time she had been prepared. She wouldn't allow herself to be tricked into accepting something she didn't want. She'd refused a party, a celebration of any sort. In any case, it wouldn't have been possible to celebrate with the war raging all around them, with the Khmer Rouge closing in on the city. Still, she would not allow him to sing to her, as a gift or otherwise. If she couldn't make him stay, then she would not be serenaded into accepting his departure.

C'est aussi simple qu'une phrase musicale. The Old Musician tries sounding out the line of poetry in his head. *Une phrase musicale.* It no longer has the power it did that first time he heard it. War is anything but simple.

Years later, in Democratic Kampuchea, toward the end of the regime, when it was rumored that Pol Pot, the head of the secret organization, the much feared Angkar, was none other than Saloth Sar, his inspiring and mild-mannered teacher at Chomroeun Vichea, he couldn't believe it. There must be a mistake, because his teacher had disappeared in 1962 and was since presumed dead. The two couldn't be the same man. He was convinced the rumor was false.

Only in 1997 when Pol Pot, his once smooth features now aged with liver spots, appeared on television in an interview with an American journalist, did the Old Musician, assured by what he both saw and heard, finally accept that this was indeed the same man who four decades earlier in his recitation of Rimbaud's "Guerre" had moved the class with the music of his voice.

How long has she been standing in this spot? Teera pulls back and moves away from the fogged glass to the desk beside her bed. Aware of her surroundings again, she hears it. The funeral music. It's playing somewhere outside the hotel compound, the melody faint, the lyrics indecipherable. Sometimes when broadcast through loudspeakers, you can hear it from miles away. It seems she hears one funeral every day, as if this tiny city is in perpetual mourning, making up for those years it couldn't grieve for its dead. Teera strains to listen, imagining her father's words in every tune she hears.

I know not how love chooses who and why—
Why I see infinity in your eyes . . .

It was a strange present to give a child, and an even stranger thing to sing on her birthday. It wasn't a funerary song, but it was still a *smoat*, which, he'd explained, was poetry sung in honor of loved ones, living or dead. She wonders now if the dead can serenade the living, seduce us with longings that are not even our own.

There's more to the song, though she can't recall beyond those two lines. She feels the rest of the lyrics always at the tip of her tongue, yet whenever she tries to voice them, they refuse formation, and she's left shaken by the knowledge that her body holds secrets it won't reveal. In moments like these, she wavers between amnesia and nostalgia, part of her here, part of her there, straddling that undemarcated landless geography of the dispossessed. She wants to forget it all and, at the same time, longs for something she can't even remember. What is it that she's reaching for? At times, she feels the journey, this ceaseless search, is her only true country.

As for what she truly knows, much is borrowed knowledge, collective hindsight. If pressed, she fears she won't be able to separate what she actually recalls from what she's learned over the years. What's clear is that memories—the bits and pieces that are hers—fuel the desire to know more, to probe deeper, and the more she knows, the more she's able to recall. A small, random spark can floret into full luminosity, like a pilot light igniting a halo of flame. And in such bright, short-lived moments, she sees not a portal providing immediate access to the past, a shortcut to truth and certainty, but a road map, an entente cordiale, as if time has called a truce so that she can carefully tread the battlefields of the self to find what may have survived, what may be worth treasuring. Of her father's disappearance, Amara said that he had joined the insurgent underground movement and that when he reemerged a year later, in March 1975, it was to tell her mother that the civil war would be won by the Revolutionary Army and that he would return then to fetch Teera and her mother to begin their life together in a newly forged Democratic Kampuchea.

For years Teera let this knowledge linger at the periphery of her understanding. Then at Cornell, while she was poring over historical documents, the truth of his affiliation with the Khmer Rouge sank in. But the shock of such a discovery was too much to bear, the weight of admission more devastating than omission. So she shoved history back to where it belonged, on the dusty old shelves of the unread and unexamined. She convinced herself that the past couldn't be altered. She couldn't help who her father was, the path he took, who he became, and the nightmare he might've taken part in engineering. All the same, she continued to wonder.

Even now the questions persist. Where did he go when he disappeared again? Did he stay close by in the city or go back to the jungle? And always, *Why?—Why did he leave?* What unhappiness or hope pushed him to make this choice? He gave up everything for nothing, absolutely nothing, as all would be destroyed in the end.

Shortly after his final departure, on that April morning when her grandparents and Amara were rushing to pack and lock up the house, after the Khmer Rouge had ordered them to leave, she asked her mother if they oughtn't wait for him. Her mother replied in haste, *Your father is dead. To me, he is dead, do you understand?* Teera didn't believe it—couldn't yet accept it. She had no idea whether she would see him again, but she also sensed he was alive somewhere. Somewhere he must be waiting for them. Still, her mother's words, more than the mayhem around them, shattered her world, ended her childhood, the certainty of it made clear by her father's total absence in the moment they needed him most.

Had he been captured en route during his clandestine travels back to his hiding place? Was he killed in battle somewhere, or forced by his comrades—by fractious internal politics and ideology—to disassociate himself completely from his family and its privileged background when he reentered the underground movement?

These questions surfaced for Teera years later, in America, when Amara revealed to her what she had learned from Channara—that her father was supposed to come back before the Khmer Rouge takeover. It was just a matter of a few short weeks before they would join him in his new life. But he never returned at the beginning of April as he'd promised. He'd left Channara pregnant with another child, who would be born into hunger and suffering.

Whether her father remained at large or met his demise, her mother would never forgive him for the death of their second born, a son he didn't know, would never know he had.

Again, Teera reaches for her shoulder bag and extracts her journal. Sitting down at the desk, she feels the bone-aching need to write but doesn't know where to begin. Her mind hums, abuzz with thoughts, afraid of what it will discover in stillness. She flips the journal over, noting the imprint of its flowered logo, with the words "White Hibiscus" etched into the leather cover. From the inner pocket of the back flap, she pulls out the black-and-white photograph she carries from journal to journal, each time giving it a new home between the pages. It's the only image of her parents Amara managed to smuggle out and retain, and over the years it's turned jaundiced and papery, its edges frayed, its surface spidery with wrinkles and cracks, all the vulnerabilities of age, while her parents remain forever young.

They are at a party of some sort—perhaps a soirée, as Amara was fond of saying, a word so out of context in their Section 8 housing when Teera first noted her aunt's incessant use of it. *Oh, I remember the soirées we used to have*, Amara would reminisce, pronouncing it with a proper French accent. *There was this one soirée where I sipped my first champagne . . . I was twelve, and I didn't know that champagne was not made from champignons!*

In the captured soirée, her mother is the only one wearing the traditional *sampot phamuong*—a long embroidered silk sarong—and matching court blouse, with three strands of pearls resting on the square neckline, while everyone else sports Western attire, the women in those black dresses so emblematic of the 1960s and the men in suits and ties. The young Channara—who looks to be in her early twenties, but with a confidence that makes her seem older, worldly wise—embodies what Teera has come to see as the paradox of much of the educated Cambodian elite at the time, ideologically progressive yet morally conservative.

Teera notes the correct way her mother carries herself, the self-possessed uprightness that calls to mind the arrogant superiority of another educated woman she saw in a newspaper article recently. Ieng Thirith, the former Khmer Rouge minister of social affairs, appeared in a photograph alongside her husband, Ieng Sary, and other surviving regime leaders who would be tried if the proposed tribunal ever takes place. Teera wonders if her mother ever crossed paths with this woman. Did Channara consider herself a Marxist? A Communist? Had Suteera's father returned in those couple of weeks before the Khmer Rouge takeover, would her mother have gone with him? Teera remembers her mother as steely resolute about everything she believed in. In the black-and-white photograph she's holding now, the youthful Channara stares at the camera with a sternness and austerity softened only by her extraordinary beauty.

Teera's eyes shift to the young man next to her mother in the photograph. Her father, his face turned so that only his profile is captured, smiles adoringly at his beautiful young wife. Her parents, happy and in love—or so Teera imagines—are surrounded by friends and intimates. A man has his arm around her father's shoulder, pulling him so that he leans slightly to one side. From behind, a woman pitches forward to whisper something in her mother's ear. And a bit off to the right, a group of festively dressed children gather in a semicircle, with Amara in the middle cupping something in her hand, maybe a butterfly or bug, Teera imagines. Even as a little girl, it seems her aunt could summon a crowd. This makes Teera smile, and she imagines Amara's gentle but firm voice explaining to the throng of tiny listeners how to handle a delicate creature, a fragile life.

Ah, Sangkhum. Teera remembers how Amara would sigh with happy nostalgia whenever they looked at the photo together, as if this one word brought to life a time, before war and revolution and genocide, when there was indeed evidence of "Society," a time when art and culture thrived, when ideas marked your sophistication, allowed you to move with ease from one circle into another. *You must study hard and do better than your American classmates*, her aunt would then add, as if it was all part of the same conversation. *Your mother was right. Education makes all boundaries porous, crossable.*

In this lush setting, Teera sees it so clearly now, the cultivated sophistication of her parents' milieu, the vibrant atmosphere of learning that seems to lie just beneath the dull, filmy coat of the monochrome paper. As she continues to stare at the photograph, she half expects the surface fissures and tears to mend themselves and the stilled scene to burst into life, in the full brilliant colors of the tropics.

They are all outside on the pillared marble veranda Teera recognizes as her childhood home. *Mon rêve sur le précipice*, her polyglot grandfather would rhapsodize, holding her tiny hand as they walked the grounds, always with a touch of sadness in his tone, as if speaking of something long passed. The sprawling estate stretched across the outermost tip of what her grandfather nicknamed Chrung Pich—"Diamond's Point"—facing the confluence of the country's three principal rivers: the Mekong, the Tonle Sap, and the Bassac. *1962?* Amara had written on the back of the photo, the question mark in pencil, as if added later, doubting the indelible assertion in ink.

If it was 1962, that would mean her aunt was seven, thirteen years younger than her mother, and her grandfather had just returned from his post as senior advisor to the ambassador at the Cambodian Embassy in Washington, DC. Le Conseiller, a title he would've retained in perpetuity, Amara explained, had it not been for the Khmer Rouge. Amara said she had little recollection of those first seven years of her life in the States, or—when Teera asked—why they suddenly left after such a long sojourn abroad to return home. But Teera knew this couldn't be true. Amara had to remember, or at least had to have some inkling why the patriarch abruptly gave up his highly prized diplomatic post in the embassy and moved the entire family back to Phnom Penh.

Whenever Teera and Amara managed to talk about the past, their cautious exchange was riddled with "I don't remember . . ." which was often code for "I don't want to talk about it . . . at least not yet." Teera guesses that for Amara to recall those early years in the States would inevitably lead her aunt to wonder what life might have been like had the family never returned to Cambodia. What if they had all survived?

The danger, Teera realizes, is not in remembering but in longing for what never was, leaping into vague possibilities that multiply into even more obscure possibilities. In reality, her grandfather, an ardent patriot and staunch monarchist, would never abandon his country for another. If anything, he was the kind who would return in times of upheaval to try to help steer the country back to stability, and, according to Amara, that was exactly what he had done.

Knowing what she knows now, Teera is convinced that even back then, in the early sixties, with student demonstrations and leftist politics on the rise and the underground movement gaining membership and momentum, her politically astute grandfather must've discerned the fault lines, the rifts and ruptures around his tightly cordoned enclave of privilege and power. He must've known her mother's role in augmenting those rifts, her infatuation with the left, and he must've used all his weight and influence to try to keep his country from sliding toward the abyss.

Précipice. Teera loved the sound of it as a child, without knowing what it meant. It wasn't the kind of word one learned in primary school—even at the elite École Miche—but through her grandfather's refrain, his lament, it became firmly rooted in her memory. A lifetime later and in an entirely new geography, she encountered its English equivalent in her high school AP Literature class, and only then did she realize her grandfather had been speaking for all of them, for all Cambodia, a nation on the brink of its own destruction, its willful suicide.

The temple officiant lights the candle on a *popil*, a carved wooden holder shaped like a banyan leaf, and gestures for the Rattanaks and their boy to scoot forward. A group of elders, representing the eight cardinal directions, encircles Makara. They pass the lit candle around in a clockwise direction, each drawing a half-moon over the flame before offering it to the next person, weaving a symbolic wreath of protection around the boy. Last in the circle, the spiritual medium receives the candle in one hand, opens the lid of the clay vessel with the other, and blows out the flame in one decisive breath, sending the strand of smoke dancing in Makara's face. When the smoke enters his nostrils, Makara lets out a series of coughs, as if to suggest that indeed his spirit has united with his body. The jolt sends a sprig of cowlick straight up at the back of his head.

The Old Musician smiles, remembering Prama's cowlick, the spiky hair his friend was forever trying to tame with coconut oil, the prickly strands that earned him the pet name Kamprama—"Porcupine"—a playful spin-off on his grandiose formal name, Pramaborisoth, one of "True and Pure Knowledge."

He last saw his friend alive that misty morning, in 1971, when he—then Tun—waited with his daughter outside their Citroën on Sisowath Quay along the river. By then Prama had joined the Communist Party and was preparing to go into hiding. His friend wanted to meet at the promenade in front of the Royal Palace, an open and public place, which would give the illusion of a serendipitous encounter between two old friends, so as not to stir any suspicion from patrolling police. It was normal for people to park their cars on the streets and then go for a jog or stroll on the promenade along the Tonle Sap River.

Tun himself had come in running shorts, though it was a nippy morning. To keep himself warm while he waited for this so-called chance meeting with Prama, Tun stretched and sprinted back and forth between a pair of coconut trees. On the curb, his daughter stood with her back to him, drawing pictures on the car window, observing his opaque reflection through the fogged pane. Earlier at home, she had woken to the sound of his footsteps walking past her room and then, trailing him through the hallway, insisted on accompanying him.

Now, worried she'd get sick from the mist falling on her head and the chilly breeze from the river, Tun suggested she go back inside the Citroën. She refused, telling him that the fine spray was *tik phka chouk*— the shower falling from the lotus-shaped faucet they had at home, under which she'd lose herself every morning, singing his funerary *smoat* to herself, happy as a sparrow trilling in its birdbath, oblivious to the mournfulness her invocation inspired.

The Old Musician swallows, pushing down the grief rising to his throat at this last image—the happy innocence with which she embraced the world—and he wants to weep but cannot.

The monks have reached the final incantation, pausing to allow the group to repeat each line after them. Dr. Narunn dips the sacred brush made from a bundle of finely pared coconut spines into the bronze bowl and sprinkles water on the throng before him. The drops make the Old Musician think of the tiny beads gathering on his daughter's long locks that morning, like strands of infinitesimal pearls materializing and melting in rapid succession.

He closes his eyes, remembering the mossy dampness of her hair when he placed his hand on her head. He'd caught sight of Prama at the far end of the promenade. He ordered her to wait inside the car. She reluctantly obeyed, noting his hardened voice, which he almost never used with her. In subtle protest, she sat in the back instead of reclaiming the passenger seat where she'd always sit with him, as if to say, *If you don't want me near you, then I won't sit next to you!* He gave her a rueful smile. She did not smile back.

Prama appeared on a rickety old bicycle, less a symbol of his fallen economic status as the disinherited heir of a silk fortune than a statement of his identification with the laboring masses. The two friends mimed surprise at running into each other. *Here of all places! How are you doing? Where do you live now? Well, let me give you my address!* Prama pulled from his breast pocket a pen and folded paper, pretended to scribble down his address, and handed Tun the paper, which in reality was a letter to his father, from whom he was now estranged. The silk merchant had disowned Prama due to his associations with those "loathed Communists." But Prama, ever boyishly affable and good-natured in spite of his serious political agenda, never begrudged his father for cutting him off. That morning, preparing to join the insurgency, he told Tun he wanted his father to understand his decision, his chosen path, a course he believed the entire country would one day be forced to take. This was the dawn of a bright new decade, his friend told him, sounding a bit naive, Tun thought. Prama, having taken another nickname, an alias he refused to reveal, parted by saying that he hoped Tun would reconsider following him.

Several months later Tun did join Prama. At his funeral. Prama was killed during the crossfire between the insurgents and the government army at a jungle-shrouded temple outside of Siem Reap. It was never really clear whether he was killed during battle or captured by the other side and executed. Either way, his body was abandoned in an open field and reclaimed by the government soldiers who identified him as Kim Pramaborisoth, the son of the silk merchant Kim Houng. Neither Prama's alias nor his role in the revolutionary movement was ever known. It was better this way for all concerned. The body was brought back to Phnom Penh, where Tun had joined the family for the funeral, taking his daughter with him. It was the first funeral she would attend.

Sorrow floods his chest, and the Old Musician lets it overtake him.

Eyes still closed, he shuts out the present completely. His mind swings back to that morning on the promenade when his friend was still alive, when, before jumping back on his bicycle, Prama grabbed him and hugged him hard, his fist affectionately pounding Tun's back as if to say, *Stay strong, pal.* Tun, facing the car, looked up from his friend's shoulder and saw his daughter watching them. He waved to her playfully, mouthing he would soon be done, but she blew on the window, fogging the glass with her breath, shutting him out.

By March 1974, he was indeed a full-fledged member of the resistance and would soon go underground, leaving his daughter behind. He would come back for her, but during his long absence she'd outgrown a father's coddling adoration. *Oh, Papa, I'm not a baby anymore.* Her one reprimand was enough to leave a permanent bruise on his heart.

He feels a stream of water from Dr. Narunn's brush landing on his face. He opens his eyes. To his surprise, he sees only the young physician in the ceremony hall with him. The ceremony has finished, everyone is gone—as are all traces of sunlight—and night has made its pale appearance in gray.

Smiling from across a lit candle, Dr. Narunn teases, a hint of concern in his voice, "I didn't think my chanting was so melodic as to induce such melancholia. You're crying, my friend."

Interlude

Morning comes
    soft
        steps
            on
                liquid-green
                    marble
        tiptoeing
            toward
            my bed
                    _____dragging
                a thin beam of sunlight
    like the magic wand
        of a child at play.

I sleep . . .
        dreaming of you—
                a sanctuary
        tucked
                in the landscape of childhood
        memories—
                a daughter's prayer nipped
                    in the bud by
                        whizzing bullets
        shouts of revolution
                        A father's disappearance.

A bird calls
                from the walled garden
                                whistling
                                        its morning song
                Coffee-colored salamanders
                cross paths, nod, How do you do? I'm fine, thank you,
                        and scurry away like two arrows
                shooting   in opposite directions.

Fear tosses and turns, fighting a battle already lost,
                Old hurts seep through layers of selves,
                        travel the river of histories,
                                remembered voices,
                                        then, like grains of sand,
                                                vanish into oblivion.

And I . . . I wait for you in the calm
                and silence
                        of a thousand textures and hues
I wait for you
                in the folds of white hibiscus.

Second Movement

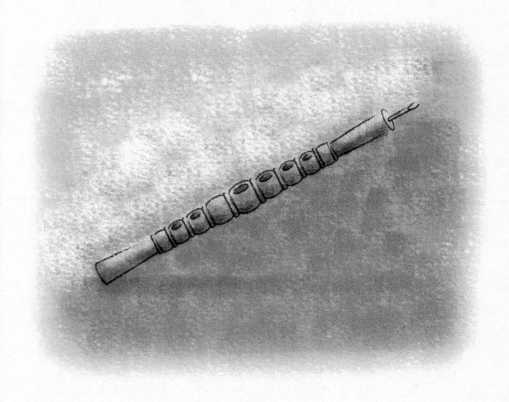

Her gaze falls on the young man, and it's like staring at a silhouette she's known all her life, a figure she's encountered repeatedly in her disparate dreams. His head is bowed so that she can't quite make out his face, but the rest of him is clearly delineated through the incense smoke wafting in the *vihear*. Tall and lean, with broad shoulders and elongated collarbones that seem to exaggerate the width of his exposed chest, this prince-like figure appears statuesque, chiseled from stone, his mannerisms and movements stylized, choreographed by some ancient code.

Covered only from the waist down with a swath of white cotton knotted into a loose *kben*, he bows three times to the principal image of the Buddha at the center of the prayer hall and once in each of the four cardinal directions. And only then, as he turns, does Teera feel certain she's met him before. "He's beautiful," she murmurs.

"Well, yes, and maybe it's okay to say so, since soon he'll no longer be a monk."

Teera turns to Mr. Chum standing beside her and stammers, "W-what, he's a monk?" No wonder he appears so strikingly familiar. She looks again and realizes now where she met him, on these same stairs, when she visited the temple the first time a week or two ago, when she ran fleeing from him like an idiot. "I'm sorry . . . I don't mean to offend." Sometimes she forgets the culture she's returned to, its rules of behavior, what a woman can or cannot express aloud.

"Oh, I don't mind!" Mr. Chum lets out a soft chuckle. "If only some pretty young lady thought that of me!"

Teera is grateful for his lightness, his easygoing attitude. Then, unable to help it, she ventures further, "How do you know he'll no longer be a monk?" She reddens in spite of herself.

"He's wearing the white garb of a novice who's just been given permission to disrobe."

Disrobe. Stop it!—He's a monk. Or was. All the same, she feels scandalized at the sight of those bare shoulders. She looks away, upset with herself. *You have no shame.*

Mr. Chum continues, oblivious to her inner monologue, "He's paying final respects before he puts on regular clothes again and returns to lay life. Let's go introduce ourselves."

"No!" Teera blurts out, and promptly silences herself lest they disturb the man in the *vihear*. "He should have his solitude, don't you think? Maybe we can come back afterward. I'm—I'm afraid I'll change my mind again if I don't do this now."

Mr. Chum nods. "I'll wait for you here, then? Are you sure you don't want me to come along?"

"Y-yes." She dithers, overwhelmed by the sense she doesn't know what she's doing.

In the car on the way over, she managed to explain her earlier confusion and fear, why she'd panicked and run the last time they came to Wat Nagara, what this place held for her, what it holds for her still, and, despite her persistent apprehension, the reasons that compel her to revisit the temple.

"I have to do this alone," she tries to reiterate with more conviction than before.

"All right then," Mr. Chum says decisively, as if to push her along. "Just signal if you need me."

He's referring to the routine that has served them well when they venture out together: she speed-dials him on her cell phone, allows just one ring, and he comes to their agreed meeting place. He's grown protective of her, assuming the avuncular role accorded him through the familial titles they use for each other, and getting a local mobile number was his idea, for the convenience as well as for her safety.

The old driver understands the importance of this visit. It's not every day, he told Teera in the car, that you cross paths with someone who might be able to shed light on what happened to your loved ones, who may have witnessed their last days, their final breaths. To know for certain they died, even without the proof of bones and ashes, is its own kind of peace, for it allows us to separate the missed from the missing. He himself would walk to the ends of the earth to meet another who could tell him what became of his wife and children, his first family, whose silhouettes he still searches for in crowds, whose voices he imagines hearing through the market din. *The strange thing is I wouldn't know if I bumped into them right now.* Afterward, he seemed surprised that he'd shared so much with her.

Likewise, Teera is astonished by how much she's come to rely on him, to trust him. Once he was a Khmer Rouge soldier whose shadow she would've feared. Now it's clear to her they are on the same journey, her search becomes his, and he is utterly invested in the mundane task of ferrying her around, always ready for their next quest.

As Teera makes her way down the steps, she realizes there remains very little of the temple she remembers from her childhood. All the structures seem to have been built only recently, and the grounds are smaller than she recalls, perhaps because of the brick walls, the fresh clay texture not yet sullied by the blackish-green algae veining other surfaces. There are some ancient-looking trees, at least old enough to have preceded the Khmer Rouge, but no structure stands out or strikes her memory with ringing clarity. Yet, the resonances of what once existed are all around her, and she feels in her steps the imprints of her childhood strolls upon these grounds; she senses walking beside her the *pralung* of her young self, that little girl she once was, at times running ahead, leading the way. She remembers that then, as now, it was lush and harboring, and that during festivals vibrant colors glittered across the seemingly infinite expanse—before there were walls—where land reshaped itself into water and water into forests and forests into clouds.

Fiery specks flood her vision. Orange, cinnamon, and deep earthy red of the monastic cloths flutter among leaves and branches, calling to mind the brilliant swaths of autumn when she left Minneapolis several weeks ago, and Teera remembers in turn how struck she was by the fall season, its tropical tinges, when she and Amara arrived in America that October in 1980. The hues of one love simmer in another, she thinks.

She realizes with a pang of guilt that before she was even aware she loved her father, her mother, loved another human being, she had loved a place—this land, which, in her innocence, she didn't understand as defined by borders and geography, its relationship to other countries, only in the intimate sense of family, safety, and home. The world then contracted and expanded, nimble and borderless as her imagination. As she grew older, she learned of territories with clearly marked perimeters, often drawn and redrawn by wars and revolutions, by blood. Yet, as Teera takes these steps, she knows she has never stopped loving this place. Its people, its landscape. She has never let it go. She's learned to embrace another as her home only because once she knew how it felt to be embraced by a land, to be rooted and safe.

She heads toward the cluster of wooden dwellings, the monks' private quarters, where, she was told, young women are not normally permitted to enter unless they are *nhome*—family of the ordained. *In your case, though, it's perfectly all right*, the Venerable Kong Oul said when they spoke on the phone early this morning. *Your reunion is long awaited.* Teera found it curious that the abbot used the word "reunion" rather than "visit." Did he know she'd come before? *The two of you will have much to talk about*, he told her, and then prophetically added, *And you'll know then what course you must take.*

What has the Old Musician revealed to the abbot? Did he speak of her father, their imprisonment in Slak Daek, how they had suffered together, what might have been their crimes? Or is she hoping for too much? Perhaps the Old Musician has nothing to offer her beyond the cryptic fragments he's already shared in the letter, and those tired old instruments.

But something nudges her. A thought, a feeling. No, even less than that. Some vague yearning she can't begin to articulate.

Teera spots the "cottage" the abbot has described for her, perplexed that he used so grand a name for this weather-beaten hovel squatting in the dirt, with its walls of thin wood planks crudely tacked together, leaving huge gaps in between. She looks from it to the pristine white stupa bearing her father's name in gold lettering at the far end of the compound, then back at the cottage. Her heart flutters. She tells herself he's waiting for her now inside that cramped, dank space. How can this be his home? How can it be anyone's? Yet, in these past weeks she's come to see all too clearly that to have any shelter at all separates you from the countless whose only claim to home is a corner of sidewalk or a small patch of public ground.

Now, looking around the temple grounds, Teera questions the value of building stupas, or any such dwellings constructed for the dead, when the living lack the dignity of shelter, the privacy afforded by simple walls and a roof. She thinks of the street corner near her hotel where a family has set up shelter. Every time she goes out for her evening walk she encounters them—a young couple and their school-aged daughter. Last night the father had parked his cyclo against a lamppost so that his small daughter could do her schoolwork under the light. As it started to drizzle, the little girl pulled the clear plastic hood of the cyclo forward and clasped it in place with a clothespin, leaving open the pair of rectangular air holes cut in the sides like tiny windows. There, the girl cocooned herself inside the bubble-like sphere, poring over her schoolbook, arms around her backpack—a Clifford the Big Red Dog bag, the kind of item sold at the open-air market among piles of donated used clothes that have made their way from America. Teera has learned this is where cast-off belongings end up, unacceptable even to charity organizations like the Salvation Army and Goodwill. Leftover hand-me-downs for leftover lives.

But the way the little girl wore the backpack on her chest, hugging it, made clear how much she cherished it. The bag doubled as her doll, and as she rocked back and forth, memorizing her lesson, Clifford bobbed up and down, ears flopping, nodding agreeably with the recited lesson, his once bright synthetic fur dulled by poverty but softened by ceaseless love.

The child kept reading, even as the light from the lamppost grew dimmer in the gathering mists. Outside, her parents moved around the cyclo and fastened a blue tarp around its metal frame to create a space for themselves underneath. As Teera approached them, she stepped off the sidewalk, not wanting to trespass upon their private space, the sanctity of home however vagrant and lacking, and continued the rest of her evening stroll on the street.

She pauses on the narrow footpath leading directly to the cottage. She wants to turn back, to run away again, feeling ridiculous and small-minded in her quest. What is it that she hopes to reclaim? Hasn't her life, all she's been able to rebuild in America, made up for what was lost and destroyed? What more could she demand when others have so little, almost nothing to live on?

"Hello, sir!" a voice suddenly calls out, and she turns toward it. A young monk pokes his head from beneath a saffron robe hanging on a line between two bowed hibiscus saplings. Teera looks left and right only to realize that the "sir" was directed at her. She hesitates, unsure what language to respond with, but finally in English reciprocates, "Oh, hello there!—Sir," she adds, almost an afterthought.

This pleases her greeter immensely. He offers her a wide grin, made more comical by his shaven head and big elfish ears. He turns to another shadow beside him, the tethered saplings bowing even deeper from the tugs and pulls of the laundered robe, and suddenly another young novice pops up, exclaiming, "How are you I'm fine sankyou sir!" The two giggle, covering their mouths with their hands, clearly delighted that they get to experiment on a complete stranger. "I'm fine sankyou sir!" the first echoes, and again they both giggle.

Everywhere she goes, Teera witnesses this—the easy laughter, the abundant lightness. When she gives the proper greetings for monks, they promptly duck back into hiding, so now she sees only their silhouettes behind the transparent glow of the saffron robe, like two characters in a shadow-puppet play. "Khmer Amerikan!" they exclaim in hushed excitement. "Khmer Anaekajun!" She's heard this repeatedly since her arrival, a term that seems to convey, *One of us . . . but not quite.* Teera couldn't have imagined that in her own country, where everyone looks like her, she'd be labeled again and again an outsider. It unsettles her.

Suddenly she is standing in front of the cottage. Her heart thumps, and she feels the odd sensation of being a child again, loitering in front of her father's music room, straining to hear if he was practicing behind the closed door. How did she get there? How has she come here?

Again, Teera is struck by the collapsibility of time and space, the melding of worlds and selves, and before she can work out how to announce her arrival—whether to call out a greeting or rap on the frame, as there's no door to speak of—the burlap curtain on the doorway parts.

He stands before her. A shadow mangled and maimed, a patch over one eye, a scar across his face. The contour of a rivulet drawn by tears. *I know not how love chooses who and why— Why I see infinity in your eyes . . .*

She catches her breath, stunned, suddenly remembering. *I dream of an alternate existence, a world parallel to this for you and me . . . where birth's not a moment but eternity.*

Finding her voice, she struggles. "I—" The large sun hat held to her chest trembles. "I am . . ."

"Suteera," he murmurs. "Yes, I know."

There's no place even to invite her to sit, not a single piece of furniture besides the bamboo bed. Even if there were, even if he could afford something, arrange somehow for it to be brought to him, where would he put it? The cottage perhaps has room in one corner for a small bamboo chair and table, the collapsible kind sold on street corners and sidewalks. But a chair alone, he recalls from his time wandering among the city's homeless, costs at least ten American dollars, more than he's had in years. There wasn't much he could've arranged beforehand to prepare for this visit. He can barely arrange himself, the placement of his heart, in these past hours since the Venerable Kong Oul came to offer him the news. *I've just got off the telephone!* the old monk relayed excitedly, abandoning his usual pious calm. *The gods have granted you the reunion you've so longed for!* The Old Musician's immediate unthinking response was, *You were on the phone with the gods?* The abbot let out a riotous laugh. *No, my friend, Miss Suteera! She's in Cambodia—in Phnom Penh!* His heart stopped then, for how long, he's not sure, but when he became aware of it again, it was pounding inside his chest. She came. She's here, in this same city. Now she's inside his cottage. Right in front of him. Not a dream but a vision nonetheless.

For the first interminable seconds, he shuffles about in the tight half-lit space, picking one thing up and setting another down. He'd like to offer her tea, but he has only a single chipped cup, the same one he himself drinks out of every day, the inside stained dark brown, its surface spidered with cracks. Perhaps Dr. Narunn will come by and he can then oblige his young friend to aid in the hosting. But, he remembers, the physician is leaving today—might've already left. He chastises himself, *You old fool.* He should've had the foresight to borrow a cup and saucer from the temple. Or at least a clean glass to offer her the cool rainwater from his cistern. It's especially sweet and refreshing after the sustained downpours of the past months.

He pauses, backtracks, and scoffs, *Rainwater?—Don't be ridiculous, you'll get her sick.* He stands ramrod in his spot, wondering if she can hear him, if inadvertently he's spoken aloud. He feels her gaze piercing him, traveling the length of his scar, resting on the black eye patch Dr. Narunn has given him, as if trying to see past it. He dares not meet her eyes, look into those dark, lash-laden depths. "May I offer you something to drink?" The words fly from his mouth in perfect-pitched American English, surprising them both. They are still for a moment. Then she looks away. He is mortified by what he's uttered—the language, the lavish offer, the carelessness of his tongue. As if he could give whatever she desires! *Old fool.*

"Thank you," she says finally, in English no less, her voice guileless, thinking nothing of his momentary confusion with time and space. "But I don't need anything." Returning her gaze to him, she switches back to Khmer. "I—I've come to see *you.*" She smiles, the sun hat still pressed against her chest, as if hiding something fragile.

His heart tears, bleeding inside. Has he misheard the emphasis, the empathy in her voice? He mustn't allow himself to believe she regards him any way other than with suspicion.

"May I sit?" She gestures to the foot of the bamboo bed.

He stands shaken for a second, then mumbles apologetically, "Yes, of course," and makes as if to clear away the instruments he's neatly arranged to await her arrival.

"It's all right, there's room."

He doesn't know what wounds him more—the girl, the voice, or the tenderness these simple words evoke. His mind rushes back to that singular moment when the young Channara, his secret love—his only love—appeared in his cramped apartment in Washington, DC, speaking almost these same words. *May I sit?—Right here on your bed?* They had planned this moment, desired it for so long. Still, how nervous they both were, like children. He was terrified that she'd taken such risk to come to him, to be with him at all. Yet, in his heart, love beat infinitely stronger than fear. He sensed the same was true in her heart when he knelt in front of her, pressing his head to her chest, letting her legs and arms enfold him. They remained like this, on the edge of the bed, until they were both calm. It was a lifetime ago, but the moment still pulses inside of him.

Now the daughter stands before him, an echo of her mother, sunglasses atop her head, her shoulder-length hair gathered in a loose braid to one side, the strayed wisps coiling around her ears, sticking to her damp skin. So tenuous her presence, she seems barely a brushstroke. A calligrapher's exhalation, the sweep of hand across parchment. He fears she will fade away, as magically as she arrived.

She perches tentatively on the edge, her long legs extended, toes pivoting, as if ready to leap and flee. How many times has he rehearsed this moment, the things he wanted to say, the truths he must purge? Now she's here and he cannot think where to begin.

He senses she understands his helplessness, his disbelief and shame—the indignity of his impoverished surroundings—for she drops her gaze and turns instead to the instruments beside her. The sun hat, now placed on her thighs, continues its nervous jiggle, and he can't tell what part of her is shaking—her legs, her hands hidden underneath it, her abdomen. His own stomach hollows and heaves, a capacious cave swarmed with bats suddenly awakened and beating their wings. "Was your drive here agreeable?" he finally manages stiltedly.

"It was lovely, thank you. My driver took me on a small road near Chrung Pich." A pause, as if she expects him to say something, and when he doesn't, she continues, "Then we drove the rest of the way along the river. It's especially beautiful today." Another pause. "The water calm and glittering."

He nods vigorously, pleased by the lightness of her voice. He considers asking her when she arrived, how long she's been in Cambodia, and how much of Phnom Penh she's seen. He swallows and the words, the simplest expressions, plunge to irretrievable depth. She's been here for some time, he's almost certain, long enough that it would only grieve him to know she's been so close yet unreachable. She seems like one who has landed and found a footing on familiar ground, a migrating bird, one of those long-legged white egrets rediscovering its abandoned nest among the rice fields. The important thing, he tells himself, is that she's here now. She's here. *Speak with her, you mute!*

"And how do you find the climate?" He winces at the banality of his effort. "The heat can be draining when one's not used to it." He remembers he found the air suffocating after his return from abroad.

"I forgot how hot and humid it could be. I'm grateful when it rains."

Yes, rain, that elixir of renewal. He longs for it now to close the wounds her appearance has reopened, cut anew into his heart. "Perhaps it'll rain while you're here," he offers, noticing the beads of sweat forming on the tip of her nose. Her mother's exquisite nose. The narrow rise of its bridge made him think of ascension. Yes, once he thought this, once when he was that young student in America, when he dared to reach so high for love, when he thought of love not as something you fall into but something you rise toward—the sky and its limitless mystery.

"Perhaps it'll rain," he murmurs, not sure whether he has already said it. *Did he just now hear thunder?* Perhaps he's imagined it in thinking about the sky, the vast geography of longing.

"I hope so," she says, looking perplexed.

They are both silent. He sees that this trite conversation pains her as much as it does him. Yet, he does not know where to go from here. He keeps still and mute.

She reaches for the instruments. "We who are left behind . . ." Her hand flutters for a second above the lute before alighting on the slender oboe. "You know, when I was very small," she commences again, the tremor barely perceptible now in her voice, "I used to think the *sralai* was female."

He wonders whether "you know" is something she inveterately uses, a phrase of habit, or whether she is testing him to see if he does know, if he does remember, if he is who he claims to be. He braces himself.

She rests the oboe on the sun hat. "It was the only instrument I thought of that way, as having a specific gender. Srey Lai, I called it. Lady Lai," she adds in English, half whispering, as if the translation is for her own benefit; then back to Khmer again: "So lovely and feminine, don't you think?"

He doesn't know how to respond.

"Yes, I thought it a woman." She grows more composed, and he has the curious sensation that they've talked for hours already, that somehow they've always been in each other's life and this is another of their frequent ruminations. "A mother with child." She taps her forefinger on the rise where, counting from the top, the fourth air hole is bored. "Because of this bulge here, you see. I imagined she'd given birth first to these four notes, one immediately after another, and then sometime later two more, each note a gift to the world. That's how music must have originated, I thought. At least the kind of music we're able to hear, the kind we can share with one another. A universal melody, in other words."

Is this something he ought to have remembered? Frantically, he searches his memories. Nothing. Was it never told to him?

"But there's another kind of music, you see." Her finger moves to the solid space below the fourth air hole, outlined as if meant for another note. "An unborn melody, I think."

He swallows and waits for her to continue.

"Like the *sralai*, I've come to believe, every person carries the seed of this melody inside himself. A truth he alone knows."

He feels himself unraveling.

She returns the oboe to its place between the lute and the drum. Then, looking up, she says, "My father is gone." Her voice catches. "But I have come hoping the truth did not die with him."

Crossing Monivong Bridge over the Bassac River, they head back to the city, and in the far distance to the east, the Mekong shimmers in the sunlight like one long, exquisite poem.

Before leaving the temple, as she was thanking the Venerable Kong Oul for arranging the meeting with the Old Musician, the abbot asked whether she might do a favor by letting her driver give the departing monk—now ex-monk—a ride home with his few belongings. *Dr. Narunn*, Mr. Chum calls him, his tone emphatic with respect and admiration, using, as is customary, the first name even in formal salutation. It's clear to Teera now that no one here is ever just one thing, what appears on first encounter. She supposes this is true to some extent of any place, and anyone, but feels it especially so in this landscape of evolving *pralung*. Aurora borealis. She recalls the Northern Lights she once saw from a friend's lakeshore cabin in the depths of the woods near Ely, Minnesota. Here, among paddies and palms, where the dead walk and sit beside you, their heaves and sighs mingling with your breaths, you witness a similar phenomenon. *Aurora spiritus.*

"I hope it's all right with you . . ."

It takes a second or two before Teera realizes the doctor is speaking to her from the passenger's seat. "I'm sorry . . . my mind was elsewhere," she admits ruefully.

"I should be the one apologizing." He turns to look at her, then just as quickly faces front again, embarrassed by their proximity, the mirroring of their expressions. "I should've just flagged down a *motodup* instead of troubling you."

"No trouble at all." In truth, she would prefer to be alone with Mr. Chum, who by now is used to her long stretches of silence, her way of receding deep into her thoughts. But when a whole family often squeezes onto the narrow seat of a moped, Teera can't bring herself to tell Mr. Chum she'd like the car to herself, at least not in the presence of a holy man who needs a ride. With his hair shorn and the smell of incense permeating his clothes, not to mention a palpable aura of tranquillity about him, she finds it difficult not to think of him as a monk. Any other time, under different circumstances, she would wholeheartedly welcome the doctor's company, even desire it. His closeness only augments the sense of familiarity, the feeling that she's met him in another time, another life.

"See, nothing to worry about!" Mr. Chum asserts jovially. He explains to Teera that it's not far out of the way to Dr. Narunn's home, someplace called the "White Building."

"Well, thank you again," Dr. Narunn says, hand sweeping the top of his head, brushing back the hair that's not there, as if for the first time feeling self-conscious of his looks, the strangeness of his appearance, a bald man in everyday clothes. "You're both very kind."

Teera manages only a halfhearted smile in response, still trying to make sense of what transpired moments earlier. Until reaching the front of the cottage, she hadn't been conscious of it, and only as she faced the Old Musician—the forgotten lyrics of her birthday *smoat* coming back to her—did the irrational question flash in her mind, unexpected. *Could he be my father?* For one brief moment as their gazes met, as they stood considering each other, the impossibility ripped through her. She knew it couldn't be, and yet the long-buried accusation flared in her mind. *The last time you held me, Papa, you left me shattering in the wake of your footfalls . . .* She could barely imagine the words without trembling.

Following him into the cottage, Teera could hardly stand, shaken by her childish longing. She asked if she could sit, and having found a steady perch on the edge of his bamboo bed, she studied him: the patch on his left eye, the permanent squint in his right one, the scar bisecting his face, the evidence of cruelty branding his skin. At one point, exchanging pleasantries, she mentioned their home, the name of their family estate, and waited for that flicker of sorrow for its loss in his face. It never surfaced. It was foolish for her to hope, even for one brief moment.

They continued their polite, strained conversation, and she noted his movements, his profile as he turned, his frame and height. *He's not a towering figure by any measure*, she thought, *but neither is he small for a Cambodian man*. She couldn't understand why he appeared reduced, compromised in some profound way. Age and suffering diminish a person's stature, or perhaps it was that low, dark space of the cottage. She'd imagined him tall, the way she had once thought her father towering, able to reach beyond the soaring palms to catch for her a bird flying in the sky. She was certain she had never met him before, yet he seemed familiar somehow.

Who then is this broken old man, this ragged and tormented being she's just met? What depth or darkness has he risen from? What message from the dead does he carry for her? Where *is* her father? Does he lie beneath the soil like the rest of her family? Or is he among the living somewhere, existing as the palimpsest of his long-ago self, altered beyond recognition? What memory, what history does this old musician carry in the depths of his occluded vision? What new sorrows will he bring to her?

"Is it too much air-conditioning?" Mr. Chum cuts into her thoughts, looking at her through the rearview mirror. "You're shaking."

Teera stares, confused, unsure whether the chill surrounds her or rises from within. All the same, her cotton white dress, with its billowing half sleeves, which she thought was ideal for a temple because it's both comfortable and modest, feels somehow inadequate now. She rubs her forearms and hugs herself tighter. "Yes, a little."

Mr. Chum promptly turns off the AC. Dr. Narunn unwinds the

kroma from his neck and offers it to her. "Please," he says and, seeing her hesitate, jokes, "It's only a little dirty, I promise."

She thanks him, embarrassed she can't engage more fully, can't reciprocate his lightheartedness, and wraps the blue-and-white checkered scarf around her shoulders. It smells of candle and incense, incantation whispered into its folds, the musky warmth of another's skin. She has the urge to gather it and press it to her nose.

They've reached an intersection. There are neither traffic lights nor stop signs. But like all the cars around them, they slow to a crawl. Looking past the couple of cars ahead of them, Teera expects to see a motorcade escorting a convoy of armored Ford Rangers favored by high-ranking officials and oligarchs, or worse, a Hummer barreling down at sixty, eighty kilometers an hour in a zone marked twenty. No such vehicle emerges. Instead she notices an old man, tall and stately but otherwise dressed in the patch-filled clothes of a mendicant, a bamboo cane in one hand and a cotton satchel on his shoulder. He takes a cautious step from the sidewalk into the humming traffic, then pauses, tapping the bamboo cane on the asphalt, swinging it from right to left, his head cocked to one side, listening, observing with all his senses. Then he lifts his free hand straight past his head and proceeds forward, weaving across the intersection.

He's blind, Teera realizes in astonishment. Though he can't see, he raises his arm in the air so *others* can see him. Everything stills inside her. In this chaotic little city where traffic stops for no one, except out of fear for those with power, and fatal accidents occur daily, so it can seem human lives are as dispensable as those of chickens and pigs on their way to slaughter, this mute gesture feels like a revelation of sorts.

I have come hoping the truth did not die with him. What truth is that? What is she seeking? She's no longer sure what she meant. Though she knows in this very instant that if all she has to take with her when she leaves this land is the image of the raised hand, she'll have gained more than what she came with. She may never fully grasp the source of inhumanity, what drives a people to massacre one another, the potential for hate that lurks in every heart, or at what point ideals turn rancid with venom so that they poison and corrupt, murder the very beauty they aspire to create. What is clear before her is the simple fact that it takes conviction to do what this blind man does. In the absence of sight, when all is dark around you, it takes a deep-seated belief that others will answer your appeal, that their humanity will rise to meet your lifted hand, your raised hope, and in that brief moment, you cross the otherwise arbitrary divide between death and life.

On the other side, a middle-aged woman, cradling a basket of steamed peanuts she's selling, takes a firm hold of the old man's wrist and helps him onto the sidewalk, just as traffic weaves again around him. Teera's eyes follow him, until their own car makes a turn and he disappears from her field of vision.

If her father lived to old age, would this be his life? Would a stranger look kindly upon him? Do others see what she sees—these small, unheralded testimonies to the ineradicable bonds holding together a society, affixing its shattered pieces despite the persistent aftershocks that add to its myriad strains and cracks?

"How old is he?" she asks, her thoughts leaping again, from one person to another.

"Hmm, I'm not sure." Dr. Narunn seems to be thinking it over. "Maybe in his late seventies? For someone who can't see, he crossed that road with such sense of direction and purpose. What do you think, uncle?" The physician turns to Mr. Chum.

"He could be much younger," Mr. Chum says, hands on the steering wheel, mindful of the vehicles around them. "It's hard to tell how old anyone is these days. *Khmer yeung chap chas.* Poverty and suffering age us. We all look older than we really are. Take me, for example!"

Dr. Narunn, not missing a beat—"Forgive me, uncle, how old are you? Twenty-nine?"

Mr. Chum laughs, head bobbing appreciatively.

"I meant the Old Musician," Teera says.

A brief silence. The two men exchange surprised glances. Teera expects this. Until now she hasn't said a word about her meeting.

"We don't know really," Dr. Narunn says after a moment. "We don't even know his name. At the temple, we all call him Lokta Pleng—'the Old Musician'—and he's never objected to it, never once corrected us."

"He spoke English to me." In the cottage, she dismissed the Old Musician's slip of the tongue as the result of thinking her an American, the way people here randomly blurt out English greetings—*Hello! How are you?*—when they sense she might be a foreigner, eager to test what they know, perhaps to demonstrate that Cambodians are catching up with the rest of the world. "I mean, he's not just some homeless old musician, is he? He was once somebody, a learned man."

Again, Dr. Narunn and Mr. Chum seem taken aback. After another awkward silence, the doctor says, "Well, yes, and he must've suffered horribly for who he was. Sometimes, I can't help but think that his anonymity—this absence of name and history, or as we Buddhists say, this self-less existence—is the only way he's able to continue."

"Does he not have any family at all?"

"I'm afraid not. He's never spoken of a single relative, friend, or anyone outside the temple community. Certainly not to me. He doesn't speak at all of his life before he came to Wat Nagara. I believe he lost everyone to Pol Pot."

Teera is silent.

"Sometimes, walking past his cottage," Dr. Narunn continues, "I hear him speak, very tenderly, to the instruments, as if they were people, his children. He's very attached to them."

In the cottage, Teera also sensed this—the Old Musician's love for the instruments, his almost parental protectiveness toward these inanimate objects. *If it's all right with you,* she'd said before leaving, *I'd like to keep them in your care awhile longer.* He nodded. It seemed to her he could only nod.

Tentatively, Dr. Narunn says, "There's only one person I'm aware of who might have some connection to his past. And even this I only guessed while helping him with a task." Again, the doctor hesitates before continuing. "You see, several months back, he asked for my help in writing you."

Teera is startled, more than she lets on. How many lives are connected to our own in these small ways without us knowing?

"You are destined to meet, then!" Mr. Chum exclaims.

Dr. Narunn flushes and, clearing his throat, says, "I've wanted to mention it since we got in the car." He gives Teera an apologetic glance.

"So it was you who wrote the letter," she murmurs, understanding now why it looked to her as if it had been written by one person and signed by another.

"No, I was the scribe—I merely took down his words. He was very exact in what he wanted to convey."

"Are you close to him?" Teera asks.

"As close as one can be, I suppose, to someone extremely private, essentially unknowable."

It suddenly occurs to Teera whom Dr. Narunn reminds her of. Chea, the young soldier who scurried them across the border to Thailand, quietly comforting her as he guided her steps. Dr. Narunn has that same soothing way of speaking. Though she barely recalls Chea's face, she knows the doctor—who seems her age, thirty-seven, or maybe a bit older—is too young to be the soldier. She steals a quick glance at his profile anyway. *The thing about loss,* Amara once said to her, *is that it rims the silhouette of every face you encounter.* In a way they'd lost Chea too. After he'd guided them safely to the refugee camp in Thailand, he immediately turned around with the intention of helping others out of Cambodia. That was the last time she and her aunt saw the young soldier. Later they left for the refugee camp in the Philippines, their orientation site before immigrating to the United States. Once in the States, Amara made countless inquiries among friends who'd arrived after they did, as well as those who remained in the refugee camps. But no one had news of him. Stories abounded, and the most pervasive belief was that Chea never made it out of Cambodia again.

"How do you go about looking for lost ones?" she asks, fingering the gold necklace she's worn for so long that most of the time she doesn't feel it there.

"It depends." Dr. Narunn turns to face Teera, eyes probing hers for a second or two before facing front again. "If you think they're still alive, you can make an appeal for information in the newspaper, on the radio or TV, and so forth . . ."

In the refugee camps, they never had to barter the necklace for food, and after arriving in America, once it became clear that they would never go hungry again, Amara fastened it on Teera's neck, with the solemnity of passing down a family heirloom, explaining she'd had it "blessed." When Teera wanted to know how, as there was neither a Buddhist monk nor temple in Minnesota at the time, her aunt said that she'd gone to the copper-domed Cathedral in St. Paul on Summit Avenue, surreptitiously lit a candle for it, and prayed to the statue of Christ on the cross. *We make do*, she'd told Teera. *And so must the gods.*

"You can also go to their home village or town, their birthplace, if you know where. Most survivors tried to get back home as the regime fell, believing their loved ones—if they also survived—would do the same. They're likely to still be there."

Since then Teera has considered the necklace a kind of talisman, her protection against forgetfulness, a reminder always of how close she was to death, how close she still is to the dead. Could the soldier have made it all the way back to his home village? Phum Kruos, she remembers Amara telling her. In Siem Reap. Dead or alive, she feels him with her now.

"There's also Tuol Sleng," Mr. Chum says, so quietly Teera almost misses it.

Tuol Sleng, Pol Pot's most ruthless secret security prison and torture center. During the regime, it was known to the top echelon of the party leadership and those who worked there by the cryptic code S-21. Out of more than fourteen thousand men, women, and children sent there, only a handful of adults survived, none of the children. It's been turned into a museum, with thousands of photos of victims on display.

"It's not a place we can step into lightly," Dr. Narunn says, "and when we do, it stays with us, lives inside us forever. Most Cambodians, I believe, have not seen it still, and those of us who have, it is for one reason only—to look for our lost."

Teera asks no more. They continue the rest of the drive in silence. She feels they've arrived at the end of a long, shadowy corridor, only to find impenetrable darkness. She fears a bottomless drop on the other side.

August 1973 . . .

He steps into her room and, lifting the edge of her mosquito net, bends down to kiss her, to smell her hair. Breathe in the scent of innocence against the stink of underground politics, dark and addictive as nicotine, clinging to his clothes and skin. She must have inhaled a whiff of it, the poisonous odor he's dragged in, or at least must have sensed his movement, for she stirs and murmurs in her half-conscious state, "I waited for you, Papa. You didn't come. You broke my feelings."

She turns on her stomach, relinquishing him like a dream. At times Tun feels she owns and disowns him as only a child can, without malice or marking, without the complication of adult feelings. To her, love must not be any trickier than a blanket: she can wrap it around herself, or shed it for the time being—kick it off when it becomes too weighty—and it will always be just within reach, warm and versatile, when she needs it. In the morning when she wakes, she'll love him as before, as she always has, with all her feelings intact, her heart whole.

In the dark living room, the illuminated hands of the clock on the console table by the entrance say it's almost ten. He has plenty of time to pack and get to the appointed place by the ferry dock near Chruay Chongvar Bridge. He feels like an intruder these past few months, an interloper in his own existence, stealing into one shadow and sliding out another, his steps caught in the choreography of secrecy, the slow yet sure dance of disappearance. *Leak kluan. Lup kluan. Kasang pravatarup thmei.* Hide yourself. Erase yourself. Construct a new autobiography.

He lights the kerosene lantern beside the clock and brings it with him. Shadows loom, turning as he turns, clamoring along the walls and ceiling like phantom dissonances.

In his room, he lowers himself onto the cushion in front of the teak coffee table that served as his writing desk. On the floor beside it, his straw mat and pillow and stack of books beckon him, and he longs to lie down, to lose himself in some history or story, then slip unconsciously from the worded pages into the uncharted landscape of reverie. But neither sleep nor rest will be his tonight. He turns up the wick, fighting the exhaustion that threatens to incapacitate him, and sets the lantern down on the table, his body mirroring the trembling blue flame inside the glass. He grabs a blank music sheet from the untidy pile in front of him.

August 6, 1973, Tun writes at the top, only to realize it is the wrong date. More than a week has passed since, but this date will forever be burnt into his memory. He takes another sheet and attempts to restart the letter afresh, his vision seared with images of death and destruction. He can't begin to comprehend the devastation that has descended upon their world, let alone explain it to his small daughter.

A third of Neak Leung—his hometown—razed by a B-52 bomber when it unleashed its twenty tons of metal and fire. A mistaken target, the papers said. But this brings him no comfort. Such a blunder only augments the horror. It all comes down to this simple truth: no matter the intended target, lives would be lost, homes obliterated. Two of his childhood buddies, soldiers, with their wives and small children. An elderly bedridden couple, bosom friends of his mother, people who'd loved him as their own. The woman he had been engaged to, whose heart he broke when shortly after his own mother's death four years earlier he rescinded his promise to marry. Other friends and neighbors he'd visited every time he returned to his hometown. All dead, pulverized, their bones and flesh mixed into the pummeled earth.

Over thirty craters, one after another stretching from north to south, have sundered the center of town, as if some monster had prowled through unseen in the hours before dawn, leaving tracks more than two kilometers long. He will never forget it, the devastation he witnessed in the aftermath. Every death, every life scathed by it, left behind to endure this scorch, to bury its own dead. A mother bent over the edge of a crater, her entire being quaking at the scattered remains of her children—a wooden rattle here; an overturned bassinet there; a chubby, silver-bangled wrist beneath a layer of broken dirt, fist clutching at the air, at the breath that had already slipped away. The young mother clawed at her throat, gasping, grasping, when a group of townsmen began the work of covering up the pit. "Noooo!" She let out a long wail. "Leave it! I want them to *see*! I want them to see from their planes what they've done! I want them to see! Make them see!"

She lost everything, her entire family and home, Tun later learned as he made his way through the wreckage, the absolute stillness that had enshrouded the town. Anger, bewilderment, despair. *How could they have done this? They said they were here as our friends—to defend us. Then they arrive to kill us in the middle of the night? They've succeeded in their mission. They've murdered our children in their sleep!*

As of today—August 15, Tun remembers now—the Americans have officially ended their airstrikes in Cambodia. Other nations quickly condemned this denouement as irresponsible, leaving in its wake a massive refugee crisis and a government military, a supposed US ally, now far outmatched by the insurgent army. A clear indication of how the United States will treat the rest of its Asian allies, and perhaps the rest of the world. When the going gets tough, one diplomat decried, the tough abscond.

Morally vacuous, Tun thinks, swallowing the bitterness coating his throat. *Unforgivable.* You wreak havoc on a place, leaving it strewn with limbs and body parts, devastated buildings and debris and denuded trees, then you abandon it for those you've wounded and maimed to clean up. You cover your tracks, your mistakes and disorder, with the disarray of a mother's grief. You try to seal her mouth, silence her rage, with your American dollar bills. A few hundred for a family dead, a bit less for a limb lost, and even less for a home destroyed. How much then would you pay for my shattered faith! I once believed in you Americans! Was filled with admiration for your land and your race, the wisdom of your democracy, the power of your technology. *Your progress was the justice I dreamt for my country. The right that would've eradicated the wrongs of my history* . . .

A melody emerges, and Tun forcefully stills it, the heel of his palm pressed against his chest, muting his heartstrings—the sudden tides of sharp pain—as one might mute the string of a guitar. Now . . . Now all he feels is disgust. Utter revulsion for a people whose conscience is as misdirected as their weapons.

What other sentiments could he summon to dampen the ill—this hate inflaming him? The word gives him pause. *Hate.* It's not an emotion he assumes lightly. It's not one that offers him light. To be inflamed is incorrect then. He feels absorbed by it. Hate would be his endless night, his covered grave. He's not ready to die yet. He must hold on to some shred of hope. There is decency still in this world. He has to believe this, for his daughter's sake.

Once again, he is aware of her presence on the other side of the thin wall, senses her breathing like a vibrato originating somewhere deep in his being, his consciousness—the silence that precedes voice. He often feels she is the current, that inaudible music just beyond hearing, slipping through this world, and he's merely one of those things, like a leaf or a laundered sheet, that take on movement, flutter to life, when she brushes past. Yet, here he is, the sojourner tonight, ready to leave her and sneak away into another existence.

Survival by separation, he reasons. He's doing this for her. What parent does not want a better place for his child? It's been two years since Prama's death, and he fears if he makes no sacrifices, if he does not take sides, more lives will be lost, and his country will be obliterated in the firestorm of another's making.

The irony does not escape him that the tragedy forcing him out of his daughter's life now is the same that brought her into his. Four years ago—1969—her home was also bombed, the entire commune of a dozen

villages or so, including hers, completely decimated, along with the only
school and what little there was of a clinic. She survived only by hiding
in the hollow of an ancient rain tree, around which she'd been playing,
while her mother was cooking outside their hut, keeping an occasional
eye on the girl, who appeared in the distance no bigger than a starling
flitting about in the open fields. Perhaps, Tun pauses to think for a moment, it should've been the other way around. The child should've kept
her eyes on the mother. But then what? She would've only been witness
to the blast that destroyed her mother and home, her entire world.

When the child heard the awful drone of the Stratofortress, she'd
looked up and glimpsed the sleek silhouette of a winged minnow slipping in and out of the clouds. This troubled her, for she'd only begun to
learn that while some creatures are aerial, others are bound to land and
water. *You're not a bird*, her mother would always warn. *Don't jump from
that tree.* Fish, the child thought, don't belong in the sky. *Or do they?* But
before she could rearrange the image in her head, there were other min-
nows—itsy-bitsy baby ones—dropping suddenly from the belly of the
larger fish in neat little rows. The air vibrated with their descent. The
coppery, translucent downy hairs on her arms and neck bristled. She
began to run, paused to pick up a ripened kapok pod that had fallen to
the ground, by some instinct broke it in half and sealed her ears with the
white fibers inside, and kept running. She found cover, crawling into the
womb of the giant rain tree, with her legs pulled up to her chest, arms
around her knees, curled like a fetus, as the world erupted around her.

Tun would come to learn these details bit by bit, from the child herself and others like her who had barely escaped the bombing and were
brought to the hospital in Phnom Penh. She was so small he'd missed
her entirely when he'd first walked into Calmette, where she was lost in
the gauzes of misery that had unraveled from the waiting room into the
anemically lit corridor.

The hospital was short of staff; thus Tun and Prama—his friend was
still alive then in '69—and others from their political group had come
to volunteer. With no medical knowledge or skills to offer, their task

was mainly to escort the wounded—those who could still walk—to the correct treatment room. They were told from the start that some of the smaller children did not understand they'd lost their homes and families, and therefore great care should be taken when communicating with these little ones. Arrangements were being made for temporary shelters in the city where the children would remain until permanent guardians could be found. Perhaps distant relatives somewhere would eventually emerge to claim the orphans. In the meantime, boys would be placed in a temple, but girls would have to be relegated to an orphanage. Ignored and forgotten by all, a life there, everyone knew, would be a life in perpetual limbo, with no possibility of a future.

As Tun came into the corridor to help the next patient to treatment, he spotted her among the wounded and shell-shocked. A face so small and perfectly round, the first thought that popped to mind was "pea pod." Indeed, she appeared to him like a tiny seed, a life whole and self-contained, needing only love and care to bud. And yet here she was, lost in this cramped tunnel of blood-soaked bandages and last breaths.

Feeling his gaze, she looked up, her eyes lit with such fierce hope it was akin to recognition, like the mirror reflection of an encounter the previous month that had arrested him as profoundly.

Their reunion took place on the street in front of La Salle de Conférence Chaktomuk, the new performance hall from which he'd emerged after a long morning of grueling rehearsal in preparation for that evening's opening-night performance of *Tum Tiev*. He was among the lead musicians, and the main lyricist, for a stage adaptation of the revered classic of thwarted young love. Tun stepped into the afternoon glare, his vision assaulted by the sudden brightness, his temples still throbbing from the thick clouds of incense and candles burning with the *baisei tvay kru*—offerings made to the guardians of Music and Art—that accompanied every rehearsal. He needed fresh air. Behind the conference hall, the river water susurrated, wooing him, and he wished for nothing more than to plunge into its depths and be borne away by its liquid melody.

On the sidewalk in front of him, vendors paraded hand-painted kites, sparrows chirping in tiny bamboo cages, snacks wrapped in banana leaves. A crowd had gathered around a cart selling fresh sugarcane juice, like bees inebriated by the mist sugaring the air. *Two cones for us, please!* one called out above the collective drone, and another, *Three over here!* The vendor acknowledged the orders as he fed two or three cut stalks at a time into the hand-cranked extractor, each stalk wrapped with a twirl of citrus rind—the famed virescent Pusat orange. Tun's nostrils smarted at the thick, sweet scent. He was suddenly aware of his parched throat. So instead of veering right toward the river, he swung left into the crowd, much too forcefully, nearly knocking a little girl, who looked up startled, the banana-leaf cone full of juice wobbling in her hand. Before he could apologize, the girl's mother turned, and his heart stopped.

"Oh!" exclaimed Channara.

Failing to find the proper greeting, he stammered breathlessly, stupidly, the wind knocked out of him, "*It's you.*"

"Yes."

Eternity stood between them, and neither knew what else to say. Then finally, Channara spoke again. "This is Suteera, our"—she faltered, then, steadying herself, proceeded—"my daughter. Suteera, darling, say hello to Uncle Tun. *Il est un vieux ami de Maman.*"

The little one did not speak but, palms together and bowing slightly, offered him an elegant *sampeah.* He didn't expect such grace from someone so small. *She's much too young to be mine*—the thought insinuated itself. He chased it away. *Our,* Channara had started to say. She must've not wanted to bring her husband into the conversation. He was touched by this attempt to protect him from her life, from the happiness he could not share. Had Suteera been his child, she would've been eight or nine now. Still, in this little girl, he glimpsed what might have been.

"Suteera is three," Channara said, and, smiling at her daughter, teased, "and terribly shy."

"Three!" Tun exclaimed, feigning lightness. The girl was born in 1966, he quickly calculated, four years after Channara married, a long time for a married Khmer woman to be without child. He could well imagine the pressure she must've endured from her family, particularly her imperious father, Le Conseiller. But knowing Channara's character, her fierce desire for independence, he guessed she didn't want to be tied down right away.

The last he'd seen her was on her wedding day in December 1962, a year after his return from America. He'd come to her family estate as part of the *plengkar* ensemble hired to play at the wedding. Somehow he'd found the courage to step into her bedroom, the sanctity of her solitude, the final moments of her singlehood before she would share her bed with a man other than himself. *You broke my heart*, she'd said. *And you my soul*, he replied, standing at arm's length, unable to move closer, to embrace her as he would've liked, paralyzed by his own anguish. *So we're even now*, she murmured. *Never*, he shot back. It was their last exchange, and he regretted each syllable as he spoke it, as it emerged forcefully of its own will from his lips. He hadn't been able to forgive himself since.

As he stood facing her again on the sidewalk in front of Chaktomuk, he thought perhaps this unexpected collision was an opportunity to rectify their terse parting. He had to find his way into her graces again, if not her heart. Perhaps he could win her daughter's affection. "My, you're so tall for your age!" He winced at the falsetto of his flattery but couldn't stop himself. "Such a young lady already!"

Suteera stared at him, unblinking. He shifted uncomfortably.

Everything about the child was a replica of the mother, only in much tinier utterances. The long, slender limbs that seemed to accentuate an inborn aloofness, already so apparent even at this tender age. Eyes veiled in an abundance of lashes that gave the impression of bottomless pools rimmed with ferns. Hair that borrowed the intonation of the sea, rising and falling in continuous waves. He could not believe what he was seeing. A double epiphany. The way they stood there holding hands, while he hovered just outside their sphere of intimacy, pierced him with such magnificent agony he believed he would never heal from it. Pain, he would come to learn, has its own afterlife.

He suffers it even now.

Tun looks down at the music sheet before him, its muted glow under the lantern. Besides the date, he has not been able to write another word. Again, he turns up the wick for more light.

"Sita, *pralung pa* . . ." he murmurs aloud, tearing himself from the memory of Channara's daughter and turning his mind instead to his own child.

Sita, my soul, my breath . . . He invokes again the atmosphere of their chance meeting, which felt somehow predestined. He remembers thinking he was witnessing a birth, a life coming into being, though she was already a little girl, independently whole and self-aware, when he spotted her that afternoon in the hospital corridor. There was something prescient in the way she focused her gaze on him, as if she intuited the path he couldn't yet see.

Beside him, Prama was whispering to another volunteer, something about how this was the perfect opportunity to recruit more villagers into the underground movement. But Tun was no longer listening. He felt every step he took was meant for her and her alone.

She rose to meet him. "You are my papa?" she asked in a small voice.

He floundered, confused. It wasn't really a question. He recalled the term he'd learned from the music dictionary he'd purchased while studying in America years before. *Messa di voce.* That was the quality of her voice. Loss and reclamation sustained in a single pure note.

Next to the child, a man with a slight wound on his left shoulder let out a dry, derisive chuckle. Tun suddenly felt Prama leaning into him. "Her mother died in the blast," his friend whispered. "A village outcast." Tun gave his friend a quizzical look, to which Prama responded, "The story is that she had the child out of marriage. It seems the girl never knew her father but was constantly told he'd come should she ever need him. They said the mother was not quite right in the head. Her mind, I suspect, was worn down by the persistent ridicule. Both mother and daughter were severely ostracized. No one will ever claim this child."

It always amazed Tun, Prama's exceptional ability to inspire instant trust in people, who would tell him things they might not share with their own family. He attributed this to his friend's boyish charm, a sincerity of spirit. Prama genuinely loved people, and they responded likewise, a quality—*mien prayauy*—that made him extremely useful in the revolutionary movement.

"How old is the child?" Tun asked.

"She can't be more than four," Prama said, shrugging, as if to remind him it didn't matter, as birthdates are rarely recorded in villages. "I don't know. Maybe younger?—Three?"

But her eyes, Tun thought, belonged to someone much older. They intimated a loss that made his own seem trite in comparison. Looking into them, he had the unerring sense he was staring at his future, his entire life. Or rather, the life that would fill the chasm in his own.

"Papa has come to get Sita," she said, referring to herself by name, as small children are taught to speak, a way of endearing themselves. Certainly this worked on him as never before.

Sita. Suteera. The closeness of the two names, not to mention the nearness in age of the two girls, renewed that sense of loss he'd felt upon seeing Channara with her daughter, a child he could never share. He did not believe in fate, and yet, for the first time, he thought it might be this: the unspoken longing in one's heart reciprocated in the longing of another. *You are my papa.* He felt certain now it wasn't a question but a declaration of heightened conviction.

Her next gesture sealed their fates together. She stepped forward and, her arms lifted toward him, fell into his awaiting embrace.

"Can we go home now?—I want to go home, Papa."

What could he say? She'd already known unimaginable loss for a child her age; how could such a lie add to her misery? He held her against his chest, the crescent of her neck fitting perfectly into his, her pulse in rhythm with his own. As she tightened her arms around him, he noticed that, despite her weight and solidity, her breaths were shallow, wispy as a newborn's. He felt somehow responsible for the very air she inhaled and exhaled, as if he himself had given birth to her, had selfishly brought her into this precarious world by his very wish for her, for a family to call his own, for a life lived in parallel to Channara's.

It was all so new to him, this feeling of knowing that he would lay down his life in an instant for another, for this child. *His* child. *She could be my daughter.* The words encircled him, again and again. *My daughter.* He could hardly believe it.

"Yes." His heart tightened, opened, and filled, all in the same moment. "I've come to take you home."

Sita. Tun can barely say her name now without choking, let alone write it down. He claws at the music sheet, his fingertips leaving elliptical sweat marks like notes on a scale chart. Sorrow and regret lead the way before he even begins the journey. But words, whose attendance he most needs, desert him. He mustn't fool himself. No matter the noble intention, there is no gentle way for a father to tell a child he is abandoning her.

"I'm an impostor."

"Excuse me?"

"I'm not who you think I am."

Teera feels her heart constricting. Not again. Not another loss. Not before he even belongs to her, before she even grasps what it is they share, what they are to each other. She proceeds cautiously: "Who are you then?"

Narunn sighs. "I'm not really a doctor . . ."

Teera keeps silent, suddenly unable to breathe, the air utterly still around her.

"At least, not as good as I'd like to be. Of course I went to medical school, did my training"—he deepens his voice in a mock serious tone—"at the Faculty of Medicine, at the Royal University of Phnom Penh. Sounds rather fancy. But in those early days after the Khmer Rouge, it wasn't much of a school, let alone for medicine—"

"You!" She cuts him off, letting out a breath. Relieved, she makes as if to whack the side of his head, but instead pulls the tuft rounding the curve of his ear. "I thought you were serious!"

"I *am* serious. Seeing the kind of training medical students get today, I often feel inadequate."

"Never mind," she says, smoothing back the ruffled strands. His hair, now fully regrown since he'd resumed life outside the temple, still surprises her, its sprinkle of gray incongruous with his youth. Yet, it's the part of him she finds most endearing, for it testifies to the possibility of old age, his pact with time—their conspired assertion against the stranglehold of history. Teera curbs the urge to grab his entire face and kiss him in the way that Cambodians kiss, which is not a kiss at all but a kind of inhalation—if you love someone you breathe into your body his smell and atmosphere, his joy and sorrow, his pride and poverty.

She looks around Narunn's one-bedroom apartment, which is both his home and his clinic, where he serves some of the poorest in the city. Most, like him, reside here in the White Building, the gargantuan ghostly structure that haunts the sight of passersby, as the Royal Palace or the National Museum just a few blocks away might dazzle.

Constructed in six four-story blocks, connected by open staircases, with more than 460 apartments, the complex was initially conceived in the early 1960s as housing for the rapidly emerging lower middle class. In the years following its completion, as the urban population swelled even further, with the influx of families fleeing their provincial homes to escape the bombing and war in the countryside, it quickly became over-crowded. Not long after, when the Khmer Rouge took over and the city was emptied, the White Building was abandoned, its residents banished to the countryside.

Now, decades later, within its crumbling, mold-infested walls, amidst ruined plumbing and dangerously exposed electrical wires, it shelters nearly three thousand disparate souls—multiple-generation families and single mothers, students and teachers, struggling artists and surviv-ing music masters, civil servants and street vendors, professionals and prostitutes, addicts and drug dealers—each impoverished in some way. Narunn makes his home in this notorious slum not because he lacks the means to get out but, as he told Teera simply, *My work keeps me here.* His work anchors him. It is his pride and conviction, his chosen poverty.

Still, every time she visits he apologizes for the things he lacks to make her comfortable. If only he knew the wealth he embodies, the richness he harbors in his heart. She's never loved anyone quite like she loves him.

Love. Teera catches herself. Does she love him then? How can it be this easy, this fast and certain? Yet, love no longer scares her, bewilders her as it once did, makes her want to retreat and seal herself from what she's come to believe is its natural, inescapable conclusion—loss. Yes, she loves him. And yes, it is this easy to love and be certain of it, even at the risk of heartbreak and inevitable separation. It's been a month since that day they left the temple after her visit with the Old Musician, and this entire time she and Narunn have been together, seeing each other almost every day, alternating between his place and her hotel.

"Is something wrong?" Narunn asks.

"N-no. Why?"

He laughs. "Because you haven't heard a word I said."

"Sorry. Tell me again. Please?"

"Forensics."

She blinks in confusion.

He laughs louder. "I was saying if I could do it all over again, if I were young enough to go back to medical school, I'd study forensics."

"Oh, really?—Forensics? Why?"

"Well, I was reading an article in a medical journal the other day, about forensics and genocide, and what it would mean for Cambodia if a tribunal is established. But what fascinates me is the idea that the medical narratives of the dead can be used to help the living. Utterly amazing. It seems such a powerful and necessary tool. If the deceased could speak, what stories would they tell, what evidence would they reveal to help prevent another death? Astounding!" His enthusiasm is untainted, infectious. "Think about it, medicine as a kind of nonviolent dialogue between the dead and the living!"

"Wow." She laughs, running her fingers through his hair, so perfectly trimmed by a roadside barber whose shop is a rickety bamboo stool under a tree, with a mirror nailed to its trunk. "Here I thought you were going to tell me you're a drug smuggler, or a hired assassin for one of those Excellencies."

"Now *you're* not being serious." He kisses her, his nose to the curve of her neck, a deep inhalation.

She is suddenly aware of his hair prickling the hollow of her palm. Aroused, she promptly jerks her hand away. Again, she remembers the cultural landscape she's in, the self she must inhabit, the traditions and beliefs imprinted on her like birthmarks. *The head is a temple*, she hears Amara admonishing. She has yet to lose the habit of commiserating with her aunt about everything. *I know. I'm sorry, but.* She abruptly ends the conversation, and for the first time banishes Amara's ghost from her mind, from the room. Her aunt cannot see her like this, wrapped in a stranger's *kroma*, in his arms, yielding to his bed, his desires, her own.

In the refugee camps, Teera remembers, she was astounded to learn that in their culture it was better to have strangers assume Amara was widowed, that she had lost a husband to starvation or execution, like countless other women, than to have them know the reality of their situation—that here was a young unmarried woman with a niece to look after on her own. It wasn't proper, Amara explained, as if forgetting they'd just emerged from a hell where they hardly owned enough clothes to cover their skin and bones, let alone the strength or dignity to shoulder the mantle of a culture in ruins. *People will assume you're my daughter, and if they're going to think that, it's better for them to believe you're a child conceived in marriage rather than outside.* Teera thought angrily, *Who cares!* They had no country, no home, no family to speak of; anyone important to them was dead and gone. Who cared what these people, every bit as broken and rootless as they were, thought about them, about anything? It never occurred to either to just speak the truth—that out of their whole family only the two of them, girls at that, made it out of the country alive—because by then the truth no longer mattered.

"*Allô allô . . .*" Narunn croons, tapping the tip of her nose with his forefinger. "*Leu bong niyeay te oun?*"—*Do you hear me calling, darling?*

Teera recognizes the popular song of Sinn Sisamouth and Ros Sereysothea, which, according to Amara, made wooing on the telephone de rigueur among young lovers during her aunt's teenage years. "You reversed it," she tells Narunn. "The girl is calling him, not the other way around. The telephone rings three times in the middle of the night, he picks up, and she's the first to speak, *Allô bong . . .*" Teera hums the melody, hearing the electric guitar, the keyboard.

"Impressive!—You certainly know the song."

"Of course," she can't help but boast. "I know every word of it by heart."

For the longest time, Teera remembers, music had been her only doorway back to Cambodia. During her high school years, these Khmer rock ballads from the decades before the war resonated with her more viscerally than the American pop her classmates and peers were listening to.

Teera closes her eyes, and suddenly a scene flashes in her mind—her mother at the river's edge releasing a caged sparrow from a bamboo netting, while her father stands holding what looked like a banana-leaf cone. She shuts her eyes tighter, willing them to turn so she might see more than just their silhouettes. But, hard as she tries, they remain as they are, side by side, so close to each other that she's almost certain they're touching. She wonders, *Where was I at that moment?* She must have been there with her parents for her to recall the scene. She imagines they were in an exalted state, their moods lifted with the flight of the tiny bird released.

Teera stills the image in her mind and, for the time being, pushes it to where it will be safe. She supposes it's only natural that the longer she stays, the more she will experience these flashes from the past. She must learn to take each as it comes, to save it for when she has the solitude to examine it, to expand it, to nudge the boundaries of her own memory.

She opens her eyes, turning her attention back to Narunn, to the lightness of their conversation. "You know, because of this one song," she says, recalling what Amara once told her, "because of this innocent exchange of '*Hello hello*' across the night, my grandfather wanted to ban all of Sinn Sisamouth's songs from the house."

"But why?—Everyone loved Sinn Sisamouth!"

"Well, the girl starting the call caused quite a stir, especially among the older generations, traditionalists like my grandfather. *Srey kromum* telephoning a man in the dark of the night, from her bed no less. Simply scandalous!"

"But are we sure she's a virginal maiden?" Narunn bats his brows with mischief.

"Stop it, I'm trying to educate you!"

"How do you know so much about this?"

"If you haven't noticed, Doctor, I'm Khmer."

"Khmer?—Are you really?"

Teera turns somber. That question, the very notion of Khmer or not Khmer, led to countless deaths and disappearances in her village during the last year or so of the Khmer Rouge rule. *Communism unites us all!— But not if you're Vietnamese! Filth, rags—those* yuon*!* So those with any perceived connection to Vietnam were purged.

Narunn pinches her nose. "You're an impostor like me."

She smiles sadly.

"Hey, I'm only kidding!"

"But you're right. I *am* an impostor of sorts. An itinerant outsider. Never the person I'm supposed to be."

"Aren't we all?"

"I suppose . . ."

"Yes?"

"Well, in America, I feel most Cambodian, and here, I feel more American than I remember ever feeling in all the years I've lived in the States." Teera's gaze darkens, receding into itself, and she sees a child, a little girl, walking in a long, narrow corridor much like the one outside Narunn's apartment. Ever since she first set foot in this place, she's had the unsettling feeling that she'd walked this space before, or somewhere like it. "There's this Welsh word," she continues after a moment, "I learned years ago in a poetry class at Cornell. *Hiraeth*. It has no exact equivalent in English. Or Khmer, I think."

"But it's something translatable," Narunn offers tentatively, "to every heart that's ever known loss, desired the impossible." He grins. "Am I right?"

Teera gives him a strange look. "You could say that. It's this deep longing for a home that never was. An ailment that brings both a sense of estrangement and a haunting familiarity."

"Ah, I know this ailment. I've seen it in countless patients. Indeed, I have it myself—as a matter of fact, our entire people suffer from it. A disease of incompleteness, disconnection."

"Yes!" She feels a sudden rush of love for this man who understands her so effortlessly.

"You're wrong, though. There is a name for it in our language."

"Oh, really?"

"Memory sickness, which, as you know, the Khmer Rouge deeply feared, so much that they attacked it like an epidemic."

Teera nods, remembering. She wonders if there's such a word or phrase for the self. Can you grieve for the person you've never been? A wholeness, a singularity, you've never known? Is *pralung*, or any such concept of the soul, its antidote? Her thoughts drift. *Where is Amara's pralung now? Where is mine? Whose ghost or spirit is calling to me this very moment?*

"*Allô allô* . . ." Narunn cuts in, laughing. "Calling you back to me."

"Sorry."

"Are you always like this, lost to your reverie? It's impossible to compete with a dream, you know."

Teera props herself up on one elbow, her curls brushing his shoulder and chin, her chest pressing against his upper arm. They are skin to skin, stretching in nearly equal lengths, the *kroma* now twisted in the crevice between them. When they make love, she notices, he breaks out in goose bumps, his body a canvas of impressionism, all ripples and resonances, pleasures bestrewn in dots, the shifting luster of passion evoked. Culminated. She lets her forefinger ghost his collarbone, moving from left to right, lingering, pirouetting in the ellipse beneath his Adam's apple. *An unborn melody . . . every person carries the seed of this melody inside himself.* She recalls the tracery of the air hole on the oboe and wonders if love has its own note, its inexpressible truth.

"I can't see you behind all these waves and lashes," Narunn teases, blowing the curls from her face, looking deep into her eyes. "And who can you possibly be daydreaming about when I'm right here?"

Teera stares at his moving lips, not quite hearing him, this beautiful lighthearted man beside her. Narunn Nim. *Nim was my mother's first name, but since she didn't make it, I took it as my surname.* A way to carry her forward, he told her. How easy to be with him, Teera thinks. He embraces the living and the departed with such serenity, as if his entire being, not just his head, were a temple, an altar where both burial and rebirth are possible.

"Anyone I know?" he asks again when she remains silent, preoccupied. "Someone very special?"

She nods.

"Your aunt."

Tears flood her eyes, and before she knows what to do, a drop rolls out. Narunn promptly rises up on both elbows, collarbones protruding in the effort, and stops the drop midtrack, lips pressed to the side of her nose. He holds himself there, a floodgate, braced to inhale the torrent.

Teera lowers her head, burying her face in his neck, sobbing into that hollow note, and the boat-shaped reservoir of his clavicle. It's the first time she's mourned Amara in the presence of another this way, with the ungraceful, abandoned refrain of hiccups and hypoxia.

Narunn lowers them both back onto the pillow. "My training was rather scant and rushed," he murmurs, returning to the subject of medicine, as if sensing that his voice is the only thing that will soothe her. "Right after Pol Pot, everything was destroyed. There was no real health system to speak of—no functioning modern clinics, no hospitals. For our training, we scavenged, gathering whatever textbooks and equipment could be found amidst the shattered remnants of the university classrooms. Out of hundreds of doctors, forty-five survived—*forty-five*—and half of them fled the country as soon as they could. The few remaining doctors pooled their efforts for the near impossible task of rebuilding a health system from scratch, appealing for assistance from the Red Cross, enlisting the help of Vietnamese experts still present in the country.

Young Cambodians who had begun medical training before the war were recruited as 'teachers,' others finished a course one semester and turned around to teach it the next. We shared a hodgepodge of Russian, French, and Vietnamese language texts, which you were lucky if even the teacher could decipher. So literally we had to pick up from the dust and bones. We had to find our way back to some semblance of a society, to some means of healing, by retracing those disappearing footprints with our own."

Teera listens, his chest like a seashell against her ear, a chamber of echoes and currents, ancient rivers and tears, timeless sorrow.

"Let me tell you about them, these footprints, and their haunted path . . ."

Tun has finished packing. A bundle that he will carry on his shoulder. No valise, nothing unnecessary, not even his name. When he walks out his door, he will no longer be Tun. He'll assume an alias, a new identity unknown to people he loves, fellow musicians in the various ensembles to which he belongs, the friends and neighbors who share the Municipal Apartments complex, or the White Building, as some have taken to calling it. He hears movement coming into the living room. The night accentuates every sound and brings it closer, makes even an insubstantial echo seem embraceable, somatic. The whoosh of an object, the sense of something suspended, oscillating in midair. His daughter swinging a toy in her hand? A wooden yo-yo perhaps? Or maybe one of his instruments? No, she'd be humming or singing to herself, as is her habit when she wakes. This is how one should always reenter the world from whatever sojourn, he thinks. With music.

He listens more carefully, recognizing now the nanny's footsteps coming toward his room. He feels her calm the moment she appears at his door, a lotus-leaf packet swinging on a string from her hand. Earlier in his daughter's room, he wondered where Om Paan was, noting the empty straw mat on the floor across the room. All the while she's been in the kitchen, packing food for him to take, abetting his escape. She's known for some time now he's leaving. He told her only the fact of his inevitable departure, nothing else. Not why, not when. But it's clear she intuits the choreography of his every step, its direction and intention. Sometimes he feels she can hear his heartbeats from a distance.

"Are you ready, sir?" she inquires.

"Will I ever be?" he replies, trying to be light.

She gives him a solemn smile. "No, sir."

He nods. She is a tiny woman, standing no taller than his chest. A child's height. But she possesses the solidity of a rock, the stability of a mountain. He met her on the street a year or so after he'd brought Sita home from the hospital. Her infant, an eight-month-old boy, had just died from dysentery he caught as they made their escape from Chantrea, a village in southern Cambodia near the Vietnamese border, heavily bombed by the Americans on suspicion that it was an enclave for Vietcong and other Communists. Her husband had been killed some months earlier by an unexploded ordnance he'd stepped on while plowing their fields. When he encountered her on the street in her solitude, she appeared to Tun a mound of grief and bones. Beside him, Sita tugged at his shirtsleeve, insisting they bring her home. When he suggested that perhaps they could just buy her food and clothes, his daughter said, "But, Papa, she's an orphan like me." Tun realized then that his daughter knew her mother had died, and how. So they brought Om Paan home. Her stay was supposed to be temporary, until she was strong enough to be on her feet again. It's turned out he and Sita aren't strong enough to be without her.

He often wonders what he would do without Om Paan's steady presence these past years, what he would do without her now. Certainly he would never think of leaving if she weren't here to look after Sita. It seems she sees herself here for the singular purpose of caring for his daughter. She passes no judgment on his politics, and interferes in no other aspect of his life. Only once she treaded the periphery of his heart, light-footed as a skimmer, and discerned its fragmentation. *You've been hurt by love.* That was all she said. She's never ventured further. And he does not tell her that one afternoon this love—who had so thoroughly wounded him—occupied the very spot where she now stands.

That day after he'd bumped into Channara in front of Chaktomuk Hall, after they'd taken their cones of sugarcane juice and strolled along the promenade and spoken at length, with little Suteera contentedly following close behind, Channara suddenly asked if they could see where he lived, and, not wanting the moment to end, he was more than happy to oblige. But he regretted it the moment they stepped inside, when Suteera, honest in the innocent yet brutal way that children often are, murmured, "It's . . . it's so small." Channara did not hear her daughter, her eyes taking in his sparse solitary existence, her mind lost to thoughts he could not ascertain. Tun knew then he could never hope to give this woman he loved the life she was accustomed to, deserved.

"Om . . ." he starts to say, his voice trailing. *Elder aunt.* He addresses her as his daughter does, though she's only in her early forties. She could be his older sister, and he treats her as such, with respect and gratitude and love.

"It's nothing special, just rice and fish," she says, lifting the stringed packet toward him. A brief silence, as they try to avoid each other's eyes. "Please be careful," she says after a moment, sparse with her advice, which only increases his apprehension.

He thanks her, slipping the packet into his bundle. His gaze momentarily flits to Sita's room, and panic seizes him again. Catching this, Om Paan says, "You know I've loved her as my own."

"I've never doubted this. It's just that I . . . I can't . . ." He fumbles. Takes a deep breath. Then starts over: "I've tried to write a letter explaining my leaving. I want to make it simple. Something she can understand. But—"

He stops, conscious of the rising agitation in his voice, afraid of waking his daughter in her room just a few feet away.

"I will do my best to comfort her," Om Paan offers quietly. "Until you return."

He takes the nanny's hand and squeezes it. He doesn't trust himself to say more, least of all make a promise. He might not be able to return. He might well be captured by the government tonight and shot on the spot. The execution of Preap In, a decade ago in '63, is still fresh in his mind. The young insurgent belonged to a group called Khmer Serei, a nationalist movement in opposition to both the Communists and the monarchy. Preap In was arrested en route from South Vietnam to Cambodia to negotiate his group's participation in the government, after having been guaranteed safe passage on the authority of Prince Norodom Sihanouk, head of state at the time. The prince, determined to make an example of the young insurgent in order to sow fear in the rising opposition, ordered the execution filmed and then broadcast for a month in every cinema, seen by adults and children alike. Lasting fifteen minutes, the film showed Preap In shackled and caged like an animal, assaulted with imprecation and refuse of every kind, then shot by a firing squad. A spectacle of cruelty from beginning to end, it impressed upon Tun as nothing before the savagery his countrymen are capable of inflicting on one another. This was what frightened him most—the game, the shameless parade we make of our inhumanity.

The government has since changed hands. Prince Sihanouk is in exile, shuttling between Beijing and Paris, deposed three years earlier, in 1970, in the military coup led by his first cousin Prince Sisowath Sirik Matak, and his former commander in chief and defense minister, Lon Nol, now president of the fledgling republic. While espousing liberal democracy, Lon Nol jails and tortures his enemies in growing numbers. Despite American military aid to bolster the government, the opposition forces continue to strengthen, feeding off the sharpening climate of repression. Violence has become the primary means of political expression. Tun fears this is only the surface of what's to come.

In the dark, narrow corridor outside his apartment door, he stills his heart and gathers his final resolve. He can almost hear Om Paan breathing on the other side. She lingers at the door, listening, grieving. A moment passes, and he hears her walking away toward his daughter's room. But he knows, like him, she will not sleep tonight.

He walks to the end of the corridor and descends the wide, open stairwell, weaving back and forth in a continuous zigzag pattern. He pauses now and then on a landing to remember conversations he has

had over the years with his neighbors, the civil servants and professionals who made living in an apartment setting—so different from that of
the traditional Khmer home or Chinese shop house—seem modern. He
remembers the time his daughter cut her foot on a piece of broken glass
and the entire floor came to her rescue. She is without a mother, but she
does not lack for maternal care and affection. This comforts him, eases
his steps forward. Perhaps she won't miss him all that much, he tells
himself.

On the ground, he hears a bamboo flute playing faintly from the
landscaped gardens on the east side paralleling the Bassac River six or
seven hundred meters away, recalling for him the innumerable hours he
spent composing music outside when it was too hot inside his apartment, or when electricity failed and the only source of light was the sky
above. Tonight electricity is out again in this part of the city—a constant
during wartime—but the stairwell from top to bottom is awash with
moonlight. Looking at the latticework of masonry covering the walls,
he once again marvels at the way the design plays with angles and silhouettes, how it makes use of *sramaol*—shadows and shades—to frame
natural light, harnessing it into focus, illuminating an enclosed space
while keeping it ventilated and cool. There's lightness to the modernist
architecture that has begun to reshape Phnom Penh in the years since
independence. The White Building is no exception, and tonight, with
the full moon shining, it appears ethereal as an apparition, mournful and
chalky as its name.

This is his daughter's home, he tells himself. She's survived the
bombing of her village. She is meant to live. Their home will endure. It
has to, or his leaving will have been for nothing. He will do whatever it
takes to return to this spot again, if not to hold his daughter, then to see,
to know for himself, that she is safe inside.

He crosses the triangular stretch of ground behind the apartment
complex to a corner of the street where he's most likely to find a ride
late in the night. Even at this hour, even without electricity, people are
up and about, moving with subdued gaits and gestures, their silhou-

ettes like shadow puppets outlined against the pearly night. Most are refugees from the countryside who have made the streets and sidewalks their homes. Lon Nol and his government are incapable of curbing the havoc they've created, so these families make do, pitching their tarps and spreading their straw mats wherever they can, surrounding themselves with sandbags—if they're lucky enough to have even that much—for when the sirens sound, signaling another air raid.

Food stalls offering different varieties of porridge and soup scent the air, making the open space feel somehow less exposed, less dangerous, and, in some corners, as familiar as one's own outdoor kitchen. A Chinese boy beats his chopsticks together in rapid succession, like a pair of drumsticks rattling out *pek-pok pek-pok*, the rhythm that's earned the nighttime snack its name, "Pekpok Noodles." The boy walks ahead of his father, who wheels their wooden cart, heavy with ceramic bowls and spoons, noodles and vegetables, and a large tin pot of steaming broth. At the end of a short block, they stop to fill the orders that have already come in, the father preparing the soup, and the son carrying one bowl after another to the customers waiting in their homes or shelters.

Tun takes it all in—the night scene, the mingled smells, the quiet music of life being lived and enjoyed despite the threat of death, the possibility of an airstrike always looming. Normality. As strained as it may be under the circumstances, he will sorely miss it. There will be none of this where he's going. No food stalls to satisfy his late-night cravings. No markets. No restaurants. No home, no family. Only the jungle.

He doesn't even know where he and his comrades are going, only that there should be a guide at each of the handoff points, the first of which will be in Chruay Chongvar once they've crossed the Tonle Sap River. The precise location of any encampment or base must be kept secret throughout the journey, in case they are captured.

Again Tun hesitates, fighting the overwhelming urge to turn around and walk back to the only life that holds any meaning for him. His daughter is all that matters, she gives value and purpose to everything he does, and, paradoxically, the very thought of her at this instant reminds him why he must proceed. In war one must choose sides, he feels. If caught in the middle, one risks being massacred by fire from all directions.

Still, greater than his fear is the belief that a more just world—if not a gentler one—awaits to be built. Here then lies his ineradicable faith in the future, even as the present crumbles around him, even as one regime fails and another emerges only to prove more corrupt, more vicious, than the previous. He could blame America for the current maelstrom, but the truth is, since his student days, those brief months in that great nation's capital, where he glimpsed at close range a government and its Constitution in practice, he hasn't been able to let go of his hope for what Cambodia could become. Surely if a nation as enormous and disparate as the United States can hold itself together around a single ideal without falling into fiefdoms, a small, relatively homogenous country like his has as much chance, if not more.

Democracy. There is no more viable system to govern a society. He fervently believes this even now, even when his own government has made a shambles of it. The Republic is a joke, doomed to fail, but propped with America's might, it has become a sustained hypocrisy. What choice does he have except to pin his hope on a yet unseen future? So he joins those who are battling for that future, even as he questions the blunt specificities of Communist ideology, its literalness, its lack of metaphor and music.

Stop. He mustn't reason too much, or everything will fall apart, as it inevitably does when one philosophizes. He must do what needs to be done. Simple as that.

He sees a cyclo and beckons it toward him. "Chruay Chongvar Bridge," he tells the peddler, a sinewy adolescent who looks as wiry as his vehicle.

"Yes, sir, thank you, sir," the boy enthuses, lacking the ease and confidence of a seasoned peddler. He doesn't seem to belong in this urban landscape.

It's obvious to Tun the boy is too soft-spoken, too polite to be a peddler of any sort. Here in the city, boys of this age are being recruited into the militia in a patriotic call to Bamreur Jiat—"Serve the Nation"—enticed with a choice of an M1 rifle, an M16, or an AK47. One sees these youngsters everywhere, at any hour, balancing their weapons next to their schoolbooks on the handlebars of their bicycles, as they rush from school or from home in a round-the-clock duty of patrolling the city for possible "leftist activities." Perhaps it's not wise for Tun to converse with this strange boy, but for some reason he desires a connection, however tenuous. Once they're well on their way, and sensing the boy is harmless, he asks, "Where are you from?"

"Banaam, sir."

He turns to have a better look. "Banaam is near Neak Leung."

"Yes, sir."

"When did you come to Phnom Penh?"

"The day after Neak Leung was hit. My mother forced me to leave. She was afraid we'd be next. Though, she herself is still there . . ."

Tun is silent. Another life displaced, another family torn.

"Were you a cyclo driver in Banaam?"

"No, sir. My mother took her entire savings to buy me this so that I could have some means to support myself in the city. Once I've saved enough, then I can bring her." His voice grows soft, resigned. "But everything here costs money, even chilies and lemongrass. In the countryside, we simply trade herbs and vegetables and fruits with our neighbors. Here I live on rice and salt. On a good day I allow myself a bit of *prahoc*."

At the corner on Sisowath Quay, just before the bridge, Tun gets out, empties his pockets of the few bills he's brought with him, having left his savings behind with Om Paan. He offers the bills to the cyclo driver, who hesitates, seeming nonplussed by the generosity, this gesture of extravagance at a time of extreme scarcity. Tun thrusts the money into the boy's hands. "Thank you, sir," the youth mutters. "Thank you."

Tun takes in the scene. There are even more people here, even at this late hour of the night, and the din resonates more thickly, one sound hardly distinguishable from another. A few paces away to the right, the Tonle Sap laps languidly against the shore, lulling those who are still awake into a kind of lassitude, inattentiveness. High above him the massive concrete remains of Chruay Chongvar Bridge extend out into the night. The previous year, insurgents succeeded in planting bombs that destroyed three spans of the bridge, which jut from the water still in jagged disarray. The ferry has become, once again, the only means across.

Tun and his comrades couldn't ask for a more ideal place to slip out unnoticed. Straight ahead across the road, a pair of headlights from a station wagon parked in the shadow of a cassia tree flashes three times in rapid succession. He recognizes the signal and the vehicle—a rented dark green Peugeot 404, a popular and reliable family car, ubiquitous and therefore unlikely to draw attention. Inside await his comrades, two men and a woman. They will cross the river in the station wagon by ferry, and if stopped by a guard patrolling the dock area, they are to let their female comrade speak, use her charm. *Some things never change*, Comrade Nuon had grumbled at their exit plan when it was discussed at the meeting earlier that night. *I suppose equality for women will have to come later.* This comment drew a severe critique from a high-ranking cadre in attendance. It showed a lack of faith not only in the revolutionary movement but in the party. The Organization, he told her, never errs.

Looking around, Tun is not overly worried about the crossing. The government is much more vigilant of movements into the city, so it's easier to leave than to enter. Besides, the men relegated to these non-fighting roles are often young, barely out of their teens, undisciplined and minimally trained. They are easily bribed, and nothing charms a young boy with a gun more than another treasure of shiny steel. The watch on Tun's wrist should come in handy in such a situation. It's a good thing he didn't give the watch away to the cyclo driver, he thinks. Had he remembered it in that moment, Tun might've felt compelled to relinquish this last *sompirak sivilai*, this frivolous "object of civilization," which will have no value in the jungle, as time there will cease to exist. In some way, it already has for him.

But he must hurry. His comrades are signaling him again. This is it, he thinks. He closes his eyes and takes a deep breath. *Lokta, Lokta!* a child calls from somewhere behind him as he's about to cross the road.

His eyes flutter open.

Narunn tells Teera he was sixteen when the Khmer Rouge fell, and his extended family—more than twenty members, including his father, grandparents, five siblings, cousins, uncles and aunts, nephews and nieces—were all wiped out. His mother was the last to go. She died trying to give birth to a life conceived by force. The man who'd raped her, a stranger housed in a neighboring village, was dragged to the fields and executed, one bullet in his head, another in his crotch for good measure. Such crimes were not tolerated by the Organization.

After admitting her own fault in a public self-criticism session— failing to look modest enough, revolutionary enough, and therefore inviting unwanted male attention—Narunn's mother had been allowed to live. A different kind of punishment. She'd hoped against hope that the absence of menstruation for the next several months was a sign she was menopausal. She was after all nearing fifty. But her belly grew and grew even as the rest of her became more emaciated. Then the ninth month arrived, she went into labor, and after a night of sweat, blood, and blinding pain, the life inside her gave up trying to find its way out, as if sensing it stood no chance outside her womb. Even so Nim had no strength to grieve, to feel anger or regret, to fear. She too would die, and she was ready. She curled up on the wood floor, holding her stomach, the lifelessness within. A body inside a body, the mother a coffin for her child. She took comfort in this, in the knowledge that out of all her dead children at least this one had her protection, her permanent embrace. She calmed her heart, slowing her breaths, saving them for Narunn, the only one of her five children—*six* counting this one in her womb—and the only member of her family still alive.

At dawn's first light when he returned as usual with his work unit from quarrying stones at a mountain in the neighboring district, she gathered her remaining strength to give voice to the thoughts that had kept her alive the past hour as she waited for him. "I've made peace with death," she murmured, her voice faint but tranquil, her eyes traveling the silent, parallel rivers down the sides of his nose. "I'd like you, in my place, to reconcile with life. Take it beyond what I can give you. Go forward, my son. I will see you on the other side."

But grief made going forward impossible, even long after the regime had collapsed. There remained the danger of unexploded mines, the risk of being kidnapped and brutally killed by Khmer Rouge bandits, the utter lack of resources, and most important, the feeling that if he left, he would be relinquishing his duty as the family's sole survivor—to be the signpost to their unmarked graves. This kept Narunn bound to his village at the water's edge for a while longer, during which he made every effort to teach himself, to make up for the lost years in his education.

As there were no books for him to learn from, he sought the monks, the artists and musicians, the village elders for whatever knowledge they could impart, whatever wisdom had survived with them. Through the recitation of the Buddhist dharma in Pali and Sanskrit, he plumbed the depths of language, ascertained the roots of words and their relations, their inevitable rotation and return—*anatta, anantakol, avasana, anicca.* Selflessness. Eternity. Termination. Impermanence. Nothing is static. Even death is a kind of continuity. There is no end, no beginning. Only *analay*—homelessness—this continual search for a self that belongs.

From *neak smoat*, these soulful singers of poetry, he discovered that music can heal, that a human's voice is a most potent medicine: it can stir even the dead. And from a medicine man, he learned that healing is a dialogue, a peace talk of give-and-take, an age-old negotiation between life and death. At a birthing ceremony, he watched a midwife reverse a baby in breech position, turning the infant's head toward the birth canal, with movements of her hands that mimicked the improvised gestures of the accompanying spiritual medium, as she danced to the music of *khmer leu*, the mountain nomads of Ratanakiri who passed through his village, their ensemble of instruments ranging from a single leaf to the *amvaet*, a wind instrument with sweeps and curves as ostentatious as a peacock's. He thought of the ordeal his mother had endured in labor while he was absent. Had there been a doctor, a hospital or clinic, perhaps her death might have been prevented. Had there been medicine, even the most basic analgesic, her pain and suffering could've been palliated.

In countless conversations with an old pharmacist who'd been dislocated from his home in Phnom Penh to the countryside during the mass exodus and who'd kept his identity hidden to survive the Khmer Rouge regime, Narunn often wondered if healing is as much a leap of faith as it is a science, a paradox that embodies the inescapable knowledge of ourselves—death's inevitability—and the desire to be tethered to this world, to be in the selfless service of others, to prolong what is essentially short-lived. *You'd make an excellent doctor*, the pharmacist said, encouraging Narunn to go to the capital, where such pursuit might be possible now that the country's reconstruction had begun. If his own health hadn't been irretrievably broken by the years of hard labor and starvation, the elder would certainly return to the city himself. While it was too late for him, he urged Narunn not to confine himself to this small village. He must continue learning—strive to expand his mind beyond the limit of his geography and birth. Ignorance, the old man told him, is its own kind of hell.

Thus, at the urgent behest of this mentor, Narunn set out for Phnom Penh, first by boat, then walking from one village to the next, hitching rides in oxcarts whenever possible, crossing rivers and streams in fishermen's canoes, and once, to his amazement and delight, accompanying a mahout high up on the back of an elephant. Along railroad tracks overgrown with grass and saplings, he caught up with the slow-moving carcass of what remained of a train, and because he had no gold or any-thing of value to trade for a seat inside one of the cars, he was told he could climb atop the engine, where there was still space near the radia-tor vent at the front. *It's free*, said the conductor, nodding at the flock of men perched there. *You should know, though, that those who take the risk might never make it to their destination. This front of the train will be the first to explode if it runs over mines laid by Khmer Rouge bandits, or if we hit an ambush.* Narunn surveyed the hardened expressions of his would-be traveling companions, then climbed on. He had to make a leap into the unknown. There could be no destination without first a journey. His mother's words came back to him. *I will see you on the other side.* At the time, he'd thought she meant she would see him in death, the inescap-able end to all existence, but gradually he came to believe "the other side" of the nightmare they'd endured was *life. Go forward, my son.* She would live through him.

Once in the city, Narunn searched for the apartment building that the pharmacist had told him about. Based on the elder's descriptions, he imagined something grand and modern, indestructible. He asked every-one he encountered, reciting by rote the part of its name his mind was able to retain, but no one had any clue of a place called the White Build-ing. Narunn would soon come to learn that most of the city dwellers were villagers themselves who had come to the city because it was one of the few places in the country safe from the Khmer Rouge. Most were just as lost as he. As for the original residents of Phnom Penh, a great number had perished during those four years in rural exile, and those who'd survived and returned to the city were too afraid to speak, to give out any information, so they lived in feigned ignorance.

Narunn didn't know all this, however, on that first day. He contin-ued searching in vain, and by late afternoon, exhausted and hungry, he was ready to give up when a deranged beggar, who had been shadowing him for some time, beckoned him to follow. Speaking an unintelligible mix of Khmer and what sounded like French, the beggar led Narunn to a mammoth, crumbling structure along the riverfront. *Boeding sar,* the beggar whispered, as if the place might be haunted, as if this "white building" was itself a ghost.

Inside, Narunn found indeed it was. A ghost of a building with its ghost inhabitants. *I am afraid . . . So quiet here . . .* Messages in charcoal crawled across the walls and floors. *Only the soldiers are left . . . I am afraid. I am afraid.* Some words had faded, leaving only faint outlines; others were black and sharp, with a feathery layer of charcoal dust, as if written only days before. *Where are you?—Where am I? What is this place?* The living speaking to the dead, and the dead searching for echoes of themselves, for shadows and silhouettes resembling their own, for signs they had once existed.

Names, dates, numbers. Slashes and marks in patterns decipherable only to those who had drawn them. Stick figures of a family, with every member crossed off except the last in the row. Wiggly circles on stems, like lollipops or flowers. Other scribbles made by children's hands or minds gone mad. These renderings accompanied Narunn as he walked the ground level from one apartment block to the next, until he reached the block he was looking for. Dirt-encrusted footprints wove their way up the open staircase.

Narunn followed the footprints, only to find them vanish at the first landing without a trace. He continued the journey up, in place of who-ever had left those footprints below. When he reached the intended floor, he counted the apartments from left to right, and again from right to left. Feeling certain he'd identified the correct one, he approached it. It was occupied. His heart leapt with hope. He told the people liv-ing there about the old pharmacist who had sent him to see whether his family had returned, as this had been their home before the Khmer Rouge chased them out. The middle-aged mother, with her three teen-aged children gathered warily around her, said she had never heard of this pharmacist. Her own husband had died under Pol Pot's regime, at the very end during the big purge, she explained as if to make certain there was no mistaking her and her children for the pharmacist's family. She didn't think the apartment belonged to anyone now. She had found it empty, without a single possession. She sounded suddenly guarded, afraid. Was Narunn certain this was the right unit? *Yes.* Perhaps other occupants would know then, she suggested, clearly wanting him to leave. It was a big place, with several linked blocks, and some units empty still. The new government allowed people to claim whatever home they found unoccupied, she told him. Perhaps the pharmacist's family had found a bigger home, a fancy villa that had belonged to some rich people. Narunn nodded, sensing his search was over.

Dispirited, he thanked the woman and again headed for the open stairs. It had been several years now since the fall of the regime, and if any members of the pharmacist's family were still alive, they would've already returned, as they'd promised one another when the Khmer Rouge separated them and flung them to different parts of the country. *If you find them, tell them that you're like a son to me*, his mentor had said. *If you don't, there's no need for words. I'll understand your silence.*

Yes, silence, Narunn thought, as he meandered up the concrete staircase. It was best to leave the dead undisturbed, let them rest, wherever they may be.

He wondered how much of Phnom Penh he could see the higher up he went. At the top, looking west into the city, the tiered steeple of the Independence Monument rose above the tree line, the golden roof of Wat Langka flickered as the sun passed behind it, the National Sports Complex appeared like a luminous assemblage of ivory in the evening light. Narunn did not know what he was seeing but would gradually come to learn the names of these edifices and their histories—the monument designed by the renowned modernist architect Vann Molyvann, the temple converted to a storehouse during the Khmer Rouge, the sports stadium where many executions had taken place. On the east side, in the immediate surroundings, a wide tract of unkempt ground, bearing faint traces of landscaped gardens in neat long rows, stretched the full length of the apartment complex. Narunn sensed that in the distance beyond lay the river, but he could not see past the buildings and trees. Leaning over the railing, he let his gaze wander north, where he could make out the edges of the mythical skyline. He remembered from the day's earlier wandering the shimmering domes and spires of the Royal Palace, the old National Assembly, and the ornate temple, Wat Botum Vaddey. A lovely city, Narunn thought as he stood admiring it now, despite the darkness encroaching.

A wind blew from the direction of the river, carrying the heavy scent of mud and monsoon. If it rained, the concrete overhang above would keep him dry. Maybe he ought to just sleep out here on the landing, in the open fresh air. But, on second thought, he remembered the deranged beggar's mumbled warning—*You're in the company of the hungry and the starved. You ought to be careful with your sack of rice.* Narunn felt fear all around him, in everyone he'd met, in the guarded silence and stillness of the families returning to hide behind the closed doors of these apartments in which they coexisted with ghosts. However charming and peaceful this city might have once been, he sensed the threat of violence beneath the present disquiet. He hadn't come all this way only to be robbed and killed. He'd better go inside and find a safer place.

At the end of the long hallway stood an empty apartment with the door missing. He walked across the grimy tiles of the living room to a pair of doors on the opposite side, leading out to a small open terrace, with an enclosed kitchen and bathroom adjoining it. Everything had fallen into disrepair. Yet, he felt this was more than adequate. Back inside, he entered the bedroom. Dust danced in the fading evening light cast from a tall window with broken shutters. He opened the window, pushing the shutters all the way out, then, stepping back, he saw on the wall beside the window these words—*Darling, if you are alive, come back to me . . . Come back to me.* In the same charcoal tone, the careful outline of a slender hand—a woman's left hand, with long graceful fingers—hovered above the love letter, and next to it, the half silhouette of her right hand, as if left purposely unfinished for him who would respond. The few words that followed brought Narunn to his knees. *I wait for you. Always.*

Night fell. Having no home to go to, no family to reunite with, he found this missive on the wall inexplicably welcoming. He felt safe and cared for in the presence of the partially rendered embrace. The apartment became his home. Where else could he find a place that echoed with such intimacy? The walls spoke to him of his own longings, his search for a love that would endure and reverberate across worlds.

Mr. Brown and Mr. Smith hover on the grass at the river's edge, happily splashing each other with water from their cupped hands. Something about them reminds the Old Musician of the freshwater dolphins he once encountered during a boat ride in Kratie. Perhaps it's the way they communicate with gurgles and codes only they understand. It's easier to think of the boys as Dara and Sok when they're not reciting their English lessons. Stripped of the sanctity of the cloth, with only the inner brown wraps for modesty, they have been turned by the water into children again. They have helped him down the *naga* stairway so that he can wash his clothes in the river. He's found a comfortable perch a couple of steps up from the bottom where he can easily reach into the river.

The two novices jump naked into the Mekong, their undergarments flung aside, and race toward a submerged water buffalo with only its head sticking out. A young girl with long black hair underneath a conical hat stands straight and tall on its back, so that from a distance it appears she's floating on water. She turns ever so slightly, her reflection like the shadow cast by the gnomon of a sundial, and remains unperturbed even as the two boys approach her with loud splashes and squeals. "Hey, where're you going? Are you Vietnamese? Is this your water buffalo? *Rất đẹp!*" Sok teases in Vietnamese, which he speaks passably, like most from his village near the border. The Old Musician himself knows a few phrases—a remnant of his days spent in forest encampments with Vietnamese comrades—and wonders whether "Very beautiful!" is meant for the girl or her water buffalo.

The two swim to the front and lift clumps of water hyacinth to the animal's mouth. "How old is he?" The girl does not answer. Her inner stillness seems godlike, immense and impermeable. The Old Musician wishes her to turn around. A familiar ache lances his heart. She's not much bigger than his daughter was when he left her to fight for a cause he now fails to comprehend.

His gaze follows the little girl as she glides erect downstream and out of view.

A small boat sputters past, loaded with pomelos and sugarcanes, prow pointing toward the city. Waves unfurl and lap toward him, hitting the steps and shore one by one, and he feels himself lulled, pulled into the tides of remembering. Just as, moments before, with the ease of a blink, he had slipped into the night of his disappearance, then, in a single imperceptible shudder, emerged to find himself back on the *naga* steps, his world divided as before, one half in shadows beneath the eye patch and the other in the brightness of the afternoon sun.

"Lokta, Lokta!" The Old Musician turns toward the voice and sees Dara wading hurriedly through chest-deep water, his raised hand clasping something dark and stiff.

A catfish, he thinks, noting its bent shape. Strangely, its stillness worries him. Then as Dara nears, he sees it's not a fish at all. Fear climbs up his spine and his first impulse is to jump into the river and seize the gun from the youngster. *Throw it away!* he wants to yell out to the boy but thinks better of it. If loaded, it could fire. Dara, knowing full well the danger of his discovery, places the revolver carefully on the steps. Sok, orphaned by guns, has gone completely mute, and the Old Musician can only imagine what's running through the youngster's mind—Who has this gun wounded or murdered? Noting its newness and shine, the Old Musician suspects the revolver recently found its way into the river. Certainly it doesn't look like it's been lost for years in the sand and silt of the Mekong.

He wipes his hands on his shirt several times before lifting it. Pointing the gun away from himself and the boys, he pulls out the chamber, careful not to touch the trigger. *Never point your weapon at anyone you're not ready to kill*, the commander at his training base seethed in the denseness of the jungle. He shakes away the memory and refocuses his attention on the weapon at hand. No bullets. Relief washes over him. He should've guessed. Even a single bullet can be easily sold on the black market for quick cash, with the added advantage that, unlike a gun, one doesn't have to fear being caught with it. *I found the bullet on the street*, a child like Dara or Sok could say to a dealer in one of the dingy alleyways off rue Confédération de la Russie, where a whole string of stalls trade in such implements of death, under the front of selling imitation US military uniforms and memorabilia.

The Old Musician recalls the abundance of weapons, the seemingly inexhaustible supplies suddenly available to the revolutionary armed forces when they took over the country that April in 1975, combining their own arsenal with that of the Lon Nol government, which had received nearly two billion dollars in military aid from the United States in those final years of the civil war. During the subsequent forced exodus, and throughout the revolutionary regime, .38 revolvers similar to the one he's holding now, along with AK47s and M16s, were copiously dispensed like toys to the young, most of whom, uneducated and illiterate, had no understanding of any doctrine or cause they were fighting for but nevertheless felt the thrill and power these weapons gave them. Now an AR15, cherished like a family heirloom, might be pawned by a former revolutionary soldier to pay for the funeral of his little daughter who died of malaria, and an unearthed grenade, sold and bought and sold again for a couple of dollars, is finally thrown by a farmer to be rid of a neighbor vying for a tiny strip of farmland bordering their two properties. A young mother employed as a deminer routinely replants land mines she's extracted, fearing that if all the mines were removed she would have no work to provide for her young ones, even with the knowledge that a Bouncing Betty has already made her a widow and that a silent killer left in the ground can remain active for decades.

The Old Musician has met them all, these fragmented souls, at once helpless and hazardous, each both a victim of their circumstances and a weapon by the choices they make. All it takes is a single tripped wire— fear, anger, desperation—for them to detonate and cause irreparable harm.

"What should we do, Lokta?" Dara asks, while Sok continues to stare in muted horror.

"We take it to the abbot," he attempts to reassure the boys. "His Venerable will know what to do."

As they climb the stairs, what seizes the Old Musician's throat is not the discovery of a gun by two youngsters in their naked innocence but the ordinariness of weapons today as a currency for food in the cycle of poverty and violence.

He sees his culpability in everything.

"So that's how those footprints led me here, to this room." Narunn lifts Teera's chin so that he looks right into her eyes as he cradles her. "To this moment with you. Sometimes a couple's lost love is requited in the union of another pair, years or decades or a lifetime later. You called, I came, and since then I've waited for you."

Teera swallows. "Where were they . . . the hands?"

Narunn sits up, pulling her forward, and turns so that he holds her, cupping her from the back as they both face the closed window above the bed. Then, lacing his fingers into hers, he leans to place their hands on the wall.

"Here."

At the open-air ceremony hall, a throng quickly gathers around the Old Musician, the gun in the middle on the straw mat, wielding a hypnotic power, drawing every gaze to it. "Where did it come from?" one of the monks asks amidst the multitude of shorn heads and saffron robes. "*I found it in the river!*" Dara gloats, pride having replaced fear. *Where in the river? How did it get there? Whose? Can it shoot? Does it have bullets? I think it belonged to a corrupt policeman.* Questions and opinions erupt. *No, that's the kind I've seen bodyguards carry. It must be expensive . . .*

The Venerable Kong Oul appears and everyone promptly quiets down. "Such intense curiosity is better applied toward your studies," says the abbot, lowering himself onto the straw mat opposite the Old Musician. He looks around, smiling, as if this were just another gathering. "Back to your quarters, disciples."

The throng issues a collective moan. But recognizing an order, however gently expressed, they begin to disperse. Except one novice who remains rooted to the spot. Makara. His parents have recently forced his ordination to keep him out of trouble. "How much is it worth?" he asks bluntly.

"Oh, I wouldn't know." The abbot seems unperturbed by the youth's behavior. "It's not something you ought to concern yourself with."

"Probably at least fifty dollars," Makara insists, and the Old Musician can't tell whether the glint in his eyes is greed, inspired by the thought of such a large sum, or the effect of substance withdrawal.

After the ceremony to call his spirit back had failed, Makara's parents took him to a local rehabilitation center, where the method of treatment was literally to beat the drug out of the boy. Makara lasted a week there. Against his father's angry warning—*The boy will not change if we don't let him suffer!*—Makara's mother brought him home, devastated by the injuries and bruises covering their son's body. The boy swore he would give up drugs, but in no time at all he was caught stealing what little jewelry his mother had and pawning it to feed his habit. The distraught parents pleaded with the abbot to take their son in.

Now the boy stands in a monk's robe, seeming to challenge the only possibility left for his recovery. "I know where to sell it," he offers. "I mean I know who to take it to. Someone who'll probably pay more than fifty dollars . . ."

The abbot waits, saying nothing, his gaze at once gentle and unwavering. He seems to think it best to let the boy finish his thoughts.

"I-I'll bring back the money," Makara stutters, unable to keep still, body twitching, like someone about to have a seizure.

Finally the abbot says, "There's no need for your involvement, my dear *samanae.*" Then, as if suddenly remembering something, his face lights up. "Your mother was just here! She's brought you some fried noodles, along with some other snacks. She's left the tiffin with one of the nuns in the kitchen. Go and see. Perhaps you can have a nibble before dinner. Discreetly, of course."

Though monks are not allowed to take any food past noon, the Old Musician remembers that an exception is made for Makara, as the abbot believes the boy needs all the nourishment he can get to rebuild his strength and recover.

Makara fidgets and, after a moment, as if unable to bear the abbot's kind gaze, excuses himself: "*Kanah.*"

Once the boy is out of hearing range, the abbot turns to the Old Musician. "Ah, the tricks one must resort to in order to turn the mind of a youth!" He glances at the revolver on the mat, and the Old Musician notices for the first time how strained, how uncharacteristically discomposed, the old monk appears, despite his cheerful words. Perhaps this discovery bothers him more than he initially let on. "I wasn't at all sure what to think when Sok came and said there was a gun. It was all he could tell me."

"My apologies, Venerable, but I'd sent the boy to fetch you so as to give him some distance from the weapon. He was quite upset by its presence."

"Yes, he was obviously distressed. Hopefully, some calm has returned to him. I gave him a new English phrase to recite. *A breath in, a breath out, each breath a journey all its own . . .* I've found, even for myself, this often works better than chanting the ancient sutras." As if to prove the point, the abbot inhales and exhales slowly, repeating the cycle a few times. "Ah, I feel better already . . . Now, how did this come into our possession?"

The Old Musician quickly summarizes what transpired at the river, while the abbot listens, thoughtful in his disquiet. "We've poisoned our rivers with all sorts of pollutants," he laments when the Old Musician has finished.

"One hopes, Venerable, that it fell into the river accidentally, or if thrown there, that it was done with good intention, by someone who understood the harm such a weapon could cause."

"But," the abbot proffers tentatively, sensing the unspoken, "you imagine a more complicated journey for the gun?"

The Old Musician nods. "You read my thoughts, Venerable."

"Go on . . ."

"It's pure conjecture, of course, but it's just as probable that someone tossed the weapon into the river, perhaps in a moment of fear, or remorse for some crime committed. Given its value, an innocent handler would simply sell it if he wished to be rid of it. Fifty dollars—if the boy's right, it may be worth more—that's a month's wage for most, and one does not throw away that kind of money. Again, it's a leap, on my part."

The abbot sighs. "Well, your leap might be quite close to the truth, given the reality we live in . . . The question now is, how can we end its journey?"

"We cannot turn it in to the authorities, Venerable."

"Absolutely not," the abbot agrees, sounding forcefully adamant. "We can't count on them to keep it out of the wrong hands." In a calmer voice, he asks, "Do you recall the death of a young girl in the karaoke bar in Chruay Chongvar some while ago?"

The Old Musician nods. "It was all over the news, Venerable." *A beer girl*, they called her, killed by a highly decorated police officer because she was too slow bringing drinks. Barely fifteen, she was made to dress in an outfit suggesting she was as much for sale as the alcohol she offered to entice the male customers. Like most of her peers, she'd come from her village to the city hoping to earn money to support her family back home. Her family did indeed receive money, not through her work but through her death. And her life? Worth no more than a few bottles of Hennessy, which the police officer and his friends drank in abundance that afternoon he shot her. The officer paid the family to keep them from pressing charges, and they had no choice but to accept this "grief money" because even if they had gone to court, it would have come to nothing. A police officer of his rank has *khnong*, as they say, the backing of someone more powerful.

"Has something happened?" the Old Musician ventures, when the abbot appears suddenly lost in thought. "Has the family decided to press charges after all?"

"I wish it were something as valiant as that." The abbot shakes his head and lets out another melancholic sigh. "There's been yet again a fatal incident with the police." He inhales deeply. "And this time, it's brought *us* a dilemma . . . Along with the gun, we now have a girl."

"A girl?" The Old Musician frowns in confusion.

"Like so many in the city, she will be abandoned . . ."

"I'm afraid I don't follow, Venerable."

"Her mother was killed recently, and this morning a friend of the slain woman—someone who comes now and then to our temple—pleaded with me to take the girl in."

"You don't think . . ."

"No, no, the two things—the girl, and this gun you've found—are not connected."

The Old Musician lets out an audible breath. He listens patiently as the abbot struggles to explain.

"The friend, an older woman in her late fifties, has acted as the girl's temporary caretaker. But, impoverished herself and with ha1rdly a home, she will not be able to keep the child much longer . . ." The abbot gazes into the distance, his mind wandering, searching.

"What happened, Venerable?"

"I'm sorry . . ." The abbot recollects his thoughts. "Yes. Well, the child's mother was a dancer—a classical ballet dancer trained at the School of Fine Arts—but, like so many artists, could not find work and had to settle for performing at a hotel. It seems there she caught the eye of a VIP guest—a captain in the National Police Bodyguard Unit—and became his mistress. The wife of the police captain found out, and rather than confront him, she hired a gunman to kill the young woman."

A beautiful young woman is forced by a powerful man who desires her, or by her own dire needs, into becoming his lover. Whether she's a bar girl or a ballet dancer, her beauty is both an asset and a curse, drawing jealousy and danger. The city is full of accounts like these, of lives as brief and extinguishable as incense flames. But there is more to this story, and the Old Musician is beginning to discern the heart of it. "Is the little girl his?" he asks.

"Yes, the little girl is the daughter of the slain dancer and the police captain."

"How old is the child, Venerable?"

"She is three."

The Old Musician's pulse quickens. *Sita* . . . He tries to keep his voice even. "She is too young to be among us. We're mostly men and boys here . . ." The one thing he'd done right was to give his daughter Om Paan in place of her mother. "Perhaps we can help in other ways—give food and clothes, collect donations . . . It's better for the child to remain where she is, with a woman, a mother figure. She needs a strong maternal presence—"

"The caretaker fears the wife of the police captain will come after the little girl as well."

For some seconds the Old Musician can't speak, thinking he must've misunderstood the implication. Finally he manages, "And the police captain? Does he not care that this is his own daughter? Does he not want her? Or, at least, feel some sense of responsibility? Even an animal feels protective toward its young, Venerable." He stops, quieting his heart.

The abbot shakes his head in shared dismay. "From what I can surmise, having spoken with the caretaker at length, the man cannot and will not care. His wife is from a very powerful family, you see. The wife may accept that her husband cheats, may even tolerate a string of mistresses, but she expects him to know his allegiance. He can stray, but he's not permitted to leave any 'embarrassing physical traces' that can make the family lose face, threaten their position. Put plainly, the police captain will endanger his own life if he lets out word that the ballet dancer's daughter is his. At the moment, it seems the wife has no clue about the little girl, but, later, if she finds out and confronts her husband, he'll most likely deny his daughter's existence. Perhaps he'll go as far as to say the child belongs to another man, someone prior to him. We've seen how scenarios like this play out." The old monk rubs his chest with his fist, as if pained at having to speak aloud a reality they know all too well. "You see my quandary? It is greater than the question of whether or not I, a monk, should harbor something as dangerous as a gun, when my teaching forbids me to hold even money. Greater than the question of whether or not to give shelter to a girl in a place that tradition reserves for boys." The head monk pauses to catch his breath. "It is the fundamental yet most difficult question of *how* to protect a human life. A tiny fragile life now haunted by immense loss. A life that may be hunted."

The Old Musician feels himself unable to breathe. "Have you spoken with anyone else about this?" he asks, groping through a blur of emotions, his surging bewilderment.

"You're the first person I've come to with this. I must admit I'm still in a bit of shock . . . How are we to care for a little girl? As you say, we're a community of men and boys. Yes, we have some nuns at the temple, but they come and go, spending some days here and other days back home with their families, when needed. And, besides, I can't ask them to take on the risks . . ."

"Then, we must do what we can, Venerable." The Old Musician is aware that his abrupt change of tone must sound rather peculiar to the abbot. "Given the danger she faces, we have no choice but to take the girl in, until this blows over."

"I was hoping you'd say this. I feel the same way." The abbot looks once again at the revolver, as if probing it for answers, a more definitive solution. To the Old Musician, the gun appears suddenly benign, innocuous, compared to the dangers outside the temple walls. "Aside from us," the monk continues, "and some close friends of the victim, no one knows the cause of her death. No newspaper will dare publish her story, let alone link her murder to a prominent family. The truth is once again promptly silenced."

"Perhaps, Venerable, if the story is forgotten, and lost among myriad others like it, the child will have a chance, her life overlooked, out of harm's way."

"Yes, each day we must live with the lesser tragedy," the abbot gives in, sounding defeated. "Foreigners have often said ours is a 'culture of impunity.' An English phrase, as you know. A critique, a condemnation. But the reproof barely registers, let alone dents our conscience deep enough to force us to account for our wrong. What does it really mean? *Impunity.* Are we truly exempted from punishment for our crimes, when our culture, our core belief, tells us knowledge of the atrocity we commit is itself a punishment? Because who in his right mind would engage in villainy? We inflict suffering because we are afflicted. Round and round it goes. How then do we get out of this wheel, this spinning in circles, and find justice?"

"Perhaps it lies in this, Venerable. In the probing itself. We've become adept not so much at escaping punishment but at escaping reflection. We fear to plumb the dark and see ourselves in it, the role we played in its creation, because if we go to that depth again we may not be able to resurface, to return to light." The Old Musician keeps his gaze down, struggling to articulate each thought, fighting the despair that threatens to smother him, send him back into his habitual silence. "As for justice, I've tried to comfort myself with the thought that perhaps it is like love—it transcends generations. If we fail to realize it in our own lifetime, perhaps those who come after us will know it."

Finally, he looks up, needing to face the abbot now. "When I think of the unfathomable suffering, the countless lives lost and broken, I'm left with this profound hope that someday there will exist a world where justice is not simply the exchange of a life for a life, an ideal of retribution to right a wrong, but a path one walks and lives, a way of being."

The abbot stares at him, and for a moment the two old men seem a reflection of each other, a shared stillness. Taking a deep breath, the abbot says, "Until then, until that world arrives, we are forced to shelter both weapons and victims as best we can, away from harm's reach." Taking a handkerchief from the folds of his saffron robe, he wraps the revolver, shaking his head in disbelief. "You know, I never thought that one day I'd be a keeper of guns."

The two men rise, and as they turn to go their separate ways, the Old Musician says, "Perhaps, Venerable, you ought to speak with Dr. Narunn. I believe he knows of a charity that can transform such things into art."

At the main entrance of the open-air pavilion along the promenade in front of the Royal Palace, a little boy in a Spider-Man outfit cups in his hands a bamboo netting with a sparrow inside. He looks about five or six, but his wispy hair and wispier silhouette make him appear younger, fragile. His mother has bought the captured bird for him from one of the vendors. They climb the short stairway into the pavilion, the boy pressing the tiny captive to his chest, his mother a step or two behind, her palms splayed to catch him should he fall. The boy hesitates, gasping, when he spots Teera standing in one corner, her back lit by the late-afternoon sun so that she must appear to him as only a dark outline, a malignant spirit perhaps waiting to claim him.

Teera moves out of the corner to where he can see her clearly. It's obvious the little boy is sick, has been sick for some time, his eyes sunken, his entire complexion anemic, ghostly, reminding Teera of her aunt, the way Amara looked those last couple of months before her death, as if the most vital part of her had already left and what remained was just a translucent shell. The irony of his superhero ensemble, the mask off and strapped around his neck like a ruined second face, does not escape Teera. *The masquerade is over*, it seems to say.

The boy's mother, a delicate beauty with long black hair and porcelain-white skin, bears all the accoutrements of the country's new elite—expensive clothes and shoes, a Louis Vuitton satchel with gold trimmings, a great deal of jewelry on her slight frame, and most notably, armed bodyguards, one waiting outside the pavilion, another guarding the shiny silver Mercedes SUV parked on the street, with the engine running.

As they walk past, others move out of the way and keep a deferential distance, noting the wealth, the pistols glinting from the bodyguards' midriffs, their impassive faces behind the dark sunglasses. The young mother asks her son if he's ready, the little boy nods, and she carefully unties a knot on the bamboo netting still pressed to his chest. Then, like a magician opening his palms, the boy releases the sparrow into the air. The tiny bird flits up and down and circles for some seconds, confused by all the open space, its regained freedom, before it darts straight ahead and disappears into the glimmering expanse of the Tonle Sap River.

"Did you pray to the spirits and guardians?" the mother asks, her attention fully on her son as if she notices no one else, cares for nothing else.

The little boy nods.

"And what did you say?"

"I . . . asked . . . them . . . to take . . . my sickness away." Each word seems a monumental effort for the boy, a journey of labored breaths. "So that . . . Father said . . . you will laugh again."

The young mother looks at her son, her face quivering, and she appears to Teera at once vulnerable and steeled. "No," she says to him after a moment, the pools in her eyes receding, returning to the source of grief inside her, "so that *you* will laugh again. Like this!"

She makes as if to tickle him but stops midgesture when he begins to heave, his chest rising and falling, flimsy as a balloon with insufficient air.

The bodyguard waiting outside the pavilion hurries in, lifts the boy into his arms, gently but firmly, and carries him toward the Mercedes, as the other bodyguard rushes into the driver's seat. The mother trails a few steps behind, looking straight ahead, refusing to meet anyone's gaze, to see her son reflected in another's eyes.

Once she's inside, the doors shut and locked, the driver revs up the engine and forces the Mercedes through the throngs of pedestrians and vehicles that have amassed to enjoy the cool hours of late afternoon along Sisowath Quay. In no time at all they are gone, their car having turned the corner at the end of the block.

But the sound of the boy's breath stays with Teera, circling her eardrums, like the exhalation inside the spiraled chambers of a seashell, muffled but persistent, as if part of some greater susurrus. Again, Teera remembers her aunt, the last evening of Amara's life, the breath that grew more faint with each passing hour, as if inside the still, almost lifeless body under the white sheets, Amara was taking an unhurried stroll, saying her silent farewells to Teera, to the doctors and nurses, to the walls and windows, the hospital bed, the morphine drip, thanking everyone, always grateful and ever gracious.

A month or so before her death, when she was still fully coherent, not wanting the memories of her death to overwhelm their home, the life they'd shared, Amara had made Teera promise to let her die at the hospital, where she knew many staff members from having taken her clients—refugees and immigrants who did not speak enough English— for various medical visits over the years. She'd firmly refused even the offer of a hospice close to home, where it would be quieter, more peaceful. *There's nothing quieter or more peaceful than death*, she'd said good- naturedly, *and I'll go there soon enough*. The evening that was to be her last, Amara summoned enough strength through her haze of pain to utter these simple words—*Hospital. Take me.*

Teera quietly left Amara's bedside and walked to the living room, a fist in her mouth to block the howl threatening to escape her throat. She recollected herself, sucking back the tears that'd come through her nostrils, and called for an ambulance. She'd been expecting this moment, and yet when it came, it rattled her and she pushed against it, anguish- ing. *No, not now, not tonight . . .*

By the time they reached Hennepin County Medical Center, Amara had already lost consciousness. The doctor explained Teera's choices. While she knew Amara would've wanted the least struggle, Teera chose life support, to which the doctor said calmly, *You understand that this will only prolong her death*. She shook her head, unable to explain that long ago, as a child, she had learned death was inevitable—sooner or later everyone was going to die—but if she could live just a bit longer, then it was worth all the fight.

She didn't have the peace of mind to explain this to the doctor, so she kept shaking her head, until he complied with her wish. Less than an hour after they'd hooked her up, Amara took her last breath, so long and slow it sounded like a sigh, a yawn before falling into the dark void of sleep, into that silent, unobserved journey.

Death, Teera realizes now, was only a second's moment, its certainty registered on the machine with a bleep. Life is the prolonged voyage, the unhurried return to the beginning.

It is evening, and the Old Musician returns alone to the *naga* steps. He scans the shoreline, noting the debris—plastic bags, water bottles, old nylon nets, a rusted bicycle wheel—partially hidden in the mud and grass near him. He is suspicious of everything he sees, fearing a discovery much worse than a gun. In the river, where a few days earlier the little girl stood on her water buffalo, he discerns a woman standing on the stern of her boat, a metal bowl in her hand, and for a split second he is confused—*How much time has passed? Has the girl aged into a woman?*—only to realize they are not the same person. The distance between him and the woman is not much, certainly near enough for him to be privy to the choreography of her ritual, but the sense of privacy she embodies allows them each their separate solitude.

It appears she has just finished washing her face and arms, and now with her wet hand is smoothing back her hair. Then, from the waist of her sarong, she extracts a pinkish scarf and begins to cover her head in the way a Cham woman covers herself, tucking in the edges so that when she's done only the oval of her face is showing. In her colorful batik sarong and embroidered white shirt, she appears ageless, serene as a minaret at midnight. He knows her, or more accurately, she is a familiar figure, her home the brightly painted wooden sampan she shares with her husband and three small grandchildren. Despite their frequent encounters, she's never once spoken with the Old Musician, and he never dares engage her, conscious of her faith and the restrictions she must observe. But on many occasions he has spoken with the husband, who

often brings their boat to moor and seek refuge along the shore during
a particularly scorching afternoon, or when there is a violent rainstorm.
Abdul Razak. A name that would have gotten a man killed during Pol
Pot's regime. A birth name that he has reclaimed since he survived the
decimation of his people, and therefore, as he calls it, *niam chivit*. "My
life name, through which I honor Allah for every breath I take."

The Cham fisherman is as light-footed as he is soft-spoken, and
the Old Musician sees him emerging now with a broom from under
the woven rattan roof that arches over the middle section of the vessel.
Abdul Razak gathers his nets and fishing tools into one corner by the
entrance and begins sweeping the floorboard.

When he's finished sweeping, the Cham fisherman puts away his
broom, rinses himself with water from a bucket, and goes back inside. A
few minutes later he reemerges onto the bow, donning an embroidered
skullcap, a loose white shirt, and a checkered sarong. His three grandchildren trail him, two boys and a girl, between the ages of four and
eight. The little ones' parents have gone to other provinces in search of
more stable work.

At the sound of a distant call to prayer, the wife enters the roofed
enclosure. In that constricted space, she will address her God, seek His
boundless refuge. Near the prow, Abdul Razak kneels down and rolls
out his small square of mat, his grandchildren emulating his every move,
like little shadows of himself. He recites verses from the Quran, in a language he does not speak, his face to the distant Mecca. A spiritual origin.
A home that a man like Abdul Razak will never see, can never reach, but
a home nevertheless, for in believing he belongs somewhere, even in a
far-flung and unknowable geography, he has found his reason for being.

Perhaps home then, in the simplest and profoundest sense, is the
center of one's faith, the belief that shelters and moors a soul tossed
to drift in the open sea. The Old Musician longs for such certainty of
conviction.

The call to prayer grows more sonorous. The human voice and its
ancient, mysterious music. It unfurls across the Mekong where the river

narrows so that the Old Musician is able to hear it, catch its refrain and loop, even as the words are indecipherable to him. It must be coming from somewhere in Arei Ksatre, where, Abdul Razak told him, a small community of Muslim nomads living on the edge of the Mekong has erected a makeshift mosque of tarp and bamboo so that those like themselves without land or permanent homes can come to worship. While most humbly constructed, the mosque boasts a pair of loudspeakers, a small wooden board listing the precise times for the five daily prayers, and a bronze carving of the crescent moon and star, which the imam carries with him everywhere, Abdul Razak said, the only permanent feature of their "wandering mosque."

The singing deepens in resonance. Judging from the light, it is the call that precedes the setting sun. The Old Musician has returned to the river, hoping to catch a glimpse of the little girl and her water buffalo, that faint reverberation of his daughter, and hold it still. But this mournful echo of the soul resonating across water and sky, stretching as if toward its source, its longed-for infinity, seems providential. Then again, the mind perceives what it desires, a pattern or importance where perhaps there is none. For the moment, he feels everything—the appearance of the Razaks and their boat, the wind sending a continuous ripple in the direction of the peninsula, the porousness of the evening that makes time seem mutable—conspires to draw him back to that night, which for so long has existed only as an outline in his memory, like the missing note on the *sralai*, its tone and timbre muted, until now.

With the headlights off, Tun and his comrades eased their car slowly off the ferry to the makeshift landing on the other side of the abandoned bridge. They turned right and drove south for about two kilometers until they came to a throng of open-air huts on stilts at the river's edge, reached by bamboo walkways. During peacetime, this outdoor yet secluded eating place, frequented by young lovers, would be open from early evening to the small hours of the morning, but the fear of monsoon floods and mortar shells had left it mostly empty, abandoned. Under the moonlight, it appeared like a ghost settlement awaiting some impending arrival, an exodus from the world of the living.

Tun and his comrades got out of the Peugeot, locked the doors, and threw the key into the marsh below. Hopefully, by the time someone noticed the ditched vehicle and pried the doors open, they would've already been long gone, their path untraceable. They'd chosen a good month to journey, despite the worsening road conditions, the ground muddy and puddled with craters of rain. During monsoon season, particularly in July or August when the rain began to intensify, fighting between revolutionary forces and government troops occurred less frequently, with each side waiting for respite from the deluge to launch their attacks. On a night like this, impregnated with the possibility of a heavy downpour, the only battles were distant ones, episodically flaring the night sky with a muted glow. In the momentary quiet, one could almost believe peace was possible, imminent.

The four comrades walked back in the direction they'd just driven, weaving through the interstices of trees, their silhouettes camouflaged in the surrounding shadows, their path lit by only the moon and stars, which appeared even brighter above the darkness of the peninsula, most of it yet to be electrified. Somewhere in one of the bigger trees an owl hooted, and every time they passed a bamboo thicket, one cicada would chirp and then a whole throng would follow in a deafening symphony, as if colluding to hide the sound of their footsteps, abetting their escape. Fully aware of possible buried mines, they stuck to the routes they had carefully cased out and mapped with the help of their comrades based in clandestine cells on the peninsula. Through the dense woods, away from houses and busy roads, they risked only contact with poisonous plants and wild animals. At one point, Comrade Nuon let out a surprised shriek and promptly silenced herself with a hand over her mouth. "I think a snake just slithered across my feet," she said, by way of apology, looking embarrassed. Tun felt something bulbous and slimy—a snail most likely—clinging to the strap of his left sandal. He shook it loose.

As they proceeded, he offered his arm to Comrade Nuon, and she took it without hesitation, pressing close to him when something startled her—a branch falling in the stillness around them, a human-shaped shadow that seemed too large to be human, the meow of a kitten in the middle of nowhere. She was a young bride, following her husband, who had gone underground six months earlier, shortly after their marriage. Both had been civil engineering students, drawn to the promise that in the new Cambodia they would be able to use their education to serve the common good, designing dikes and dams that would allow for rice planting all year round.

Tun had never met Comrade Nuon's husband and yet he felt envious of the man, wondering what it was like to be loved by a woman who, even without full knowledge of where her husband was based, would give up everything to follow him into the forest. Would Channara have made such a sacrifice? Would she have blindly followed him anywhere? Left her privileged diplomatic life in Washington, DC, to join him as a penniless student returning to Cambodia those many years ago? *You'll never know now, will you?* he chastised himself. *You never gave her the chance to consider such a choice.*

He'd left America without so much as a note to her, simply vanishing, as he'd been instructed to do. *There is no future for you here,* Le Conseiller had said to him over the telephone, speaking in the even tone of those assured in their words, their power. *If you wish to have a future at all, you will return home for your father's funeral, and you will remain, give up your studies in America. I'm giving you a graceful exit from your folly. You will not say a word. You will simply vanish from her life.* The senior diplomat had refrained from mentioning Channara's name in his directive, as if it would defile his daughter by uttering it in the same breath he'd spoken Tun's name. A year later, on Channara's wedding day, standing in her room as she accused him of breaking her heart, Tun could not bring himself to tell her the reason for his silence without revealing the mute cowardice with which he had submitted to her father's demand. Even if she could forgive him for the cowardly way he'd ended their love, by then it was already too late, for she had decided on someone more deserving of her respect, a doctoral student of music at one of the universities in Washington, DC, another Cambodian who had arrived in the American capital in the fall of 1960—a year before Tun—under the auspices of Her Majesty Queen Kossamak, Cambodia's preeminent patron of the arts. Aung Sokhon, though from a humble background like Tun, possessed the serious courage of a true artist, who dared to push not only the boundary of music but that of love, trespassing class barriers and defying fearsome statesmen, to ask Channara's father for her hand in marriage.

Tun could only imagine how thoroughly Sokhon must've impressed Le Conseiller for such a union to even be considered. A less brave man would have been reduced to nothing, his future ruined before it began. During his brief sojourn in America, Tun had met Sokhon once, and though it was only in passing at an embassy function, it was clear that this reserved, contemplative young scholar, whose musical talents surpassed those of any other Cambodian musician of their generation, possessed an enormous sense of purpose as he cut through a room full of diplomats and dignitaries to greet the Cambodian ambassador and impress upon the attending throng the necessity for those who called themselves "envoys of culture" to respect the culture they purported to represent. *Your Excellency must offer a platform where artists could perform with dignity. A venue does not make a stage,* Sokhon had said, alluding to the numerous occasions when musicians like himself and Tun had had to play during an embassy dinner, amidst the din of the meal itself, their beautifully crafted melodies lost to the clatters of knives and forks, the cacophony of competing conversations. *If we do not stop to listen to our own music, how can we expect the foreigners to?* There was a sudden hush among those who had heard Sokhon's incisive words, and for a moment the Cambodian ambassador looked as if he was considering putting Sokhon in his place, but, to the relief of the crowd, he responded affably, *You are right, of course, you are absolutely right.*

During the entire exchange, Tun noted, Sokhon's composure never once flickered, as if the young scholar were standing inside an impermeable bubble. Tun realized in that moment Sokhon would become someone important, for he possessed that unassailable sense of self and vision so necessary in the pursuit of art. To a man like Sokhon, there were no boundaries, except those he drew around himself to protect his dignity and ability to create.

Tun did not have Sokhon's inviolability or courage. At times he wondered if his decision to leave, to take sides in the war, was a mislaid attempt to rectify his own failure of character. He had been unable to stand up to Le Conseiller, a weakness that had cost him the only woman he had ever loved—would ever love—and now he was taking a stance against all the injustices of his society, against the cruel tyranny of a class to which a man like Le Conseiller belonged.

The four comrades had reached an intersection between a temple and another ferry dock, smaller than the ones by the bridge, and quickly turned left to avoid exposure on the open road. Finding the narrow footpath they'd noted during their reconnaissance visit, they slipped into it single file, like ants into a crack, moving in sequence through untamed woods and carefully cultivated orchards. Last in the queue—with Comrade Nuon and the other two men a meter or so ahead of him—Tun had the complete solitude to examine the course he had traveled these past years. He searched his memory for overlooked opportunities, possible second chances.

During Channara's visit to his apartment that day after their chance encounter at Chaktomuk, Tun could hardly resist the desire to take her into his room and make love to her. If Suteera had not been with them, he might've found the mad courage to do just that, for in that mined, embattled geography of his heart, she was never his *songsa* but his wife. *You should've married me*, he wanted to tell her. *You should've been my wife.* Channara must have felt his insanity for she suddenly brought Sokhon into the conversation, mentioning how her husband had finally received his doctorate in musicology and was now teaching at the University of Phnom Penh, as well as holding an advisory post in the Ministry of Culture. Tun felt a jab of regret, remembering his abandoned studies, his unrealized dreams. Channara, conscious of what she had done, mumbled an apology, explaining she hadn't meant anything by it. *Oh, la bonté, regardez l'heure! Où est passé l'après-midi?* She took the opportunity then to say good-bye. *Au revoir, monsieur,* Suteera murmured solemnly, echoing her mother, who had suddenly chosen to speak in a foreign tongue, as if this would somehow make their farewell seem less intimate. Tun could only offer a silent nod in return. That was the last time he'd seen Channara.

Second chances, he realized now, favor the brave. The four had reached Al-Azhar Mosque on the eastern shore of Chruay Chongvar. A shadow emerged from the thicket of banana trees across the road and introduced himself as their "comrade in the movement." There was no exchange of aliases, for aliases were numerous and deciduous as leaves. The young revolutionary, who looked to be in his early twenties, examined their clothing and, judging the simple cotton pants and shirts—peasant clothes—to be appropriate for the journey, handed the men each an embroidered skullcap and Comrade Nuon a white cotton head scarf. "Just in case," he said, and they understood this to mean that when necessary they would put on the head wear and pretend to be Cham fisher folk. It was an effective disguise, as fishermen traversed the river at all hours, and Chams were not usually suspected of being Communists. Those who joined the underground movement, like the young comrade before them, felt that for too long their people were pushed to the periphery, their history and culture effaced, and now, with talk of revolution and a just, egalitarian society emerging from the chaos, saw the opportunity to play a more central role. But the recent attacks on their religion from within the movement, particularly the ban on praying five times a day, had led to numerous defections and kept countless other Chams away.

Nodding for them to follow, the young revolutionary ducked back into the banana thicket and led them down an incline to a long canoe covered and hidden beneath the curve of a mangrove, whose twisted roots were partly swallowed by the rising water from the monsoon. An old fisherman stepped forward, blinking at their tilted silhouettes on uneven ground, and, recognizing the young Cham, beckoned them onto the canoe. Tun sensed the old fisherman was not one of them, not a Communist, but someone sympathetic to their cause. The two Muslims exchanged greetings, *Salaamu alaikum, Alaikum es-salaam.* An alliteration of goodwill and wishes, Tun heard in the emotion, the words foreign to his ears. Then, with nothing more said, the old fisherman took to the oars and, slowly, they glided from under the shadow of the mangrove out onto the open water, its smooth surface illuminated by the heavens and the intermittent flares of distant explosions.

Tun kept his eyes on the peninsula, peaceful and seemingly unreachable as another world despite its nearness. Through a clearing he glimpsed the minaret of Al-Azhar Mosque, the carved crescent moon cradling the star at the top, in the aureole of the real moon, full and encompassing. A dream, he told himself. He'd journeyed into a landscape that harbored not one moon but two, where a self could exist both as a fragmented sliver and as a complete whole, not contradictions but inverted reflections of the same truth. Yes, it was possible to love someone and at the same time let her go. First Channara. Now his daughter. He thought of her curled up in her bed, her body embracing sleep. *Sita . . . my soul, my shattered self.*

Teera hears a familiar, playful *beep-beep* from a motorcycle and spots Narunn among the crowds, waving to her from the back of his black Honda Nighthawk. She recognizes him even with his face hidden inside his helmet. They have agreed to meet at the pavilion and will later choose a restaurant nearby for dinner. He wedges the Nighthawk—the one extravagance in his otherwise self-deprived existence—into a space between two parked cars, alights from his seat, secures his helmet to the handlebar next to the spare one he always carries, and strolls toward the pavilion.

"Oun," he greets, hand smoothing his hair into place, eyes luminous as if drawing light from the silvery strands at his temples.

Oun. As always, her heart flutters at the word. Its familial tenderness, its shy intimations. Little Sister. Darling. Wife. You peel away the concentric layers of meaning and find your place in its folds. And the way Narunn says it—in its breathless wholeness as if the sentiment is vastly larger than the word can ever contain—makes Teera feel she is all these.

"I drove by a bit earlier, honked and waved," Narunn tells her, "but you seemed completely preoccupied with a little boy. My competition, perhaps?"

She shrugs noncommittally.

"Anyway, I went around the block several times, until a space opened up to park. Didn't mean to keep you waiting."

Teera does not tell him that she came a good bit earlier than planned, hoping that by walking around the riverfront she would remember more of the scene with her parents that had flashed across her mind several days ago when she was with Narunn at his apartment. Instead she blurts out—"I think the boy has cancer! Or something grave like that. He just has that look, like he's never going to get better, and he knows it, and his mother knows it. I think they're important, powerful people. Certainly very wealthy." Confusion furrows her brow. "But they seemed utterly at the mercy of fortune, or in this case, misfortune. *Oun anet*," she adds guiltily.

Narunn inclines his head a bit, looks at her, smiles. "You feel for everyone."

"Shouldn't I?" she murmurs, somewhat to herself, her heart pulled in a conflict of empathy. "Is it wrong?"

"Why?—Because they are rich?"

"I don't know."

"In a place like this," Narunn says, surreptitiously hooking his little finger into hers, "illness seems the only constant democracy. It affects everyone the same way. And in the absence of reason—when we don't know how or why one is afflicted, or what's the cure—compassion is the only appropriate response."

They stand now side by side, their gazes on a dinner-cruise boat gliding downstream, his small finger swinging hers. She's been careful not to touch him in public, conscious of tradition, how they'd be perceived. Yet, she can't look at him without feeling a surge of desire, this ever-growing belief that she is meant to love him, he who shares her history, who understands her loss and yet carries his wisdom with such levity that his nearness makes her feel she can rise above any sorrow.

"Are you sure you're a doctor, and not a monk?" she says after a moment, keeping a straight face, her gaze still on the water.

"I told you I was an impostor." He takes full hold of her hand and pulls her toward the side entrance of the pavilion, as if suddenly forgetting their age, the restraint they've tried so hard to maintain. "Come—let's get some juice!"

They cross the street to a row of carts selling fruits and drinks at the corner of the grassy park directly opposite the Royal Palace. All the vendors seem to know Narunn, greeting him with warmth and affection.

"Ah, we thought you'd given up on the rest of us and joined the sangha for good." He is their brother, their nephew, their son. "Can't you see he's married now?" Eyes wide, Teera turns to Narunn, expecting him to correct their mistaken assumption, and when he doesn't, looking as mischievous as they are, she reddens.

Noticing this, the coconut vendor, with limbs as sinewy and brown as coconut trunks, intercepts: "Who will you make rich today?" Narunn chuckles. "I believe you are the lucky man, uncle. Two coconuts, please." He looks to Teera for confirmation; she nods, grateful for the change of subject. The vendor pulls out the smallest pair hidden beneath a pile of young green fruits, expertly slices the tops off with his cleaver, plunges a fat straw inside each, and hands them to Teera and Narunn. "Dwarf coconuts, you remember?" he says, sensing Teera's forgetfulness, her time away from this land, which they all seem to have guessed. "The last two from my tree this season." Teera takes a sip, eyebrow raised when the intensity of the sweetness hits her. She nods. *Yes, I remember now.* And just as she thinks this, she recalls a similar scene from childhood of her drinking juice from a banana-leaf cone on a busy street corner. Something citrusy tickles her nostrils. Is it an actual orange she smells? Or a memory? She takes another sip from the coconut. Waits . . . but nothing.

Narunn tries to pay, but the vendor won't hear of it. "My treat today," he says, with a toothless grin to Teera. "See, you've brought me luck already," Narunn tells her.

They thank the coconut vendor, and as they turn to leave, a young man in a wooden wheelchair rolls toward them. "Vichet!" Narunn greets. "How are you?—Would you like a coconut?—Or some other fruits, perhaps?" The young man shakes his head, laughing, his eyes soulful, melancholy, despite his youth and outward cheerfulness. "Thank you, but I just want to say hello to your wife." Teera opens her mouth to correct him, but Narunn exclaims, "It has been a while since we last saw each other!" He turns to Teera, gesturing at the young man's collection of grasshoppers made from woven palm leaves bobbing on sticks as thin as wires. "Oun, Vichet is an excellent craftsman. You can give him straw and he'll turn it into something wonderful." The young man blushes and, taking a grasshopper from the bamboo column tied to the front of his wheelchair, gives it to Teera. "May I pay for this?" she asks. Vichet shakes his head—"That one is not for sale." Their gazes meet for a second, and then he looks away, seeming suddenly conscious of the short stumps that are left of his legs. "Vichet works for an organization that trains the disabled to make traditional handicrafts," Narunn explains, obviously proud. "His grasshoppers are quite popular among tourists. Perfect traveling companions. The grasshoppers, I mean. Not the tourists."

"Your wife is lovely," Vichet murmurs, stealing a glance at Teera.

"You flirt!" Narunn slaps him on the shoulder, and to her says, "I'd better take you away before this boy breaks your heart, and mine." Behind them the other vendors laugh, echoing Vichet's sentiments—"Lovely indeed! No wonder you've kept her hidden from us! Bring her back soon, Doctor."

"Not a chance!" Narunn waves. "Good-bye, everyone!" He guides Teera across the traffic, one hand holding the coconut, the other protectively on the small of her back. They trace a straight line along the pedestrian crossing—which no one respects—giving way to cars and trucks, letting the motorbikes and *tuk-tuks* and other smaller vehicles weave around them. "You know everybody!" Teera exclaims through the din, the grasshopper bobbing on its stick above her coconut, as if attempting to drink from it.

"That's what happens when you've lived in one place for as long as I have. You could say I was among the original inhabitants, when Phnom Penh was still a ghost city. Everyone knew me as the orphaned bachelor—*komlos komprea*—and now I'm gray-haired, still living alone, unmarried. Forever an orphan in their eyes. Naturally, they're all worried, and more than a bit curious."

They reach the other side of the road. "But you *told* them you are. Married, I mean." Teera tries not to show her bafflement, but her voice betrays her. "It seems . . . unnecessary, not to mention untruthful." The grasshopper nods, agreeing.

"Oun, I'm sorry." Narunn turns to face her, palm grazing her forearm.

"I got carried by the moment. I really am sorry. But I didn't want to ruin their happiness." He looks down at his feet. "Nor mine, I suppose."

Teera doesn't know what to say to this, so she takes another sip of the coconut juice.

"I know you'll leave," he continues after a moment, his voice even quieter now. "Return to America. Your life is not here. I know this. When that time comes, if needed I'll find a way to explain your absence. But they won't ask, beyond, *How is your wife? Why are there no babies?*—In a teasing way, of course! We—the Cambodians here—have learned to live with a permanent sense of impermanency. Any one of us could lose our life—or, like Vichet, the one thing that matters most to us—just crossing this traffic. So we've become a bit greedy: we seize whatever happiness we can, in the moment." He looks at her, eyes pleading. "Forgive me?"

Teera nods but does not tell him she has no plan to return to America just yet, that this morning she went to a travel agency a few blocks from here to change her return ticket to an open date, that she's not offended, just cautious, for she too knows what it's like to live with an abiding sense of loss. She takes his hand, and they walk along the promenade, sipping their coconut juice, at times loudly, like children. She knows also that his letting everyone believe they are husband and wife is a way of respecting her, giving her a place in his life. In their language, *songsa*—"lover"—is a word that prefigures heartbreak, separation.

"What happened to Vichet?" she asks after a while.

Narunn heaves, shaking his head. "A long story. A sad one. But, to put it simply, he was a runner, out running in a city with hardly any sidewalks, and where there are, they're overtaken by cars and trucks. The bigger the vehicle the more rights you claim and, as you've witnessed, those on their feet have no rights whatsoever. But here's the crazy thing—Vichet *was* on a sidewalk when he ran that morning. A Hummer thundered down the street in the wrong direction, and a Land Cruiser, trying to get out of the way, veered onto the sidewalk, lost control, crushed his legs. It happened near the White Building. A boy from my same block rushed in to alert me. When I arrived at the scene of the accident, I saw there was little I could do, except to bind and bandage the legs to minimize the bleeding as much as possible, and give him local anesthesia for the pain. He needed to be taken to a hospital to be operated on, by proper surgeons."

"How awful!"

"The one miracle is that he came out alive, if not altogether intact, physically or emotionally. But gone are his hopes of ever competing internationally in a race."

"When Amara was sick but still working, I had to fill in for her one time and took her client—a Cambodian man affected by childhood polio—to have him fitted for one of these new graphite leg braces. It was amazing to see how well he walked in it. It could still be possible for Vichet to run, to compete again."

"Yes, perhaps in America anything is possible. But here . . ."

Here, it's a different reality. How could she forget? She feels astoundingly American, ridiculous in her obstinate hope. It was the one thing that Amara, in her role as a surrogate parent, had cultivated in her while she was growing up. *Good grades aren't enough.* In her junior year of high school, bending over college applications, she related to Amara what her high school guidance counselor had told her. *If I wanted to go to an Ivy League school, we'd have to have a lot of money saved up in a trust fund.* Teera didn't even know what a trust fund was. *You will go,* Amara replied simply, never pausing in her task as she stood washing rice at the kitchen sink before setting it to cook. *You just have to get in.* Quiet, stubborn hope, even in the face of seemingly irreversible defeat, is Teera's inexhaustible inheritance.

"He can't reclaim what he lost, but the NGO he's with now is his best chance for recovery. They're teaching him, and others like him, to live with the loss, to discover a hidden talent and nurture it. Funny, with his legs gone, Vichet has learned he's quite skilled with his hands. You know he built that wheelchair himself."

"He does seem remarkably skilled." After a moment's thought, she asks, "What happened to the drivers?"

"The Hummer never stopped, never even slowed down to see what had taken place in the wake of its reckless power. The owner of the Land Cruiser was utterly distraught, scared out of his wits. He could barely drive when he took us—Vichet and myself—to Calmette Hospital. He was the one who paid for everything."

Teera shakes her head, confounded. "There's so much cruelty, so much generosity. I don't think I will ever understand our country, our people."

"Neither will I," Narunn echoes. "Yet, to hear you say this gives me a strange serenity . . . you know, like I'm not alone . . . you see what I see." He draws her attention toward a bird vendor with a collection of bamboo cages around her, and a little girl standing nearby contently blowing bubbles. "You see them? They are mother and daughter, a team. The little one catches the birds, and the mother brings them to sell, to be released by those seeking to make merits, answers to their prayers. At times, I feel we—all of us—are like those sparrows, our imprisonment and our freedom intimately linked, willed by the same hands, the same forces."

They come to one of the concrete benches spaced at long intervals along the promenade, remnants of the old days. They toss the empty coconuts into the garbage can nearby and sit down on the bench. High above them, the flags of various nations hemming the length of the promenade flap in the steady breeze, the sound reminiscent of distant helicopters, the pulse of war. Now that others might be assuming them husband and wife, Teera feels brave enough to rest her head on Narunn's shoulder. She looks up, tapping the grasshopper against her leg, and searches among the fluttering colors. She spots France, Japan, China, Vietnam, Russia, the United Nations, a chronicle of power imposed and contested on this land. The US flag flies several poles down to their right. Operation Menu, the initial phase of intense bombing was called. US forces had been bombing Cambodian territory for four years already when, in March 1969, Operation Menu took this to a new level with carpet bombing by heavily loaded B-52s, first in the border region, targeting Vietcong supply routes. Richard Nixon had ordered a lavish banquet for Cambodia, one incendiary feast after another. The first was code-named Breakfast, followed by Lunch, then Supper, Dinner, Dessert, and Snack.

These only served to whet the appetite for destruction, and the bombing intensified further over the following years, extending deep into the country, including the tragically mistaken target of Neak Leung.

"You are right," Teera tells him, her gaze on the river again, following the dinner-cruise boat gliding downstream.

"About what?"

"Captivity and escape, how they intertwine." Her eyes catch sight of a flock of birds moving south, past the confluence of the three rivers, and she knows that if they keep going, tracing the curvature of the Mekong, they will reach Neak Leung. "A government that ensnared us into its grand war has given so many of our people their freedom."

"The Americans did not create the Khmer Rouge," Narunn says. "We can't escape responsibility for that violence, that madness which is our own."

"I know that. Yes, as a people, perhaps we would've suffered anyway, sooner or later."

"But you're saying the American bombing brought it sooner."

She nods, and then shakes her head, entangled by all she can't express. "I look at my life and feel unlucky to have been born into that time, that suffering. I want to lay blame but I don't know where, on what or whom. Then I think I was so lucky to survive it, and escape. There are moments I'm convinced that my escape would not have happened if not for the American role in the war. It feels both consoling and *wrong* to think this way. Yet, it's what I cling to when nothing can pull me out of despair. I know it doesn't make sense. But anger . . . sinks me even deeper. So I feel grateful because sometimes it's the only lifeline, the only way to live."

They sit in silence for a long while, her head on his shoulder, his face buried in her hair. She feels him softly kissing her—inhaling her scent, her entire self, through the strands.

"One day we will try the dinner cruise," he whispers, "but now I want to take you somewhere more special."

After a seemingly endless journey by both water and land, Tun arrived at his base, a partially cleared area under the cover of a dense teak forest. It seemed like an ancient world, a landscape of centuries before, and he had to remind himself it was still 1973. *August 1973.* It was a brilliant morning, with sunlight bouncing off the foliage bejeweled in raindrops left from the early dawn. Campfires dotted the ground, with tendrils of smoke rising in the heat and humidity. Hammocks clustered beneath large swaths of army tarps tenting from branches like the wings of giant bats at rest. On his left, a stream ran parallel to the encampment, the water clear as glass so that he could see through to the rocks and pebbles lining the streambed, an undulation of blues and grays. A young soldier clad in black perched on the edge, drinking from his cupped hand, his gun cradled in the crook between his abdomen and thighs. Another knelt on a crossing made of felled young teaks, head bowed, contemplating his reflection amidst the lily pads. A lone dark pink blossom appeared almost red against the black of his uniform and the surrounding forest.

Tun walked past a group gathered around a fire, sharing a large cooked tuber they'd just extracted from the embers, the brown, bark-like skin partly burned and dusted with ashes. Each broke off a piece, hot with steam, and passed it to the next. He nodded at them; one or two returned his greeting, while the rest just stared. How young they were, many barely into their teens, a few appearing no more than nine or ten, including the soldier leading him now through the encampment. There was a hardness to these boys; they seemed interchangeable, disconnected from one another, without perceivable rearing or roots. Tun imagined they had been hewn from the dark gray rocks jutting out of the earth like half-buried giant tortoiseshells from a prehistoric time.

Despite the soldiers everywhere, a sense of stillness and silence pervaded, as if the immensity of the forest muted all human endeavor and expression. Likewise, Tun felt minuscule, a speck in the formidable verdure, where young teak leaves unfurled three times bigger than his hands. To his right, beyond the clearing, he discerned some huts, barely visible through the screen of trees, and he guessed that they housed more senior soldiers, commanders, and cadres. Weapons and ammunition were gathered in small mounds, scattered across the encampment, some covered with tarps, some with twigs and leaves, others left exposed to the elements so that the words painted on the wooden crates had begun to bleed or fade away.

He followed the boy soldier past a storage depot, a rectangular roof of woven teak leaves anchored by four posts. Underneath were large plastic bags of rice and stashes of *boîtes de conserve*, as his friends in the military would refer to the canned goods, which they secretly sold by the truckload to the insurgent forces. He couldn't be certain whether this stockpile had been captured from defeated government troops, but judging by the condition, he guessed it had arrived through an exchange between supposed "enemies." Tun remembered one particular night many months earlier when he and another comrade—assigned as escorts by the leader of their underground cell—had ridden in a jeep with a colonel in the Lon Nol army, guiding a camion full of supplies with "US" markings on the canvas bags and tin boxes to a secret drop-off site atop a hill along the national road to Kampot Province. At the appointed hour, the government soldiers had emptied the truckload carefully at the edge of the ravine, where a group of revolutionary fighters waited to receive the *cadeau*. There was no shortage of corrupt high-ranking army officers ready to sell whatever stashes they could get their hands on, but there were also those, like the colonel, who were sympathetic to the cause and, with insurgent forces now controlling most of the country's territory, had put their stake with the inevitable victors.

Tun's gaze flitted again to the soldier kneeling on the crossing over the stream. There was something devotional to his posture, his arms together in front of him, as if in prayer, hands tucked between his knees. No one paid attention to the figure, and for a moment Tun wondered if he was looking at a mirage. He blinked, but the soldier remained where he was, head bowed, his entire being expectant, waiting. Despite the temporary stillness, Tun suspected at any moment they would all pick up and leave, taking whatever supplies they could carry, leaving the rest to be swallowed by the seething, tangled mass of vines and undergrowth. And for the first time he was grateful that his daughter was not with him. Once or twice during his travels he wondered if it had been a fatal mistake not to bring her along. He knew of others who had gone underground with their family members in tow. Had he demanded it of Om Paan, she would've packed up Sita and come with him. But after all they'd been through, he could not uproot them again, take away the home and stability they both so cherished. Besides, if all proceeded as planned, he would go back to Phnom Penh to fetch them in a year's time, and by then he would've seen for himself what he was asking them to abandon their life for. Presently, there was only this forest and the battle-gutted landscape he'd traversed to arrive.

In Kompong Cham, in a district known as "Jewels of the Bees," where he'd parted ways with Comrade Nuon and the two others, Tun had walked through a village like the surface of the moon. Huge bomb craters transformed by the rains into ponds where children swam and hunted for frogs among colossal chunks of shrapnel. Hillocks sliced by rocket-propelled grenades, their tips half plunged into the earth like banana flower heads pitched from a great height by some immortal strength. Inundated rice paddies harboring overturned tanks and armored personnel carriers that resembled the carapaces of gargantuan crabs. In another district, he'd charged through a burning village caught in the crossfire. A mother, running from the village, pausing to collect pieces of meat from the carcass of a water buffalo blown up by a hand grenade, salvaging what food she could to later feed her children. A father screaming for someone to shoot him, cursing soldiers on all sides, his dead boy in his outstretched arms. *Why don't you kill me too?—Kill me, you cowards!*

After what he'd seen, Tun felt the encampment was a kind of sanctuary, however imposing the forest might appear. He wondered where the others had ended up, if they'd arrived at places as untamable, as concealed. They were separated so no permanent bond would form among the four of them, as tended to happen with traveling companions. From the start, they had all understood that there was to be no friendship, only camaraderie; no loyalty, except to the Organization. Loyalty was absolute, secrecy paramount. These were the most palpable fortifications—aside from the jungle itself—surrounding the encampment. He'd been shocked to observe that the soldiers, most of them rangy and underfed, would confine themselves to sharing a single burnt wild root, or even forgo food altogether, while the supplies of rice and canned goods gathered layers of twigs and leaves and dirt. What he'd understood as ideological rhetoric—*We do not take from the communal pile; we eat when our brothers eat*—appeared to command inviolable allegiance, restraining them from siphoning a can here, a can there. On top of this, Tun did not know where he was, and he imagined the same was true of the others.

In the final leg of his journey, under the dawn's drizzle, he'd been driven blindfolded in a partially covered oxcart, and when he alighted a short while later, landing unsteadily on soft earth cushioned with tiny scaly leaves, the black cloth removed from his eyes by fingers as weightless as feathers, he found himself kneeling under a thick dome of overgrown bamboo, the rain replaced by bright morning light filtering through the sieve-like canopy, the oxcart disappearing through a narrow opening in the forest, the squeaks and moans of its wheels growing more distant with each rotation. Tun had blinked in confusion, thinking himself inside an enormous cage, an aviary one might encounter in a myth or dream, as sparrows hopped from branch to branch all around him. Had he been captured? Was his enemy a giant?

A young boy had stepped from behind him and stood off to one side, waiting and watching, the black cloth that had been Tun's blindfold now dangling in his small hand, an AK47 cradled across his stomach in that intimate way a peasant boy might hold a newborn calf. Tun recalled the lightness of the boy's fingers when he'd untied the blindfold, and now it was obvious to him that these fingers, long and agile, were more suited to a musical instrument and its intricate choreography of notes than the monotonous dissonance of the battlefield. He suddenly regretted not having brought with him at least a simple bamboo flute. Yet, he couldn't imagine playing any of those instruments from home without the presence of his daughter, for she'd made them her own, addressing each like a beloved sibling. To the *sralai*, the tiny ivory oboe he'd brought her from Ratanakiri, he'd once heard her ask: "*Sralai srey oun somlanh*—you little one I love—what song will you sing me today?" This memory alone nearly knocked him off balance again.

The boy nodded for Tun to get up and follow. Without further exchange, they pushed deeper into the canopy, tracing its curve and narrowing cavity, until the bamboo gave way to hardwood trees, a forest dominated by ancient teaks, and, in the midst of it, the encampment.

Finally, Tun felt safe to ask where he was, and in reply the soldier mumbled some letters and numbers designating the region and zone, but nothing more. Silence appeared to be the boy's native tongue. Tun had decided then it was best to observe, take in as much as he could. Things would become clear soon enough. So he'd hoped.

Now, making his way through the encampment, he wondered where their leader was, who among these half-starved, inured fighters was the commanding cadre. Could it be the soldier on the teak crossing? For the third time, his gaze strayed toward the figure bowing over the water: he certainly had the adult patience to hold himself in such prolonged stillness. As they got closer Tun realized the soldier did indeed seem older than he had earlier appeared at a distance, perhaps in his twenties or possibly thirties, with a physique more sculpted, more muscled than the flat geometry of a young adolescent. He wished the soldier would look up, and just as he thought this, a shot reverberated in the forest across the stream. Perhaps an engine had misfired, but there was no car or truck anywhere, no road in that impenetrable wilderness. For some seconds it became even more silent and still, the forest seeming to hold its breath.

Even more curious, the boy leading him paused in his steps and turned opposite from where the shot had echoed. Tun could not catch his gaze, and when he looked around at the others he noted that they were doing the same, turning away from the origin of the firing sound, as if denying the sound. Before he could make sense of it, a soldier emerged from the forest across the stream, a pistol in his hand, and strode angrily toward the crossing. One of the camp leaders, Tun thought. A battalion commander. Everything about him spoke of war; he was all combat and rage. "Your turn!" he shouted, but the soldier on the crossing did not flinch and kept his head bowed. His uniform—the loose-fitting black pajamas of the revolution—told Tun he was not a captured enemy from the government side, a prisoner of war, but one of their own. But what was his crime? What had he stolen? A can of sardines or condensed milk, a Zippo lighter from one of the boxes strewn on the ground among the supplies? And what did it mean, "your turn"? Was there another offender, another captive? The commander stood over the bowed man, the gun now pointing at his head. "Get up!" Still, the offender remained, immovable as the gray boulder a few feet behind him in the middle of the stream. Tun looked around, stunned that not a single person acknowledged what was happening. The commander caught Tun's gaze, their eyes locked, then all of sudden he lifted his pistol, arm outstretched and straight as an arrow, and pointed the gun at Tun—"You, over here!" Tun froze. The commander eyed the boy soldier, a flicker of exchange passed between them, and the boy scrambled over to Tun, nudging him forward with the barrel of his AK47.

"Shoot him," the commander ordered, thrusting his pistol into Tun's hands, and it was then, standing on the crossing, that Tun saw the wrists of the man kneeling before them were bound tightly with rope. "I said shoot the traitor!"

Tun felt his limbs go numb, heavy as lead, his entire body inert with fear. *This cannot be happening.* And yet, he knew it *was* happening: this was not some nightmare he could wake up from but madness in the making. The commander grabbed his hands, imprisoned them inside his own, and, lacing their fingers around the pistol, shot the kneeling offender in the side of his head. The man fell on his side, a chunk of his skull gone, blood splattering, seeping into the tight crevices between the felled teaks. "Anyone else want to defect?" the commander thundered, eyes sweeping all gathered, his pistol back in his hand. Silence. Every face was a blank. "I didn't think so," he murmured, and then to Tun— "Never point your weapon at anyone you're not ready to kill. Let this be your first lesson." He looked at the lifeless body at their feet and kicked it into the water. The lily pads sank beneath it, lost in the ballooning of black clothes, and then, as if by some madness or miracle, the lone dark pink blossom broke through the surface again, wrestling to recover the rays of the sun.

Narunn has brought Teera to a house on the southern shore of Chruay Chongvar, one of the few traditional teak homes still standing, and beautifully preserved, amidst throngs of new construction. It belongs, he told her, to a magnificent woman who has taken him in as one of her own. Yaya, everyone calls her, short for Lokyay Tuat—"Great-Grandmother." When they are introduced, Teera is surprised to find that the tiny soul hunching before her, with back curved like a sickle and head shaved bald in keeping with Buddhist tradition for the elderly, is the same formidable woman she pictured through Narunn's description. It is only when Yaya embraces her that Teera feels the elder's strength, her ageless fortitude. Even more astonishing, as she holds Teera's face between her thin, fanlike hands, Yaya sticks out her tongue, revealing a hairline scar across its midsection. This wordless greeting moves Teera deeply.

Despite the long-ago injury, the elder can still speak but chooses not to say much. Instead, she smiles endlessly, lips permanently puckered between two caved cheeks as if always ready to kiss and be kissed. As she sits on the carved wooden platform under the raised teak house, the younger generations—from a middle-aged grandson who can scale the tallest palm tree on their property in mere seconds to a little baby, a great-granddaughter, just learning to walk—whirl around the diminutive matriarch like tributaries of a Great Lake, meandering in numerous directions yet always returning to their source, bringing to her the earth's treasures: berries to freshen her palate, a coronet of wild jasmines sprinkled with water to cool her exposed head, unknown bugs and beetles for her to identify, roots to add to her lacquered box of traditional cures. Yaya repays these gestures by taking her loved ones into her arms and pressing their faces into hers, inhaling their scents, as if doing so guards their lives, or some essential part of them, with her own breath.

In no time at all, Teera learns from the loquacious clan that Yaya had thirteen children, none of whom survived the Khmer Rouge. Yet, some of her grandchildren did, and they have multiplied, through marriages and births and other tenuous connections. As for Narunn, he came one day to Chruay Chongvar looking for a distant relative of his mother's who might've had a home around here, at the southern tip of the peninsula. When Yaya encountered him on the dirt road in front of their property she invited him in to meet her family, a brood of grandchildren, who explained that they were new to the land and did not know which house had belonged to whom before the war, who among their neighbors were original residents, and who were refugees like themselves. At the fall of the regime, fearing kidnappings by the remnant Khmer Rouge rebels, they had fled their village in a remote area east of the Mekong and come near the city, where it would be safer. They found the rustic setting of the peninsula preferable to the city itself, and, to their good fortune, discovered this house among overgrown trees and bushes, with a few shutters missing but otherwise in remarkable condition. They couldn't tell Narunn for certain whether the house had belonged to his kinsmen, as no one had ever come to claim it. In any case, he was welcome to stay with them, be part of their family.

"Now we welcome you also!" they declare, pulling Teera into their midst. "You're one of us!—Our foreign sister." Through their eyes, Teera begins to glimpse the melding of her divided self, the stranger to this land and the child who never left.

True to their words, they treat her like family, like she'd always been part of their clan, drawing her into competing conversations, as they dash about orchestrating a traditional country feast—food of the peasants, they say—to welcome her back to her Khmer roots. *M'rum! M'reah!*

M'ras! They take turns holding up to Teera the edible leaves, flowers, and buds sprouting wildly on their land, singing the names for her benefit in case she's forgotten, before tossing them into the various pots simmering over the clay braziers in the outdoor cooking area off the side of the house. Teera takes out the journal she carries with her everywhere in her shoulder bag, asks whether it's all right for her to jot these names down, and, when they chorus their consent, begins to scribble, feeling strangely at home with her thoughts, as if it's a natural thing, writing in such company. *Romdaeng . . . romduol . . . kjol rodek . . .*

There is music to their words, a rhythm connecting a familiar spice to a rare mountain flower and the flower to the harvest wind, whose name bears the resonance of a child's laugh. One day, she tells herself, she wants a family as large and boisterous as this, a home open to all who pass. She notes the rows of solid round teak columns holding up the house so that it appears an abode rising from the earth, an indestructible entity, protected through the years of war and abandonment by the surrounding trees, by the spirits and ghosts that took up residence. "You've dug a pond since I was last here!" she hears Narunn exclaim, and, turning, sees him pointing to a field of lotuses blooming in one corner of the property. Ravi, the eldest of Yaya's granddaughters, explains, "Yes, to give our land a breath of water"—*dangherm tik.*

Teera echoes the words in her mind, writing them down lest they escape her completely. And as she does so, one explains to the others that this scribbling of hers is the way of the *sas sar*, something she must've developed living among the "white race." Another agrees, "Yes, they read and write all the time. They record everything, not like us; we don't know our own history." Ravi's husband, the palm climber, retorts, "Oh, we know, but we'd rather not! We *choose* to forget." His cousin interjects, "*Min bomphlich kae bomphlanh*," harking back to the adage of the Khmer Rouge years. "What we can't forget they will destroy. It's self-preservation, pure and simple. We're like *prahoc*, rotten to the bone but prepared to last." Laughter erupts, and the rowdiest of the bunch offers Teera a jar of the pungent pickled fish—the quintessential condiment in

Khmer cuisine—and, gesturing to Narunn, advises, "Make sure the doctor has the courage to stomach this thing raw before you trust him with your heart." Narunn grabs him, and they tussle like boys—"You water buffalo, I'm going to make you eat mud!"

Amidst the continuing jest, Yaya beckons Teera to her. On the way here, Narunn told her that during the Khmer Rouge, Yaya, by virtue of her peasant background, was ordered to identify who among the city people exiled to her village were enemies of the Organization. She refused, instead offering her tongue to be cut off. Better, she told the soldier, than telling a lie.

Beholding this whisper of a woman on the wooden platform, Teera is amazed that Yaya not only survived that ordeal but that she has lived to such an age, her skin so deeply grooved and veined that she seems inseparable from the land. What's even more amazing is that the elder has long outlasted the soldier who grazed her tongue with his razor-sharp knife that day, who was later purged, a victim of the revolutionary cleansing he had instigated in the village.

Teera takes a seat on the wooden platform facing Yaya, her legs folded to one side, feet tucked beneath her, a gesture of propriety and respect toward the elder. Between them sits a bamboo tray of fresh spices—a profusion of scents, textures, and colors. Yaya looks past it to the journal, nodding for Teera to read. Teera is unsure if she's understood correctly. Narunn catches her eye and winks.

"It's mostly in English," she tells Yaya. "Except for a few Khmer words here and there."

Yaya smiles. It doesn't matter the language. The creases in her forehead, the delight in her eyes, the crosshatched lines around her mouth, the stillness of her hands—Teera has never met anyone who speaks with every part of her body, who conveys so much with silence.

She opens the journal to where she's tucked her pen, clears her throat, and reads—"'A breath of water' . . . So many expressions I've forgotten. I am like this land, each word recalled, excavated, lends me its breath, its life, and I hear a voice echoing the story I want to tell . . ."

Words, Teera loves them. If pressed, she will probably admit that her longest love affair has been with language. Even as a child—a quiet one at that—she was besotted by words, the way they looked and sounded, the way they caressed her ears. Eavesdropping on adult conversations, she'd snatch phrases she didn't understand, words too big for her, exceeding her emotion and years. She'd store them in her memory and, when opportunities arose, toss them like pebbles to see where they landed. Later, a refugee in America reaching to grasp the nuances and subtleties of another's tongue, she wanted not just to survive in this borrowed voice but to thrive. She studied hard, read ferociously, made daily lists of vocabulary to conquer, signed up for Speech and Debate even though she was terrified of public speaking and couldn't begin to formulate her thoughts, least of all in proper English. *You're like a sponge—you soak up everything. Your language is remarkable. And your mind . . . your mind is a steel trap*, her drama coach had said. *A steel trap*, Teera would later note in the spiral journal she kept for English class, her repository of unfamiliar phrases.

In a volunteer internship at the county courthouse, bending over the Xerox machine, leafing through applications, affidavits, and dossiers, Teera was introduced to the specificity of the legal vernacular, its exactitude and restriction. It spoke to her desire for clarity. Later, at Cornell, she entertained the possibility of studying toward a law degree. Poring over casebooks and law manuals, she'd ponder the frailty of "deposition," its merit and value relative to "interrogatories," or the providential definitiveness of "judgment." She'd fall in love too with a phrase like "description of notes," twirling it around her tongue, around the silhouette of a poem emerging in her mind, as she absentmindedly twirled a lock of hair around her pen, dreaming, composing . . . It was as if, without knowing its shape or direction, she sensed she had a story to tell, and she was keen to equip herself with the elements of exposition. As she studied history, however, submerging herself in that era whose very name was a matter of debate—the Vietnam War, the American War, the "conflict" in Southeast Asia—she learned that the things she wanted most to write about lacked fixed definition, defied simple clarity. They were only hinted at in the books she was reading, if not ignored altogether. These, she felt, are the things that gain brilliance only in darkness, acquire solidity and wholeness only when your world is destroyed, when all you have left are fragments of the life you once knew.

Love . . . hope . . . humanity. Intangible, yes, but also the building blocks of self-preservation, renewal. *These are the most durable possessions I have . . .*

Teera glances up, confused as to what she's read aloud, what she's recalled silently in her mind. Beside her, Yaya nods and, seeing Teera's hesitation, says, "*Taw tiat, chao*"—continue, grandchild. Teera's eyes smart at the last word. Fighting back the tears, she returns her gaze to the pages of her journal. *I walk into a family scene, and find the scent of home cradled in a tray of spices. A cut of fresh galangal releases a bouquet of memories. The air is filled with the aromas of my childhood, fragrances that envelop and linger, haunt my senses like ghosts . . .*

How strange, she thinks, to give voice to these words and to hear something unlike her own voice, something that has acquired a timbre of its own, as if the sentiment belongs to all who listen, not just she who's written. *I take a deep breath, inhaling the* pralung *of a lemongrass, and I feel nourished, healed, even if only in this moment.*

Teera looks up and sees that Yaya has had her eyes closed. When she opens them again, she cups Teera's face in her hands, peers deep into her eyes for what feels like an eternity, and then, as when they first greeted, sticks out her tongue, head bobbing from side to side, in the same flow and inflection as Teera's reading. It suddenly occurs to her that perhaps Yaya isn't simply showing her the scar, that perhaps this is the elder's way of taking in all the words she can't form, the truth she can't articulate. Teera is reminded of how when learning English she'd stretch and flex her tongue, preparing to sound out a new word, shaping the space for what was to come, even if in that moment she couldn't voice it.

Perhaps, Teera thinks, silence is its own voice.

Yaya lets out a laugh, a bubbling brook gushing upward from her belly, sending her sunken cheeks puffing with transient youth. From the tray of spices, she plucks out a green sprig similar to lavender, with tiny purple flowers, and gives it to Teera.

"*Ma-orm*," Teera says, smelling it. She doesn't need to write this one down. She remembers it, the earthy fragrance that recalls for her the smell of the first rain when it hits the earth and assumes its dry, sultry breath. There's a word for it in English. "Petrichor!" she exclaims, and then repeats it more slowly for Yaya.

Yaya smacks her lips, tries to articulate it, twirling her tongue round and round like a child licking ice cream, and finally gives up in a fit of giggles.

Narunn emerges from the tussle, dirt smeared across his forehead and nose, and the words of the victor chiding him—"Hah, who's eating mud now!" Narunn fires back, "I'll get you next time, brother!" And to Teera and Yaya, "What's so funny?"

Again, Yaya bubbles with laughter, leaning as if about to tip over with too much happiness. "You!" Teera tells him.

Narunn sulks off, shoulders slumped in a pretense of hurt, heading for the clay cistern by the back stairway. When he's finished cleaning himself up, he returns to the wooden platform, mopping up the excess water on his face with his shirtsleeves. The cell phone in his pants pocket begins to ring. He answers, sitting down next to Teera, and after a few seconds silently mouths to her, "Wat Nagara," before turning to give the caller his full attention.

Teera's heart lurches. The Old Musician. She hasn't been back to see him since their first confrontation. She pauses at the thought. *Was it a confrontation?* She didn't think of it that way at the time, but in retrospect it was like walking into a minefield, where a single wrong step could detonate some buried secret, destroy the fragile existence they each had built for themselves. The careful choreography of her words around his had exhausted her, and afterward she knew she would have to collect herself, summon her strength anew before another encounter. But the longer she stays away, the more she feels unkind. For all his restraint during that first meeting, she sensed his attachment to her, and for her part, she hasn't been able since to separate him from her thoughts of her father. Perhaps this is the reason she's stayed away. Melancholy fills her, pushing out the earlier gaiety.

"Yes, Venerable," Narunn says, and Teera realizes he's talking to a monk. "I'm sure it can be arranged. And yes, I'll speak with Miss Suteera . . ." At the mention of her name, Narunn turns to Teera and smiles. But she's not convinced, his solemn tone worrying her. "*Tvay bangkum*, Venerable." With this formal salutation, Narunn disconnects and slips the phone back into his pocket. "That was the Venerable Kong Oul."

"Is everything all right?" Teera asks, stopping short of blurting out, *Has something happened to the Old Musician?*

"There's a child at the temple, a new orphan, in need of a little escape from her ordeal—she has recently lost her mother—and the abbot is wondering if we could find a day to take her somewhere outside the city, somewhere fun for a three-year-old."

Three. Teera remembers that she was twelve when her mother died. "Oh, the poor thing must be so scared, so sad."

"Yes, which is why the abbot thought it might be good if I ask you to come along, to have a woman's presence. He tried to call you but there was no answer."

Teera reaches into her bag for her cell phone but then realizes she left it on the desk in her hotel room. "What happened to the child's mother?" she asks, turning back to Narunn.

He tells them what the abbot told him about the shooting that ended in the young mother's death, and the delicacy of the situation, the little girl whose life may still be in danger. Teera listens, silently horrified.

"Do you mind making an excursion to the countryside?—I know how you feel about going too far out of the city . . ."

Teera shakes her head. "Never mind. Anything I can do to help."

Narunn squeezes her hand. "Thank you."

"The little one might like Phnom Tamao," Yaya says, as she works through the tray of spices, plucking out what can be saved for another meal. "The sun bears are precious. And the gibbons . . . they make me laugh!" It's the most the elder has said all evening.

"Ah, yes, good idea!" Narunn kisses Yaya on the cheek, and to Teera explains, "There's a wildlife sanctuary in Phnom Tamao."

Just then, Ravi, presiding over the cluster of pots, announces that the dinner is ready. A bustle of movement follows, as everyone gathers on the straw mats laid out on the cleanly swept ground around the wooden platform. Excitement accompanies the parade of dishes—lemongrass snail, whole fish baked in a blanket of sea salt over charcoal, *prahoc* with kaffir lime grilled in banana leaf, the famous coconut *amok*, a variety of curries and soups.

Teera takes a deep breath, letting the aromas fill her lungs, assuage and renew her for another day. Perhaps this is all she can ever hope for—a momentary restoration to gather her strength and move forward. To live as courageously and willfully as she can in the company of those who've also suffered, and triumphed.

He keeps returning to the river. The Mekong rolls languidly, serenely, belying the dangerous undercurrents far below the surface. Even with his deteriorating sight, the Old Musician can still make out the opposite shore, where water ends and land begins, where the blue-black clumps of distant forest meet the gray patches of clouds. A landscape in silhouettes. Light contours the dark, and the dark seeps into everything.

For decades now, he has traversed the murky, treacherous terrain of his conscience, tracing and retracing countless times the routes he had taken. There had to have been such a divide—much like the mighty river before him—a chasm he crossed separating one existence from another, the known from the unknown, right from wrong.

At what point in his journey did he make the crossing to that other side from where there could be no return? The question plagues him. He is convinced it was at the encampment that morning of his arrival. That was the moment when everything changed. What human being commits a murder and afterward remains unaltered, whole? It was his first execution, the first life he'd extinguished. It does not matter that another soldier had pulled the trigger. There, on the teak crossing, his own fingers gripped the gun as surely as those of the young commander, and he felt the pulse of the metal, heard the unmistakable click, absorbed the smooth reverberation of the bullet through the compact steel chamber, as if the weapon were part of his body, as if it drew energy from him alone.

Could he have said, *No, I won't do this*? Could he have tried to reason with the young commander? Could he have fought back, wrestled free from the grip, angled the gun in a different direction? Could he have nudged or kicked the kneeling captive into the stream and let him try to escape? Even with his hands bound, the prisoner could have run. His legs were not tied. Or were they? . . . Still. He—Tun—could've done something. Anything. But instead he froze, allowing the will of another to overtake him completely. And, in his numb silence, in his inaction, he became an abettor. A murderer.

That moment then, that brief instant in which he could have acted but did nothing, was the chasm, the moral void where he slipped and fell, plunging into a vicious depth, only to emerge on the opposite shore, unable to return to who he had been, the self that believed he'd left his daughter to fight for something good.

What happened next hardly mattered to him at the time. He remembers vaguely being led off the teak crossing, a shove on his shoulder, the tip of a gun nudging him—*left, right, straight head, right again . . . Move faster!* Whose gun it was, he didn't know. He dared not look back. He heard the voice of the commander from far behind him, ordering the soldiers to remove the "body of the traitor" from the stream so that it would not poison the water. *Throw it in the forest with the other one!* A shuffle of feet, the sound of water lapping, the collective heave of effort pulling the corpse ashore, hauling it away through leaves and branches.

How was it possible that he was able to keep walking, to take one step after another? He arrived at a hut cordoned off from the rest of the camp by a fence made of roughly hewn bamboo stakes and barbed wire. A prison, he thought. But it had an almost lived-in feel to it. Within the barbed fence, in one corner a scraggly vegetable patch persisted, with tiny nascent leaves among old ones, resuscitated by the onset of rains, it seemed. He noted some pumpkin vines, tomato and chili shrubs, a clump of lemongrass, and random sprouts of *ma-orm*. A domestic plot. A home, amidst the untamed, untamable jungle. How was this possible? He could not think straight. Were his eyes deceiving him? What day was this? Where was he? Was it only this morning that he'd arrived? It seemed a lifetime had passed. No, he reminded himself, a *life* had passed. A man had lived and died, and time did not hasten or slow; it moved with the same steady gait. His mind whirled.

In another corner sat a pair of plastic gasoline containers with their mouths sawed off and a bamboo yoke fastened to the handles. Buckets to draw water from the stream. Blood filled his vision. He saw again the body falling, breaking the mirrorlike surface, the water lily radiant in its singular, ostentatious beauty.

Inside the hut, a horrible stench hit him, and in the semidark he thought he must've walked into an outhouse. They'd brought him here to let him defecate before shooting him. But why? So he wouldn't soil his clothes? Clothes they would salvage after he was dead. His eyes adjusted to the dark and he saw that the hut was completely bare except for a plank of wood covering a hole in one corner of the dirt floor. Flies buzzed around it, and an incessant hum rose from beneath. He held his breath, quelling the urge to retch.

"This is where you'll start," a voice said from behind him. Tun turned around and saw a young soldier, older than the one who'd led him into the camp, a face he recognized from among the crowd eating the burnt tuber earlier. "You can't leave the hut for any reason," the soldier muttered. "You'll do all your business there." He nodded to the wood plank. A brief pause, and then he added, in a tone that sounded almost conciliatory, "You'll stay put until your time is up, and this will depend on how well you're taking it."

Until my time is up? The question formed in his head but he could not summon the voice to express it. His throat felt tight, blocked, and he knew if he opened his mouth only a prolonged scream would emerge. But when had he last screamed aloud? Long ago he'd learned from his father to bear the anguish, to prove his strength against the pain. If he screamed now, it would reach all the way to that time, when he was a boy crouching under his father's whip.

The soldier walked to the doorway, pistol hanging at his side. A handgun similar to the commander's. "*Lutdom kluan,*" he said, using the revolutionary lingo, then switching to the gentler everyday language. "*Ot thmut.*" With this, the youth left, barring the door shut from the outside.

Discipline yourself. Endure. Tun puzzled over the ambiguity—the duplicity of words. Was the soldier trying to help him? Was this advice, cloaked in the tone of a command?—*Do what it takes, and you will survive.* Or was it merely an order?—*Endure. Live.*

Tun continued to stand there, rooted to the spot where he'd been left. If he moved, he would buckle. He must first find something to hang on to. A thought. A melody. Even a single note would do. *Dtum. Dtum. Dtum.* He tries mimicking the beats of a drum, a large bass drum that leads a funerary procession. A man had died—not someone he had known, not a friend but a comrade in the movement nevertheless—and if there was to be no funeral, then at the very least a note to signal his departure, to acknowledge the silent space left by a breath. But nothing emerged from Tun's throat. He tried again. Still nothing. He had the odd sensation he was caught in a sleep paralysis. Yet, there was no doubt in his mind he was awake, and though he was standing upright, he saw himself recumbent, felt something pressing down on his chest. A presence, a weight. A sadness. But whose? His own? Was he dead? If it was his own lifeless body he was seeing, then *he* could not be grieving, mourning his own death. When his friend Prama died, he remembered, he'd tried to explain death to his daughter, at the funeral they'd attended together. He didn't have the heart to tell her what he believed, what he knew to be true—that the moment we are born, each step we take is toward death. Instead, he resorted to telling her about the songs and melodies performed at different stages of a funeral. *There's music, you see, to awake the soul of the deceased, music to comfort it when it becomes aware that it's no longer part of the human world, music to lead it into the otherworld . . .* He knew he was veering from the truth, making it sound as if death too was a journey, much gentler and more poetic than life itself, and in some way preferable. He told her about the instruments in a "music of the ghosts" ensemble—the small oboe whose airy exhalation mimics the wind, the eternal breath; the crescent-shaped nine-gong gamelan whose rippling notes, when struck in continuous succession, echo the circling of time; the drum that marks the ending of one journey and the beginning of another, hastening the footsteps of the deceased toward the spirit realm. Once he'd finished, his daughter declared, "When I die, I want you to play all the instruments of the world one by one! I want you to sing me every song you know! Do you promise me, Papa, do you?" He nodded, and she said quietly, "Good, because I don't ever want to leave you." He'd wanted to abandon the funeral then, to spirit her as far from the presence of death as possible.

Tun realized now the weight on his chest was his longing for her. Again, he heard his daughter's voice, as if she were inside the hut with him. His pulse quickened—*What are you doing here? Go back home.* But then it felt like they were already home, that he'd arrived back somehow, because there she was inside his room, surrounded by musical instruments, blowing this, tapping that, plucking a random string, curious about the new ones he'd brought to add to the collection. *What's this one, Papa?* she inquired, her voice and words so gentle he dared believe he was forgiven for having left in the first place, for abandoning her in the middle of the night. *It's a leaf from a teak sapling. Sapling?—Is it a baby tree? Yes, a baby teak, one as tall as you. What's it for, Papa?* She held the leaf by its tiny stem between her thumb and forefinger, twirling it. *For music. Music!—But how?* He took the leaf from her and placed it between his lips, as one would a reed in the mouthpiece of a woodwind, his body the instrument. He blew on it, weaving a simple tune with his breath. The leaf vibrated, buzzing like a cicada. *It's alive, Papa, it's alive!* She clapped, enchanted. *Yes,* he agreed. *Give anything the soul of music and it will sing.* She turned to a drum and tapped on it. *DTUM!* Just once but loud enough.

Tun woke from his trance. He felt released, no longer paralyzed, although alone in the hut once more. *Of course,* he kept thinking, *of course* . . . He should've realized it. It was the wrong note, the wrong pitch, the wrong instrument altogether. He voiced the rhythm aloud— *dtum dtak da-rum dtum dtak da-rum dtum dtak dtak dtum*—invoking the double-headed *sampho*, a sacred drum regarded as the instrument of the Teacher, the Master. Once when he explained to her that the larger head was called the "teacher" and the smaller head the "child," his daughter had laughed and thought the *sampho* was created specifically for the two of them, that it was *their* instrument.

He'd found what he was looking for. A reason to endure. He kept to one thought and one thought only—*Sita, Sita, Sita.* He had to stay alive. This was the only way to get back to her. No matter what it would take. He had to stay alive.

It's Saturday morning and the otherwise tranquil atmosphere of Hotel Le Royal is abuzz, as if the hotel existed at a portal between past and present, most days retreating nearly a century back in time, ensconced in French Indochina semblance, and then on the weekends reemerging into the hectic modern world, with cell phones ringing in every corner, computers clacking away. A few seconds' stroll through the lobby exposes Teera to a diversity of languages and nationalities, and the possible journeys that might have brought these sojourners to her homeland. On one sofa, a blond-haired, blue-eyed child sporting a UNESCO T-shirt speaks Khmer to her Cambodian nanny as fluently as she does some Scandinavian language to her siblings. A few seats away, an impeccably dressed designer of African descent, with a slight British accent and a profile as regal as that of any Angkorian king depicted on the ancient temples, looks over samples of Cambodian silk with his clients, a group of well-heeled Spanish-speaking women. In a discreet corner, a young interracial gay couple leans into each other, shoulders touching, as one peruses his laptop and the other the *Wall Street Journal*, an array of emptied espresso cups scattered on the coffee table before them.

Knowing that Café Monivong, where she usually takes her breakfast, will be crowded, Teera heads in the opposite direction for the bookshop café overlooking the pool garden. In the cool, echoing hallway, she passes the prominent glass display of the champagne cocktail stemware specially made to welcome the widowed Jacqueline Kennedy decades earlier, in November 1967. The visit, *Life* magazine claimed in its glossy spread that Teera came across long ago at Cornell, was the realization of Mrs. Kennedy's "lifelong dream" to see the ancient, ruined monuments of Angkor. But for all its glamorous facade, history tells us the journey had a serious political intent—to repair the fractured relations that resulted when Sihanouk, enraged by the war spilling over from Vietnam, had severed diplomatic ties with the United States in 1965.

Camelot in the Kingdom of Wonder, Teera thinks every time she happens by the display. What politics shatter, myth can mend and recast anew. Not only did these glasses survive war and revolution, they were exhumed from the abandoned cellars en masse with barely a scratch. Among them one in particular supposedly even bears the lipstick of the former first lady, preserved somehow all too clearly.

Teera turns into a narrow room with books lining one wall and souvenirs the other. Easily overlooked among the hotel's glitzier shops, it appears more like a secret nook than a café, which, when she first discovered it, appealed to her solitary nature, her desire for quiet and privacy. Morning light streams through the tall windows behind the counter and bounces off the glass display offering an array of sandwiches, baked goods, and sweets so decadent that Teera's teeth throb at the mere sight. A young waitress greets her, a face she has not seen before, obviously someone new to the staff. The young woman seems shy, even more reticent than Teera. Relieved at not being drawn into extended pleasantries, Teera makes a quick order and then walks past the dark wood counter out onto the small balcony. She settles into a corner seat, pleased to be the only guest here. Her mind returns to the cocktail glasses and she wonders vaguely if her grandfather was among the dignitaries gathered that evening to listen to Sihanouk's original jazz renditions in honor of Mrs. Kennedy. It's easy to imagine he might have been, given the important advisory role he'd held in the Cambodian Embassy in DC. The thought that one of those glasses—these very grounds—could bear some imprint of her grandfather sends a shiver down her spine.

The ghosts are everywhere, crossing paths with her, joining her at the small table. Perhaps she is not alone after all.

Her coffee and croissants arrive. The waitress bows slightly and hurries back indoors, seeming glad to escape the curious scrutiny of her guest. Teera is equally grateful for the solitude, a moment to ease the nervousness, the apprehension that has accompanied her since waking.

She pulls out her cell phone, noting the time, and sets it on the table to not miss Mr. Chum's call. She has enlisted his service for the long drive to Phnom Tamao. They will fetch Narunn from the White Building, go to Wat Nagara to meet the little girl, and together take her to see the hooting gibbons and sun bears at the wildlife sanctuary, as Yaya has suggested. While Teera is looking forward to the trip, she is also anxious about spending a whole day with a little girl whose name she's yet to know, who has just lost her mother. How do you comfort a child whose parent, the only one she knew, was gunned down? *I'm so sorry for your loss* . . . Such words seem both formal and trite. Does the little one even know her mother's dead? How do you explain such violence to a child? And then there's the Old Musician. Teera can't think of him without mourning her own loss.

She takes a sip of her coffee, as if caffeine would calm her nerves; tears a piece of croissant and nibbles on it, her gaze finding distraction at the far side of the children's pool. Early on weekend mornings, outside guests as well as those staying at the hotel begin to lay claim to their favorite spots to linger for hours on end. Always among the first to arrive are Luna and her mother, Emma, who Teera now shares an easy exchange with whenever they cross paths at the pools. Emma, a single woman in her late forties, with exuberant red hair that seems a token of her strong personality, has lived and worked in Cambodia for many years. She'd adopted Luna three years earlier from an orphanage, an infant abandoned at the door of a clinic in an area known for its brothel scene. Luna, in the sagging two-piece swimsuit she practically lives in, bounces through the lounge area, closely followed by her mother, towing books and bags and various bottles. At the corner of the pool nearest the changing rooms, Emma dumps everything onto a pair of green-cushioned lounge chairs beneath a matching umbrella.

In the next seats over, a white-haired elderly couple, distracted by Luna's cuteness, does not see that a monkey has lowered itself from a frangipani tree behind them, one arm grasping a branch, another reaching for their books and spectacles on the low table beneath the tree. Only when Luna lets out a gasp, clapping as if to spur the monkey on, does the couple become alert to the crime in progress. The husband shoos the monkey with his bathrobe, while the wife jumps several steps away, one hand over her mouth, the other on her heart. Judging by their reactions, this must be their first encounter with the furry fellow residents. After a few hissing threats between man and monkey, the apparent peacemaker relents, disappearing once again into the branches, though not without securing a conspiratorial nod from Luna.

The old couple resettles into their chairs, visibly relieved. Emma leans over, as if to reassure them, and though Teera can't hear from this distance, she imagines her repeating what everyone has come to accept—that, while a nuisance at times, the monkeys add to the old-world charm of the hotel, and guests should expect to have their belongings brazenly snatched at least once during their stay. Keys, sunglasses, and cell phones are among the most coveted novelties. These are after all city monkeys, as an old gardener working at the hotel once told Teera, not too different from us *svar pteah*—"house apes."

A stir ripples through the leafy treetops, and the monkey reemerges, leaping onto the balustrade of a balcony two floors up. Teera can see him clearly now. Hanuman, she's nicknamed him, the palest of the long-tailed macaques that roam the hotel grounds, his fur so supple and silvery that he appears almost white in the sunlight. Something familiar is slung across his tiny shoulders like the end of a kite's tail. Teera's gaze darts back to the ground, and after a quick search, she spies Luna's brown silhouette partly concealed behind the half-raised back of an empty lounge chair. It seems that while Emma was busy chatting with the old couple, Luna took off her bikini top and gave it to her cross-dressing friend. Still deep in conversation, Emma remains oblivious to her daughter's escapade.

A laugh escapes Teera, and she feels her apprehension begin to subside. *You love children*, she hears Amara say. *You'll have fun with this little girl.* She wishes her aunt were here with her. They should have made this journey together. There are so many things she failed to ask. Why didn't Amara ever marry, have children of her own? Teera would've loved a young cousin. But in truth, she knows, this was not possible. A scene emerges in her mind, and Teera sees herself again as that eleven- or twelve-year-old peering from behind a screen of leaves, discovering something she didn't quite understand.

It was evening and, after a long day of laboring in the mud and sun, everyone had washed and gone home. Only Amara remained with the leader of their *kong chalat*, a mobile work unit responsible for digging ditches to irrigate the rice fields. The two women stood side by side, with water up to their chests, in a clear pond surrounded by bamboo thickets, the unit leader still fully dressed, it appeared, and Amara wrapped in her sarong, dyed a deep black, as with all revolutionary clothes. The unit leader suddenly turned toward Amara so that their faces almost touched, gathered Amara's drenched hair to the front over one shoulder, and then pressed her nose into it, into Amara's chest, her wet skin, before she lowered herself completely into the water.

At first Suteera was confused, unsure what to do, but then understood she ought to remove herself from the vicinity, leave Amara and the unit leader their privacy. Amara must've assumed that she had gone home like everyone else, when in fact she had been slow in coming to wash. She'd dawdled in the rice fields, looking for crabs and crickets she could add to their sparse evening meal. Finding none, she meandered lazily along the dirt path, stopping finally at the bamboo grove at the mouth of the pond.

Suteera did not stay to see if the unit leader would resurface. It wasn't drowning she feared, because both women knew how to swim well. Later—weeks, or maybe months—when the unit leader was taken away, branded an "enemy" of the Organization for reasons unclear to anyone,

Suteera thought it was her fault, that because she hadn't stayed that evening to keep the others away from the pond, the unit leader got caught, her love for Amara discovered somehow. But this reasoning didn't make sense. Amara too would've been eliminated.

It was years before Teera would come to comprehend the intimacy, the love shared. She and her aunt were already in America, well adjusted to their new life, and Teera had wondered why Amara never paid heed to the men interested in her. *You ought to marry one of them*, she teased. *Even our sponsor is hopelessly in love with you.* Amara did not respond to her baiting. She stayed quiet for a long moment, and just as Teera started to think that she might've offended her aunt, Amara asked, her voice and gaze distant, *Do you remember Comrade Sovann? The leader of our irrigation unit?* Teera felt suddenly caught off guard, and she was afraid that saying yes would betray what she'd seen at the pond those many years before. So she told Amara she didn't remember. Again, Amara fell into silence. Then, shaking her head, she finally murmured, *When you've known love, you can't settle for its substitute.* It was the closest Amara ever came to opening that locked compartment of her heart.

Teera's gaze follows Luna into the pool. Emma is beside her, seeming to have noted and accepted that the little sprite's bikini top is lost. There's something easy and natural about their relationship, as if they had always been mother and daughter. If the two were more physically alike, Teera would never have guessed Luna was adopted. It is the kind of bond Teera imagines Amara would've had with her own children, deep-rooted and yet undemanding.

She recalls now those weekends when she and Amara would go jogging together, then afterward stop at a park to watch the babies play with their mothers. *That one is so fat I want to eat him!* With the cancer, they no longer went running but would still go to the park to watch the children or, as Amara put it, to inhale the plumpness of life. During one of the last few visits before Amara became bedridden, she said, *I won't be*

*here to see it, but I know you'll make a great mother one day . . . Love doesn't
die, Teera. It never leaves our side. From the very beginning, long before we
knew who among us would live and who would die, your mother made me
promise to love you for both of us. And I have, for her, for our whole family.
You were never an orphan. Love was always your guardian. You have its
abiding protection. It never abandoned you.*

A lump forms in her throat, and Teera realizes what she has been
dreading isn't meeting the child at the temple, the little girl whose
mother was slain, but herself, the girl whose mother ended her own life.
She is terrified of coming face-to-face again with abandonment.

This admission releases her. She finishes her breakfast and, with her
small belongings, walks back into the café to purchase sandwiches, pas-
tries, drinks, desserts—enough food for a picnic party at the wildlife
sanctuary. Her cell phone rings inside her handbag, a single cheery tune,
and she knows it is Mr. Chum signaling her. He has arrived and is waiting in the parking lot out front. With the food in hand, she retraces
her steps through the hallway and, as she passes the display of cocktail
glasses once again, she catches a reflection of her mother in herself. She
pauses, smiles at the reflection, and then rushes toward the sunlight.
The ghosts follow her everywhere, yet for the first time, she does not
feel haunted.

The last time the Old Musician saw the White Building was in 1974, the night he returned to the city to fetch his daughter. Three decades seems like a blink, but the transformation is complete, the decay irreversible. A mass tomb that appears neither for the dead nor the living but for those disavowed by both. Grime and mildew lay siege to it so that even its nondescript sobriquet bodes its vanishing. Aside from its sprawling silhouette, he does not recognize the Municipal Apartments, and it is unlikely that his erstwhile home bears any trace of him.

Still, even from a block away, he is shaken by the sight of it and dares not venture any closer. He leans on the high wall gating the villa at the street corner onto which he's accidentally wandered, one arm pressed to his stomach to stop the quaking. At dawn this morning, he caught a ride on a *tuk-tuk* with some monks from the temple who often come to the city on the weekends for their alms rounds. He thought the change of scenery would do him good and decided to wander awhile longer on his own. He would be all right, he assured the monks. He knew his way. But now he wonders how he's gotten here. Has the city changed so much that he no longer knows the streets, which turns to avoid? He's come to where he should not have. Yet, he can neither backtrack nor move forward. A recurrent pattern in his life.

Breathe. You are here now. He lowers himself onto the sidewalk, sitting on the bare concrete like a beggar, his cotton satchel on his lap. *Just look, and you might catch a glimpse of her.* A cat rounds the corner and slinks past him, a moped whizzes through the intersection, a dog yawns

and rubs itself against a lamppost across the street, and a vendor pushes
her cart filled with breakfast buns toward a market area. The morning is
still calm, the streets have been freshly swept of detritus, and the city has
yet to be overwhelmed by noise and movement. In the clean early light,
the Old Musician can almost believe that it's possible to peel away the
decades, the decay, and find her once again standing before him.

She stood in the dark living room, framed by the doorway, arms stretched
wide. To embrace him or to block him from reentering their home, Tun
couldn't tell. Just seconds earlier, before unlocking the door with the key
he'd carried close to his body all these months, he'd paused, reminding
himself why he'd come this far, despite the danger ahead. With the fighting encroaching on the capital, Tun couldn't leave Sita and Om Paan
unprotected, at the mercy of either side. Given the government's violent
crackdown on collaborators and even relatives of suspected rebels, shepherding his family into the rebel-controlled zone seemed the safer path.

Tun had chosen this time of the night when most would be lost to
dreams, when the need for sleep held sway, stopping all activities, even
the battles. But there his daughter stood, wide awake, looking up at him.
She'd padded from her room at the precise moment when he pushed the
door open. Had she heard the movements of key and lock? Or had she
by some mysterious intuition sensed his return, heard his footsteps long
before he arrived?

Tun dropped to his knees so that he was at eye level with her, a finger
over his lips so she would know to make no noise that might wake the
neighbors. "Sita, I've come back . . ." he whispered, taking her into his
arms, pressing her hard against his chest to stanch the tide of emotions
threatening to flood his heart. She was soft, like down or a cloud, and
for a moment he forgot himself, forgot the long months they'd been
separated. "I see that your moonlets have been spinning away," he teased,
recalling the explanation she'd given long ago for her tenderness, this
supple outer shell cushioning her inner self.

She pulled back, bewildered, and then, heaving as if to gather her bearings, murmured, "Oh, Papa, I'm not a baby anymore," in a voice so composed that for a split second he was unsure whether it was hers or an echo of someone else's. She stepped away from him, arms crossed in front of her chest now, as if to bar further affection.

Tun reeled at her self-possession, falling back on his haunches. Almost a year had passed since he left home, and he knew he ought to explain his absence, but there was no time. Besides, how could he even begin?

He looked to Om Paan standing behind her, a second silhouette in the night. The three of them, he thought, must look like a prop crew stealing onto a darkened stage, making unseen arrangements to an otherwise witnessed life. "We have to leave," he stammered, the words tumbling out awkwardly like a command. Om Paan nodded, disappeared into the room she shared with Sita, and a few seconds later reappeared with two bundles. "I knew you'd come back, sir, so I prepared," she told him with a calm that could only mean that during his absence the two of them had rehearsed this moment countless times, anticipating his return and their hurried departure, preparing the youngster to say good-bye to her home, her life. "We are ready."

Tun picked up his daughter, sensing her slight resistance at being carried like a small child when it was obvious she no longer regarded herself as such. Om Paan closed the door soundlessly behind them, and though she knew they might never return, she locked it anyway, so as to delay others from discovering their absence.

With shoes off to mute their steps, they stole through the pitch-dark corridor and then, crouching low, weaved down the open stairwell. Outside, with their shoes back on, they dashed toward a pair of cyclos under one of the leafy trees in a row along the road. Roeun, the cyclo driver, was the same young man from Banaam whom Tun had met ten months earlier, in August of '73. Back then Roeun hadn't known he was aiding Tun to slip into hiding. This past March, Tun had made the initial inquiry from Oudong, the nearest provincial capital controlled by the insurgent forces, and, once Roeun was located, had reestablished connection.

It was now the beginning of June, and while government troops had launched attacks to reclaim Oudong, this one calm night afforded Tun an opportunity to extract his daughter and Om Paan from the city.

As requested, Roeun had brought along another cyclo driver, someone they could trust, a "comrade brother" in the network of insurgent sympathizers and collaborators, which, in the past year or so, had expanded to include a staggering array of people, from powerful government ministers and influential bankers to policemen and military officers to street sweepers and maimed beggars. Tun, with Sita still in his arms, climbed into one cyclo, while Om Paan settled into the other with their belongings, the bundles hidden from view beneath her feet. Tun turned briefly for one final look at their home, a tiny dark recess among rows and rows of other tiny dark recesses in the night's catacomb. He had no regret leaving it now. His daughter was with him. He'd endured his trial, bartered a part of himself, for this reunion.

As they knitted their way through the familiar streets, passing well-known sites and landmarks, the city enveloped them in an eerie silence, as if it were empty, inhabited only by shadows, and Tun recalled the evacuation of Oudong, in which the entire population of the town was herded like animals to resettle in a makeshift commune deep in an uninhabitable forest. He and his small unit of soldiers had arrived at the tail end of that evacuation, when the town was nearly emptied. He heard talk that the same thing could happen to Phnom Penh in the event of their victory, though he always dismissed it as rumor. The city's population—perhaps more than two million now—was simply too big for such an undertaking. Even so, the momentous silence unsettled him, gave him a premonition, though he knew not what it was.

Tun wrapped his arms tighter around his daughter, one hand cupping her face. She'd given way to sleep, relaxing against his body. He could hardly believe he was holding her. He would do it all over again. For her, he would endure an ordeal far worse than what he'd gone through at the forest encampment. Yet, how could he possibly explain what had happened, why it had taken him this long to come back?

For some weeks—maybe a whole month, maybe less—he had not been allowed outside that hut. From one day to the next he would sleep, wake, eat, shit, breathe his own foulness and ruin, all within the dark confines of the mosquito-infested thatch. Food and water were slid under a gap beneath the door. There was no discernible schedule. A day or two could go by during which he would receive neither, and he would have to rely on the grasshoppers or crickets that found their way into the hut, the raindrops he'd managed to collect in a cut section of bamboo. He had no means to wash, except during a storm when rivulets of water pierced the roof. Most days he festered in the heat. On nights when it rained without pause, he shivered. He was given no blanket, no mat or mosquito net, no hammock, nothing, not even a *kroma*. The only essentials at his disposal were those he'd brought with him from home. To his surprise, they did not confiscate these belongings. He resisted the urge to ask for anything, fearing they would take what little he had away or, worse, end it all for him. In any case, there was no one to ask. He would hear voices, laughter, and shouts floating from the middle of the encampment. Methodical plinks and echoes of target practice. Sometimes even singing, an out-of-tune but boisterous chorus of young male voices. But the area surrounding his hut was always silent save for the din of the jungle.

A soldier would come and go, mutely delivering the scant meal, walking around the hut checking to see that nothing was amiss, and Tun would detect only a partial silhouette or bare feet circling the ground, the sleek outline of an AK47 or a pistol pointed downward nonchalantly from a hand. The closest he received to an explanation was when a voice once said, "This is not a punishment. The Organization needs proof, you see." He thought it might be the battalion commander, but it sounded like someone older, more solemn and somehow cultivated. In any case, Tun silenced his rage, quelled the urge to claw his way out like an animal. At times, his hunger for human contact was so great he wished that it *were* punishment, that a soldier would just come and beat him, shout threats and abuses. A punishment would've been simple and clear, and Tun would've known for certain that he was still alive.

One day the door finally swung open. It had been unbarred from outside, by whom or when, Tun had no idea. He suspected it was a test. So
he remained inside, glued to his corner, bracing for death, his impending
execution. But no one came. Two days later a figure walked in, the intense
sunlight from behind making the silhouette appear porous, spectral. A
hallucination, Tun thought. Then the figure said, "Comrade, your trial
is over." It was the same voice that had spoken to him days earlier. "The
isolation was necessary. You've proven your loyalty. You will now join the
rest of us." The figure stepped forward to reveal a man who looked to
be in his late forties, with, as Tun had surmised, an educated manner to
match his speech.

Comrade Im was the leader of the encampment, a high-ranking
cadre with access to the Central Committee, the core leadership of the
Communist Party, or, as it was now more commonly referred to, the Organization. These extreme measures had to be taken, he later told Tun
once it was clear that Tun could be trusted, his inviolable allegiance to
the Organization demonstrated. The revolution, Comrade Im went on
to explain, was entering a period of intense radicalization. Those joining
the movement must be made to understand that they were soldiers, and
soldiers must embrace suffering and hardship on every front. It was easy
to teach new recruits to handle guns, pull the pins of grenades, launch
rockets, but far more challenging to teach them discipline and loyalty.
Often it proved impossible. In the case of loyalty, it was not a trainable
skill at all but a character trait that had to be coaxed out of people by
putting them in a trial such as the isolation Tun had endured, with no
explanation given whatsoever, except the vague knowledge that this was
the Organization's design. Initially, it had not been so strict. Newcomers
were allowed outside the hut, so long as they stayed within the marked
perimeter. Some even took to planting vegetables and herbs while being
"broken in." Now, with the war intensifying, there was no room for question, for doubt, for sentiment. Only absolute devotion. Those who tried
to defect were invariably executed.

What Tun had witnessed on the teak crossing, Comrade Im said, would happen to anyone suspected of collaborating with the enemy. Yet—Comrade Im pointed out—the execution had been a kind one, compassionate even, given the battalion commander's predilection for cruelty. It was immediate and without torture, because the offender was a high-ranking cadre, one of the encampment leaders, respected and loved by many. Other traitors were disemboweled or had their throats sliced, writhing slowly toward death.

"Now do you see that your trial was not at all a punishment?" Comrade Im said, smiling charitably. Tun nodded but kept silent, forging his resolve to stay alive, which, during his isolation, had solidified into a trait all its own. For him, there could be no loyalty without love. It had always been this way. With his music. With Channara. With Sita. In the absence of love, loyalty was merely obedience, what one owed one's captor. He'd known obedience with his father. He could summon it again.

In the meantime, if becoming a soldier was the only way back to his daughter, he would learn to fight, he would cross one battlefield after another until he reached her again.

So he became a soldier. To his great relief, there was a new battalion commander. The old one, he was told, had been called to the "Special Zone," the area around Phnom Penh, closer to the enemy. Under the new commander—who worked jointly with a Khmer-speaking Vietnamese combat specialist—Tun learned to handle weapons, to aim and shoot at targets called out to him impromptu; to sense danger by the slightest sounds and stirrings in the forest; to crawl in the grass, under barbed wires, in torrential downpours; to dig trenches and build barricades; to sit still as throngs of red ants bit into his flesh; and, most important, to feel nothing in these moments and to remember only that bloodshed was a cause for exaltation, the closest feeling to joy one would experience in the presence of the Organization.

After a few short months, Tun was told these military exercises were adequate, considering that most soldiers received none at all and learned to fight during actual combat. He had received as much because he was deemed capable of being a leader—he understood maps, could make sense of diagrams and charts, knew how to use a compass, could read and write. And thus, at the end of his training, Tun was put in charge of about thirty soldiers. His own ragtag platoon of half-starved illiterates. Many of the new recruits were terrified by their first battles, but they remained with him, loyal to the insurgency, because the fear of being killed in the line of fire was secondary to the fear of being tortured and brutally murdered by their own. They had seen it happen to their own friends caught trying to defect. In short, they had been unequivocally forewarned.

For Tun, it was neither fear nor blind allegiance that kept him moving. He dodged countless bullets, narrowly escaped explosions, and several times even broke through enemy lines, only to be baffled by how he'd managed to do so, how he had survived, with the occasional slight wound. He had only one goal—with each victory to get closer to his daughter. In that sense, perhaps love had been at the forefront of all his battles. But he had not dared express such sentiment, or even think it, until now. Until this very moment when he sat looking down at her sleeping face, when he felt her in his arms and, unlike those tormented nights when he'd only dreamt of her, knew that she was real.

Tun turned to Om Paan in the other cyclo moving in tandem with his. She smiled at him, nodding silently, as if to say there would be time later for words. They'd reached the edge of the city. They thanked Roeun and the other cyclo driver, said a solemn good-bye, and quickly transferred to a prearranged oxcart loaded with hay and clay pots. They continued like this the rest of the way, furtively hopping out of one ride into another, following a route mapped out in advance, avoiding government checkpoints through the help of various guides and "eyes." They raced against time, aiming to reach Oudong, about forty kilometers north of the city, before battles resumed at dawn.

That night they reached Oudong as planned, but not all of them made it out. A few days later, after the government troops had virtually reclaimed the former royal capital, Om Paan was killed in crossfire during the final battle. As Tun's unit retreated with the rest of the insurgent forces, she crouched beside him, shielding Sita while he fought, and when the bullet came she took it—a single definitive shot in the side of her neck. Tun had no time to think, feel, or even react, except to seize Sita from Om Paan's lifeless clutch. Only later when they were safe in a forest did he note the silent scream trapped in his daughter's eyes. It was a look that would never quite leave her. Again and again, he would be privy to it. Her horror. A hint of which he glimpsed decades later in Suteera's eyes when they met.

He is not ready to see it again. Not yet. She is probably on the way to the temple this very moment with Dr. Narunn, to pick up little Lah for their outing. He knows now why he has come to the city, why he wandered this far, along these particular streets, arriving as if by accident at his former home. If he were to recount his life to Suteera, he could do so up to this point, the final year before the country fell, knowing that someone of her compassion would be sympathetic to his mistakes, all the possible wrong turns he had made, the many moral lapses he'd fallen into. Shocked as she might be, she could probably bear to hear of his love for her mother, Channara, and forgive him for it. Or, if not that, at least pity him. And he . . . he could probably go on to tell her about the next several years, knowing that everything he did, vile or forgivable, was to keep his daughter alive. But how can he tell her the one truth she seeks and still bear the horror in her eyes? *What do you know of my father?* he can almost hear her asking. *What happened to him? Who are you?*

The answer is simple, and yet how can he tell her?

I am your father's executioner.

Third Movement

L ah. There is a cheerful ring to the child's name, and as though she were a musical note, the little one hums continuously. In the driver's seat, Mr. Chum taps his fingers on the steering wheel, and beside him, Narunn shakes his head gently from side to side as he whistles along. They've been driving for some time now, withstanding breath-halting lurches and bumps, the calamitous swerves of vehicles overburdened with passengers and belongings, the continuous edging of oxcarts and tractors onto the already crowded narrow lanes. Lah seems unperturbed by it all, perfectly content in the backseat as she snuggles into Teera's shoulder, her tiny arm around Teera's waist. When she catches a glimpse or a sound of something interesting, the girl will poke her head up and take in the full scene—a *chhayam* drum carnival with giant dancing puppets at the entrance to a temple, a stream of schoolgirls in blue-and-white uniforms pedaling their bicycles along the dikes of dry paddy fields, a wedding party buzzing with bamboo flutes and coconut *tros*. When it's just flat country scenery, the child dips down again, curling her body like a snail into its shell, attaching herself to comfort and safety, the shelter of another's body. The apprehension Teera felt back at the hotel has long vanished, and in its place something stronger, more certain, is taking root, though she does not yet know what it is.

Earlier this morning at the temple, when they were introduced, the first words to emerge from the little one's lips were: "I'm four today!" The girl counted aloud to herself and then, with one hand pinning down the thumb of the other, uncurled the correct number of chubby fingers for them all to see. Teera had expected someone willowy and broken, but the face gazing up at hers beamed with a curiosity that eclipsed loss. "Are you the auntie from America?" Lah scrutinized, her dark round eyes rimmed with lashes as jet-black and silken as the hair framing her tiny-moon face. The Venerable Kong Oul standing nearby gave a hopeful smile, and Teera, lowering herself to the child's level, said, "Yes . . . and I've come to take you for your birthday outing. Would you like to see some gibbons and sun bears?" Lah nodded vigorously, and then broke into a giggle when Narunn stepped aside and started making muted hoots and scratching himself like an ape. "Are you from America too, uncle?" Lah asked, hands cupping her mouth to suppress her amusement.

Narunn grumbled with indignation, "Oh no, somewhere much more glamorous!"

"Where?"

"The jungle, of course!"

Lah narrowed her eyes for a moment before appearing to reach the same conclusion. Narunn and Mr. Chum each took her by the arm and swung her toward the car. The Venerable Kong Oul and Teera followed a few steps behind. "I told her you were an auntie from America," the abbot said. "It's kind of you to play along. I wanted to give her something exciting to look forward to, a day with someone who has no connection whatsoever to her ordeal."

"She seems all right," Teera told him. "Surprisingly joyful."

"A child this young is resilient, and she is remarkably so. She bounces around like a bubble, and the little novices trail her everywhere, as you can see." The abbot nodded to the clusters of monks gathering here and there to watch, curious, vigilant. "They feel protective of her but maintain an appropriate distance, in accordance with the monastic rule. I'm the only transgressor here." He chuckled. "I've made a small place for her in my room. It's far from ideal, but it'll have to do for now."

"Have you told her what happened?"

The old monk nodded. "Yes, simply that her mother has passed, not the details of how and why. And, as with most children her age, she takes it to mean her mother is 'gone,' at least physically. How she makes sense of this is hard to know . . . Every now and then she'll ask when her mother is coming back, and I tell her more or less that her mother is on a long journey to find a better life, and that for the time being she is to remain at the temple with us. It's clear she senses something is wrong but does not ask to know more. Such is the wisdom of innocence—it does not seek the answer it cannot accept."

They walked in silence for a while, and, as they neared the car, the abbot said, "Also, I'd asked you to come along because I felt the Old Musician would want to see you. He knew you were coming today but must have forgotten, because he's gone into the city with the monks on their alms rounds. Perhaps you'll see him later today when you return from Phnom Tamao." The monk stood still for a moment, hands clasped behind his back in a contemplative bow. "He's the only one who seems shattered by the little one's presence. He tries to stay out of her path as much as possible, though it was he who insisted we bring her here."

Teera gave him a surprised look. "Shattered?"

The abbot shook his head. "I don't know . . . Perhaps 'shattered' is the wrong word. He's deeply affected by her loss. Anyway, I thought seeing you again might be a good thing."

Though they'd only met recently, Teera felt she knew the Venerable Kong Oul in some deep way, having read his extended correspondence with her aunt. *When misfortune befalls us*, he'd written in one of the last letters to Amara, *whether a collective one like war, or a personal one like illness, it is tempting to see religion as the answer. In all my years as a monk, I've come to believe that religion is only another way of asking the question, why? Why is there suffering? Why are we here?* In Teera's own interaction with him, the abbot had always been able to fathom the unspoken, and she thought this the mark of his spirituality—the ability to reach deep into another's soul without seeming to trespass. She could see why Amara had sought his counsel from afar over the years. Teera felt at ease with him, in a way she'd never been able to feel in the presence of other monks. "I'm sorry, I've been meaning to plan another visit," she said after a moment, "but the time never seems right."

"I understand." The abbot held her gaze. "Until then, off you go now, *nhome atmah*. Be mindful on the road."

Teera hears a deep sigh from the passenger's seat and then a softer one against her chest. Both Narunn and Lah have fallen asleep, their breaths weaving a hypnotic rhythm around her heart. She lowers the little one's head onto her lap, letting her stretch out. Lah stirs, unconsciously humming some residual notes. In these brief hours together, it's become painfully clear to Teera that this is a child who has learned to sing herself to sleep, who knows loneliness and solitude, who senses the permanency of her mother's absence even without knowing the meaning of death.

The car bounces over a large pothole in the road. Lah turns on her side so that her face is lost in the folds of Teera's shirt. Teera caresses her until she is tranquil again. *Nhome atmah*, the abbot called them. Certainly, these three odd people in the car are the closest thing to a family she's recovered since her return to Cambodia.

They've turned off the main route onto a dirt road lined with leafless brown saplings. Plumes of red dust rise up and surround the car, making it hard to see out. Mr. Chum proceeds cautiously, even though no other vehicle is in sight on this stretch of the road. Glancing at Teera through the rearview mirror, the old driver says in a low voice so as not to wake Narunn and Lah, "It gets like this during the dry season. Nothing but dirt. Like Pol Pot's time."

Teera nods, glimpsing the starved, skeletal landscape through the billowing sieves. Dust rises and falls, rains have washed away the blood, the seasons spin into decades, and yet, the past is but half a breath away. She has only to exhale, and that long-ago desolation, such as she'd never known before that day, unfurls into a vast, unconquerable terrain.

They were on a similar dirt road, her oxcart moving in one direction and her mother's in another, each receding into the dust. Channara's supine form was covered with a *kroma*, and her bare feet sticking out the back of the cart were the last things Suteera saw.

It had been a quiet, wordless death. Channara died from consuming the same small green fruits that weeks earlier had poisoned Rin, Suteera's little brother, who'd probably mistaken the fruits for baby mangoes. Her brother was hungry—starving like the rest of them—and, being only two or three, had no way of knowing what was edible, what was not. They found him on the riverbank behind their hut one evening after returning from the fields. He was lying under a row of trees that one of the village elders identified as *dao krapoeu*—"crocodile's sword"—with long green lance-like leaves. Her brother was only partially breathing by then, and when Channara picked him up, asking, "Why, why, why?" as she pried from his mouth the remaining bits of what he'd already swallowed, her little brother murmured, "Rice. Mama . . . rice." Channara lost any semblance of composure then—she screamed, "It's not rice, baby, it's not rice!—*It's not even food*." Hours later, Rin stopped breathing altogether, his mouth agape, as if still awaiting the rice that never came.

After his death, Channara disappeared into herself, in the same way she'd done back home whenever she wrote. Except now, Suteera was certain, her mother would never reemerge, because there was no story to share, no words that could bring her brother back. So, day after day, the silence thickened, and Channara sank deeper into it. Then one day, Suteera found her mother with a bowl of the same green fruits and a dipping mixture of crushed fresh chilies and salt. The desolation in Channara's eyes as she looked up from her eating told Suteera that it was too late. Grief was its own poison, and Channara's body was flooded with it.

Suteera sat down opposite her mother, rocking gently back and forth. Silent rivers cut their faces, plunging into the gulf between them. They did not speak. What could they have said? The same two words knocked at Suteera's heart—*Don't die*. She couldn't even begin to imagine what was going through her mother's mind. Until that moment Suteera had not seen Channara's vulnerability, a parent's childlike fragility. *Don't die*.

Aside from her own impossible wish, she wanted only to comfort her
mother in these last hours.

Sometime in the night Channara died, and Suteera let out a single
audible sob when she woke to find her mother breathless beside her on
the straw mat.

When the village cadres learned of the death, they assigned a soldier
to take Channara's corpse away to fertilize the fields, in keeping with
revolutionary practice. Suteera, they said, could now go live with her
grandparents and aunt in the village where they'd been sent. It would
only take a morning to get there by oxcart, but because of what happened, Suteera would be allowed the whole day off from working. She
ought to use this time, they told her, to examine her mother's choice,
as she may be called upon to give a critique at the next commune-wide
political meeting. *Choice? There's no choice. Death is all there is.* Suteera
raged against the emptiness, the hateful landscape. The dust rose and
silenced her. The only sounds came from the oxcart wheels grinding the
bones of the earth.

Teera hears beeping, only to realize it's from their car. Mr. Chum keeps
pressing the horn as they trundle ever cautiously along, passing the
flimsy skeleton of a thatched hut on the right and a desiccated palm on
the left. The dust has thinned, but it's still a challenge to see far ahead,
and Teera thinks he must be alerting an unsuspecting cow or water buffalo wandering too close to graze on the sporadic clumps of brown grass.
Or perhaps there are wild animals on the loose in the vicinity of the
sanctuary. Troops of macaques waiting to ambush them. Khmer Rouge
soldiers, with AK47s and rocket launchers, belts of bullets draped from
their bodies—

Teera blinks away her fear.

Mr. Chum's honking grows insistent. Narunn murmurs something,
rising from his slouch, his voice husky with sleep. Lah follows suit, sitting upright in the backseat, rubbing her eyes. "There they are," Mr.

Chum says, sounding suddenly relieved. "Didn't want to bump into them by mistake in these dirt clouds."

The dust slowly begins to settle, and it's clear why the old driver has been so vigilant. Straight ahead, in a row on either side of the road, dusty gaunt figures crouch with buckets and bowls in hand, tossing water in repeated arcs that wet the ground, their gestures ceremonial—funereal. Teera's breath catches, and for some seconds she is unsure whether they are phantoms from the past—mere mirage—or actual ghosts rising from the splintered earth. What time period has memory dragged her into now? What unfinished graves have they disturbed? As their car moves nearer, she sees that the figures are mostly elders and children, but their haggardness, their destitution, makes them at first glance indistinguishable one from another.

"What are they doing?" Teera asks, when at last she finds her voice.

There is silence in the car, as if such things are inexplicable, defy expression. Teera asks again. Finally Narunn says, "They're watering the road to keep the dust down. So we can see." He pauses, clearing his throat. "In return, they hope we'll give them food, some small change, whatever we can spare."

"I don't understand. How can this be? How can they live . . ." Teera hears the despair in her own voice, something breaking inside herself.

"*Srok yeung* . . ." Mr. Chum murmurs, as if "this country of ours" were explanation enough.

"But where are their homes? There are no huts here, not even trees to offer shade. Where do they come from? And where are their children?— Who cares for them? . . ." Teera grows more agitated with each word.

"They come from villages around here," Narunn says, keeping his voice even. "To some who pass by, they are just beggars. But they are grandparents, and the little ones are their grandchildren. Many are orphans because their parents have died."

"Of what?"

"Disease. Hunger. Poverty."

"But their heads are shaven . . . Are they in mourning?"

"Perhaps some are. It's possible that some have recently lost loved ones. But it's also because they've taken the Buddhist vow of renunciation and, as you know, under normal circumstances, they would be meditating at temples, trying to find peace in their old age."

"But the heat—it's too hot for them to be out there. It's too hot. They should not be out here. They shouldn't."

"But there they are."

There they are. Forfeiting their comfort to stoop on this dusty road and beg for food to feed their children's children. The simple truth of it slices Teera. She remembers her grandparents, sees them now among these living ghosts in the path of the car—her proud, powerful grandfather hiding stolen grains in his mouth to keep for her when he returned home from the fields; her grandmother tentatively tasting this fruit or that leaf to make sure it wasn't poison before giving it to her. *What kind of mother can't keep her child alive?* her grandmother had wept bitterly that afternoon upon learning the fate of her grandson and elder daughter. At first Suteera thought it an accusation against Channara, but over time—as she watched her grief-stricken grandmother, witnessed her unfaltering gentleness toward others in spite of her own anguish—she would come to understand it as a mother's indictment against herself. Perhaps, like Channara, her grandmother wanted to die, to punish herself for failing to keep her child alive. Certainly it would've been easier for her to let go, to renounce this world with its interminable suffering. But her grandmother lived, carried on, because she had Suteera to look after. Just as Yaya, Teera realizes all of a sudden, must've fought to live in order to care for her brood of grandchildren, even as she mourned her own children in the ground.

Perhaps the question isn't *how* anyone can live like this, bearing a lifetime of cruelty and deprivation, but what makes them *want* to live in a world indifferent to their struggle. What? Is it the recognition that life extends beyond your own being—that it doesn't reside in you alone but in everyone and everything you wish to see endure?

A river surges through Teera, flooding her face, the desolation around her. "Please stop the car," she says, barely able to speak. "I— W-we can't just drive past them."

Lah, seeing the tears, pulls Teera to her chest. "It's okay, Mommy," she says. The child, in her bewilderment, must be confusing Teera with her absent mother. "It's okay. Don't look, Mommy. They make you sad. Don't look at them."

"But they have nothing," Teera sobs, in the way she never could, would never allow herself, when she witnessed her brother's starvation, the hunger that would kill him. "They have no food, no shade. They have nothing, and they're giving us their water." She knows she's not making any sense.

"Please don't cry." Lah presses Teera's face tighter against her tiny chest, caressing her. "We can give them our picnic food—I don't need any! I'm not hungry."

Both men are silent. Mr. Chum has managed to pull the car onto the side of the road, parking it on a patch of scraggly, dried-up leafy vines. Lah continues to caress Teera, humming softly now.

When Teera regains her composure, Narunn, reaching for her hand, asks, "Should we get out and say hello?" Teera hesitates, heart fluttering, then nods.

As they approach, a throng gathers around them, puzzled, curious. Lah passes out the food Teera brought from the hotel café and the fresh fruits they'd purchased along the way. Mr. Chum, who knew what to expect from having driven this road many times before, starts dispensing the stack of hundred-riel notes Teera saw him change at a gas station earlier. Narunn and Teera contribute some bills of their own to the pile. It's not enough. It's never going to be enough, Teera realizes with dismay.

How is it that even decades after the war the suffering seems ineradicable? In the beginning Teera thought she might become used to it, that its sheer breadth and magnitude would simply numb her. But the longer she stays, the more she struggles with it. A child bathing in an open sewage canal. A mother raking through mounds of trash to feed and clothe her little ones, beneath billboards advertising luxury watches, all-you-can-eat buffets. A sightless father playing his instrument, as his exquisitely poised daughter sings beside him in rags, offering beautiful music to a world that does not deserve it. Each time she encounters them, Teera is gripped by the desire to give away everything. Some days she is driven mad with despair, the sense that there's not a single thing she can do. Then there are moments, like this, when she feels enraged and inspired in equal measure, because the struggle for breath, for meaning and purpose, is never more courageous than amidst insurmountable injustice.

They've done what they can for the moment. There's nothing more to give. As they say good-bye, Teera feels a hand grasp hers. She turns toward it, and a toothless grandmother says, "My daughter . . . she was about your age." *The thing about loss is that it rims the silhouette of every face you encounter.* "I'm sorry," Teera tells her, thinking now of the grandmother she abandoned to die in a cave. She says again, "I'm so sorry."

The elder nods, lets go.

At the wildlife sanctuary, Lah quickly forgets their earlier sorrow on the road, delighted by every creature they encounter. A baby elephant with a partially ruined ear greets them, extending its trunk toward the little girl in that exhalation of a Cambodian kiss. A peacock shows off its iridescent plumage, and they note that one of its legs is missing. A sun bear with a bandaged paw nuzzles an opened coconut, licking it again and again, savoring every drop of juice. The bear falls on its back, rolling in the dust, the coconut stuck to its face, like a toddler with his bottle.

In front of a large wired cage, a ragtag group of village children are gearing up for some sort of showdown with the gibbons. One of the boys, with hair as wild and dusty as the monkeys, presses his lips to the cage, gives a little hoot at a solemn-looking female, she hoots back, he does it again, she gets excited, hooting until her body shakes—revved up like an engine for some long minutes—so that she has to hug herself in order to stop. The boy bows, conceding loss, and offers the crowd's thundering applause to her.

Narunn goes up to the cage and tries to repeat the boy's feat, but the gibbon he's baiting turns its back in gruff defiance. The children laugh, telling him that the male gibbons are stingy and less likely to fall for human tricks. Seizing the opportunity, the boy with wild copper-colored hair quickly appoints himself as their "tour guide," offering facts and tidbits about the animals they've just seen. Teera learns that the animals, like the humans here, have suffered much. They are former victims of one cruelty or another, rescued from illegal trade, from those who sought to sell them for profit, for game and pleasure, or for some misconceived cure for human afflictions. The baby elephant was wounded when a poacher shot and killed its mother. The peacock lost its leg in a trap set up by those who kill such birds for medicine. The sun bear had its paw broken by an owner who thought it a difficult pet because the cub didn't like being chained by its neck. The owner had sold the cub to a Chinese restaurant specializing in bear paw soup for wealthy Asian businessmen. Seeing the terrified expression on Lah's face, the boy quickly assures, "But it's safe now—and happy!" And to prove his point, he raises his arms high and whistles to the sun bear. The little cub stares at him for a moment, then reluctantly abandons the coconut, slowly stands up, and raises its unhurt arm, keeping his bandaged paw lowered. The boy gives the sun bear a triumphant whoop.

They've noticed that the boy has burn scars all over his body, and as they meander along, Lah stares and stares at him, then finally blurts out, "Little uncle, why is your skin wrinkly like tree bark?" Unfazed, their guide says, addressing the grown-ups, as if all this time aware of their persistent but muted curiosity, "When I was little I got gasoline mixed up with cooking oil. When I poured the gasoline into the frying pan, flames leapt up and swallowed me whole!" A shadow darkens his face for a few seconds. Then, banishing it with a shake of his wild hair, he declares, "But I was only five then—now I'm nine!"

They walk past a large enclosed muddy pit with what at first resembles a group of cement statues but on closer look turns out to be a cluster of live crocodiles lazing about in the muck. One has its jaws wide open. The boy informs them, "It'll snap at whatever you toss its way—bananas, mangoes, monkeys." He glances at Lah, and then, winking at Mr. Chum, pretends to whisper—in a voice loud enough for all to hear—"And little girls who ask too many questions!" Mr. Chum lets out an uproarious laugh, only to be promptly silenced by a look from Teera. Lah scurries away from the mud pit and attaches herself to Narunn.

The two walk hand in hand for a while, one very tall and the other very small, and as they approach the reptile den, he lifts her up and perches her on his shoulders so that she can see inside—a clutch of pythons curled like giant painted pretzels, the near stillness of their breathing belying the strength of their grip.

"Nineteen . . . seventy . . . eight," the man murmurs aloud, saying each number slowly, as he scribbles the year across a paper on the stack in front of him. He puts down his pen, looks up, and asks, motioning to the tray atop his desk, "Would you like some tea?"

Tun makes no reply, and his host pours some from the pot into the only cup. To Tun's relief, the tea appears to be cool, not scalding hot as he feared. The man ponders the faintly brown liquid, takes a sip, and sets the cup down, nodding to his young colleagues, his directive barely perceptible. The boys escort Tun into a chair facing the man's desk in the middle of the room. His head spins, his vision wavers, and Tun feels he might pitch forward, falling flat on his face onto the smeared tile floor, if not for the hands gripping his shoulders. Irrationally, he's grateful to be sitting down—on a chair no less, and in a room with a writing desk, the very implement of education, reason. Maybe it'll be different this time. His faint heartbeat rises.

"How can we make this easier, less painful, for both of us?" his host murmurs from behind the desk, his head turning to the window that frames the expansive trunk of a tree. Tun wants to speak, tell the man how grateful he is, but his mouth will not open, his jaws throb in resistance. He can only swallow, tasting the tea against his parched throat, his body's thirst overwhelming. *It's not hunger that will kill you . . .* His mind strays, and he wonders what else besides the giant tree exists beyond the small square window lined with iron bars. Earlier, he was blindfolded as they pushed him across the compound, and now inside the room, with the door shut, he is allowed to see again. Other rooms they've taken him to were stripped of furniture, and without windows. This one seems strangely civilized, ordinary. *How can we make this easier, less painful, for both of us?* Tun reins his thoughts back in, trying to make sense of the question, what more they want from him. He has told them everything, his entire biography. Exhausted the list of possible traitors and enemies he can name.

"Nothing?" The host keeps his gaze fixed on the tree trunk. To Tun, the bark appears to be rippling, like the skin of a moving animal, a python perhaps. Or maybe they are armies of ants marching along the grooves. Again, his vision wavers, burns, and when he tries to blink, he sees the contour of the steel cable that eviscerated his face in the predawn hours. The ants circle his encumbered ankles, prickling his skin. How did they get in? He glimpses a trail stretching from the doorway to him. Blood. On the floor and walls. Everywhere. It assaults him, colors everything he sees, seeps into everything he tastes—his own saliva, the sweat on his lips, the air.

His host turns from the window and begins to shuffle through the stack of papers on his desk, glancing at each page, the sweep of his hand sometimes brusque, sometimes drawn out. He appears angry—no, impatient, annoyed. But never angry. "Nothing," the man repeats, even-tempered. "Absolutely nothing we can use."

Tun tries to remember this is someone who is fastidiously disciplined. Someone who in a former life taught literature, or maybe law, or the literature of law. In any case, a man of honed intelligence, not at all a barbarian.

"Mostly blank," the man continues monotonously. "You've left most of these pages blank. You haven't told us the truth we already know."

There is something strange about the phrasing. Every word sounds like a trap. *If you already know, why ask?* He dares not voice his rebellion. Instead, he focuses on a black revolutionary cap hanging from a loose nail in the wall above the man's head. A still object. Weightless, benign. It exerts no harm, even if hurled with force. To the far right, in the periphery of his vision, hover familiar objects. A cow's rope, frayed from overuse. Steel cables of varied length and diameter. Electric cords with exposed copper wires, metal clamps. A clear plastic bag, soiled with condensation and spit. A pair of pliers. All in a tidy row, each tool on its own hook, secure in its purpose. Beneath, a phrase drawn in charcoal. Even without turning his head, Tun knows what it says—*You must not scream under any circumstance.* The rule is scrawled across the wall of every such room. Beaten into him.

"Is there nothing more you can write, Comrade? Nothing more you want to tell us?"

My hands . . . Just as he thinks this, Tun feels the metal band coming off one wrist; his arms swiftly pulled back behind the chair, manacles clanging, banging against wood; then his hands bound once more. They are quick, unlocking and locking him in mere seconds, the two guard dogs. No, guards. *Boys.* They are boys. Humans like him. He has to believe this. They're capable of reason. If not that, then at least pity. Some part of them must pity him. One bends down now and straps his already shackled legs to the chair. Fear makes Tun delirious. So he hopes, as he always does, that this time will be different. Hope is his body's last defense before the inevitable final defeat, which will come at the hour they alone decide. Along with the written rules are the unwritten ones—*You must not die under torture. You will suffer as long as we deem necessary. If you die, then another will suffer on your behalf.*

"Let us be like brothers," his host susurrates. "With no secrets between us. You confess, and I write it down. Will this be easier, less painful?"

His host. This too, Tun must believe. That the man facing him is capable of human decency. A person who invites you into his space and offers you tea cannot be completely dispossessed of kindness. Tun's mind splits in two, one half arguing with the other. There must be a sliver of humanity one can appeal to. *Let us be like brothers* . . . Yes, brothers. Tun tries to nod but pain shoots from the base of his neck to the top of his skull. He remembers the club that caused it. He desperately wants to please his host—to cooperate, as they say. But silence fills his throat. Fear mocks him, laughing. *You think you can overcome me?*

Suddenly a current of air rises, and with it the man in front of him, palms slamming the desk, tea tray rattling—"Talk!" The black cap drops to the floor behind him, the nail clattering briefly across the tile floor, revealing a fractured hole in the plaster of the wall. Tun feels like that hole, barely visible yet thoroughly worn. His body an orifice of pain.

When all is still again, the chief interrogator says, returning to his practiced monotony, "Let's begin with a simple question." He takes another sip of tea, swooshing it in his mouth as if ridding his tongue of some bad taste before swallowing. "What is today's date, Comrade?"

He cannot remember. The year, yes—1978, as the chief interrogator announced earlier—but today's date he doesn't know. *He doesn't know.* Another tide of panic seizes him, and he can only recall that he was in a similar room earlier—this morning, yesterday, the day before, the whole of this week? Round it goes, the same questioning, the same illogic. *You're here because you're guilty, you're guilty because you're here.* He feels a sudden tightening around his ankles and recognizes it now. Not ants. Wires attached to him. Somewhere in the room, he knows, is a car battery. His torso jerks involuntarily. The residual shudder of electricity from an earlier session. The body remembers, even as the mind makes no sense. *What is today's date, Comrade?* Time ceases in hell. Only the cycle of torture. His nerves brace, his throat clamps shut. *You must not scream under any circumstance.* A jolt of electricity rattles his core, splitting him in half. Fire surges through his blood and all he wants is water. Water, please. Water. Just a drop on his tongue. Yes, the tea, the tea. Just a sip. A brief clarity—they put the tea in his direct vision yet out of his reach, knowing this is what he will want after the jolt. The liquid is meant to torment him. Everything can be a tool. *Confess your crimes, and you can go back to your cell! CONFESS!* Tun's head explodes. He cannot separate thoughts from speech, his own howling from the scream of his tormentors, from the roar of flames scourging his insides. Words escape his throat, burning as they go, splintering into myriad bright points, needles and spears. Lightning rods. Another jolt. Then another. His world blackens.

Back in his cell, Tun remembers the date. It was something he ought to have easily recalled. They'd told him earlier, at the predawn interrogation, during which he'd signed and dated his confession. Did he not remember? *No.* He couldn't utter even this single response, let alone offer more. Panic took precedence, and pain became his sole consciousness. So they accused him once again of deliberately withholding information. Undoubtedly then, he would conceal more sensitive matters, such as plots to overthrow the Organization and countless other treasons. *You've betrayed the party. If you deny it, then you're claiming the party is wrong, and this in itself is treason. No matter what you say, you are guilty, you stinking corpse! There's no escaping it!*

The last bit is the only truth they speak. He cannot escape. The certainty of it hit him again when he woke and realized he did not die as he'd hoped. Death is the only way out of Slak Daek, the only mercy granted, if any, and the party alone decides when it will come. They will keep him alive for as long as they need him to confirm their suspicions, give proof to their fears, feed their paranoia. There's always another name, another traitor he can point them to. Another life he can exchange for one more gulp of air. But he does not want to live. There is no reason to. She is gone. His anchor and compass. His life's purpose.

Perhaps this is the "truth" they say they already know and he need only admit—that it was never the Organization he'd fought for and loved. To that, he must confess. He's been a traitor all along.

The date, he now recalls, is September 5, 1978—that is if it's still the same day. He's not certain how long he blacked out. It doesn't matter. Time serves no purpose, brings no splinter of light into his interminable nights blindfolded in a coffinlike cell, except as reminder of the sustained lie he told himself. He believed he could protect her, despite the grim reality, the total transformation of his land and people, the metamorphosis of idealism into depravity. After all, he'd kept her safe and alive even in those terrible months after Om Paan was killed, even through the countless battles in that last year before the Revolutionary Army won and seized control of the entire country. If she survived the war as it raged around her, escaping explosions and gunfire only meters away, while his soldiers smoldered like termites in a farmer's field fire, then she would survive anything. It was a matter of luck, reinforced by love, his fierce determination to safeguard her life with his own. On the battleground one learns to believe in such things as luck and destiny, when time and again a skilled commander falls to a single bullet and a clumsy foot soldier survives a blast that has obliterated his entire infantry. It was his daughter's destiny to live.

When the Revolutionary Army captured Phnom Penh that April in 1975 and the long, bloody civil war came to a close, Tun thought the most dangerous part of his journey was over. Even amidst the devastation caused by the conflict, the chaos that followed as cities were emptied and people arbitrarily flung to rural areas all over the country, he remained assured that order would be restored, that peace and calm would eventually come. Out of the maelstrom, the country would remake itself, and so would he. Mistakes could not be undone; nonetheless, he resolved to do good, because, having glimpsed barbarity at close range, it was the only way he knew to be human again.

During the mass evacuation, while patrolling a district some distance from Phnom Penh, he would find ways for families to stay together when they were threatened with separation. He'd send city dwellers toward towns and villages where they had family connections so they'd be welcome. He'd help lost children find their parents or, if they were orphaned, assign them to people who seemed good and kind, and likely to care for them. When transport became available, he'd give a place to the elderly and the disabled first. He tried to set an example for the company under his command. Though he did not always succeed. Once several soldiers marched into a small temple and ordered the monks out at gunpoint. While the battle-crazed adolescents shot at sacred shrines and statues, he herded the monks into a recently evacuated villa outside the temple ground and told them to shed their monastic robes and put on whatever ordinary clothes they could find. It was for their safety, he explained. Another time he had been unable to stop a soldier from shooting a man who'd tried to flee, apparently an officer from the defeated government army. Tun heard shouting behind him, then a shot, and as he spun around, he saw that the officer had already fallen to the ground, his face in the dirt, a bullet through the back of his head.

In situations like these, he was grateful that his daughter was back at the temporary base, cared for now by female comrades in a platoon assigned to provide backup support to his company during the evacuation period. Weeks after Om Paan's death on the battleground in Oudong, his daughter tried to ask him why her beloved nanny had died in that horrible manner, why she'd died at all, and he could offer only this feeble explanation: "Because there's a war." She nodded, as if agreeing, as if she understood the cold injustice of warfare. Then after a moment she said, "It's your fault, Papa. It's your fault." She never spoke again of Om Paan, or asked him why soldiers as young as herself were killed before her eyes in the subsequent battles she was forced to witness at his side. But she wouldn't have needed to say another word, for he'd come to accept her judgment as irrevocable truth. When one engages in war, one must take responsibility for every life lost.

He no longer wanted to be a soldier, revolutionary or otherwise. He wanted only what the Organization promised to every citizen in Democratic Kampuchea: a simple life in the countryside. At the end of '75, six or seven months into the new regime, the first "purifying" campaign was launched in an effort to cleanse the insidious bourgeois tendencies within the party membership itself. Art was unequivocally bourgeois, so Tun, a former musician and an intellectual, was stripped of his cadre rank, as were countless other party members of similar background. Henceforth, he was told, to sharpen his proletarian consciousness he had to work in the fields as a rice farmer. Yet, because of his valuable contribution during the insurgency against the Lon Nol government, he could transfer to a village of his own choosing.

Tun could hardly believe his luck, as if the Organization had heard and granted his wish. Many others were not so fortunate. Comrade Im— the commandant of the forest encampment where Tun had received his training—was eliminated; his previous collaborations with Vietnamese comrades marked him ideologically impure.

Tun took his daughter to Chhlong, his mother's birthplace in Kratie. They were assigned a traditional wooden house on stilts facing east to the Mekong. The house was small but sturdy, with one big room in front and a long, narrow cooking area in back. His daughter's favorite spot was at the top of the stairs, where she would sit in the doorway and search the currents for the Irrawaddy dolphins known in that part of the river. Once, shortly after they'd arrived, he took her on a boat at sunrise and they encountered a pod of the dolphins playing with the light bouncing off the water just meters away. The smallest one—a calf not much bigger than a bolster pillow—flipped and swam backward, seeming to wave gleefully to them with its stubby fins. His daughter was utterly delighted, the happiest she'd ever been since they left home. He couldn't return to her everything she'd lost—their home in Phnom Penh, Om Paan, her childhood—but he could give her this momentary joy. So at sunrise before joining others at the rice fields each morning, they'd slide out in the palm dugout and wait for the dolphins.

In this way, they became father and daughter again, taking pleasure in the newness of their surroundings, the reassuring pattern of village life, the company of kindhearted villagers who noted his daughter was without a mother and he was without a wife. Some of the village elders remembered Tun's mother from her youth, before she married and moved away to Neak Leung, and this knowledge was enough for Tun and his daughter to be regarded by the village cadres as peasants rather than former city dwellers, the less desirable class. Residents of Chhlong were charmed to see how this "widower" was so devoted to his only child, and how the motherless girl in turn seemed protective of her father. At work in the fields, they would sometimes spot her hugging him with innocent exuberance, and despite knowing the rules against familial affection, many could not help wishing their children might show them similar tenderness.

As the revolution intensified, with rumors of extreme hardship and starvation in other parts of the country, Chhlong was buffered from the most radical policies. Comrade So Phim, secretary of the East Zone that included this corner of Kratie, had a reputation for being lenient, seeing no need to enforce communal eating or revolutionary attire, at least not until much later. He was a hugely popular party leader, whom Tun first heard of when fighting in Kompong Cham, in an area east of the Mekong under Comrade So's military command. It was this tenuous connection with a man he'd never met that would later prove perilous.

Since the first "purifying" campaign that stripped Tun of his rank, the Party Center had launched successive nationwide purges, each rooting out and eliminating tens of thousands of "traitors." By April or May of '77, two years into the regime, rumors of mass killings had become indisputable reality. Whole families disappeared from Chhlong, as others arrived, heaving like colonies of the undead, emaciated and tormented, only to be carted away again. Severe rice shortages plagued the country, most shockingly in the Northwest Zone, once the most fertile land. The Party Center blamed the bad harvests on "certain internal enemies" plotting to overthrow the Organization and undermine the regime. Entire communes came under suspicion, accused of harboring traitors, and villagers were massacred en masse.

Then, only three or four months ago, Comrade So, rumored to be among the accused, disappeared. Some said he shot and killed himself when the Party Center ordered his arrest. It was impossible for Tun to know with certainty. So much was kept from ordinary people, with impenetrable layers of secrecy woven around the Organization. He didn't want to ask questions that would draw attention, or do anything that could brand him an enemy of the regime. Like all, he lived in terror from one day to the next.

One evening at the beginning of August, he was at home with his daughter. Together they had returned from the fields, the sunset magical after the rain, casting a shimmering rainbow over the water, so they thought they'd go down to the river to wash and possibly catch a glimpse of the dolphins. She'd stepped inside to collect a change of clothes for them each, and while waiting he scanned the river for bobbing heads or the flick of a tail. So absorbed was he in his search that he did not notice the three revolutionary guards approaching until they'd already surrounded him.

"The Organization summons you," they said. Tun went completely cold. Those four unmistakable words were his death sentence, and to ask what crime might warrant such a punishment would only have provoked his execution on the spot. He recognized them as new guards, recently posted to his village, so he could not rely on familiarity. Instead he tried pleading, but his words came out muddled—"Comrades, my daughter . . . she's only twelve." She was still a child, he'd meant to say, and she needed him. Their response was equally obscure: "Yes, we know, and that is exactly your crime. Your *own* daughter!"

"Papa." He heard her whisper from the top of the stairs. A bourgeois term. She hadn't called him this in a long time. Since liberation, it'd always been "Father," and, more recently, "Comrade Father." He saw the fear in her eyes, heard it in her voice. He summoned what was left of his own courage and responded in kind, abandoning her revolutionary name: "Sita, my love." If this was to be the last time, he wanted her to know what she'd meant to him. "My life—" His throat swelled. He couldn't say more.

They ordered her back inside the house and pulled him away. He made no attempt to resist. By now he'd stopped thinking of his own life. If she was to survive without him, he mustn't give them any reason to punish her. He kept walking without once turning back. The villagers would care for her. She was deeply loved. She would know who to go to.

At a crossroad outside the village, an oxcart waited for them. Tun climbed in, and the guards quickly bound his wrists and ankles, blindfolded him. He didn't understand the need for all this—it would've been simpler to end his life with a bullet.

As the cart trundled along uneven paths, the evening turned to night, the darkness beneath his blindfold deepened, the crickets came out and tuned their ensembles. Several hours must've passed before the oxcart finally stopped. Tun felt a pair of hands loosen the rope around his ankles. Another hand urged him off the cart. He stood swaying for a moment before regaining his balance. They took turns shoving him forward and he waddled barefooted, his car-tire sandals abandoned on the oxcart, until they paused at what sounded like a wooden door creaking open. A final shove, and the door banged shut. The rattle of metal chain and lock. He was on a hard cement floor, alone in pitch-blackness, imprisoned within layer upon layer of incomprehensibility.

The first blow came in the middle of the night. He thought the roof had collapsed. A white brightness flooded the room, blinding him. A flashlight in his eyes, the blindfold having slipped to his nose. Then came the second blow, a rifle butt to the side of his head. Blood seeped through his hair and down his cheekbone. *Confess your crime!* He tried to tell them he'd committed no crime, but this only earned him a kick in his chest. Still he persisted, and still they were not convinced. More kicks, more blows, until he heaved against the cement with only enough breath to utter, *W-w-what crime?* The answer was more devastating than the violence they'd rained down on him: *You've had an immoral relationship with your daughter. We've seen you hug. As you said, she is twelve, not a little baby. She doesn't need to be comforted in such a way. It is immoral. This kind of love—between father and daughter—is impure. She's also arrested, and if you don't want her to suffer like you, then you must confess your crime— all your crimes, including your traitorous connections, everyone in your* ksae kbot, *your string of traitors and betrayals . . .*

By then, his heart had stopped.

What is today's date, Comrade? Now that the answer has come to him, he wishes he could laugh. Memory is the enemy, the serial traitor. It betrays him again and again. Yet, he never learns. He forgets. He forgets that no one is safe—no man, woman, or child. He forgets that anything you do, or do *not* do, can be seen as a crime. He forgets that once accused, you are guilty, and everyone you know is culpable by association. He forgets, he forgot. He told them what they wanted to know—how he came to be linked to the traitor So Phim, where he'd first heard of the man, why he'd chosen to settle in Chhlong . . . He told them the truths and the lies, all they wanted him to admit. *Isn't it true that you'd been under that traitor's command from the beginning? Wasn't this the reason you chose Chhlong, a district in his zone, so that you could continue to plot against the Organization with him and others in his network? Who else do you know? Give us names— everyone you once knew, everyone you know now, all the people you've ever known. If you don't give us enough names to add to your* ksae *. . . Let's put it this way—do you want your daughter to die? It is as simple as that, you see.*

Again, memory deserted him, and he forgot all over again the evil they could do. So he told them, writing confession after confession, list after list. Countless names. Some real, others invented. But it made no difference. All the truths he'd purged, the lies he'd conjured. They murdered her anyway and threw her in the Mekong. Now she could swim with the dolphins, they told him, laughing. They'd defiled her, he learned in another round of beating. In this way, they made truth of their lies. The party *is* that powerful. He ought to remember.

Tun turns in his cell, bumping into a wall either way. It's not the same cell they threw him into that night after his arrest. This is Sala Slak Daek. They've brought him from Kratie to Kompong Thom, to a proper *santebal*—a security center. Chhlong is far away, and he would like to forget it, forget his entire life. But he cannot. Memory is deceitful.

He hears a moan in the adjacent cell and, against his will, remembers it is Sokhon. Aung Sokhon. One of the many names his memory be-trayed. A life he exchanged in the desperate hope to save his daughter's. He loved her. Purely, profoundly. Innocently.

But love is no excuse.

A single throb in her heart, like a drumbeat. She wakes. *Where am I? . . .* It takes Teera some seconds to be fully conscious of her surroundings. Beside her, Lah is facedown under the cover, one arm around the purple silk elephant they bought at the hotel gift shop, the other hanging off the side of the bed. Seeing the child in her bed, Teera wonders, how can so small a life exert such hold, such sense of anchoring, upon her own?

She leans over the child to look, and sure enough, Narunn has been edged off and is napping on the floor, elbow draped over his forehead, hand tentatively clasping Lah's. Again, Teera's heart throbs, the cartography of love, its ever-expanding frontiers.

A drum echoes, the same sound that woke her, that she'd mistaken for her own heartbeat. Quietly, she rises and steps through the glass door onto the balcony, following the sound. On the grassy lawn adjacent to the children's pool, a group of adolescents are arranging musical instruments on a raised platform for a performance later this evening, it seems. The large placard on an easel to the side says it is an ensemble of "former street children" trained by a local NGO specializing in traditional music. In the middle of the arrangement, the oldest-looking of the children—a boy about fourteen—hits a painted *sampho*, first with his left hand, then his right, alternately testing each head of the barrel drum. It's twice as big as the one in the Old Musician's care.

The Old Musician. He lingers always at the periphery of consciousness, more persistent than the ghosts. Teera sighs . . . She hasn't been able to stop thinking of him since their return several hours ago from Phnom Tamao.

Leaving the wildlife sanctuary, they'd intended to drop Lah back at the temple as planned, but when they telephoned the Venerable Kong Oul to say they were on their way, he informed them that the Old Musician hadn't yet come back from the city, which meant Teera wouldn't be able to see him. Just as well, she thought. She was tired, they all were, so she asked the abbot if it would be all right to take Lah to the hotel and keep her for the night. The abbot couldn't have been more delighted. It is now dusk, and Teera wonders if the Old Musician has returned to the temple. She'd been dreaming of him when she suddenly woke to the sound of the drum. She can't recall a single detail of the dream. Surely the abbot would call if anything happened.

She goes back inside and checks her cell phone. There's no missed call. She unmutes it, just in case. Then she walks to where Narunn lies on the floor and, brushing her lips against his, whispers, "Hey, sleepy head."

He stirs, opens one eye, then the other. "Hey, sleepy heart . . ."

She laughs. He gives a quick glance at the child, whose hand is still in his, and to Teera says, his voice unusually clear for someone just waking, "Let's go to Siem Reap. Let's take her with us."

"What?"

Narunn lets go of Lah's hand and pulls Teera to him. They lie in each other's arms, her head on his chest, and he says softly, exhaling sleep from his body, "I was just now dreaming of home . . . You remember, I told you it's on the Tonle Sap Lake, not far from Siem Reap. A fishing village." Teera nods. "The two of you were there with me. You met my mother, my whole family. They'd been waiting for us. They were still alive . . . It was all so real."

They are both still, and even without looking, Teera knows his eyes are closed as he tries to imagine them again, tries to bring back the dream. She listens to his heart, its music. Now and then the *sampho* answers, setting the rhythm, leading the way.

He has remained, unable to move, shackled to his corner by remembering. On several occasions during the day, strangers kindly stopped to ask if he was lost and needed help to find his way home, or if he had a home at all. When the Old Musician assured them he was all right, thanking them for their concern, some tried to offer money, which he humbly refused. But when a little girl from a noodle shop across the street came in the heat of the day with a packet of fried noodles and a bottle of water, he accepted this timely generosity, nodding in muted gratitude toward her parents, the proprietors of the shop. It is now evening, and in the gathering dusk the White Building appears less imposing, as if it might vanish completely when night arrives. But he knows it will survive the dark, as it has for decades.

In recent years, the aging structure has provoked an ever-intensifying debate among disparate groups—activists fighting to preserve it for the historic value, developers maneuvering to demolish it and erect something new on one of the city's most valuable plots of land, residents still living inside because it is the only home they've ever known. Several months back Dr. Narunn read to him a magazine feature on the White Building's architect, Lu Ban Hap, who—second only to the renowned Vann Molyvann—was a driving force behind the New Khmer Architecture movement of the post-independence period.

In 1949, the feature said, Lu Ban Hap traveled with other students on a steam ocean liner from Saigon to Marseilles. In Paris, many of his fellow Cambodian students became enthralled with Marxism. Yet Lu Ban Hap—

encouraged by Vann Molyvann, who had arrived a few years earlier—pursued a different sort of revolutionary education at the École nationale supérieure des Beaux-Arts, where he became a disciple of Le Corbusier, the famed leader of modernist architecture. Whereas Marx advocated political mobilization as the path to social transformation, Le Corbusier's modernism espoused a reimagining of the physical environments that structure social interaction, eschewing ornamentation in favor of mathematical order and harmony. The article went on to translate into Khmer a quote from Le Corbusier's manifesto *Vers une architecture*—"At the root of today's social unrest is a question of building: architecture or revolution."

Absorbing every word read to him, the Old Musician had the odd sensation that this line was a reprise from a forgotten conversation. Days later, it came to him. *Music . . . or revolution. Before us lay these two paths, my friend . . . We made a terrible mistake. But choice was always there. It's available to us even now, even here . . .*

Here in Slak Daek. This was what Sokhon meant. When Tun first learned that they had ended up in adjoining cells, he could hardly believe it. Yet, he had only to remind himself that those with a shared history were often brought to the same prison, even from different provinces. According to the brutal logic of the Organization, witnessing the torture of a friend or loved one would make a victim more likely to confess to any crime. Why then should Tun be surprised that their separate paths had suddenly converged? After all, on the list of people he'd implicated, he'd declared Sokhon a "friend of a friend."

Once in Slak Daek—in those last months of 1978—he and Sokhon did indeed become friends. That too was a choice. For in that hellhole where they festered as condemned enemies of the state, friendship was an act of rebellion, their joint sabotage, the only possible shadow of escape. They stole every chance they could to talk, to mourn, to remember. Though they couldn't see through the wall of wood planks separating their two cells, they heard each other's moans and cries, half-choked breaths, silent entreaties for death to come. A strange intimacy grew between them, as if pain—the agony of the body—exposes the heart as only love should. In this way, each man knew as much as he could bear to know about the other.

In March 1974, the night of his daughter's eighth birthday, Sokhon had gone underground, leaving his family behind. For months, he and Channara had talked it through, deciding that the birthday celebration would provide the perfect cover and, most important, prove his commitment to the cause. Why else would he abandon his daughter on such a special day? Given the family background—their privilege and status, their time in America—it was crucial for Sokhon to demonstrate his revolutionary zeal, Channara advised, if he was to come back for her and Suteera without eliciting suspicion. Sokhon's entry into the movement was facilitated by a prominent party intellectual and commander of the North Zone, Comrade Kuon, who, shunning the austerity of the typical Communist military commander, enveloped himself with an atmosphere of art and festivity. It was this love of art—in particular music—that had connected the two men. Sokhon would spend the next year in various forest encampments in the liberated North Zone, crafting revolutionary songs with words to incite the masses, molding his own artistic sensibilities to party doctrine. Art is not born of inspiration, he learned, but of blood and sweat, the proletariat aspiration. An artist is merely another weapon of the revolution.

The following March, on the week of Suteera's ninth birthday, he returned to Phnom Penh as planned. The war had reached its climax, with insurgent forces closing in on the capital, poised for victory. The American and other foreign embassies were preparing to evacuate. It was only a matter of weeks, possibly days, before the old regime would collapse and a new, brighter Cambodia rise in its place. In the meantime, Sokhon told Channara, he could not risk capture by staying in the city longer than he already had. Although a revolutionary, he was only a civil cadre, and had to rely on the help of soldier comrades to scurry safely through combat zones. He would return once the city had been fully liberated, and Channara should be prepared then to leave with him and journey to an area of Kompong Cham in the North Zone where their new home would be. They would take Suteera but must cut ties with the rest of the family. Would Channara be able to make this ultimate sacrifice? Yes, came her firm reply. Amidst a relentless siege, Sokhon slipped back out of the city, abandoning them as he'd done before.

Liberation came a few short weeks later, but, to his bewilderment, Sokhon could not return to the city, having been ordered to stay put. He was given no explanation, only this firm warning: *A great deal is uncertain, alliances are shifting, and many are scrutinized. If you make the wrong move, we cannot guarantee your safety, let alone that of your family or anyone connected to you.* Sokhon waited, clutching to the wan hope that Channara had remembered and would try to make her way to him with Suteera somehow. One month passed, then another, then many more . . . Finally, 1975 was coming to a close, and the only news he received concerned his own fate—he would be posted to a remote labor camp in the upper reach of Kompong Thom, his membership in the party revoked. He was advised by a sympathetic comrade not to seek help from any high-ranking cadres he knew, as they may already be implicated in some web of accusation. Instead, he should use this opportunity to disappear, go to Kompong Thom as ordered, and wait it out, until the party had purged itself of traitors. So Sokhon went, he disappeared, motivated by the fear that if he stayed in Kompong Cham, he might very well encounter his family and jeopardize their lives, now that he himself was somehow marked. Surely the party would right itself and everything would calm down soon.

The purge continued, seemingly without pause. One campaign hardly ended before another was launched, the supposed enemies multiplying like lice, connected in an indecipherable tangle of strands. Comrade Kuon seemed to have vanished, his zone divided and passed on to others. The rhetoric following his disappearance suggested that he had come under suspicion of the party leadership.

In Kompong Thom, Sokhon was no longer a musician and composer but was assigned to be an instrument maker, a man with far humbler skills, more like a carpenter, which put him in the laboring class, kept him safe. When not digging irrigation ditches or clearing bamboo forests for rice fields, he would make instruments for the village's revolutionary musical troupe. This earned him a favorable nod now and then from the local cadres, the kinder of whom would furtively reward him with an extra ration of rice, a wedge of palm sugar, an ear of corn. Like most, he was starving, but the flimsiest stories suggesting the possibility that his family might still be alive would renew his reach for life. Even dreams fueled his hope, giving him energy to endure. He had only to close his eyes and they would appear before him—Channara, Suteera, his parents-in-law, Amara—all so real. His only family. He'd never known another.

Orphaned since boyhood and brought up by the monks at Wat Nagara, Sokhon had come under the guardianship of the temple's most illustrious devotee. Le Conseiller first took note of Sokhon through the mournful lyricism of his sung poetry, and later, as the boy matured into adolescence, through his thoughtful commentary on the dharma with respect to equality and social justice. At the behest of the temple's abbot, Le Conseiller assumed the full responsibility of Sokhon's education, paving the way for the young man's schooling in Cambodia and abroad. While Sokhon's intellectual acuity earned him respect among his peers, it was Le Conseiller's powerful influence that procured him the royal government scholarship to study in America. Sokhon owed his every achievement to Le Conseiller, and when the formidable diplomat conceded to his request to marry Channara, he felt his existence couldn't have been more fortunately endowed. Though intimate friends of the family had long foreseen the union—as it was common for a wealthy patriarch to take in a promising young boy and groom him for his daughter—Sokhon viewed it as nothing less than a miracle.

He had loved Channara for most of his life, starting with his first glimpse of her when the family visited Wat Nagara during their annual return from America, where, he'd later learn, her father was an official in the Cambodian Embassy. She was five, a celestial creature with hair almost to her knees, and he was nine, a newly ordained novice with no hair at all. Orphaned and poor, he could only dream from a distance . . .

And through the years he dreamt of her, feeling she was with him all the while, even when far away in another land. Every year he would wait for her return, thrilled about her month-long stay. Every year he would grow to love her more—silently, secretly. For all Sokhon dared to dream, he never presumed, never overstepped the boundary of generosity. Even the confidence he embodied was a bestowal of sorts from Le Conseiller, who, with a keen sense for self-invention, maintained an appearance of distance and impartiality so that Sokhon could make his own mark, earn the respect necessary to move in their milieu.

In his early twenties, while taking a respite from his studies in America, Sokhon married Channara. During the first few months of marriage, he would often wake in the middle of the night, slightly shaken, unsure if it was his heartbeat or hers that had stirred him to wakefulness. Staring at Channara, he could hardly believe she was his wife. She had not only accepted him but, by her own admission, loved him. He felt it. In some mysterious way, she loved him. Sokhon would fall back to sleep, thinking perhaps he was still dreaming. Later he would tell himself that certain dreams acquire the pulse of reality. His had throbbed into existence when he was that nine-year-old novice reciting the sutras, forgetting his line, falling out of rhythm with the other monks, as he caught sight of her hopping about the temple grounds, each leap pounding his heart. Several years into their marriage, when their daughter Suteera was born, he felt that his dream was complete, fully realized, becoming the life he lived and breathed.

So in Kompong Thom, separated from his family, Sokhon dreamt again, fiercely, feverishly. In his mind's eye, he saw that they were still alive. He had to believe this because a reality without them was not one he could accept. He pictured countless moments of reunion, imagined all the possible ways in which they could survive, promised himself that once they were together again he would beg Le Conseiller for forgiveness . . . He rehearsed the words he'd say to the man who'd been like a father to him, who'd given him everything—*We were all caught up in the war, you see. The American bombing shook the very foundation of our existence. Cracks and fissures appeared everywhere, and as you said, our hopes and dreams tilted on the precipice. Yet, had I heeded your counsel and paid close attention, I would've seen what you saw—that the politics of anger and hate only hastened the rupture, consuming the last remnants of stability we had. I've betrayed my education, my talent. I betrayed our family. I betrayed you who loved and nurtured me as if I were your own son. How can I begin to express . . .*

Sokhon dreamt. Even as the nightmare around him spun out of control. He hoped. He yearned for his wife and daughter. Then, one day he was awakened to reality, finding himself shackled to names and lives he barely knew, while the fate of his own family remained unknown.

"You say I am in here because of you," he told Tun in one of their earliest whispered conversations through the wall. "You named me. But others did as well. I appear in multiple dossiers, the chief interrogator assured me, and therefore I could only be guilty . . . Do you know he studied law and literature, our inquisitive comrade? A former classmate of mine. Wrote a brilliant essay on the literature of justice, examining the feudal system of crime and punishment through the lens of classics like *Tum Teav* and *Thmenh Chey*. And now, years later, here we are, on the other side of that brilliance. You and I held captive to his blinding logic."

Even if Sokhon absolved him of blame, Tun remained certain of his culpability. He recalled now that, while feverishly scribbling down names of people he'd known, he had thought of Channara, had been on the verge of declaring her name out of longing, but something had stopped him, as if even in pain his heart had known to keep her secret, to protect her. Instead, he'd written down her husband's name. How many times had he wished Sokhon dead, wished the man had never lived at all? There was no doubt in his mind. His confession alone would've led to Sokhon's arrest, concluded his fate.

At the start of November, a couple of months into their incarceration at Slak Daek, the two men were hauled from solitary confinement and shoved into a chamber with a dozen or so other prisoners. No longer blindfolded and shackled in place—but with their legs and arms still bound in chains—they could see and drag themselves about. Faint traces of words in Pali and Sanskrit floated across the plastered walls, like half-uttered prayers. Someone said they were inside the compound of a temple, and this had once been a classroom where little monks learned to read and write, memorized the sutras. Amidst the stench of shit and urine, blood and sweat, intractable excretions of pain and fear, it was impossible to believe the room had been anything other than the bowel of hell. "A temple?" Sokhon scoffed in hushed indignation, he who'd been a monk in his early youth. "What kind of name is Slak Daek for a place of worship?" Tun made no reply, having learned that like any alias it hid a dreadful truth.

"Choke on metal" was not only the meaning of Slak Daek but in the prison it was their daily staple. *Confess, or do you want to choke on metal, you rotting maggot!* Slak Daek was filling up, they overheard the guards saying, and the single cells were needed for those yet to endure their first sessions with the chief interrogator. They couldn't see beyond the room, with the windows boarded up, the double wooden doors locked and always guarded, as evident from the echo of footfalls pacing the pathway outside.

Tun didn't want to see, didn't want to know. As it was, the sight of the other victims filled him with renewed horror. Every prisoner was bruised, bloody and broken, festered by wounds decaying to the whiteness of bone. Flies alighted on their open sores, intoxicated by the freshness of flesh. One prisoner could hardly breathe, his back against the stained floor, mouth agape and eyes glued to the ceiling, pupils permanently dilated. Two of the prisoners—one looking no more than sixteen, another perhaps in his early twenties—had no nails on their fingers and toes, their hands and feet splayed with abscesses. Former guards of the prison, Tun recognized. It could mean only one thing—they had failed to follow orders. A middle-aged man heaved in one corner like a chained beast, his residual heft suggesting he'd been eating well until only recently, until he was caught and starved like the rest of them. Tun felt certain the man had been a cadre of some rank. Occasionally, the prisoner would lift his head, turning it slowly in that exaggerated gesture of the blind, his eyes so swollen that he seemed to have no eyes at all beneath a giant throbbing forehead. A sightless monster. They were all becoming monsters through the monstrosity they endured.

As for Sokhon, Tun could barely look at him. Both men became suddenly hesitant toward each other, as if the wall between their former cells—the physical barrier—had precipitated their profound intimacy, and now without it, they were doubly vulnerable, doubly at risk, each suffering not only his own torment but the other's. It took a long moment to finally look each other in the eye. And, despite the violence done to them, it was painfully clear that each was a life—heart, breath, and soul—still pulsing beneath the landscape of injuries. Tears welled up in Tun's eyes and a second later spilled forth from Sokhon's. They were connected in ways they couldn't begin to describe, individually shattered but together somehow whole.

The cycle continued, unremitting. Every day someone was towed out for interrogation and, hours later, brought back more devastated than before. A victim was left alone only long enough to recover the energy to withstand further interrogation. If suspected of faking weakness, he would be deprived the daily cup of watery gruel. On a night that might've been Tun's or Sokhon's turn, a pair of guards burst into the chamber, as another pair stood with flashlights guarding the double wooden doors. They began kicking the immobile prisoner sprawled on the floor. "Time for another talk, you useless cur. Get up! What?—We can't hear you. Oh, His Highness wants us to carry him on a dais!" The prisoner, his eyes still glued to the ceiling and unblinking, began to convulse, chest contracting, the valley beneath his protruding bones dipping and rising, until his breaths turned to hiccups. One of the guards kicked him again and marched out of the room, followed by his partner. They couldn't risk being blamed if the prisoner were to die in their presence. For the rest of the night, Tun and Sokhon and the other inmates listened to the man's hiccups, the soft rasping more horrifying than anything they'd heard inside the prison. In the morning, he finally died. Two days passed before guards removed the swollen corpse. They were not the same guards.

Afterward, Tun sought a quiet corner by himself, trying to calm his heart—a sudden, unreasonable convulsion of hope. As if sensing something out of the ordinary, Sokhon shuffled beside him, chains clanging. They crouched in silence for a moment, then Sokhon said, barely a whisper, "I don't want to end that way."

Tun was only half listening. He'd recognized one of the new guards—a former trainee of his from those early days in the insurgency. The boy had grown into a man, but his face was unmistakable. Tun couldn't be certain if the boy had recognized him in his horribly altered state. Still, hope knocked against his breastbone, in silent delirium.

Sokhon lifted his manacled wrists and crossed them in front of his chest, staring down at the loop of metal chain. "Should I get to that point, where it's neither life nor death, I am asking . . ." He paused, swallowing. "I am asking you to have mercy. To do for me what I wouldn't have the strength to do myself."

Tun regained his attention and stared at Sokhon. *What are you saying?*

"I still want to live. In spite of everything, I want to live. Yet there comes a point—"

"*But . . . how?*" Tun cut him off.

Sokhon, nodding at Tun's wrists, said, "With that . . . the chain of your manacles. Wrap it around my throat, release me from the suffering." He spoke so evenly that it terrified Tun all the more. "I would do the same for you . . . I want us to decide while we still have our wits, while we can still think at all. Whoever should reach that point first, the other will execute this last wish. Can you promise me this?"

Tun could not bring himself to open his mouth.

"You know, several months ago when one of the village cadres—a man in charge of the musical troupe—warned me of my possible arrest, I started to put together an ensemble of instruments I would bury, as one buries the cherished possessions of the dead to accompany them on their journey. Except in my case it would be the instruments first, a kind of pre-burial. Some part of me still believed it a mistake. But if it turned out not to be, I thought, then I'd have the instruments ready for my passage into the otherworld. I already had the *sadiev*, an antique one given to me by a village elder in Kompong Cham. I'd made several kinds of oboes for the musical troupe, and kept a favorite, the *sralai*, for myself.

I would use the rest of the time to make other instruments, bringing together those for the dead and those for the living, fusing two disparate ensembles to create a unique one for myself. Yes, sacrilegious, I know. But then again, I had yet to die. There was still hope. I'd barely finished a *sampho* when they came for me."

In spite of his confusion, Tun found a strange comfort in Sokhon's words, as if they echoed some covert longing of his own. His curiosity surprised him. "Did you bury them?"

Sokhon shook his head. "There was no time." He receded into thought for a moment. "Music . . . or revolution. Before us lay these two paths, my friend. We chose wrong. We made a terrible mistake. But choice was always there. It's available to us even now, even here . . ."

Tun faced Sokhon for the first time. "But what about the one of us left behind? If you reached that point first, I would fulfill your request . . . But *who* would bestow upon me the same mercy? Who would put me out of my misery?"

"I've no answer to that . . . Yet, if it were the other way around, I who had to take your life, only to then be tortured to the point where the only part of me still alive was pain, then I'd hope my last thought to be that once in my life I'd made the right choice—to cut short the terrible suffering of a friend. It would be small comfort, but in this place, I can't ask for more."

Tun nodded, then, after a brief silence, said, "I understand."

Night arrives, shadowy and fluttering like a moth. The Old Musician rises from his corner, barely able to discern the shapes about him. He searches for a *motodup* to take him back to Wat Nagara, where he will seek refuge in the dark of his cottage. His memories trail him.

Narunn heaves himself from the river onto the ironwood dug-out, a blue checkered *kroma* tightly wound around his hips, the rest of him coppery brown and glistening in the first morning light. Teera pauses in her writing and watches from the veranda of the raised wooden house where they've been staying, its stilts and stairway almost completely submerged in the high water. She closes her journal, needing no paper and pen; she could sketch him with her breath alone.

Rivulets flow down the length of his body, and he seems a being molded from the elements—wind, water, earth, sun. The long, narrow dugout rocks under his movements, prompting Lah to grab her seat with both hands. Narunn shifts his legs, straddling the vessel, like some ancient warrior taming the mythical *naga* serpent with the grip of his bare feet. When all is still again, he kneels down in front of the little girl, a baby turtle in his open palm—"Someone wants to meet you." Lah looks skeptically at the inert brown shell no bigger than her own palm. "He's in there," Narunn whispers. "He's just shy." Tentatively, Lah runs the tip of her forefinger across the hatchling's back, tracing the barely visible ridges, the minute squared pattern like stitching on a quilt. "Where's his mama?" she asks after a moment. Narunn nods toward a clump of bright green water hyacinth bobbing nearby. "In there. Waiting for him. With his brothers and sisters."

Teera's heart tugs. She senses the sorrow beneath the child's question, the loss too big to comprehend. *You met my mother, my whole family. They'd been waiting for us. They were still alive*, Narunn said when waking from the dream that brought them here to his native village on a tribu-tary of the Tonle Sap Lake. *It was all so real.* As she surveys the flooded geography, with the sky reflected in the water so that trees and houses and all earthbound things appear afloat on clouds, Teera thinks perhaps this is all a beautiful dream.

"Elephant Tusk Landing." The village took its name from a legend that recounts an epic war between two mighty elephant kingdoms. As the mammoth armies marched into battle, they created a furrowed path that would become a river, and along the river rose a strip of land shaped like an elephant's tusk, a sign that buried deep in an unreachable layer of the earth lay the petrified remnant of the elephant king who'd died in battle, his troops defeated and subsumed into the victorious parade. As a little boy, Narunn would plumb the depths of the river and lake with his gangly band of naked pals, overturn anthills and termite mounds in the hope of finding the fabled relic, the possession of which—even a tiny shard—was thought to bring great luck not just to the finder but to the whole village. It'd never occurred to the stripling Narunn that one day he, a grown man, would scour the same earth and water for the remains of his family. Aside from his mother, who took her last breaths in his arms, his other family members had died without him as witness, and he could only guess where they might've been taken and killed. After the Khmer Rouge, whatever skull or bone he chanced upon, he would take to the village temple so that the monks could accord them the proper ceremony. As for the rest—his loved ones and the countless lost—he allowed himself the consolation that they'd become inseparable from the terrain, woven into the story of this place.

"Let's return him to his family," he says, placing the turtle in Lah's palm so she can lower the creature back into the water. Again, Narunn rises, unfurling in one sinewy movement, one arm extended to Teera. She slips the journal safely into the hammock behind her, descends the few planks of the stairway unclaimed by the water, and steps into the dugout, steadying herself against his weight. Cautiously, she proceeds to the middle and lowers herself next to Lah on the seat. He smiles, one brow raised in question—*Ready?* The two nod vigorously, eager to begin their voyage.

Narunn walks to the bow, where he takes command of the criss-crossed oars pivoted on a pole near the prow, and begins to row. Beneath them the river rolls like a mirrored walkway, opening ever wider in the distance ahead. He is tuned to the rhythm of boat and water, the physical memory that flows through him, his body recalling each stroke forward and back. *Tuk tov . . . kompong nov*, they've all said, those who remember him from his childhood when he first learned to navigate this flooded terrain. Teera understands it now, sees it so clearly. In just a few short days, he has completely shed his urban, educated sheen, stripping down to the bare-bone tautness of one in constant movement with the water. Even his speech is reduced to mostly susurrus and smile, as if all words lead back to the same basic truths. If she came upon him now as a stranger, she wouldn't be able to tell him apart from the other fishermen. He appears not just part of the landscape but deeply steeped in it.

They arrived in Siem Reap more than a week ago and spent the first few days at a hotel in town, taking time to see some of the ancient ruins of Angkor, until Narunn finally located a childhood buddy of his from the village, one of the boys he used to roam the terrain with. They visited him and his wife—a childless couple—as they were about to set out on their sampan to cast their nets in the vast expanse of the Tonle Sap Lake. Given the itinerant nature of their livelihood, the couple would be gone for some time, but, as they'd already conveyed to Narunn on the phone, they wished the three visitors would enjoy their home on the water. "I'm afraid it's just this one room," the wife apologized, gesturing to the modest but neatly kept space. "And the area in the back, for cooking and washing. And of course, the veranda—our bit of luxury!" It was lovely, Teera told her, thanking them both for their generosity. Again, the couple expressed their regret, wishing they'd known sooner Narunn was coming, but at this point it was too late for them to reverse course: they had to check on traps set days earlier. If they didn't, they could lose the bulk of their catch, the main source of their income for the year.

The Great Lake is at its most bountiful, most generous, the husband explained. Now, at the beginning of the dry season, with the rains having only just disappeared, the water remains high but not churning with silt and sediment, as in those turbulent months of the monsoon. Some parts are so tranquil they reflect the forest and sky in astonishing detail. "Quite majestic, in fact," their host concluded. "You must see it for yourself."

Teera needed no further convincing, and by then, hardly an hour into the visit, Narunn had already changed into a *kroma*, ready to take his first plunge. He saw his friends off, swimming alongside their sampan, slaking his body's long-forgotten thirst.

News of his return traveled fast, and soon a cluster of boats gathered around the house, carrying old friends and neighbors eager to be reacquainted. Some had brought along food, explaining the strict instructions from the fisher couple to feed their guests well, to look after them during their sojourn. The stream of visitors continued into the evening, and throughout the next day, and the next, bearing a continuous variety of dishes just prepared—local specialties Teera and Lah might enjoy, Narunn might have long craved. Even strangers came, and though they'd never met Narunn until that moment, they felt they knew him in some way, knew of his great loss—his large family—and his brave continuation in the face of that loss. It was as if he'd never left, nearly two decades of absence barely a ripple in this estuary of timelessness. He was remembered, he was deeply missed, and, as far as they were concerned, he was family, as if the borders of their hearts were as fluid as the terrain shaping them.

Teera contemplates now the topography before her—the man and his landscape. Narunn moves with the oars, his narrow back rippling with its own runnels and rivers, a force of strength at once quiet and resolute. In his company, she's learned to let words and perceptions slide, as easily as water slides off the skin. Here, in the eyes of the villagers, she is his "wife," and Lah their "daughter." In her heart, there is no name, no spoken language, for the love she feels, the immediate and profound connection she shares with these two, each a life as adrift as hers, and yet together—the sight of them together—a kind of harbor all its own. Teera dares not cling or hope for more, dares not peer too far into the future, the vast unknown.

They glide past other boats, and houses on stilts, most painted blue or green, deepening the hues of the water. Past a vendor with her boatload of fresh fruits and flowers and vegetables for the morning market. Past a "minimart" afloat under the shade of a giant umbrella offering individual packets of Nescafé and instant noodles, tin pots and pans and plastic dishes, hats and sunglasses, prepaid phone cards and, incredibly, international call services. Past a little boy rowing his even littler sisters in an oversize aluminum bowl—the kind used for laundering clothes— all three dressed in crisply ironed uniforms, heading toward a school buoyant on pontoons of rusted oil drums. The boy winks at Narunn, as one man would to another, acknowledging the concentrated effort required to ferry one's family safely across the water.

On they go, exchanging silent greetings with those they meet. A nod, a smile, a gesture of recognition. A deep bow to a row of monks receiving alms on a phoenix-shaped vessel near the steps of a temple of white-and-gold pillars. The monks do not stir from their contemplation, do not look up, do not chant or speak to the villagers giving alms from their boats. Speech is an incursion. Only the oars are loquacious, their rhythmic whisper and whoosh permissible, a welcome sutra in this birthing light.

It is their last morning here, and Narunn is determined to take them all the way to the end of the mile-long stretch through the flooded forest, where the Tonle Sap Lake awaits. His previous attempts had been unsuccessful, their trip prolonged by countless things to see, drawn-out greetings, more old friends to reacquaint with. But starting out early like this, they should be able to make it there without too much disruption and turn back before the sun gets too hot. Lah scoots from the seat to the bottom of the dugout, where she can safely delight in the water. She drapes her arm over the hull and lets her fingers skim the surface, creating rills and rifts that mimic the patterns of the oars. Narunn whistles toward a group of fishermen with their nets and traps extending into the inundated mangroves. Recognizing the birdlike call, they whistle back, a tune all the more haunting amidst the drowning trees.

A narrow winding path weaves ahead through an archipelago of water hyacinth. To the left, a thatched hut rocks gently in the breeze, surrounded by rafts of spices drying in the sun, and amidst the bold profusion of colors, three naked siblings stand in a line from tallest to shortest, a live fat snake wound around their shoulders like a ropy scarf, a shared comfort blanket, all twisted and tensile. Nearby on a raft with buckets and bowls and scattered bars of soap, their mother is washing their baby brother, dunking him right into the river, while the three children await their turns, faces still full of sleep. They exchange long, silent stares with Lah. To the right in a clearing, a man balances on a bamboo coracle, jabbing the water with his spear.

As they glide farther now, without others in sight, Teera follows the rhythm of the oars breaking the water, and her thoughts turn to the quiet of another narrow winding path they traveled just a few days before . . . a footpath under giant strangling fig trees, leading from an ancient ruin, the last of the Angkor temples they'd seen that day. They were tired and wanted to find a quiet place to rest before catching their *tuk-tuk* back to the hotel. Halfway along the footpath, Teera heard the sound of a wind instrument emerging faintly from the surrounding woods. She stopped in her tracks, looked around, and, aside from Narunn and Lah walking a few steps ahead, saw no other souls. She listened for it again but heard only the rustling of leaves. She must've imagined it. She hadn't slept well the night before, waking in the dark to the sound of a child's crying, only to realize it wasn't Lah's but her own. She'd then lain awake, silencing herself against the pillow, until the pitch-blackness lightened to dawn.

Her tiredness was making her hallucinate, she thought, standing stock-still on the path.

"Something the matter?" Narunn asked, walking back to her, Lah high on his shoulders.

"I thought I heard music . . ." A chill ran through her as soon as she said it, and then came the reply, echoing across ancient forests, across time—*Out here, there's only music of the ghosts.*

Teera felt weak. She needed to sit down. Narunn lifted Lah off his shoulders, unwound the *kroma* from his neck, and spread it for them under the canopy of the giant strangling figs.

The instrument resurfaced, louder now, the unmistakable lament of a coconut *tro*. Other instruments emerged, joining in one by one—a bamboo flute or an oboe, a drum, a zither, a xylophone, cymbals and bells—until a whole ensemble resounded through the forest. The three listened, Teera and Narunn leaning into each other, heads and shoulders touching; Lah sprawled in front of them, her tiny head in Narunn's lap. The melody shimmered, bloomed, and cascaded. Then, gradually, it evaporated. Only the echoes of the drum remained, like the footfalls of some unseen guardian enjoying a late-afternoon stroll, taking pleasure in the sunlight coruscating from the leaves.

The three listeners rose and headed toward the source of the music. Something magical and divine. Teera let her imagination indulge. An ensemble of forest sprites, or *apsaras* and *devatas*, those deities depicted on the bas-relief of the temple they'd just seen. What inspired beings had rendered such a beguiling, ethereal tune?

A small thatched roof came into view, and in its shelter, on a raised bamboo platform, a group of musicians were retuning their instruments. One of them looked up and slowly turned toward the crackle of feet on pebbles and leaves. He was blind, the lids of his eyes sealed shut into two ridged lines. Sensing approaching listeners, he lifted the bow of his three-stringed *tro*, which, in fact, had only one working string. He tuned his entire body to listen again, and then, as if sensing something else—the quiver of another's heart, the current of sorrow from a long-forgotten time—placed the bow back down on his lap.

Narunn offered greetings to the men, whose clothes were so threadbare they assumed the color of earth and straw. He introduced himself by way of his village—"a child of Elephant Tusk Landing"—and Teera and Lah as his "family." He conversed with them as though they were brothers and uncles, smiled and laughed in response to their questions, and asked what Teera was too overcome to ask. *How long have you been playing together as a group? Were you musicians before your injuries? How were you injured?* The last question, Teera was certain, Narunn knew the answer to, just by looking at the scars, the patterns of healing, but he asked anyway for her sake, sensing her wonder. An amputee, who handled his worn prosthetic as though it were a priceless musical instrument, said he had been a rice farmer; another a fisherman who'd explored every tributary of the Tonle Sap; one a soldier in the government army after the Khmer Rouge; another a soldier *during* the Khmer Rouge, forced to fight as the regime was falling. The *tro* player had been a teacher, until he couldn't see, couldn't read and write, not even for himself, let alone teach another to do so. Land mines were their common enemy. Their scars, their wounds, their missing limbs, and these partially broken instruments salvaged from the city's refuse—all brought them together. Teera listened mutely, moved beyond words by this ensemble of disfigurement, dearth, and undiminished dignity.

They wanted to play another piece for the three visitors. As the *tro* player swept the bow across the only remaining string of his upright fiddle, Teera suddenly realized why the night before she'd woken up crying in the dark: she was bringing to completion something she'd started decades earlier, something interrupted at the borderland by the fear of death around her. A lamentation for the homeland she was about to abandon.

As they walked slowly back to the entrance where their ride awaited, meandering the long way around, Teera told Narunn about her desperate flight a lifetime ago from Kompong Cham to the jungle of Siem Reap, the ghostly tremor that'd stirred her to waking, the quiver of her own heart she'd mistaken for phantom music. About a boy named Chea, a soldier who, at the fall of the Khmer Rouge, had scurried her and Amara across the rice fields and forests not so far from where they were now, guiding their steps through the interstices of land mines, and delivered them to safety at the refugee camp in Thailand, only to turn around again to help others. Chea was from Siem Reap, a native of

Phum Kruos. For years, once the country had become stable again, her aunt had sent letter after letter from America to government offices here, inquiring about him. She'd pursued every possible contact, paid people to search for him, but all led to nothing. When Teera herself had first arrived in Cambodia, she too had contacted the census office in Siem Reap to see whether they had any records of anyone with that name and history. And she'd been forced to accept anew that there were those whose fates she would never know. Now, having heard the musicians and their stories, she feared Chea, who'd carried her as explosives detonated all around, and had probably helped many others escape in the same way, might've lost his own life to those remnants of abandoned battlefields. The injustice of it was more than Teera could bear.

Narunn took her hand and squeezed it. "But perhaps like them, like these musicians, your friend could've survived an explosion. If he's still alive, if he's somewhere in the country—or in this world—it's not impossible to cross paths with him again."

Teera stared at him, astounded by the steadiness with which he clung to every possibility of life, seen and unseen, despite all he'd lost, or perhaps because of it. An emotion overwhelmed her. She felt profoundly indebted to the forces that had kept him alive, that had willed his path toward hers.

"In the meantime, we keep searching . . ."

The river widens, spreading open like a fan. Suddenly they emerge into the oceanic vastness of the Tonle Sap Lake. There is no discernible shoreline in front of them, only the boundless undulation of blue and green, interspersed with reflections of the clouds, birds in flight. Here and there outlines of something solid materialize—shoals, sandbars?— only to dissolve completely when a flock of cranes or ibis break the surface of the water. Narunn stops rowing, letting the tips of the oars drop like anchors. He turns to face Teera, and a look passes between them. *Tuk tov . . . kompong nov.*

The boat departs . . . but the harbor remains.

As always, there were two guards, one keeping watch at the closed door, and the other doing the interrogator's bidding. A moment earlier, with his blindfold removed, Tun had noticed that the small square window lined with iron bars was now boarded up. Aside from a muted sliver of sunlight piercing through a gap between the boards, he could no longer see the expansive tree trunk whose rooted presence he'd often fixed his gaze on as violence rained down upon him. He noticed always with renewed horror the wall of instruments, their ready compliance, the singular inviolable code of conduct. *You must not scream under any circumstance.* The words mocked him. His eyes frantically searched for something to focus on—some sign that there existed a world beyond this absolute hell. He found nothing, save for the sliver of light. He heard their question but couldn't bring himself to open his mouth to speak.

They were asking whether or not he wanted to eat. *Cee reu min cee?* His first impulse was to shield his face, clamp his hands over his lips, shut them tight. But his wrists, like his ankles, were bound behind him, as he was made to kneel on the tile floor. He shook his head vehemently, idiotically, anticipating the excrement they would feed him, as they had the last few sessions. Yet, he didn't remember seeing the bucket in the room, couldn't detect any fresh stench besides his own fear. Still, they could beat him until he defecated and make him eat his own shit. "*Arh'aing cee reu min cee?*" the guard standing next to him demanded, echoing the chief interrogator. They no longer addressed him as "comrade." *Arh'aing* was what you'd call a leech, a worm, anything other than a human. The guard grabbed his hair and pulled his head back so that his mouth was agape to receive whatever they would force down his throat. Tun wanted to plead, but he could barely swallow, his windpipe suddenly hardened as if coated with cement. Again, the chief interrogator murmured, with violent calm, "*Cee reu min cee?* It's a simple question. And really, there's only one answer. Just say it, and it'll be over."

Suddenly the end of a bludgeon smashed his left eye, like the force of a steel ball. "*CEE!*" he screamed in agony, falling to the floor, the side of his face smacking the hard tiles, his protruding cheekbone shattering as if bones were made of powder. "*CEE!*" Yes, he'd devour his own excrement like the cur he was! He'd eat anything! His own rotting flesh if he must! Whatever they said, he'd obey.

He whimpered, disgusted by his weakness, yet unable to rise from the floor, from his debasement. He wanted only to press his smashed eye to the guard's bare foot and still the pain against the warmth of another's flesh. He was certain his eyeball had detached and embedded itself in the back of his skull. The freshness of pain, its rawness and intensity, shocked him as much as it hurt. He'd expected that by now he'd be used to it, his nerves numbed by the repetition of abuse, the severity of impact. He'd thought that at some point pain would reach a level the body could no longer translate into words or awareness. That he would no longer be able to identify it, just lose himself in a paroxysm, like a splinter in an immense explosion.

The guard kicked him, shaking his foot loose of the despicable heap he'd become. "Now you've admitted the truth," the chief interrogator said from his perch on the edge of his desk, one leg swinging nonchalantly, "what exactly did you do for the CIA?"

Tun reeled. He'd misunderstood. A trick of the tongue. A foreign intrusion into his own language, a language, though innate as breathing itself, that had become alien to him. *C*, not *cee*. Even a single letter could be a trap, ensnaring a victim into self-condemnation.

"Everything," Tun lied through his shattered skull, his battered eye, already swollen shut. "Everything the CIA wanted me to do. I was their lackey, their spying dog . . ."

Satisfied, the interrogator got up and left the room. The two guards remained. Then the one at the door said to the one who had beat him, "Is he dead, Comrade?"

"If only he were that lucky." The older guard spat, disgusted, the bludgeon still in his hand. "We can't take him back to the cell now, short of carrying him."

The younger one moved from the door, stood over Tun, and, with the butt of his rifle, pushed him on the shoulder so that Tun fell flat on his back. "I'll stay with him. Until he can move again," the boy offered. The older guard hesitated, then reluctantly nodded. "Make sure you call me when he's ready."

Once they were alone, the younger guard lowered himself onto his haunches, his AK47 in the crook between his abdomen and thighs. Tun recalled this was how the boy had held his gun when he'd first laid eyes on him that long-ago morning by the stream at the forest encampment. How the boy would always hold his gun when not fighting, as if cradling it. "Why won't you die?" his former trainee growled, leaning low into Tun's face. "Why are you so pigheaded? Why do you still hang on?"

Tun struggled to express himself. "You . . ." *I know you. You were once under my command, my care . . .* It was obvious from the look in his eyes that the guard remembered. Tun said the only thing that mattered— "Why . . . don't you . . . help me then? To die."

Back in the chamber with the other prisoners, Tun slowly came to his senses, and he began to regret his words. He imagined what would happen if they reached the chief interrogator's ears. *Who do you think you are? Only the party will decide how and when you die!* It would be one thing if they killed him for having spoken so boldly, but he knew they could make him suffer far more terribly than he already had. Each time he thought he'd endured the worst, they shoved him deeper into the abyss, reminding him there was no limit to their evil. Tun told no one, not even Sohkon, whom he trusted with his life—whom he'd entrusted with ending it, should such a moment present itself.

Weeks passed, his injured eye began to heal, the swelling reduced bit by bit, though it still throbbed painfully, and he could no longer see clearly with it. His right cheekbone did not shatter, as he'd believed, but was badly bruised. His body vigorously healed itself. While others around him died, Tun, to his utter dismay, continued to live. He kept waiting for something to happen, and yet he knew not what . . . Lightning to strike this whole place down? A miracle, a greater force than this evil to wipe them all out? At times he wondered if he'd imagined the whole exchange with the boy.

Then the day arrived when it was his turn again in the interrogation room. Like countless times before, they brought him in blindfolded, but before they even had a chance to position him as they wanted, commotion broke out in another part of the prison. At first all he heard was the sound of gunshots, then running footsteps, and the breathless voice of a guard at the door, addressing the chief interrogator: "Elder Brother!—A prisoner's stabbed his own throat!"

The interrogator allowed the guard to catch his breath, and then asked, "Did he die?" his placid tone in stark contrast to the guard's excitable words.

"No, Elder Brother. Well, almost . . . I don't know."

"I heard a gunshot."

"Yes, Elder Brother, one of us fired our gun to warn him not to die . . . he must wait for you. It's not our fault. He asked for pen and paper. He said he wanted to confess. We told him you were busy now with another prisoner, he must wait his turn. He insisted. So we sharpened a stick— a fake pencil—and tossed it to him. 'Here, you dog, write your shit!' A joke, Elder Brother. We meant it as a joke. He used—"

"*Enough!*"

Dead silence.

With his blindfold still on, Tun could not see beyond shadows. But he felt the fear around him thick as walls.

"How unfortunate," the chief interrogator murmured. His calm pronouncement sent a shiver through the room. Tun could feel him rising from his desk. At the door, the interrogator paused and said, "You two come with me. And you, take this prisoner back to his cell."

The guard gripping hold of Tun's arm replied, "Yes, Elder Brother." It was the boy.

For a moment there was absolute stillness, and then Tun sensed the boy fidgeting beside him, adjusting the collar of his shirt, or perhaps a *kroma* around his neck, the checkered pattern breaking the solid black of his pajama-like uniform. Tun heard the soft timbre of thread breaking, and a second later felt the hard, cold press of steel at the center of his palm.

"Here's your way out," the boy whispered. "Do it right. Otherwise, we both pay."

Tun stared at the tiny blade, so delicate it resembled a piece of jewelry. A pendant perhaps. A spear-shaped amulet for protection. There was even a hole at the base one could thread a string through and wear it around the neck. Keep it hidden beneath a collared shirt. The top edge was smooth and linear, the cutting edge angled and tapered to an arrow tip. If he ran his thumb against it, even lightly, it would cut. The circle of rust around the hole suggested that it had been previously attached to some kind of handle with a tiny screw or bolt. Aside from the rust, it was in perfect condition. An artisan blade. A rare weapon. At Slak Daek, it could only have come from the cache of implements. That it should be in a prisoner's possession was unheard of. Yet, here it was, in Tun's own hand. A gift to end his life.

He had kept the blade for two days now. He could not risk keeping it much longer. So far he'd hidden it by inserting it in the hem of his ragged shirt. This was the first time he'd taken it out to examine, and he did so surreptitiously, wedging it between his thumb and palm. Even Sokhon had yet to know. His friend was gone, taken to interrogation. Many times Tun had been on the verge of telling, but he couldn't bring himself to it. It would have made their pact so much more real, brought them that much closer to committing the terrible act, choosing who should go and who should stay . . .

Do it right. Otherwise, we both pay. The youth's words came back to him and Tun suddenly wondered, *What guides a person's hand? His heart? What has made the boy endanger his own life for a life nearly gone? Does compassion still find its way into hell? As sometimes a sliver of light steals through a crack in a sealed window* . . . The thought filled him with hope for a second, and he thought, if only he could vanish carrying this sliver of light inside him.

It looks to be an overcast day, the river phantom gray, the sky endlessly somber. For the Old Musician, it's cold, bone-chilling at times, especially in the night and early dawn. But for Teera, it's perfect, the most pleasant weather she's experienced in these past few months. She dresses lightly but modestly for the temple, a simple silk sarong and cotton blouse, a soft organza scarf draped diagonally across her chest, a mantle of humility in this place of worship. He is bundled in several layers, one loose tunic on top of the other over a pair of wraparound pants, a grayish *kroma* wound around his neck to protect his throat from the seasonal chill. A thermos of hot water sits in front of him, along with a couple of tall, thick glasses, which this time he's had the foresight to borrow from the temple. He offers her plain hot water and apologizes for having nothing else. She tells him she's gotten used to drinking it again, no matter the weather, like a real *koan* Khmer. He fills her glass, and then his, wondering whether she's just being kind, or whether indeed she's acclimating. Steam rises and evaporates.

The water is still too hot, he tells her, so they ought to let it sit. She tells him that in Minnesota this is summer temperature, but here everyone freezes. As if to concur, he brings his palms over his glass, cradling the warmth. How fragile he looks, Teera thinks, remembering the last time they were face-to-face, the marks of history riddling his body, the weight of it upon him. Yet, he also appears somehow lightened. Just as she, to the Old Musician, appears transformed—more rooted in some way by her journeys.

Only moments ago he arrived, waiting in the ceremony hall, and she came soon after, lowering herself on the straw mat in front of him to his right so that he could see her with his good eye. *Channara*, he thought for a breathless second. In traditional attire, she looked exactly like her mother. The long tamarind-colored skirt and cream blouse, cut to fit her slender frame as was popular in the 1960s, intimated a preference for classic simplicity, an inherited sense of elegance. She greeted him, palms together in the customary *sampeah*, and he saw too her father, the eyes that seemed at once intensely focused and endlessly seeking. Sokhon's resolute will, the pinprick flicker of light he'd taken with him when he closed his eyes for the last time.

She carries it now, this piercing luminosity. It radiates as she speaks. A beacon turning, turning, turning . . . Dispelling the shadows and gloom so that he feels his sight has been momentarily restored. The world around him becomes less mottled, less mangled. He listens without a word, without moving. He could listen to her forever.

"Narunn sends you his greetings," she tells him, flushing whenever she says the doctor's name, a secret happiness making her glow all the more. "He's purchasing a piece of land on Chruay Chongvar. Something he's thought about for a long time, but never found a compelling reason for until now. He wants to build a home." Her voice chimes with nervous joy. "He's there now, signing the contract, having a final survey. Lah is with him. They're inseparable." She blossoms at this image.

He's not surprised by her words. When Dr. Narunn offered to take the child and look after her for however long necessary, the Venerable Kong Oul felt his prayers had been answered. *I never once thought to ask the doctor*, the abbot had confided, *at least not to become a full-time caretaker of the girl, given he's a man on his own. It's a weighty responsibility, not to mention fraught with uncertainty. Yet, I can't think of anyone more suited, more heaven-sent.* The heart loves in spite of uncertainty, he thought of telling the abbot then. It continues to love in spite of danger and loss. Instead, he said, *Sometimes, Venerable, the smallest, most vulnerable life has the power to move the heavens.*

He returns his attention to the heart blooming before him. She goes on to recount the trip she took several weeks ago to Siem Reap. How she and Narunn had decided spontaneously, telephoned the abbot and received permission to take Lah with them, packed in a mad rush, then left that very evening on the last flight, afraid that if they waited until the next morning, they'd change their minds.

She tells him how they'd landed in the small airport amidst fields of tall grass, greeted by fireflies blinking in the peripheral darkness, mimicking the stars in the night sky. She tells him about the small boutique hotel with traditional wooden houses where in pitch-blackness she woke one night to the presence of her own ghost, its unfinished weeping.

The timbre of her voice, the flow of words, her calm and generous revelation, this unreserved sharing that feels like forgiveness. He takes it all in, drinks it like fluid, the glass of water in front of him forgotten. How like her mother she is—gracious, wise. And yet, unlike her also—gentle and open.

Teera, undeterred by his silence, keeps talking. All this time she's feared to trespass, even as she hungers to understand. But, if she doesn't push against the door, how will she know whether it's locked? She tells him about their visits to the temples of Angkor, and to Banteay Srei, its delicate yet splendidly carved red sandstones, its libraries with ornate real doorways as well as illusory ones, intimating perhaps that learning is a gathering of knowledge, the known and the manifested, as well as a leap of imagination, a reach for the mysterious, the invisible. Walking around the concentric courtyards, you certainly feel the ghosts of ancient scholars, hear the echoes of their ruminations.

As she says this, he espies the ghost beside her, one of many now in their midst. He's often wondered when Channara died, whether at the beginning of the regime or toward the end, and how. What was her state of mind as she succumbed to death? What surged through her heart? Love, anger, bitterness . . . regret, that most pernicious poison? He considers briefly whether he should ask, but just as quickly changes his mind. What good would it do now to know this? Such knowledge would not stanch his bleeding, reverse his disintegration.

Teera recounts their pilgrimage to the Tonle Sap Lake, whose ebb and flow sets the pulse of the country, tracing the air with her fingers, invoking the anatomy of an organ, with its veins and valves, chambers, reservoirs and atria, which Narunn sketched in a page of her journal. "Our homeland, in his rendering, looks like the human heart." And the heart, she now realizes, having seen how life stubbornly thrives and reasserts itself wherever she travels, will continue to beat.

Watching her, he's conscious that she's surpassed her own mother's age. He feels suddenly grateful to have a glimpse of the woman he loved in this burgeoning beauty. *Suteera . . . Sita . . .* If his daughter had survived, if she lived to this day, he imagines, perhaps this is how she'd look, how she'd sound. He remembers Suteera's birthday. March, Sokhon told him. Soon she will be thirty-eight, not so young. Yet her life, he senses, is just beginning. Love is the only rebirth.

Teera pauses, and without looking up takes a sip of water from her glass before continuing. She tells him about Narunn's childhood friend and his wife, their lovely home on the water, the floating world of Elephant Tusk Landing. A place steeped in legends, memories, and love. She is hoarse from talking. Her voice fades, drawing to a close. "I wish you could've been there with us."

A flutter in his chest. She didn't have to say this. He wants to repay her tenderness with his own—*You are never far from my thoughts*. But he needs all the self-composure he can muster. It is now his turn. "I've wanted to speak with you," he says before he loses courage.

She lifts her face to meet his gaze—the one sorrowed eye, the unknowable one beneath the black cotton patch. "I'm listening."

"But, before I begin, you must promise me that you will stay, that no matter how difficult it gets, you will remain to the end."

She nods.

"You can judge me as you see fit. In return, I only ask that you witness the full extent of my crime."

A nd *so it came to this . . .*

"Choice . . ." your father said, straining with every breath, as he cowered in a corner of our communal cell, now overcrowded with new arrivals. "Remember . . . our talk?"

Our inviolable promise to each other. To choose when to die, and by whose hands. I nodded, unable to look at him, even as I crouched only inches away, my back against the wall, he on my right. Just as you sit now. Only hours earlier, your father had returned from yet another interrogation. The method of communication, it seemed, was air. Or, more precisely, its deprivation. All it took was a plastic bag to draw blood. His earlobes were coated with it, I'd noted through the corner of my eye, a dry streak running down each side of his face.

"Look . . . at . . . me," he said, summoning his strength.

In my desolation, I finally understood why the boys in my father's music troupe—close friends of mine whom I slept and ate and practiced with—would avoid me after I'd endured a beating from my father, our music master. I had believed then that they were ashamed of me, ashamed of whatever weakness of character always provoked my father's wrath. *Why couldn't he just be a better student—a better son?* I'd often imagined them grumbling to one another. *If only he was less stubborn, quicker to submit . . .* Now, in this prison chamber, witnessing without pause the suffering of a friend, I felt profoundly ashamed of myself, my incapacity, my uselessness. What good was compassion if it could not prevent, or even dampen, the violence inflicted on those around me?

"*Look at me*," your father commanded quietly but as forcefully as he could. The place was loud with the moaning and motion of other prisoners. I drew myself closer, looked at him, and he continued, "Soon . . . My time . . . will come soon."

What good was my existence if it only entrapped another in a lie?

"There's . . . nothing left," your father persisted, inhaling, reaching deeper for strength. "Even they've run out of the lies they want me to repeat. There's nothing left. Nothing more I can give them. Except my blood." He paused, steadying his voice. "I'm marked for execution, you see. A slow, drawn-out execution. Their so-called doctor will come. There is a war, I'm told. They say they need my blood to treat the wounded."

He was hallucinating, I thought. There was no war, of course. The endless reverberation of gunshots we knew to be prisoners being executed in continuous waves. Even in moments of clarity, I could hardly distinguish gunfire from the rattle of chains echoing through the cells. The other things he was saying I couldn't comprehend. I didn't want to understand, to imagine.

"How kind of them to explain it all to me. Perhaps this is their one act of courtesy."

I wanted him to stop talking, to preserve what little strength remained. But I understood all too well the mind emerging from torture, the muddle of pain. Words, even senseless words, were necessary, the struggled grasps reaching back toward sanity, toward life. Even as life had become nothing but misapprehension, an extended overture to total and permanent obliteration. I let him talk, torn by the desire for my own life to end and my desire to see him live.

"Every time—just before the first blow, the first shock, the first cut of air from my lungs—I hum. It confuses them. Makes them hesitate for a split second. They can't be sure if I'm submitting or rebelling. They think they have a monopoly on truth. But the truth will echo through, even under the weight of a mountain of forced confessions. I know that now."

He moaned, his shackled hand reaching for mine resting limply at my side, equally hindered. He tapped his fingers on my knuckles, a rhythm of sorts, and I realized he wasn't moaning but was attempting to chant—to sing. In that place, at such a moment, your father was trying to *sing*. He licked his lips, swallowed, and once more gathered his strength. "*The spirit of this land . . . lives in its fields of rice . . .*" His voice was barely audible, but I recognized the cadence of a *smoat* as I leaned in to listen. He sang the same short lyric, the single stanza, over and over, his words as labored as his breaths. When he'd finished, I repeated the refrain, giving it the melody he intended.

We were quiet for a moment, and then your father spoke again. "I wrote it . . . when I was making the *sampho*. It's part of the drum, written into its skin. A hidden invocation. A sealed truth. It's just as well . . . that I never had the chance to bury it. These fields are stained with the blood of so many . . . Yet, the music will endure, without me. I realize now I'm merely one in this ensemble. I've served my purpose, played my part—"

"No, listen to me," I said, cutting him off. "My daughter is gone, but your daughter, your wife and family, may still be alive. You must fight to your last breath."

"But when I can no longer fight, when they've siphoned my blood, and all I am is this vessel of pain. You promised me, Tun."

I lowered my head. I could not bear what he was asking me.

"Should you come out the lone victor in this battle, then find my daughter, find my wife . . . take my place."

I cradled him, his head in the nook of my arm, the long chain on my wrists encircling his torso so that it must have appeared I was trying to bind him to me. Had such a thing been possible, I would've done just that—I would've bound your father's breath to mine, given it the force of my own life. But he was beyond reach, the wounds accumulating on his arms and legs in addition to the gashes and sores covering his entire body, the sites the needle had punctured now swelling like blisters, the blood clotting beneath the bruised skin, leaking crimson, caking around him on the floor. What self or consciousness remained was undetectable, trapped inside the frozen mirrors of his eyes.

They'd come several times already to draw blood. I'd stopped counting. The same two young "doctors" would come, illiterate adolescents, fumbling over the grimy page of illustrations they'd brought along each visit to guide them through the procedure. I was certain, having seen how such things were decided, they'd been chosen for "medical" training precisely because of their youth and ignorance, which, according to revolutionary logic, made them fierce, unafraid to "experiment." When they came for the first blood collection, your father had still not recovered from the previous ordeal; the streaks of red coating his earlobes had yet to peel away completely. His effort to speak to me, moreover, had drained him of every ounce of physical strength so that he lay there on the floor as if waiting for them, as if complying with the cruelty, the demands of some beast-like appetite. This time there was no pretense of taking him out for interrogation. The bloodletting would be performed there in the room, in front of the other prisoners, as the chief interrogator had instructed. The two doctors—children really—started off arguing in hushed voices over which arm to try first, the difference between a vein and an artery, who should hold down the prisoner in case he struggled, and who should handle the needle. *I've only practiced on a banana stalk*, the younger of the two said, looking uncertain and scared, and the older tried to rationalize, *Well, that's why they sent us. Doesn't matter if we do it right. We just need to make sure we get some blood . . .* Despite their terrifying incompetence, their own panic and fear, they'd obtained what was needed, and more important, they had conducted their first *pisaot manuh*—"human experiment."

Now I no longer cared what they'd do to me. I gathered your father tighter in my arms, as if he were the broken pieces of myself, his bruises my battered faith, his blood my own irreversible bleeding. Even if I lived to eternity, I knew I would never recover from these wounds we shared.

I retrieved the tiny blade from its hiding place inside the hem of my shirt. I'd kept its existence concealed from your father, thinking it was meant for me, my own termination. There was no need to involve him, I'd decided. If I were to take my own life, it would be just my crime alone. I'd thought and rethought, until I could think no more, and there had never once been a doubt in my mind, or my heart, that between the two of us your father should be the one to live. But now this moment had arrived, and I realized our last conversation was not a reinstatement of our pact, an entreaty for me to hold to my promise, but was your father's farewell. There was a choice, and he'd chosen his executioner. All that remained was that I must exercise my own terrible bounded choice.

I had at my disposal this blade, a craftsman's tool no bigger than a plectrum. As your father lay still in my arms, I searched his paralyzed gaze again for any movement, any shimmer or sign, anything other than this look of transfixed agony. *I don't want to end that way*, he'd said of such entrapment. I pressed my ear to his mouth and tried to detect breathing—the cycle of exhalation and inhalation that might've suggested he was struggling to resurface. When I touched his wrists or the swollen veins on his arms I could not be sure if what I felt was a pulse or the throbbing of injured nerves. His body seemed to be sinking, collapsing on itself—his cheeks, the hollow at the base of his throat, the basin of his chest. I was witnessing the slow concaving of a life beneath the weight of unimaginable brutality, one layer of suffering amassed upon another.

With my left arm, I cradled your father as if he were an instrument, the most sacred of all, and with the blade in hand, the plectrum held firm—like the sharpened tip of a lute player's bow—I swept my right arm and, in a single clean stroke, played the only note left to play.

A sob. A howl. An animal's cry escaped my throat. I pulled him closer to me, rocking us both, burying my face in the pool of our spilled humanity.

When the guards heard Tun's anguished cry, they burst into the room, revealing a reddish full moon at twilight in the open doorway. For his unforgivable transgression, robbing the Organization of its authority to determine the time and manner of a man's death, he was punished even more savagely than before. At the height of his agony, Tun misread the changing atmosphere, the prolonged gunfire, the lapses in guard surveillance, the urgent hushed exchanges. Just weeks after Sokhon's death, Democratic Kampuchea collapsed against the invading forces from Vietnam, revealing in its retreat a ravaged land and people.

Into this broken landscape, Tun wandered, dragging his mutilated self, the limbs now unshackled but severely encumbered by injuries both recent and old. At one point, feeling the phantom weight of the chain that for so long had bound his wrists, he looked down and noted his swollen fingers, the bloody and purulent tips, some with half-torn nails, others without nails at all. They did not look like human hands, more like claws belonging to some buried creature that had dug its way out of the grave. He remembered the last few sessions as one interminable stretch, the pliers exacting payment again and again. *Such steady fingers you have, holding that blade, hiding it from us. Let's see how steady they are now* . . . Then, he regained consciousness one day to find that abruptly everything stopped. No more taunting voices, no more torture, no more guards. Just a suspended disquiet, followed by a hollow stillness, as if some monstrous presence had put down its club and trident, all its implements, and vacated the premises, disappearing into thin air.

A group of bedraggled, emaciated townsfolk appeared a day or two later, unlocking the cells, setting the surviving prisoners free. The man who unshackled Tun said, heaving in his own wretchedness, "There were rumors." He looked down, ashamed. "No, more than that . . . We heard the tormented screams, the dying pleas. We smelled the awful stench all around us. But we didn't want to believe. How could they turn a temple into such a place? Now we see." Again, he looked down in shame. "The earth will never forgive us." Among the thousands of victims brought to the prison over the months and years, Tun was one of the few to walk out of the gate that day.

Now, as he stumbled through the town, he could not tell the living from the dead. Both haunted him. Unable to bear the presence of either, he gathered what he could—a length of rope, discarded clothes, a rusty hatchet, trifling scraps of abandoned food—and headed into the hills. He knew how to survive in the jungle. He'd done it once before. Besides, it wasn't survival he sought so much as solitude. After months amidst the howls of torture, he wished for nothing more than a muted vanishing, in the way a dying tree might recede from sight, suffocated by mosses and clinging vines. There was a real chance that he may end violently: a tiger could attack and eat him alive, but still he would know that its ferocity was motivated by hunger, not hate. He'd rather confront the impartial cruelty of nature. If other human beings could do what he and his fellow countrymen had done to one another, then he wanted no part of this race. He did not understand how and why he survived, but until death arrived, he sought a humanless existence.

In the jungle, he began to heal, his strength reasserting itself, only to realize he was not alone. Another self had taken root inside of him, with a will stronger than his own. *Should you come out the lone victor in this battle, then find my daughter, find my wife . . . take my place.* At first he tried to silence it like he did the other voices in his head. When that failed, he beseeched it to go away, he reasoned and cajoled, offering explanations on the inanity of certain hopes, the merit of acceptance. *There is peace in letting go. You of all people should know this.* He argued, and argued, to the point that he often lost track of which side of the argument he was on, which identity was his own and which was subsumed—exhumed. *You promised me, Tun.* Who was he addressing now? Who was *he*, this self that survived, this body that walked and talked, arising into its own? At times, he felt like a crazed animal, a tiger stalking its tail, circling its own shadow. *It's just as well . . . that I never had the chance to bury it. The drum, and the other instruments. The music will endure . . .* Round and round it spun, invoking the cadence of another promise, a pact made all the more powerful because it was pledged to oneself. *I would use the rest of the time to make other instruments, bringing together those for the dead and those for the living, fusing two disparate ensembles to create a unique one . . . Yes, sacrilegious, I know. But then again, I had yet to die.* The words gained clarity, took on urgency, propelling him toward a path. He emerged from isolation and found his way to the village where the instruments had been left, to reclaim them, to see what remained. To know for certain that some part of him—Sokhon—lived, and triumphed. *The truth will echo through, even under the weight of a mountain of forced confessions.*

Tun found the instruments, which had been rescued and cared for by a fellow musician, the head of the village musical troupe, a former cadre himself who had barely escaped the purge. As for Sokhon's lost family, the villagers weren't even aware he had a wife and daughter to begin with. If, as Tun had once believed, there was a chance they may still be alive, then how would he confront them? The weight of what he'd done descended upon him again. What possibility had he severed? He wondered if he'd misread the signals at the end. Misread the most important thing. That sudden brief flicker in Sokhon's frozen gaze, which, Tun had thought in his confusion and agony, was a glint of light reflecting off the raised, moving blade. When it was done, the blade having dropped to the floor unnoticed, Sokhon closed his eyes. Tun howled. The strength it must've taken to close those eyes.

Tun left the village, gathering the instruments like the cherished remains of his friend. *Music . . . or revolution,* Sokhon had said. *Before us lay these two paths* . . . Perhaps it was not too late. In another village, Tun began a new life, hiding himself in music, in the anonymity of a street performer. Every now and then, he'd pick up the *sampho* and tap it gently, remembering Sokhon's hidden invocation, searching for the truth it might reveal. But he heard nothing, only the secret incantation of his own heart. *Mercy . . . or murder?* Which had he committed? Again and again, it echoed.

"For the last twenty-five years, I've asked myself this question, lived with the burden of that choice." He looks up, facing her in the gathering night. "It was mid-December 1978 when I last held your father. It was the dry season, like now . . ."

Yet, he notes in this fading light, the monsoon has descended upon her, soaking her chin, the front of her blouse, her scarf. She is shivering. Still, she stays rooted to the spot, hands clasped in her lap, fighting her own collapse. *Sita*, he wants to say, but remembers whose heart he's breaking.

"Suteera . . ." He wishes now only to hold her. "Suteera, had I known our release from Slak Daek was just breaths away, I would not have carried out our pact. But that is the terrible nature of choice—right or wrong, one only learns after, if at all."

Teera leans over the trestle desk by the window and pushes the shutters open, latching them in place against the sudden gusts of wind rising sporadically from the water surrounding the peninsula. The sun has climbed past the window, out of her direct gaze, cresting the row of tall areca palms bordering Yaya's property, and, through the drooping bracts of fruits and fronds, Teera sees Ravi, the eldest granddaughter, lighting the circle of earthen braziers in the outdoor cooking area. Tendrils of smoke coil upward and vanish with the cool breeze. The air is redolent of charcoal and firewood, the warmth of waking.

Teera takes a deep breath, stilling herself for a moment. It's a stunning location at the tip of the peninsula, facing the Mekong, with the Tonle Sap River curving behind. At the confluence, the waters of the Himalayan peaks and the Tonle Sap Lake merge, flowing on to the Delta and the South China Sea. Everything is connected, she thinks. All is reachable in some way—the discernible and the indiscernible, the past and the future . . . The plot of land is not big, but because it parallels Yaya's more spacious grounds, with no fence dividing them, the rectangular strip appears open, borderless, rolling toward the water. Even now, in the middle of the dry season, she can spot a string of floating communities clinging to the far shores, the boats swaying in the wind at low tide amidst the exposed stilts of huts perched on the slopes. During the rainy season, Teera imagines, when the fishing nomads traverse the surging rivers, their sampans and canoes popping up in spontaneous clusters, it must bear an astonishing resemblance to Elephant Tusk Landing. It's obvious why Narunn has held out for this piece of land all these years, drawn as he is to the water, the rise and fall of the flood pulse, the shifting geography of home. So close to the city, it is a rare find.

Teera surveys the tiny abode they've occupied these past several weeks—the single room with its walls and floor of aged *koki* wood, the vaulted ceiling lined with woven rattan, shuttered windows on three sides, and off to one side the open-air bathroom, with its mini-sink, tiled shower corner, and toilet nook beneath a patch of skyline. The entrance door leads down to a narrow flight of stairs wedged against the tree trunk. Everything is miniature, an existence of half steps and delicate expressions. The previous owner, a Cambodian architect trained in Thailand, had built it as his weekend studio, a retreat from the city where he could work in solitude. Set far back in one corner of the land under a giant gnarled mango tree, atop pillars painted a flat, earthy tone, the whole structure resembles an oversize spirit house where *mechas tik mechas dey*—those unseen guardians of the water and land—might seek refuge from the rapid development on the peninsula.

Teera opens the other windows. Light streams in, carpeting the floor where at night they spread out their sleeping mats, a big one for her and Narunn, and a small one for Lah, their spaces separated by a folding wooden screen. She hears the two now moving about the terra-cotta-tiled patio beneath the house, their voices mingling with the wind chime as they try to work out where to hang it—on one of the beams, or on one of the smaller trees nearby? "Pa-Om, how about there, beneath Ma-Mieng's window? So she can hear it when she writes . . ." Father-Uncle, Mother-Auntie. This is what the little one has decided on her own to call them, and every time Teera hears it, something in her breaks into a million pieces, only to coalesce anew, larger and more whole. "*Yes,*" Narunn says, lowering his voice. "This way Ma-Mieng will never get lost. When she hears it, she'll come back from her flight." Lah lets out a muffled delight, as if colluding in some subterfuge. Teera hears them walking to the storage shed attached to one side of the house and rummaging through it, looking for the ladder and tools to hang the wind chime.

She sits down at the desk, her journal opened before her. The trestle desk and chair are the only furniture in the tiny abode, parting gifts left by the architect after he learned that Teera writes. To her left, by the bathroom door, is a closet with just enough space for clothes and other essentials. To her right, small floating shelves of books and knickknacks line the wall by the window. The rest of her belongings are stored at the hotel, where she still takes Lah to swim some afternoons. They need very little, she's found.

Still, Narunn said during their ritual walk at dawn, he'd like something bigger—"a bit more of a home . . . than this beautiful birdhouse." He has just enough savings left to be able to begin constructing, and has even enlisted the generosity of the architect, who promised to draft a plan and put together a team of local artisans and builders. He'll keep the apartment at the White Building solely as his clinic so that he can see more patients. He's also applied for a trainee position with an international team of forensic scientists preparing for a possible tribunal. It's a long shot, he admits, but if it were really necessary he could always work for a government hospital. In any case, Teera should not worry, he assured her, as if sensing a fluttering in her heart and concluding that the only remedy was not to ask for or expect any commitment, anything she might take as confining. He could look after Lah on his own, he said. The little girl has become his vocation, and he is grateful to be summoned to protect a life in this time of need. He often wonders about the child in his mother's womb—whether it was a boy or a girl. He waited until Lah ran ahead, out of hearing range, before saying, "No matter what happens, whether you stay or go back to America, I want you to know that you'll always have a home and a family to return to." He made a sweeping gesture of the whole place, their joint grounds, his and Yaya's. Teera swallowed, unable to express all that was surging through her.

I came raging against the loss, she thinks now, scribbling the words in her journal, *against this land, only to be embraced by it as if I'd never left.* Five months ago, she arrived with the notion that her sojourn would be temporary, that she'd be in and out quickly, that, as stated on the various arrival forms she'd filled out on the plane, her place of residence, her home, was the United States, and so was her nationality. Yet, she remembers, all that was noted at the airport immigration check, the only detail of import, was her place of birth, and, like for all those returning from the diaspora to this tattered homeland, her American passport was stamped with a visa marked "Permanent."

I will stay . . . For how long, she can't say. The dissolution of home requires only walking away, a single flight across the borders, but finding it again takes a lifetime of returning. *For now, I will stay . . . because part of my home is you, this budding existence we share with Lah, the whole we are trying to patch together from the fragments.* She wishes Narunn to know this.

As for the tremor, this fluttering he detected, it's not fear of entrapment but the release of what has been imprisoned inside of her. She's not sure what to call it now. It ceases to be what it was—anguish, grief, despair. It surrounds her—like a florescence of dust motes in the sunlight—and yet, it no longer possesses the weight and solidity to drag her to the bottom, to the darkness within, as it did those days right after she and the Old Musician spoke. Instead, it moves with her, rising when she rises, sitting when she sits. The sorrow of knowing. It's clear that she can put the dead to rest, bury the ghosts, but not the knowledge. What she knows now will become part of her, an abiding consciousness.

Perhaps, Teera thinks, this is what we all live with as a people, the painful awareness that this history—war, atrocity, genocide, whatever its name—surrounds us persistently, at times binding like a metal chain, other times incorporeal as dust. Even so, we can still move forward, with the small choices we make each day. To love, to harbor and protect, to rebuild.

She hears playful shouting and looks up from her writing to see the men of Yaya's household carting materials—poles, ropes, stakes, tarps—to construct a canopy for the ceremony later this morning. Narunn strolls over to meet them, Lah bouncing on his shoulders, the wind chime still jangling from her hand, their endeavor to hang it postponed momentarily. After a boisterous exchange of greetings, Narunn gestures to the middle of the plot, where the future house will stand. This is where the men will raise the canopy, with a platform underneath for the monks and straw mats all around for guests. In a few short hours, the

Venerable Kong Oul, along with some novices, will arrive to bless the land. There will be chanting, and afterward the Old Musician will offer an invocation to the spirits, asking for their protection and benevolence, their forgiveness for any trespassing.

Teera thinks back to her meeting with the Old Musician only a few days ago, six weeks after the long, heartbreaking revelation they'd shared in the ceremony hall. He seemed taken aback to see her return to the temple, to hear that she'd come specifically to visit him. For a long time they sat facing each other in mutual silence. Then, he said, "What I did . . . those many years ago . . . cannot be forgiven. Still, I am profoundly sorry."

They plunged into another silence. Finally, she said, "When my mother took her own life, I blamed myself. Rin, my baby brother, had just died, you see, and she was grieving. I should've found some way to pull her out of that awful despair, I thought. I was angry at myself, and, unable to bear this anger, I lashed out at the world." The words flowed out of Teera, filling the gulf between them. "I've since learned something about anger and despair. You can always direct your anger at something—someone. And when you do, there's almost certainly a response, and thus you have company, you're not alone in anger. Eventually it grows and intensifies, depleting you of energy, but before that it can offer a certain seductive comfort." She paused, swallowing, moistening her throat. "But with despair, you are alone. You grieve in solitude. You sink deeper and deeper into it, to where no one can reach you, and you have to gather all your strength to fight your way back to the surface. So, slowly, I've had to learn to let go of anger—to feel it but not to cling to it, as Amara taught me by her example—because whatever strength I have I must reserve for the fight against that solitary descent into grief." Teera looked up and saw tears pooling in his good eye, a faint stream seeping from underneath the patch covering the injured one. "I am here because I've fought my way to the surface again."

They held each other's gaze for a moment, a confluence of the inexpressible between them. A sudden intake of breath that sounded like a sob. From whom, neither could be sure. He nodded, and for a moment, Teera glimpsed her mother beside him—his younger self, Tun—both looking as they had that day when the two of them stood side by side at the riverfront releasing a sparrow, while she, little Suteera, sipped sugarcane juice on a bench behind them. In her remembering, Teera had mistaken him for her father. The heart, she realized as she stared at him, holds its own trial. It bears witness to what the mind easily forgets, and yet it forgives every act of love.

She flips to the back pocket of her journal and pulls out the black-and-white photograph of her parents, turning it over to look at the tentative designation in Amara's handwriting—*1962?* The year her parents married, this she's always known, from her aunt's recounting of the wedding festivities. She wonders now whether the picture was taken before or after. Could it be that the captured festive scene was a party during the weeklong celebration? If so, the Old Musician was part of the scene, somewhere in the uncaptured periphery, playing music with the ensemble sent, according to Amara, by the Ministry of Culture. A gesture honoring her grandfather, Le Conseiller, a dedicated patron of the arts, on the joyous occasion of his daughter's marriage. They were all there, Teera realizes in astonishment.

Then, as if acting of its own free will, the tip of her pen begins to blot out the year. It's not important when the image was taken. She'd like to believe that somewhere in the uncharted periphery of time and memory they still are there, all together.

Music is everywhere, voices warbling amidst the reverberations of activity. Again, Teera looks up from her desk and sees that the men are busy sawing and hammering, measuring distances with their steps, pounding stakes into the ground after a certain number of paces, organizing the tall metal poles, unrolling the tarps. They sing as they work, seamlessly finishing one love duet and moving on to the next, as if taking cue from their cell phones ringing every so often. Both duets, Teera notes, are from the past, from pre–Khmer Rouge days, but the words still resonate, speaking to the challenge of romance at a distance, forbidden connections—the hazards of dialing the wrong number, mistaking the voices of strangers for those of desired ones, longings across time and space. One group croons the girl's lyric, another the boy's. *Allô, allô? Oun? . . . Ni peit chhkuat. Mien neak-na chhkuat?* Teera laughs, recognizing the comical introduction of this "Hello" song as the caller misdials—"Hello, hello? Darling? . . ." and the voice on the other end responds, "This is an asylum for the insane. Do you have anyone who's insane?" She wonders if it's a parody of the "Hello Hello" song she's hummed to Narunn.

As if sensing her thinking of him, Narunn pokes his head in the doorway and whispers, "The wind chime's up." He nods for her to listen, and Teera is suddenly aware of the melodic tinkling beneath her window. "Lah's very proud that she showed me the proper place to hang it."

Teera smiles. "I'll come down now," she tells him, closing her journal. Narunn skips back down the stairs, the whole house vibrating with his steps, the wind chime jingling louder. Teera gets up from her desk, pausing mid-motion, remembering something. She opens the journal again, takes out the black-and-white photograph, and props it up against a stack of books on one of the floating shelves. "Your new home," she murmurs to her parents, and the gathered throng, those seen and unseen. "One of many."

Outside, Lah points to the wind chime hanging from the eave extending over the patio. "Look, Ma-Mieng, it makes those croaking uncles stop singing!"

Narunn bursts out laughing. It's true. The rainlike song of the wind chime has serenaded the men into silence.

"The Venerable Kong Oul will be happy to know . . . to see it here . . . like this," Teera says, thinking of the gun the abbot gave to Narunn, its journey, this final transformation.

"Let's go see what's cooking!" Narunn exclaims. "I don't think we had breakfast."

Teera looks across to Yaya's land, where the female members of the household are now fully immersed in culinary preparations, with pots steaming, flames leaping from the earthen braziers, the fragrances of spices thickening the air.

"But, Pa-Om," Lah reminds him, "we cannot eat before the monks!"

"Oh, I'm sure Auntie Ravi has set aside some nibbles for us."

The monks have arrived, like a row of candle flames moving across the land, their saffron robes and yellow umbrellas lit by the sunlight. They enter the canopy and step barefoot onto the slightly raised platform, leaving their sandals in the grass, their closed umbrellas in a woven basket near the edge. The Venerable Kong Oul lowers himself on the cushion in the middle, his movement so tranquil and weightless that for a second he seems half afloat. Three novices assume their places on either side of him, Makara on his immediate right, a picture of stillness, spiritual discipline. The youth gathers the hem of his robe and tucks it beneath his crossed legs, his gestures restrained, deliberate. He faces the crowd but his gaze recedes inward, delving toward some deep place of solitude. Had Narunn not told Teera of the adolescent's recent struggle to overcome addiction, she would never have guessed he'd been anything other than a monk, ordained at a tender age.

Those congregated on the straw mats bow three times, murmuring prayers, then sit straight up again, keeping their gazes lowered, palms together in front of their chests, legs folded to one side so their feet point away from the monks. Most of the elders gather in front, among them Yaya, her shorn head swaying in a row of other shorn heads, their traditional black-and-white outfits juxtaposed against the monastic robes so that they appear like a string of moons below a sequence of suns.

As it's already quite late in the morning, the ceremony begins without delay, in order to give the ordained time to partake of their only meal before noon, the food specially prepared in their honor. The Venerable Kong Oul turns to Makara and gives an encouraging nod. Hands clasped tightly in his lap, Makara begins chanting, his voice tremulous, lips partially revealing a set of marred teeth, and only then does it become obvious he has yet to fully recover. Still, the Venerable Kong Oul has entrusted him with the principal chanting, filling in only when the boy falters with his memorized lines or his voice becomes so strained as to verge on disappearing. It's common for the abbot, Narunn said, to allow the most vulnerable novices to take ownership of their spiritual practice. In the case of Makara, it has so far proven the most effective path toward his recovery, diverting his attention from his own struggle to focus on the responsibility to extend care to others, learning in small measures to exercise again the neglected faculties of compassion and self-discipline.

The other novices join in the chanting, a ripple alternating on either side of the elder monk, who dips the sacred brush into the font of water and sprinkles the audience, the earth, the air. The wind chime peals, echoing their incantation. Trees yield in supplication to the breeze.

In the back of the gathering, off to one side, Teera keeps looking across the land to Yaya's house. She was inside their small house, changing into more appropriate clothes, when the monks arrived, and by the time she stepped outside, the ceremony was set to begin, so she was obliged to join and hasn't yet had a chance to greet the Old Musician. Now a large, leafy banana palm blocks her view, so she can't see to where he supposedly waits on the carved wooden platform under Yaya's house, preparing himself for the invocation he will offer.

While the land blessing ceremony is brief, joined by whoever wishes to observe the familiar ritual, the merrymaking will continue throughout the day, with friends and neighbors stopping in to offer greetings, to welcome Narunn to the neighborhood, to enjoy the evolving array of food. Teera has noticed a steady flow of guests arriving, many bringing their own specialties to contribute to the festivity. First they cluster around the cooking area, bantering with Ravi and the women in charge of the cooking, inhaling the aromas of the dishes they'll soon enjoy. Then gradually they meander to the straw mats spread across the grounds, glad to be sitting in the sun on this refreshingly cool, windy day.

From a distance she recognizes the young man in the wooden wheelchair, now in animated dialogue with the architect. Narunn asked the architect to bring Vichet here in his car, explaining the former runner's disability, and also his talent with woodwork. Perhaps, Narunn hoped, the architect could make use of such talent. The two men appear to be hitting it off, Vichet gesturing passionately as he speaks and the architect listening intently, every so often responding with equal enthusiasm. It's easy to imagine them discussing things like the pliability of bamboo and rattan, which Vichet is especially skilled at weaving, and their potential applications in home design. Mr. Chum arrives through the gate by the main road. He'd brought the monks and the Old Musician earlier in a borrowed van, and returns now accompanied by his wife, his young married daughter, and her husband and their little children. His second family, he's always referred to them, as if the first might still be alive somewhere. He and Teera exchange a nod, and after a quick word to his family and a moment of collective recognition, they all nod. Teera wonders what he's explained to them, what kind of family she might be in his eyes.

Teera lets her gaze roam over to the pond where some of Yaya's teenage great-grandchildren teeter on the edge, angling long sticks to pluck off the dry lotus pods bearing the hard, nutty seeds ideal for roasting over an open fire. She recalls Ravi explaining the purpose of the pond— to give the land "a breath of water." Now, in the dry season, it appears to do just that, infusing every gust of wind with the smell of mud and rain. She hopes the Old Musician doesn't find it too chilly in the shade under the house. This cool spell at the end of January has arrived auspiciously, according to Yaya, who believes it encourages all to seek the warmth of home and family. A perfect day for the ceremony.

There's a brief interlude between one chanted incantation and the next, as the monks pause to drink water from the glasses set for them. Narunn leans over Lah's head and whispers to Teera, sensing her need

to see the Old Musician: "Now is probably the best time to slip away."
Teera nods, telling Lah, "You stay here with Pa-Om," as she gets up and
discreetly makes her way toward Yaya's house.

The Old Musician sees her approaching and, as on every prior meeting,
her likeness to Channara sears him. He remembers Sokhon's sudden
revelation one afternoon during those weeks before his death. *You ought
to know she loved you as well.* His friend had said this of Channara, as if
to prepare him for what might come. Perhaps, the Old Musician thinks
now, this was part of the reason it had taken him so long to return to
the city. He feared he might indeed find Channara, and, after what he
and Sokhon had endured, he had no wish to betray one love for another.

Teera lowers herself onto the teak platform in front of him, arms
outstretched, and the Old Musician expects her to gather the instruments he's brought along. Instead, she embraces him. "Pa-Om," she says,
holding him a moment longer, as if to still his surprise as much as her
own. *Pa-Om,* he repeats the word to himself, to be sure he has not mistaken it, to hold on to the sound.

"I'm sorry," she says, letting him go, "I know that you are preparing . . ."

"No, I'm glad you came," he says, his heart steadying with hers, encouraged by her calm, the kindness she continues to show him. "There
is something I want to tell you. I've brought the instruments for your
safekeeping. They are yours. I hope you will accept them now, as I will
be traveling soon."

"Traveling?" She seems both delighted and worried. "But where, and
with whom?"

He tells her of his planned journey upriver to Kratie. A Cham couple
has offered to take him on their sampan, as they will be heading to
fish the valuable striped catfish in the deep pools along the northern
stretches of the Mekong. "I will be safe," he assures her, "well looked
after by the husband and wife. They are kind people." Abdul Razak is
a skilled navigator, a seasoned voyager on the river, he explains, and the

couple's grandchildren are now with their parents, so there will be room for him on the small vessel.

"Is it Chhlong? Are you going back to your mother's home village?"

"Yes."

They are silent, each afraid to say what they know in their hearts, to speak again of the suffering, the terrible loss he endured there. Teera feels that perhaps she understands his need to face that loss again.

"When will you return to Phnom Penh?" she asks.

He remains silent, holding her gaze with his one good eye.

"I'll visit you then," she declares. "There's so much of the country I've yet to see. I'd like to learn more, remember more . . . write it down."

"Write?" he asks, curious, taking the opportunity to change the subject.

"Yes, I've always written things down . . ."

He watches her blush at this admission, embarrassed somehow, as if the desire were a shameful illness, a transgression. Yet, it's obvious to him that she's inherited some part of Channara's passion. He considers telling her that her mother was a brilliant writer, though she'd had to hide her fierce intelligence under a nom de plume. *Tun Chan*, he remembers. That pseudonym, the combination of their two names, was like a love letter to him in those years after she was married, and he would read everything she'd ever written under that name. He decides to keep this memory to himself, to let her continue instead—

"Yes, you were saying, but now . . . ?"

"Well, now there's this." She looks at her surroundings. "I need to capture it all somehow." She turns from his gaze, mortified by the extravagance of her emotion, her unpolished words. Then more humbly, she adds, "Even if only in small glimpses, just for my own recollection, my own safekeeping."

Again, he watches her flush.

Then, as if prompted by the last word, she's reminded of the instruments before them. "These are as much yours as mine," she says after a moment. "Which is why I want to ask your permission to pass them along." She tells him about the ensemble she encountered in Siem Reap, describing each musician and each tattered instrument. "I'll visit them again and see what else they might need for their music, but I thought I'd start with these—a gift from you and my father, from one ensemble to another."

Something floods his heart, rising to his throat, blocking it. Sorrow, happiness. At times he cannot tell them apart. He grieves now, more than ever, that Sokhon is not here to see for himself the woman his daughter has grown into, and at the same time, he is profoundly grateful to witness her in his friend's place. Finally, he manages to say, "Yes, of course, these instruments deserve to be played. Your father would have wanted this."

"Thank you."

Just then Lah comes running. "Ma-Mieng, Ma-Mieng," the child pants, out of breath, "Pa-Om is asking for you. The chanting is almost over. You must bring Lokta along."

They become aware again of the movements and sounds around them—the laughter and bantering, the clatters of cooking, the hum of conversations, the chanting, the wind chime. As they rise from the mat, she offers her arm so that he can more easily negotiate the uneven terrain.

Beginning the slow walk together, Teera asks, "What will you offer the spirits of the land?"

"I've decided on something short and simple. A *smoat*. Your father's last composition. I hope you would agree that the words are most fitting for the occasion. When we occupy a place, we give thanks to the spirits that remain as well as the spirits that move on."

Teera nods, recalling the verse he'd shared with her. They walk together in companionable silence, Lah skipping ahead, her pigtails bouncing. They arrive just as the ceremony comes to a close, with the gathered throng bowing one last time to the monks, who remain seated. Teera looks across the land and sees a procession of food coming. Narunn helps the Old Musician onto the raised platform, where he sits at one corner so that he can see both the monks and the audience. The Venerable Kong Oul lowers his head and closes his eyes to listen, one of many unconventional gestures of respect the abbot has shown to this man others might easily mistake for a beggar.

Teera takes a seat next to Narunn on the straw mat, where his knee presses against hers as if to offer support, and prepares herself for another heartbreak and, by the same token, another healing, knowing that in the words to come, she will hear her father's voice, his song.

The spirit of this land lives in its fields of rice,
Its forest pathways, its flooded rivers,
And in the rhythms that echo
For the sojourners, already on our way . . .

Author's Note

While the principal characters in this novel are fictional, the story is set amidst historical events in Cambodia before, during, and after the Khmer Rouge regime. These include the US bombing campaign; the Khmer Rouge victory and mass evacuation of the urban population in 1975; targeted killings of the educated elite, former soldiers, scholars, monks, and artists; and the eventual waves of purges that saw hundreds of thousands imprisoned and executed. Slak Daek is a fictional prison, but the methods of torture described there are those employed by the Khmer Rouge in a network of nearly two hundred "security centers" established across the country, including at Tuol Sleng, the most thoroughly documented of these.

A Khmer Rouge survivor myself, I escaped as a child across the border to Thailand after the fall of the regime with only my mother left from among the vast extended family who'd made up my world before the war. My father was taken away in the early days of the revolution, and his disappearance, his uncertain death, has haunted me ever since. Even as a child, I was struck by the contradiction that, like many other Khmer intellectuals of that era, my father was sympathetic to the ideals of democracy that the revolutionary movement espoused, and yet became an early victim.

Today it is common to find perpetrators and victims living side by side, and even for those of us who lived through the atrocity, it is often difficult to discern a dividing line between the two. While some joined the revolutionary movement by idealistic inclination, many more were coerced or forced to take on roles as soldiers, guards, informants, and spies. Few can look back honestly without confronting questions of conscience as to what they might have done differently.

If my first novel, *In the Shadow of the Banyan*, is a story of survival, *Music of the Ghosts* is a story of survivors. The novel opens in the period before the convening of the Khmer Rouge tribunal, a long-overdue but highly restricted undertaking focused on just a handful of surviving former leaders. My motivation in writing is to explore the questions of responsibility, atonement, forgiveness, and justice in the more every-day settings in which survivors find themselves—in the chambers of the heart, and in the intimate encounters where perpetrator and victim sit face-to-face.

V.R.

Historical Chronology

1953   Cambodia wins independence from French rule. Saloth Sar (later Pol Pot) and colleagues return from studies in France.

1954   Geneva Conference delivers political and military settlement, leading to withdrawal of French and Vietnamese troops.

1963   Preap In, an insurgent in the Khmer Serei nationalist movement, is executed. Pol Pot is named party secretary and leader of the underground Communist Party.

1967   Jacqueline Kennedy visits Phnom Penh.

1968   Khmer Rouge launch armed insurgency.

1969   After four years of bombing raids on Cambodian territory, US forces launch the intensified secret bombing campaign known as Operation Menu, which continues until 1973.

1970   Prince Sihanouk is deposed in a military coup led by his first cousin Prince Sisowath Sirik Matak and his former commander in chief and defense minister, Lon Nol.

1973   Khmer Rouge advance in civil war against US-backed Lon Nol government, gaining control over most of the country's territory. US forces bomb Neak Leung.

1975   Khmer Rouge seize Phnom Penh and take power, launching a mass evacuation of the city. In the subsequent years, hundreds of thousands are tortured and executed, many in a network of secret security prisons. An estimated 1.7 million perish from violence, disease, starvation, and forced labor.

1978   Vietnamese forces invade in December.

1979   Vietnamese forces take control of Phnom Penh in January, sending remnant Khmer Rouge forces into retreat.

1989   Vietnamese forces withdraw from Cambodia.

1991   Paris peace accords are signed, setting the stage for a United Nations–led transitional authority and elections in 1993.

1997   UN Commission on Human Rights adopts a resolution asking the Secretary General to examine requests for assistance in assessing past violations of Cambodian and international law.

1998   Pol Pot dies in his jungle hideout. Senior Khmer Rouge leaders defect. Civil war gradually ends, with remaining leaders surrendering the following year.

2001   Cambodian law is passed seeking establishment of a tribunal to bring genocide charges against Khmer Rouge leaders.

2005   Khmer Rouge tribunal is approved by the United Nations after years of debate over funding.

2007   The tribunal is operational and begins questioning surviving senior Khmer Rouge leaders.

2010   Top former Khmer Rouge leaders Nuon Chea, Ieng Sary, Ieng Thirith, and Khieu Samphan are indicted for genocide, war crimes, and crimes against humanity.

Acknowledgments

S ince early childhood I have been drawn to the plaintive sounds of the traditional Khmer ensemble, and it would be impossible to thank individually the scores of unrecognized musicians who have shared with me not only their music but also their stories. Each is a story of suffering and sacrifice. These nameless musicians I encounter on street corners and forest trails, so often overlooked, continue to move me. I feel their music in my heart, and wish to honor their efforts to sustain their art and, in so doing, to sustain us all.

I offer my profoundest gratitude to my mother, who, through a lifetime of conversations, has been my abiding partner in a journey across time and continents. I am indebted to my stepfather for sharing his war experiences as a Lon Nol government soldier who, like so many of that time, brought his young family to the battlefields, convinced that it was the safest of many risky choices.

My thanks also to Hin Yuthika, Kim McDevitt, and His Excellency Oum Maknorith for the glimpses they shared of the Phnom Penh social milieu of the 1960s; Om Chhem and his fellow village elders along the shores of the Tonle Sap Lake; the demining professional and former soldier Nhiem Khon; the archaeologist Chea Socheat; the builders and artisans Kann Mony Rath, Khorn Bora, Yich Yanyan, and Touch Det; and Nen Ekneka, Prach Mara, Mak Sophea, and Chey Savry, for their insights into the struggles of contemporary youth.

I would also like to acknowledge the numerous, meticulous analyses of the Khmer Rouge period published by the Documentation Center of

Cambodia, as well as historical studies by David Chandler, Philip Short, and Ben Kiernan, which have proved indispensable in confirming key events. Reyum Publishing has provided an invaluable service in publishing Khmer language works on traditional music and ritual, including illustrated volumes by Keo Narom and Ang Choulean.

I am deeply indebted to my agent, Emma Sweeney, for her steadfast support and wise counsel; and to my editor, Trish Todd, for her astute eye and insightful probing. My journey as an author has been all the more rewarding because of these two guardian angels at my side. I offer my heartfelt thanks also to Susan Moldow and her amazing team at Touchstone—David Falk, Tara Parsons, Brian Belfiglio, Jessica Roth, Meredith Vilarello, Kaitlin Olson, Kelsey Manning, and Cherlynne Li—for shepherding this story into the world; and to Wendy Sheanin and those at Simon & Schuster for their sustained faith and enthusiasm.

My boundless gratitude to my larger family for their generous love and support always—in particular, my beautiful sisters, Leakhena and Lynda; my fellow artist and musical inspiration, Patrick; my superhero Joann; my lovely sister-in-law, Juliana, and the kindhearted Ann-Mari and Mitchell.

To my husband, Blake, I offer my heart and soul. To our daughter, Annelise, I give my unconditional, limitless love. I am inexpressibly grateful for their love in return.

About the Author

Vaddey Ratner, a survivor of the Khmer Rouge regime in Cambodia, is the author of the *New York Times* bestseller *In the Shadow of the Banyan*. Her critically acclaimed debut novel was a PEN/Hemingway Award finalist and has been translated into seventeen languages. She is a summa cum laude graduate of Cornell University, where she specialized in Southeast Asian history and literature.